The Truant Officer

By Derek Ciccone

Copyright © Derek Ciccone 2012

All rights reserved.
ISBN reserved

Interior Layout by Cheryl Perez, www.yourepublished.com

All rights are reserved. No part of this book may be reproduced, distributed, or transmitted in any form of by any means, or stored in a database or retrieval system without the prior written permission of the publisher.

This book is a work of fiction. The names, characters, places, and incidents are products of the author's imagination or have been used fictitiously and are not to be constructed as real. Any resemblance to persons, living or dead, actual events, locales or organizations is entirely coincidental.

Chapter 1

Jorge DeRosa was half watching the monotonous security feed when she pulled up to the pump.

He observed the woman step out of the pricey SUV, unable to take his eyes off the black mini-dress that hugged every curve of her toned body. All of a sudden his job didn't seem so bad.

As the dark-haired beauty began to fill the tank, her body language suddenly turned flustered, and she headed in Jorge's direction.

She entered the food mart, her heeled shoes clicking loudly on the linoleum floor. He recognized her as Mexican, like himself, but she sure didn't look like she came from the same South Phoenix neighborhood as he did.

She approached the register. "My card didn't work in the pump. A message said to see the attendant—is that what you people are calling yourselves these days?"

When Jorge looked closer, he noticed something that surprised him. She *did* come from the same neighborhood as him. He hadn't seen her in at least ten years, but despite the fancy clothes and uppity tone, he was sure it was her. "Liliana?"

His words snapped her out of distraction. "Excuse me?"

"I'm Jorge DeRosa. Our families lived in the same apartment complex on South 40th Street. You went to school with my brother, Estaban."

She smiled at the remembrance, but it seemed fake. It was obvious to Jorge that she wanted to leave her old life behind. He knew the feeling—the gang-infested section of South Phoenix was a hard place to escape, and once you got out there was no looking back. Jorge got as far as this night manager job in suburban Chandler, but by the looks of things, Liliana had gotten much further away.

As if reading his mind, she mentioned, "It's been a long time since someone called me Liliana."

She handed him her Visa card. He ran his fingers over the plastic as if he were reading Braille. The name had changed to *Lilly McLaughlin.*

She began impatiently tapping her manicured nails on the counter. People like Lilly McLaughlin always seemed to be in a hurry—perhaps by never stopping, they would never be forced to look back. Jorge didn't bother to ask her about her mother Rosie, or her six brothers. The youngest, Manuel, was killed in the crossfire of a gang war. The thought reminded Jorge of the dangers of present day.

He held up the credit card. "I'll run it in here, and watch you on the monitor."

Her eyes narrowed with suspicion, but his intentions were honorable. He pointed at the stack of Sunday editions of the *Arizona Republic* that were wedged between bags of Doritos and other assorted chips on the overstocked shelves. The headline screamed at them: *Abducted!*

It was the Valley's third such abduction in the last month, and the source was familiar to Jorge and Lilly. It was an initiation ritual in which a prospective gang member would travel to suburbia with the intent of kidnapping a woman from a public place. The first victim was an Arizona State University student who was doing some late night grocery shopping at a Safeway in Tempe. A forty-one-year-old mother of three was next, taken from a park while walking her dog, right here in Chandler. Then just yesterday, a thirty-year-old real estate agent was snatched from outside a home in Scottsdale. The good news was that the first two women were found alive. The bad news was that they were beaten and raped—their lives never to be the same—and were either unable or unwilling to identify their attackers.

The headline seemed to soften Lilly. By removing her shield of aloofness, she now more resembled the girl that Jorge remembered. The one who wore hand-me-down clothes and tirelessly helped teach English to the many immigrants in their neighborhood.

She smiled at him. This time it wasn't fake. It was a tough smile from the old neighborhood. The one where you never showed a hint of weakness. "That stuff doesn't faze us, does it, Jorge?

He smiled back at her, noticing that she dusted off the accent for his benefit. He was now talking to Liliana. "Because we're from South Phoenix?"

Her smile turned into a chuckle. "South Phoenix wasn't so tough. I teach high school English. Teenagers—now those monsters scare me."

She sauntered toward the door.

Jorge turned his attention back to the security feed, watching Liliana return to her vehicle. When she finished filling the SUV with gas, she took out her phone and appeared to be snapping a photo of herself. Jorge looked on curiously—whatever she was doing, she seemed to be enjoying herself. Now that they were homies once again, he would feel comfortable asking her about her theatrics when she returned to retrieve her credit card.

But the picture quickly changed. It happened so fast he couldn't respond. All he could do was watch in horror.

A dark figure in a ski mask rolled from underneath the car with knife in hand. Lilly's scream pierced the night.

Even without the knife, the man looked like he could tear apart the petite woman, limb by limb. In a matter of seconds, he grabbed her by the neck, opened the back door of the vehicle, and threw her in like a piece of luggage. He ripped the nozzle from the tank. He then climbed behind the wheel.

The SUV tore out of the gas station as Jorge looked on in horror.

Chapter 2

Darren McLaughlin peered into the bathroom mirror and wondered how he could have aged fifteen years in one day. He was quite certain that he was thirty-eight when he got up this morning. The flight to New York was supposed to lose hours with the time change, not gain years.

He splashed water on his weary face and attempted to maneuver his short-cropped hair into place without much luck. All he wanted to do was fall into his bed and get his sleep for tomorrow's flight—he couldn't believe he let Treadwell convince him to join him for a night on the town. Since this was their last trip together, he was unable to say no.

"You should just shave it off and go Vin Diesel," Ron Treadwell's loud, drunken voice shot through the bathroom, while he relieved himself in a grimy toilet-stall.

"What?" Darren asked, coming out his trance.

"Your hair—or should I say lack of it. Just shave it off. It will take ten years off you."

Darren took another look at himself. "I don't think it's that bad."

Treadwell snorted a laugh. "Then I must be really hammered because I'm either looking at a bald spot or you're wearing a yarmulke. And I figure you'd discuss it with your mentor before converting."

Darren hated to acknowledge that Treadwell might actually be his mentor. But he did know that despite Ron's infantile nature, numerous vices, and general obnoxiousness, he owed him his life. Not for saving the day during one of the many flights they had piloted over the years, but for introducing him to Lilly.

"Lilly says it doesn't look that bad when it's cut short."

"Lilly lies."

Darren angered. "Lilly is the most honest person I know."

"Ease off the throttle, big guy," Treadwell said, putting up his hands in surrender. Darren really was a big guy, standing a shade under six-four.

He joined Darren at the sink. "I mean she told a fib to make her aging warrior feel better about himself. A good lie."

Darren nodded acceptance, too tired to fight for his woman's honor. He took one more look in the mirror and decided to stop fighting reality and put on his navy-blue pilot's hat. "Why are we still wearing our uniforms again?" Darren asked.

"Because the only thing chicks dig more than a fighter pilot, is a man in a uniform. So that means we have the best of both worlds. Haven't I taught you anything?"

"Fighter pilot? Have you been watching *Top Gun* again?"

Ironically, Darren was the military man who did over three thousand flying hours after graduating as an officer from the Air Force Academy. Treadwell took the civilian route to commercial airlines, getting his pilot's license at just sixteen with the goal of impressing girls. His early start was why he was ahead of Darren on the pecking order of the airline they flew for.

Treadwell reclaimed the Bloody Mary he'd rested on the sink, swirled it with the celery stick, and took a sip. Darren had given up on reminding him that the rules stipulated he stop drinking at least eight hours before a flight, and they were getting close to the deadline. Treadwell looked in the mirror and played with his rat's nest of curls. "You know how I keep my hair?"

"I thought you wore a wig."

Treadwell ignored him. "Because I have remained permanently single. Marriage adds like fifteen years to people."

By permanently single, Darren assumed his friend forgot to factor in his two divorces and three kids.

"Speaking of which, what do you think of Carrie? Please fasten your seat-belts because we're preparing for landing…in my room tonight," Treadwell said with a slurred grin.

Darren just shook his head. But had to admit what Treadwell lacked in looks, intelligence, charm, and maturity, he sure made up in confidence, and did usually make that "perfect landing" with the opposite sex.

"Her name is Kelli, not Carrie. Remember, she introduced herself as Kelli-with-an-i and you responded, 'I'm Ron with an eye for you?' I also think I'm a third wheel, so I am going to take a cab back to the hotel. That way one of us will be in shape to fly tomorrow."

They had an eight a.m. sign-in for the final day of their three-leg trip. They would fly from New York to Miami and then to San Juan, before arriving home to Phoenix deep into the night.

Treadwell looked mortally wounded. "You can't leave. You're my wingman."

"I'm actually your first officer."

"Exactly. And as your captain, I order that you stay!"

Darren was promoted to captain starting next month, after four-and-a-half years as a first officer. Aside the fact that he would be making more money, it also meant that he and Treadwell wouldn't fly together again, as a captain always flies with a more junior first officer. That's why they both bid on this trip for a final voyage of student and mentor. So Darren was guilted into staying.

Treadwell dragged him back into the bar area. It was a typical sports bar filled with loud televisions and even louder patrons. Darren had been to so many cities that the only way he could tell them apart was by the sports teams the locals rooted for. In this case it was the Yankees and the Rangers—New York.

"Kelli said she has a sister who might be stopping by. If she looks anything like Kelli, then you will be flying first class tonight, my friend," Treadwell said, maintaining his mischievous grin.

"What are you talking about? If you haven't forgotten, I'm married!"

"Yeah, but you've been whining for weeks about how you're afraid the spark is gone."

"That doesn't mean I'd ever cheat on Lilly. It's until death do us part, you know, for better or worse."

Treadwell grabbed his head like a migraine had swept through it. "You just gave me a bad flashback to my first marriage. One thing you can count on is that it will always be *worse*. You know what your problem is?"

Darren braced. Nothing like getting marriage advice from the twice divorced.

"Lilly is a spicy sauce and you're mild. It's a bad mix."

Darren looked at him, perplexed. "You've been telling me for years that we're a perfect fit because she's salsa and I'm a chip. Salsa is worthless without a chip, so we complement each other like yin and yang."

"More like yin and *bor-yang*. All I'm saying is your relationship has become too much chip and not enough dip. There's a lot of chips that would like to be in that dip, and if you don't dig in then someone else will."

Darren wanted to write it off as the ramblings of a drunken fool, but the comment stirred his insecurities. Darren never fit the image of the confident pilot. Which is another reason why he and Lilly were so compatible—where he would stick his toe into life with doubts and hesitations, Lilly would leap right in to the deep end without fear. As long as he had Lilly he wouldn't need confidence—she had enough for the both of them.

But lately she'd been distant and distracted. Maybe Treadwell was right, and she had grown tired of the mild chip. Perhaps it was the middle age that had surprisingly crept up on him. Or the failure to have that baby they tried so hard for.

But the one thing he was sure of was that he couldn't lose her.

Chapter 3

Kelli was waiting for them at their table, still sipping on the same vodka tonic. Treadwell brazenly moved right in for a kiss.

Darren shook his head. Treadwell had spotted Kelli sitting alone at the bar when they arrived, declared that they'd be having a "layover" at his hotel later that night, and now he was well en route to making it happen. In his single days, it would have taken Darren a week to build up the courage to talk to a woman at a bar, and even that was a long shot.

Kelli was attractive, but lacked a usual trait of Treadwell's women—what Lilly often referred to as "stripperness." Kelli gave off a vibe of sophistication that matched her short, stylish haircut and designer suit. She also spoke with the hint of an accent that Darren couldn't identify, but didn't feel comfortable inquiring about, perhaps Eastern European. She appeared out of place in the testosterone-filled sports bar, but explained that she was a big hockey fan and had stopped off on her way home from her Manhattan office. Her work was that of a lawyer, which explained the suit and the long hours.

When Treadwell removed his lips, she announced, "My sister just called, she can't make it."

Darren was relieved. The comment also reminded him that in the rush to "hit the town," he failed to call Lilly and let her know he made it safely, as he did after every flight. She always joked that it would make the news if he crashed, so don't waste the minutes on their phone plan. But one time he didn't call and she got upset with worry.

He removed his phone from his coat pocket, realizing it had been off the whole time. When he turned it on he saw that he had a text message from Lilly—almost a half hour ago. He badly wished he'd heard her voice, but when he read her typed words he wasn't complaining. It read: *Every man's fantasy ~ ILY Lilly.*

Darren opened the attached photo and began laughing. From the intro, he expected some racy photos, but this was even better. Lilly had photographed herself pumping gas into their SUV, posing with the look of seduction. Darren had always told her that there was nothing sexier than a woman doing manual labor. Especially one who looked like she did in that little black dress he liked so much.

He typed back: LOL ~ can't wait to see you tmrw!! ILY2.

He handed the phone to Treadwell, who burst into laughter. "I told you things were fine," he said.

Darren actually remembered him saying something about finding other chips. Treadwell handed the phone to Kelli, who remarked, "Your wife is beautiful." She examined Darren more closely, obviously trying to figure out what she was doing with Mr. Average.

Darren could care less. It only mattered what Lilly thought. And with one small gesture, he felt like he had her back.

"I introduced them," Treadwell interjected, playing the sensitive matchmaker to score points with Kelli. Or as he might say—accumulating frequent flyer miles. Darren didn't mind—it was a story he never tired of hearing.

It was Darren's first commercial flight. He was teamed with Captain Ron Treadwell, flying out of their home base of Phoenix. They had returned from a similar three-leg domestic trip, and Darren planned to retire to his lonely apartment to over-analyze his first flight and be his generally boring self. But like tonight, Treadwell dragged him out. They went to the Gila River Casino on an Indian reservation south of Phoenix, a place Treadwell had lost much of his savings over the years, at least what was left after the drinking and divorces.

Darren was mesmerized by a beautiful blackjack dealer. Her name was Liliana, but she told Darren that he could call her Lilly. If he could have formed a sentence, he would have. But as time went by, and he continued to lose money, he began striking up a conversation with her. He was impressed that she worked at the casino to put herself through school, with the goal of becoming an English teacher. He was aware that she was occupying him with conversation to break his concentration—typical dealer trick—but he would've gladly signed over anything to keep talking with her.

The only reason the story had a happy ending was because of Treadwell. After another losing hand by Darren, he exclaimed, "Will you please just agree to go on a date with my friend before he ends up homeless!"

Darren turned red with embarrassment, but it was worth it when Lilly agreed. She then ordered him away from the table with her trademark grin, commenting that he better save his money because she wasn't a cheap date. Less than a year later they were married.

The volume in the bar continued to rise as the Yankees game went into extra innings. Treadwell and Kelli seemed too involved in consuming drinks and groping each other to notice. At one point, they began childishly photographing each other with Kelli's cell phone. Alcohol and pictures never mixed, but Darren agreed to take photos of the inebriated couple. They looked like those photo-booth pictures at the mall, back before everyone had a camera on their phone. Then Kelli decided that Darren should be in the pictures, and convinced a burly Italian guy at the next table to take a group shot of the three of them.

As the games ended—Yankees a thrilling win, but the local hockey team losing in disappointing fashion—the bar began to clear out. The televisions switched over to the cable news channel GNZ. Darren wasn't really interested in the latest Democratic primary that was headlining the national news, but his only other option was to watch his mentor make-out with some woman he'd just met. His mind was solely on Lilly, anyway. He checked his phone—no return of his text. He figured that she'd either gone to bed to prepare for a long Monday at school, or was feverishly working on her lesson plan. His watch was still on Arizona time, where it was just past ten.

The next news story was about a controversial Israeli pop star named Natalie Gold, who was expected to make a highly anticipated arrival in the US this week. Not everybody was thrilled by this, and certain groups had organized protests to greet her arrival. Darren had no idea who she was, or why she was controversial, but Treadwell did. He began singing the lyrics to her latest single in a drunken slur.

Darren looked at him strangely. "Where'd you learn that?"

"When you have kids, you pick up all sorts of stuff. Wait until you and Lilly start pushing out some pups." The grin on his face was permanent at this point.

Kelli seemed to instantaneously sober up. She grabbed an expensive looking handbag and rose to her feet.

"Where you going?" Treadwell asked, looking stunned.

"Kids are complicated. Sorry, I don't do complicated," she said and began walking toward the door.

"I'm divorced," he yelled desperately to her, holding up his ring-less finger.

"That's what they all say," she shouted back as she stepped out into the rainy April night.

Darren couldn't help smiling. "Crash landing."

"Very funny," Treadwell muttered and swigged down the remainder of his Bloody Mary. It was the first one all night that he really needed.

Darren refocused on the news just in time to hear the anchor state, "In other news, there has been another abduction of a woman in Arizona. It is the fourth one this month, in what's believed to be an act of gang violence."

This grabbed Darren's interest. The gang abductions had been a huge story back home.

The anchor continued, "GNZ has gained access to the security video at the Mobil station in Chandler, where the latest abduction took place."

Darren watched a dark figure roll from underneath the SUV and attack a woman with a knife. He then threw her into the backseat and drove off.

Darren felt like he just gained another ten years. His stomach gripped tight.

The woman in the video was Lilly.

Chapter 4

Not even the relentless desert heat could put a blemish on the perfectly made up face of Jessi Stafford. She applied the finishing touches—a dab of gloss on her shiny red lips, and a flip of her thick mane of blonde hair—then dug her six-inch heels into the pavement as if preparing to stand her ground against a charging army. It was just another battle in the war to regain her relevance, and now victory was in sight.

She looked into the camera and unveiled the look of a serious journalist; one she'd perfected on stops in Orlando, New York, and now Arizona.

"I am reporting from the gas station at the corner of Elliott and Alma School Road in Chandler, where a woman was abducted, just hours ago."

After a dramatic pause, she continued, "My sources have confirmed that this is another in the series of gang-related attacks that have stricken the Valley with fear."

When Jessi signed off her report, sending the coverage back to the no-talent anchors in the studio, she let out the smile she was holding back like a sneeze.

"What's so funny, Blondie? Kidnapping humor, or have the gasoline fumes finally gotten to you?" remarked her just-out-of-college cameraman, Byung Park, sporting the usual smirk that Jessi so wanted to wipe off his face. But she let it pass, knowing she'd soon be paroled from this rinky-dink station in the desert, her penance complete.

"This abduction story is my ticket back to New York—and nothing makes me smile more than the thought of getting out of here."

"I heard all the murderers back there are lonely without you—looking forward to your conjugal visit … err … riumphant return."

She had made the ascent from a college dropout to anchoring the top rated newscast in New York City by age twenty-six, proudly using all of her ample assets to get there. But the fall was sharp and unforgiving.

The "Jane Callahan Missing" story that became the "Jane Callahan Murder" story had made Jessi a local star. She was the one to receive the tip on the whereabouts of the body, along with landing the much sought after interview with Jane's husband, and the lead suspect in her murder, Wall Street icon Steve Callahan.

Before Jessi's star could enter orbit, the pictures appeared of a bikini-clad woman gallivanting with Steve Callahan by the pool of his Mt. Kisco mansion, including a particularly damaging one that featured Jessi delicately applying sun tan lotion to the murder suspect. The headline in the tabloid paper was *Killer Sex*, and things began to spiral downward from there. Jessi was sent packing, eventually landing at this nothing station in the desert. But she didn't feel sorry for herself. In fact, she immediately began plotting her rise back to the top, figuring what better place to rise from the ashes than Phoenix. Now it looked like she might get her chance.

She had no time for Byung and his smart-ass remarks—the other reporters would cover the story, but Jessi planned to uncover it. She moved into the mini mart to once again follow up with the night manager, Jorge DeRosa. He was a tough nut to crack, but as the only witness to the abduction, he held the key to the answers she needed.

He saw her coming. "I told you, I have nothing to say to any reporters."

She had tried the soft approach earlier, twice, without any luck, so now it was time to play hardball. "Let's get down to business, Jorge. Can I call you Jorge?"

"It's my name."

"I've seen the video." It was distributed to all news outlets, hoping someone had recognized the assailant, but Jessi was more interested in the victim. “I saw that the woman paid with a credit card, so you know her name. I need the name, Jorge, do you understand?”

“I understand that I handed over everything to the police, and it’s up to them what is released and what isn’t.”

“The police should have stopped these monsters months ago. I’m trying to save this woman’s life, not to mention the next one—and if we leave it up to the police, I guarantee you there will be another victim. I saw you talking to her on the video, it looks like you liked her, maybe even knew her.”

“I told you—I’ve got nothing to say.”

She moved close to him and whispered, “Perhaps you should reconsider your answer, and then I’ll reconsider bringing in INS to have you sent back over the border.”

“For your information, I’m an American citizen. I was born and raised in this country. Were you?”

Threats were working about as well as nice did, so she went to the tactic that never failed. She bent over enough so that Jorge could get a good view of her long legs, and flashed her irresistible smile. “Maybe we can work something out.”

“I don’t know what you’re getting at, lady,” he exclaimed, his attention wandering behind her.

Before she could even follow his gaze, she felt the man’s presence.

She turned quickly to see the thick gelled hair and out-of-date sideburns of Officer Brandon Longa.

“Are you cheating on me, baby?” he said in his thick Brooklyn accent, grinning from ear to ear. Longa was the lead investigator on the case, and after a few dates, had become the inside source that had leapfrogged Jessi over the competition. Like her, Longa was in the desert doing penance for things that happened back in New York, where he was once a NYPD officer, and he thirsted every day to get back there.

She gritted her teeth and forced her most flirtatious smile. “C’mon, Brandon, I need that credit card.”

"When we decide to release the name of the victim, you'll be the first to know."

"Pretty please," she begged, flipping her hair like she was trying to get out of a traffic ticket.

His smile turned sly. "I might have an idea of how we can work things out."

Jessi whispered back, "What do you have in mind?"

Longa turned to Jorge. "I'm gonna need your bathroom key."

"Excuse me?"

"Sorry, did I speak English? My bad—give me el keyo for el bathroomo."

Jorge grumbled under his breath as he handed the oversized key to the plain-clothes police officer. Longa took Jessi by the hand and escorted her to the back of the station, with Jessi receiving more than her share of dirty looks from the other reporters and police. He opened the door and led her inside the cockroach-infested restroom.

He pulled her into a tight embrace, his hands roaming over her most sought after real estate. He then started to kiss her.

"Slow down, Brandon," she cautioned, but her actions didn't match her words, as she ran her hands along his hips to the back of his tight-fitting pants.

"Don't have time to slow down, baby. You want the name, then let's get down to business."

Desperate times called for desperate measures. She took out a sanitizing spray from her purse and began spraying it profusely around the room, trying to remove the stench of urine. She covered the sticky floor with paper towels until it acted as wall-to-wall carpeting. She then awkwardly knelt on the floor and forced her most seductive look up at Brandon.

He broke into heavy laughter. "You were really going to do it! I just wanted to see how far you'd go—what wouldn't you do for a story?"

From a kneeling position, she threw a punch. She missed her target, catching him with a glancing blow on the left hip.

"Do you know what the penalty is in Arizona for assaulting a police officer?"

"When I'm finished with you, assault will be the least of your worries."

Smiling, he responded, "I guess it's your lucky day because I'm willing to call it even."

He headed toward the door, before abruptly turning back toward her and tossing the key on the floor. "Why don't you let yourself out," he said with more laughter.

Jessi rose up, balancing onto her skyscraper heels. She took out her sanitizing spray and began coating herself like it was bug spray. Once she felt she had fought off the potential bacteria, she smiled.

She had no plans to trade her assets for information, and certainly not on this filthy floor. She had gone to great lengths to get information in this business, some dirtier than this bathroom, but she never played that card with anyone, including Steve Callahan, no matter what the New York tabloids said.

She put the spray back into her purse and then pulled out the Visa card that she had lifted from Brandon's back pocket.

The name on the card was Lilly McLaughlin.

She smiled again.

Chapter 5

Darren arrived at Phoenix Sky Harbor Airport, a place that had practically become a second home to him the last few years. It looked the same with its southwestern motif and general cleanliness, but it felt like everything had changed.

After witnessing the video of Lilly on the news, he immediately called his chief pilot back in Phoenix, as was protocol in the case of an emergency. Within half an hour, he was back at JFK and booked as a passenger on the last flight out that night. They made a stop in Atlanta, where Darren picked up another red-eye to Phoenix. There was no in-flight movie, but he had a horror flick playing over and over in his head the whole way. He kept thinking of the pictures of those other women after they were found. *Beaten and raped.* He also knew that Lilly would fight her captor with every fiber of her petite body. That worried him even more.

With the two-hour time difference, he arrived in Phoenix at 5:30. The sharp morning sun was seeping through the airport windows and reflecting off the gated shops that were not yet open for Monday morning business. Darren always loved being in the airport before the crowds arrived. It normally gave him a sense of peace, but he knew he would never have peace again until he got Lilly back safe and sound.

He moved through the airport, still in a daze. But was snapped back to reality by the sight of an unusually tall woman with bright blonde hair, running at him in a pair of heels that even Lilly wouldn't attempt to wear. An Asian man half her size ran after her holding a camera.

Darren couldn't believe this. The police had told him it was imperative that Lilly's name was not released—not wanting to risk turning the abductor into a cornered animal if Lilly's picture was splashed across the television and newspapers. But while the police were nowhere to be found, the press was moving in on him. Where was airport security when you need it? Probably frisking some eighty-year-old lady from Des Moines as if she were some suicide bomber.

The woman almost knocked him over. She stuck a microphone in his face and spoke aggressively, albeit slightly out of breath, "Mr. McLaughlin—I'm Jessi Stafford of Channel-6 News. I can't even imagine what you must be feeling right now."

What he was feeling was his guts being ripped out without an anesthetic. But he also felt anger towards this reporter for the threat she posed to his wife's safety.

"I think you have the wrong person," he said as composed as possible, and kept walking.

"You are Darren McLaughlin, correct?"

"Never heard of him," he said, looking for a sign of the police officers he was supposed to meet upon arrival.

She held up a photo of Lilly. It was her school photo from South Chandler High, where she taught English. Unlike the camera-shy Darren, Lilly never took a bad photo. Even her driver's license photo was magazine-worthy.

He grabbed the photo away from her. "Don't you understand that you're putting Lilly's life in danger by showing her picture!?"

"So you *are* Darren McLaughlin," she said with a grin. She turned to the cameraman, who looked half asleep. "Are you getting this?"

"Turn the camera off," Darren demanded.

She turned back to him. "I'm going to be straight with you, Darren—can I call you Darren?"

He said nothing, which she took as a green light.

"Your wife is in danger, Darren. And it has nothing to do with a picture—it's because you think the police are going to find her. If you're counting on the police, Lilly is going to end up beaten and raped like the others—you saw the pictures of those women, right?" he again said nothing, but nodded slightly—he had. "I'm your best shot to get her back safe and sound."

He looked at her with disbelief. "What could you do to get Lilly back?"

"For one thing, the police in this case are incompetent. They tell you that Lilly could be in danger if her name gets out. But then fail to protect information that would connect her to the abduction."

She displayed a credit card and held it in front of his face. It was Lilly's Visa card. He tried to snatch it, but she pulled it back. "Where did you get that?" he asked with annoyance.

Then the card was gone. She turned quickly to see a wiry man with thick gelled hair. He wore a cheap, ill-fitting suit with no tie and too much cologne. "I'll take that, thank you very much."

"Give that back, Brandon," she ordered.

The man in the suit smiled coolly. "I'll tell you what, Jessi. You stop messing with my investigation and I'll look past this whole stolen evidence thing," he held up the credit card to make his point. "And if you release any names in regards to this investigation, you'll be heading to jail. And you don't really strike me as a prison kinda girl."

The comment extracted a laugh from her cameraman and she shot a dirty look in his direction.

The man in the suit nodded at a couple of bored airport security guards, who took great pleasure in escorting the pushy reporter and her cameraman out of the area.

He turned to Darren. "Mr. McLaughlin, I'm Officer Longa of the Chandler Police. Please come with me, we have a lot to talk about concerning your wife."

Chapter 6

Darren was led to a holding room beneath Sky Harbor. It was a place usually reserved for unruly passengers taken off flights. The potential terrorists made the headlines, but 99% of the time the cause of the disturbance was alcohol and not Jihad.

The no-frills room was made up of just a metal table surrounded by uncomfortable-looking chairs, and a water cooler. Officer Longa had said nothing during their journey to the bowels of the airport, which included numerous flights of stairs in stifling heat. But Longa turned into a smiling greeter when they reached the room. He introduced Darren to two other plain-clothes officers. One named Madkins, who looked like an aging surfer with a mop of frosted blond hair. The other, Gutierrez, was a large, menacing man with a Fu Manchu mustache.

They all sat around the table, except Longa, who continued to pace the room with nervous energy. Gutierrez and Madkins began looking through folders marked *McLaughlin.* When Darren had called to inform the local police that it was his wife on that video, they already had known her identity. It confounded him at first, but during his cross-country flight he had time to conclude that it was likely there was more surveillance footage than what was released, probably including the license plate number on the SUV she was driving. Thanks to the reporter, Darren now knew that Lilly must have given her credit card to the attendant. The surprise would have been if they didn't know her identity.

But at the same time, just seeing a police file with their name on it brought a sick feeling to his stomach. The heat began to smother his senses and he started to feel lightheaded.

Longa noticed this, and asked, "Are you all right, Mr. McLaughlin?"

"I'm fine," Darren replied. He didn't want any delays in the hunt for Lilly. "I've had a tough few hours."

"I can imagine," Madkins said. "You seem nervous, I'm guessing that is related to worry for your wife."

"I just want to get Lilly back."

"Don't we all, Mr. McLaughlin, don't we all," Gutierrez stated, then got up and filled a plastic cup with water and brought it to Darren. "Here you go, don't want you to pass out on us. We have a lot to discuss."

Longa stopped pacing and sat on the edge of the table, beside Darren. "So you're a pilot, Mr. McLaughlin?"

Darren thought the pilot uniform should have been a dead giveaway, not to mention that these guys had six hours to gather information about him. But as with his commanding officers in the Air Force, he knew it was best to keep the answers short and never question. Besides, Lilly was the one who was good with the sarcastic remarks.

"Yes."

Madkins continued to flip through the folder like he was cramming for a final exam. "I see you were in the Air Force?"

"Yes, I graduated from the Air Force Academy in Colorado Springs. I put in ten years before joining the civilian ranks. I now fly commercial."

"Air Force Academy, wow, muy impressivo, Señor McLaughlin," Gutierrez interjected.

"I'll bet you had one of those cool pilot nicknames?" Madkins said, feigning interest.

"That's only in the movies," Gutierrez shot back at his partner. "But what they do teach you in the military is how to use weapons, isn't that right, Mr. McLaughlin?"

Darren wasn't sure how this was helping, but continued to conform. "We went to basic training like all military. But I mostly flew cargo missions. I was never involved in any combat."

Longa got things back on track, "So the reason you were in New York was because you were working … as a pilot?"

"That is correct."

"Do you have a schedule set in advance?" Longa continued.

"Yes, we put in bids at the beginning of each month for our trips. They are based on seniority. So I've known about this trip for weeks. Can you please tell me what this has to do with getting my wife back?"

Longa frowned at Darren's challenge. "Getting her back means finding the person who drove off in your vehicle. I'm trying to establish if someone might have been aware that you were planning to be out of town."

Darren had assumed it was a random act. "So you're saying that her abductor—this gang member—might have been planning this and waited until I was away?"

The three of them traded curious glances.

"Who said anything about gang members?" Gutierrez asked with an incredulous look.

"Do you know something we don't know?" Madkins chipped in.

Darren remained confused. "I saw it on the news—fourth woman this month."

"If it's on the news it must be true," Madkins added with his smirk.

"Ever heard of a copycat crime, Mr. McLaughlin?" Longa asked.

"Sure—when someone makes a crime look like one that already took place—you think that might be what happened with Lilly?"

Madkins and Guitierrez broke into laughter. Longa shushed the comedy team, before continuing with a serious face, "How have things been in your marriage, Mr. McLaughlin. The spark still alive?"

"Things are fine."

"Fine, as in you're doing it five times a week, or fine as in nobody is filing charges against each other?"

"Things are fine," Darren repeated, his tone turning angry.

Longa remained serious. "Things will only be fine when we get Lilly back. And the only way we're going to do that is if you start telling us the truth. You do want us to find your wife, don't you, Mr. McLaughlin?"

Chapter 7

"We've had a little rough patch, okay? I don't know exactly what you're accusing me of, but if you don't want to find Lilly, then I'll do it myself," Darren had officially lost his cool.

"Whoa, whoa, whoa, Mr. McLaughlin. We're not accusing you of anything," Longa said with arms in the air, surrender style. "We're just covering all our bases. But we're convinced that your wife's disappearance is connected to your flight schedule."

Madkins and Gutierrez nodded their heads.

Darren did his best tough-guy nod and responded, "Good."

"When was the last time you had contact with your wife?" Longa asked.

Darren suddenly remembered the photos she attached to her text. It seemed like years ago. "She sent me these photos. I assume it was right before she was attacked," he said, reaching into his front pocket and handing them the phone.

Madkins practically drooled on the photos, "Every man's fantasy indeed, you are one lucky man."

He passed the phone to Gutierrez. "Ooo-la-la—that is one hot tamale."

The phone finally arrived in Longa's hands and he looked impressed. "A woman like that must be hard to hold onto for a simple man like yourself, Mr. McLaughlin … no offense. I'd be jealous all the time."

That sounded like another accusation. Darren understood that the husband was always the first suspect, but it wasn't helping to get Lilly back, and that's all he cared about at the moment. He then remembered something else. "She had GPS on her cell phone. Can't you use cell phone towers to trace it?"

They all laughed.

"Maybe we should get him a badge," Madkins quipped.

With a raised hand, Longa quieted his troops once again, and then said, "That's the first thing we did. It's called triangulation, and it led us to a dumpster at the local high school where your wife works. The phone was too smashed for us to positively ID it, but we are confident it was Lilly's phone. It was destroyed and ditched, so we are dealing with people who know what they're doing."

"Which makes it interesting that you would bring the cell phone up," Gutierrez said in an accusatory tone, no longer laughing.

Darren chose not to take the bait, remaining silent.

"Do you have any idea why your wife was out at that gas station on a Sunday night?" Longa asked.

Darren shrugged. "I don't know. But Lilly always let the gas gauge run low. Maybe she was filling up so she wouldn't have to worry about it in the morning."

Longa's look said he didn't buy the answer. "The night manager said she seemed in a rush. What would be the hurry if she was just filling her tank before going home to get a good night's rest?"

"She's always on the go—it's just the way she's wired. Nothing out of character," Darren replied.

Madkins took another peek at the pictures that Lilly took of herself—pictures that were only meant for Darren. "And she is dressed to impress. That doesn't look like a curl-up-with-a-book outfit."

"Lilly always dresses like that. I'm a little more conservative, but she…"

"Your wife works at South Chandler High School, correct?" Longa interrupted.

Darren assumed he already knew the answer—it was obvious that he knew a lot more than he was letting on—but continued to go with the flow. "Yes—she taught junior and senior English."

"You said she always dresses the same way. Does that include school?"

Darren had enough of them blaming the victim. "What are you getting at!?"

"I'm just saying that kids that age can be very impressionable."

"Catch a glimpse of some leg and go into hormone overload ... ah, those were the days," Madkins interjected.

"Those are still your days. Bottom line is, hormones can make these teenagers do some crazy shit," Gutierrez added.

Darren started to think along with them. Teenage hormones, knowledge that he was out of town... "Are you saying one of her students might have done this? And then made it look like a gang initiation?

Longa took out a fake pen and pretended to write down his theory. Another not-very-subtle way of letting him know they were the police and in charge. And as much as he wanted to storm out, he needed these jerks.

"Was she close to any specific students?" Longa asked.

"A lot of them. She always wanted to help—especially the ones who had tough upbringings, like herself. She certainly didn't mean to lead any of them on."

"I'm sure she didn't. Did any of her students come over to your house, or meet with her outside of school?" Longa asked.

"She held tutoring sessions at our house on the weekends. But I met all of those kids and none of them gave off the vibe that they'd be capable of something like this."

"Husbands can always tell that sort of stuff," Longa said. "Were you always present for these sessions to perform your Jedi mind tricks?"

Darren ignored the sarcasm. "No, sometimes I was away, like this weekend."

"Ever meet a Brett Buckley?"

The name surprised him. "Yes. He had moved here recently from Seattle or something like that. Do you think he was the one behind this?"

The officers had another hearty laugh at his expense, while Darren bit his tongue.

Finally Longa gathered himself enough to say, "It takes more than one person to pull off something like this."

"It takes two to tango," Madkins said, still chuckling.

"Lleva dos el tango," Gutierrez seconded. "But my guess is you already know this, Mr. McLaughlin, even if you don't want to admit it to yourself."

Darren was tiring of the code-speak and inside jokes. "Let's cut the bull. Tell me what happened to my wife!"

Longa pointed his finger in Darren's direction. "I'll tell you exactly what happened."

Just as the words were about to fly out of his mouth, the doors of the room swung open and the cavalry barged in—led by a silver-haired man in an expensive suit. "This interrogation is over," he announced.

Longa fought against it, but the man pulled rank. "This case is now officially under the jurisdiction of the FBI. One more stunt like this, and I'll personally make sure you're writing parking tickets for the next thirty years."

Longa and his team were ushered out. When the doors shut, the distinguished looking man sat beside Darren and gave him a disarming smile.

"Mr. McLaughlin, I'm Agent LaPoint of the Federal Bureau of Investigation, and I'm your new best friend."

Chapter 8

The US Attorney pounced off his chair in his Manhattan office and picked up the ringing phone. “Eicher here.”

“It’s LaPoint.”

Eicher felt a twinge of relief. He’d been waiting for this call since he got the news last night.

“Well?” he asked, having run out of patience.

“I just finished grilling the husband—the pilot. He either doesn’t know shit, or he should win the Oscar. And I don’t mean he should be happy to be nominated, he should win the damn thing.”

Eicher sighed. Another dead end. *How could he be living under the same roof and have absolutely no clue?* As a federal prosecutor, he believed in the standard of reasonable doubt, but as a card-carrying cynic, he was always skeptical of convenient coincidences. So he needed it proven beyond any reasonable doubt that the McLaughlins’ swift infiltration into Brett Buckley’s life was a random act.

“But we got lucky,” LaPoint tried to paint a bright side.

“And how would that be?”

“The local police had beat us to him, and they were going to get an arrest warrant for the wife.”

Eicher winced. He knew the type of publicity that these kinds of cases generated. Signing an arrest warrant would have been the equivalent of putting the kid before a firing squad. “I thought Fitzpatrick said that situation was under control.”

“If it was, then I wouldn’t be sweating my balls off in the Arizona desert, would I? Fitzpatrick ordered the local police to shut down their investigation weeks ago. We gave them no explanation other than our boy Buckley had a higher calling. But after last night's events, I think they saw it as a chance to ride in like heroes."

LaPoint gave the impression that Eicher should thank him for messing up his case, and probably getting Nick killed in the process. "Something sparked the kid—set him off. I interviewed him a hundred times over the past year. He was unflappable and levelheaded. This move was completely out of character. What do you think happened?"

LaPoint chuckled. "I think we both *know* what happened. And just the fact you asked means it hasn't happened for you in a while."

Eicher conceded the point. It was a logical explanation, especially when recent events were factored in. But when it came to this case, he had learned that nothing was as it seemed to be. He thought for a moment, before saying, "I think it goes deeper."

"I think you and the kid have something in common."

"Which is?"

"You're both spooked. Seeing things that aren't there. I think it's straightforward—the local cops scared him when they threatened to make an arrest on the other matter. He knows who he's dealing with—so it makes sense that he got scared. He even told Fitzpatrick that he saw Zubov scouting him out at the mall, which we both know couldn't be true, because if it was, he'd be dead. So he did what we all do when we get scared—we run to our mommy—in his case, a mother figure. Traveling in pairs gives the illusion of safety, so that's what they did."

Eicher knew that panic was the first step toward tragedy. And just the thought of the soulless killing machine named Zubov made him ill. But he also knew what the kid had been through in the past year, so maybe LaPoint was right—the fear drove him to confide in his favorite teacher. In the end, she was the only one he trusted and she helped him concoct a plan to get him out of Dodge before Zubov got him. He wasn't going to stick around to find out if he was real or imagined.

Eicher wondered if Lilly McLaughlin really understood exactly what she had gotten herself into. But then he had another thought. A troubling one. Perhaps she knew *exactly* what she'd done.

He flipped through a folder that had been sitting in the same spot on his desk for the past year. One photo was of Nick's father, Karl Zellen, who wore a fashionable bullet hole in his forehead. The next picture was of his mother, Paula, lying lifelessly in the lion's den, sprayed with bullets. But the photos that grabbed him by the throat—the ones that turned this case into an obsession for him—were the ones of Nick's girlfriend, Audrey Mays. It was a warning to Nick about the perils of testifying against Alexei Sarvydas.

The *before* was a fresh-faced twenty-something with the smile of an idealist. The *after* was just a torso. No head—no hands—no feet. A corpse that some of his more heartless colleagues repulsively referred to as "Bob." It was a favorite tactic of the Russian mob, and perfected by the Sarvydas Organizatsiya, to make identification virtually impossible.

"We need to find him ASAP," Eicher stated, attempting to hide the desperation in his voice. "If Sarvydas gets to him first, they will be picking up his pieces with a wet-vac."

"I don't know what you're talking about, counselor," LaPoint replied, deadpan. "I thought Viktor Sarvydas was just a hardworking music mogul on vacation in Israel. A heartwarming rags to riches story."

Even in jest, LaPoint outlined two of the biggest challenges in taking on Russian crime bosses like Sarvydas. First of all, they hide behind legitimate businesses. In Sarvydas' case, it was Sarvy Music, an international music empire with a knack for churning out pop stars.

The other problem was the ease of their flight. Any Russian mobster worth his vodka had Israeli citizenship and passport—taking advantage of the Israeli policy of Right of Return, which allows citizenship and safe haven to all those with Jewish heritage and doesn't bend for any extradition laws. But most Russian mobsters were Jewish in passport only. Eicher doubted that Viktor Sarvydas had ever seen the inside of a synagogue.

"Just find the kid," Eicher barked into the phone and hung up.

Chapter 9

After hanging up with LaPoint, Eicher desperately needed a fix of good news. It was just past nine in the morning in New York, and the offices in Foley Square were beginning to fill up with the wretched rumblings of Monday morning.

Eicher viewed the hustle and bustle through the glass partition of his office and noticed a man who didn't fit in with the conservative suit-and-tie attire of the US Attorney's Office. And he was headed directly into his office.

The intruder didn't alarm Eicher. In fact, he was happy to see Ivan, even if he wasn't thrilled with the heavy scent of fish he brought with him.

"Ivan—it's April, not January," he greeted his visitor, noticing his fur cap and dense beard. He carried a cooler one might use to store bait. "Going fishing?"

Ivan displayed a toothless grin and spoke in his thick Russian accent, "We already do fishing today, and I think you be interested what we caught."

Eicher nodded his head, indicating him to continue.

"Moziaf Butcher Shop was raided this morning, investigating last week's shooting. I could have saved them time, they, of course, found nothing to connect Moziafs to murder. But they came across something that might interest *you*."

Ivan was an undercover cop in Brighton Beach—a section of Brooklyn that is the home office for the Russian mob in the United States. That's not to say the majority of the residents weren't hard working and law-abiding citizens, but Eicher was only interested in those who broke the laws. Ivan was one of the rare few willing to talk, and only Eicher and a few colleagues above his pay grade knew Ivan's true identity. He very rarely showed up here—there are only so many times you can claim to being hassled by the feds without suspicions being raised—so Eicher knew this must be important.

Like many Russians, he emigrated to Brighton Beach in the 1970s, and became a popular street vendor in Little Odessa. He was known for his homemade foods that included everything from pirogi to pastry shells filled with spicy pork. Word of mouth attracted none other than the don of Brighton Beach, Viktor Sarvydas. He was so impressed with Ivan that he made him his personal caterer at his popular club, Sarvy's.

But at heart, Ivan was a man of honor. And after observing Sarvydas' unspeakable acts, Ivan chose to become what the Russians call a *musor*, or informant. While he was never able to get Sarvydas, he did have success in the arrest and prosecutions of many of his dangerous underlings. He was so successful that the NYPD offered him a full-time position.

"So what was this shooting about?" Eicher made conversation as he accepted the ice chest and set it on his cluttered desk.

Ivan shrugged. "Who knows? Moziafs are crazy. Maybe they no kill anybody this week and needed fix."

No statement could better sum up the Moziafs—a husband and wife team of killers. They had been working for Sarvydas in recent years, although their allegiance was usually with the highest bidder for their services.

Oleg, the husband, was an enormous four-hundred-pound former Olympic weightlifting champion from the Soviet Union. He loved three things—killing, steroids, and his wife, Vana. She was arguably the more ruthless of the two, and claimed that killing was like sex for them. Ivan joked if that were the case then they sure were getting more than the average couple. The shooting connected to this morning's raid was the typical work of the Moziafs—six people shot in Coney Island in the middle of the day with hundreds of people there, yet no witnesses.

Eicher was mildly surprised by the reappearance of the Moziafs on American soil, as Viktor Sarvydas and most of his henchmen had been on the next plane out of JFK after the arrest of his son, Alexei. Last Eicher had heard, the Moziafs were taking up the sport of car bombing in Moscow, and with the trial only a week away, he expected Sarvydas' troops to lay low.

"Not one person could identify them?" Eicher asked.

Ivan had a hearty laugh at his naiveté. "They interviewed fifty witnesses and they all say *ya nectevo ne znago*—I don't know nothing. There are lots of rumors. With Viktor out of country and Alexei going to trial, many think Sarvydas' deputy lieutenant, Parmalov, is making power play and Moziafs doing dirty work for him. But who knows with these people—they have no loyalty. When I first arrive, Moziafs and Zubov were rivals in war that leave bodies from New York to Moscow, and now both work for Sarvydas. Ask me this afternoon and everything be different."

Eicher understood the frustration in Ivan's voice. When it came to the Russian Mafiya, they were severely outgunned. Eicher removed the top from the cooler and immediately jumped back about a foot.

"Moziafs like to keep souvenirs," Ivan stated, matter of fact.

Eicher stared at the frozen hands that were stored in plastic Zip-lock bags like they were leftover chicken in the refrigerator. He felt sick, but his nausea turned to interest when he saw the tattoo on the left hand in the webbing between the thumb and index finger. It was an interlocking *N Z*. He instantly knew that it belonged to Audrey Mays, Nick Zellen's girlfriend.

Alexei's powerful lawyers would have a field day with the search, and it wasn't a smoking gun by any means, but it was another connection the prosecution could make between the murders and the Sarvydas family.

As Eicher looked at the amputated hands, it sure didn't feel like something to celebrate. He feared getting to that place where finding the remains of a murdered girl would constitute a good day.

He thought of Nick, remembering how devastated he was by Audrey's death. He wanted to be mad at him for the ulcer he was causing him this morning, but could only find compassion. Eicher couldn't even fathom the emotions that must have been haunting Nick as the trial grew closer. He just hoped the next hands they found wouldn't belong to him.

Chapter 10

Viktor Sarvydas lounged in the back of his stretch limo, parked outside of the Western Wall Plaza in Jerusalem. He peered out the tinted bulletproof windows and marveled at the sheer numbers, and the ferocity of those who came out to protest his latest protégé, pop sensation Natalie Gold.

The Wailing Wall was a place where Israelis had come to mourn the past since King Herod built the retaining wall over two thousand years ago. It was considered one of the most holy places in Jerusalem. And that is exactly why he chose the spot to shoot Natalie's latest video, full of all the gyrations and revealing outfits of a pop princess.

Sarvydas smiled, proud to have achieved the desired controversy once again. And it's not like the protestors could stop him—he had friends in the highest places.

The video was classic Sarvydas. It combined his ruthless business savvy with his passionate love of music. But most of all, it was fueled by his lust for power. He not only had a kingdom that ranged from Brighton Beach to Israel to Moscow, but he was also a kingmaker. A few months ago, Natalie Gold was a homeless girl named Daria Scheffer, who was singing for her supper in Tel Aviv, outside of a Russian bookstore that Sarvydas frequented. Now, only six months later, Natalie had rocketed to worldwide fame, and her first single "Vengeance" was the most downloaded song on *iTunes*.

He spotted Natalie pushing past the angry mob, surrounded by machine-gun toting bodyguards. Sarvydas was enjoying the scene before him. He checked his jet-black hair in a mirror and adjusted the ponytail that dangled at the back of his neck. He was now in his late fifties, but age hadn't lessened his vanity. He believed in being at his best, fearing the newer model that was always trying to come up behind him. And when you are the don of the Russian Mafiya, it usually comes up behind you looking to kill.

He took one more glance into the mirror and came away impressed with himself, as usual. His face wasn't the same since the shooting, but it was improving each day. "Not bad for a poor boy from Orensburg," he mumbled to himself.

His childhood dream was to be a pop star like his idol, Joseph Kozolbol. So as a teenager he left home and moved to the Black Sea port city of Odessa, known for its wealthy residents. He took a job crooning on a cruise ship, which allowed him to travel abroad—a rare opportunity in the Soviet Union at the time. Even as a young man he was always thinking business, and took advantage of his travels to bring back items that were near impossible to obtain behind the Iron Curtain. He sold them at a huge markup, showing a pretty good knowledge of the free market for a communist kid.

The cruise ship was the start of his lucrative music and business careers. Mixing his great love of music with business to create a cocktail of power.

But this past year, he learned what a toxic mix love and business could be. When his son Alexei was accused of killing his longtime friend and business partner, Karl Zellen, he was forced to leave the US and relocate to this dreadful strip of sand called Israel. Viktor knew that Alexei wasn't the one who killed Karl, but was sure that the Americans would twist Alexei's words, or lie about evidence in order to come after him. That's why he was forced to flee. America was a lot like him—they covered up their dirty deeds behind music. *America the Beautiful. God Bless America.* He spit at that—America was no different from these protestors—pledging morality, yet lusting for the dark side.

Viktor took another glance at the scene he created. He felt the crowd closing in on the limo, continuing to taunt Natalie in screaming Yiddish. It reminded him why he hated Israel. But unlike others in the region, he took no issue with their choice of deities.

His main point of contention was that they were always arguing and shouting, and when they weren't giving him a migraine with their constant volume, they were whining about their plight. Viktor didn't understand this thinking—the way he saw it, all Russians were dealt a bad hand before they left the womb. But they grabbed, clawed, and stole their way to the top. They made their own way without complaint, even if their methods were harsh.

As he watched Natalie bounce beautifully through the bloodthirsty crowd, the ringing of his phone startled him.

"It's Kelli," the voice on the other end began.

"Make it fast—I lack time," he said, watching Natalie moving toward the vehicle, surrounded by bodyguards.

"Nick's on the move."

As he processed this news, a wicked smile came over his face. "I want him to come to me in one piece. Get word out—especially to Zubov—only I deal with Nick. This is personal."

Chapter 11

Natalie Gold was whisked into the limo. Once the door slammed shut, the protestors began rocking the vehicle.

Viktor looked Natalie up and down like he was checking for scratches on a new Ferrari. She wore a transparent fishnet body stocking with only a skimpy bikini underneath. Natalie's curves were trapped underneath the body-stocking like a bear in a bag. She had a different look from most Israeli women, which besides her powerful voice, was one of the reasons he chose her. There were no doubt many exotic beauties in Israel, but he liked that Natalie looked American. The buxom blonde who oozed a take-no-prisoners sexuality. Viktor might have been forced to stay in Israel, but that didn't mean he couldn't bring a piece of Americana with him.

He kissed Natalie on her puffy lips. She returned the kiss, but it lacked any hint of love or attraction. He sensed that it was a kiss of gratitude. Natalie was young, but she was street-smart, and like himself, she understood how to mix love and business to get to the top.

Viktor had become intimate with many of his protégés over the years. He even married pop star Maria DeMaio when she was only nineteen. But Natalie was special, and he didn't have to be Freud to figure out why.

She was a replica of Paula—the one true love of his life. He could still shut his eyes and relive the first time he heard the curvaceous beauty sing at his Brooklyn club, Sarvy's. She sang like an angel—a voice he'd never heard equaled until he found Natalie singing outside of that bookstore.

The limo drove away, knocking a few protestors off along the way. They traveled through the Western Wall Tunnel, then down the cobblestone streets and out of the ancient city. About an hour later they arrived in Tel Aviv, a much more modern city than Jerusalem, and preferred by Viktor. He opened a Sarvy Music office in Tel Aviv a couple years back. It was located amongst a north-south strip of skyscrapers crowded along the coast of the Mediterranean Sea.

As the early afternoon sun shone into the limo, Viktor placed his hand on Natalie's fishnet-covered thigh. He felt her shudder at his touch, despite her forced smile. *Good thing she was a singer and not an actress,* he thought. He liked it when those around him felt a sense of fear.

"Remember that we have an important dinner guest tonight."

Natalie nodded attentively.

He handed her a box wrapped with a bow. "I think you should wear this tonight. I believe it will make a good impression on our company."

She opened the package to reveal a sequined gown. She kissed him on the cheek and exclaimed, "It's beautiful. You are so generous to me."

"And tomorrow you will be flying to the States for your video premiere," Viktor continued, all business.

"I wish you could come with me."

He smiled at the lie. "You know I can't risk that right now—with the trial starting next week. But I do have something I want you to deliver to Alexei for me," he said, not providing any details.

"Of course."

Viktor ordered his driver to stop in Ramat HaSharon, a suburb northeast of Tel Aviv, to accommodate his desire to stop at his favorite Russian bookstore—the same one he had discovered Natalie outside of. This wasn't a nostalgic trip, he wanted to buy a stack of his favorite Russian crime novels. The criminal was often the hero in Russian novels, and he liked that.

He also enjoyed visiting his old friends who ran the store. The Russians in Israel always stuck together. They were treated as lepers, and endured constant calls for their deportation. Russians made up only about a fifth of the Israeli population, yet were constantly blamed for establishing enclaves in the country and importing shallow values. *More whining*, Viktor thought—nobody had ever offered to give back the billions of dollars that Russian businessmen like himself pump into the economy.

Viktor left a fifteen hundred dollar tip for his comrades at the bookstore. A nice payday for sharing a glass of vodka and reminiscing about their youthful days in Odessa. He also had Natalie put on an impromptu performance of her new single for the few lucky souls browsing the bookshelves. Viktor had always been known as a benevolent don who held honor above cruelty. Unlike his predecessor, a man who was feared but not respected, Viktor was showered with gifts and held in great esteem within the community—a community that had spread across the globe—but they also knew not to cross him.

They left the bookstore and drove toward Netanya, a coastal city halfway between Tel Aviv and Haifa, where Viktor owned a magnificent cliffside palace that overlooked the Mediterranean Sea. His riches were legendary.

Viktor escorted Natalie inside. He began preparations for their dinner guest, but his thoughts were on his potential reunion with Nick.

Chapter 12

Darren walked out of the interrogation room beaten and dazed. Despite Agent LaPoint's claims to the contrary, Darren didn't feel like he had anybody in his corner. He would have to find Lilly by himself—he had never felt so alone.

He entered the main airport terminal through a door marked *Authorized Personnel Only*. It was now closing in on seven o'clock and the airport had woken up from its slumber. Passengers lined up for security checks, restaurants were open for overpriced breakfasts, and newspaper stands were selling Monday morning editions of the *Arizona Republic.* On the front page was the headline: *Gang Warfare!*

Darren bought a copy, and after quickly skimming it, was relieved that Lilly's name wasn't released. If she was really abducted by a student who'd tried to make it look like a copycat crime, as the police hinted, then Darren saw an advantage in the media helping to sell the gang angle. Perhaps lull her captor into a false sense of safety.

He folded the paper under his arm and began heading toward the pilot's parking area. But blocking his path was the same reporter from earlier.

"I have no comment," he replied before she even opened her mouth, and continued his walk toward the parking garage.

"I don't know where you're going, your wife dropped you off on Saturday morning. You have no car at the airport."

He had forgotten—the plan was for Lilly to pick him up when he returned. "How do you know that?"

"I'm a reporter, remember? Sounds like you have a lot on your mind, maybe you'd feel better if you talked to someone about it."

She was right—he did have a lot on his mind. He mentally pictured Brett Buckley from one of their encounters at Lilly's tutoring sessions. He stood out to Darren because he seemed much more mature than some of his classmates. Darren also remembered his intense eyes and powerful looking physique. Now he pictured him in that ski mask with a knife, throwing his wife into the back of their vehicle and driving off. Darren felt ill, causing him to stop in his tracks.

Jessi caught up to him. "So do the police have any leads?"

He doubted it would really make him feel better, and logic told him that he'd regret it if he engaged this reporter, but he felt compelled to talk to someone, and she was the most readily available. "They had some theories, but seemed to be fishing. They definitely didn't think it was gang related. Hinted that it might have been one of my wife's students, she is a…"

"Teacher at South Chandler High, I know," she informed, as if to showcase her reporter cred.

"I shouldn't be telling you anything," he said, having second thoughts, and began walking away again. But he couldn't shake her.

"So they think one of your wife's students was stalking her?" she asked. "I've had a few stalkers myself, makes you feel very alone and vulnerable. Did the police give you a name of the student they suspect?"

"No," he lied, but his thoughts were on the first task in front of him—getting home. Maybe when he saw Lilly's things or smelled her perfume he would be able to think more clearly.

"I don't know who you think you're dealing with—I'm not some local yokel, I used to work in New York—the police would've run possible suspects by you, want to know if she ever talked to you about X student or Y student. Maybe she mentioned being scared of one of them, or had some romantic overture made toward her, something along those lines. So how about we start with some honesty?"

Coming from the person who stole his wife's credit card, that was a bit rich. Darren should have left her behind, but for some reason he didn't, and continued talking, "They were throwing some theories against the wall, hoping they'd stick. The local police practically accused me of being involved in her disappearance, but then the FBI came in and acted like they were my best friends. If they can't get on the same page, then I have no idea how they expect to find Lilly."

Jessi continued to cling to his side like flypaper, and let out a condescending laugh. "Don't you get it—they were playing good-cop/bad-cop. I hope you're smart enough to figure out that they think you're involved."

"That's ridiculous! I love my wife—all I want is her to be safe."

She rolled her eyes. "Tell it to the jury. It's textbook. You're conveniently in New York, which gives you a perfect alibi, and you and your wife were obviously having problems. So you hire one of her students and make it look like one of the gang abductions."

"I'm a pilot. It was my job to be in New York. And what makes you think we were having problems?"

"Some reporters might see your sad puppy dog eyes and fall for your story, but I see a husband away and a wife strutting around in a skimpy outfit like she's heading to a club. And you seem like one of those inadequate guys who wants a bunch of kids so you can imprison her. But your wife didn't give you children, so my guess is she had a boyfriend that she was going to better-deal you for, and that's why you had her abducted, and possibly killed."

"What are you talking about?" Darren said, lowering his voice, "Boyfriend? Killed? You're crazy! And obviously you don't know Lilly. We love each other and I'm going to find her!"

Darren barged by Jessi toward a car that wasn't there. She jumped back in front of him. "You're going to need my help to find her."

"I don't know how you could help me."

"You need to make a public plea on television. I have the power to set it up."

"If you think I was involved, then why would you help me?"

"It's in both our interests to find your wife. For me, I need to break the big story that will get me back to New York. In your case, if you really had nothing to do with her disappearance, then you obviously want to find her before she ends up like those other women, or worse. But if you did hire this kid to get rid of her, then you best start playing the role of the concerned husband ASAP."

Darren gave her a dirty look. But when he met her eyes, he came to a scary realization—aligning with Jessi Stafford might be his best chance to get Lilly back.

Chapter 13

They drove in Jessi's car, a convertible VW Cabriolet, red.

The trip from Sky Harbor to South Chandler took about twenty minutes. There was always heavy traffic in the Valley, but they just beat the morning rush. Jessi spent the entire ride on her cell phone headset like a hard-edged labor negotiator, convincing her bosses to put his plea on television. From what Darren could make out, her appeal hit a roadblock. Lilly's name had yet to be released, so besides the obvious legal issues it might raise, there was no way to check if Darren really was the husband, or just another wacko trying to break into reality TV. But she finally won out and victoriously hung up.

"You're tougher than you look," Darren quipped.

"Because I'm a pretty girl?"

"Sorry, I shouldn't have stereotyped you."

"Don't be—I've been profiling you since before we met, and sadly it looks like I'm going to be right."

"What kind of person do you think I am?"

"It doesn't matter what I think of you, it matters if the audience buys your story."

Darren was already questioning their alliance. "So what now—when do we do the interview?"

"With most respectable news stations, there would be days of legal haggling, but Channel-6 is so desperate for ratings that they'll risk getting sued. A high-profile lawsuit might actually help them become relevant. So to answer your question, as soon as we get to your house."

A knot tightened in Darren's stomach as Jessi pulled into the driveway of his home in Mendoza Ranch, one of the many master-planned communities in Chandler.

Darren was always comforted by the conformity of the neighborhood—all the homes were single-family-detached built in hacienda style, with similar exteriors. When they first came with a realtor, it reminded Darren of the pristine planned community in the movie *Poltergeist* where they moved the headstones but not the bodies. He sensed that Lilly saw it as monotonous torture. She wanted to paint their home hot pink or put up a neon sign to get some differentiation, which Darren explained was in violation of the neighborhood association ordinance.

They entered through the garage. Lilly's Jetta was there, but the other spot in the garage was empty. It was too much for Darren to take—he needed to get into the safety of the house. He led Jessi through an entrance-way that featured a vaulted ceiling and the hum of a gently rotating fan.

On a typical Monday morning, he and Lilly would be sitting at the breakfast table with the warm rays of the morning sun shining off them. Lilly would go on and on about her lesson plans for the upcoming day. She loved teaching—especially helping the students with hardships and tough backgrounds—and he could listen to her for hours while sipping coffee. It seemed lonely and foreign without Lilly. He thought being back in the home they shared might give him clarity, but it just made the whole thing seem all too real.

Jessi looked around the orderly room with its plain furniture, and announced, "I see that boring has come back in style." She chuckled to herself, before adding, "I guess you tried to bore her to death and when that didn't work you hired someone to do your dirty work for you."

Darren's face scrunched in disbelief. "You really think I killed my wife?"

He couldn't get past that.

"It wasn't even that creative. It's like you stole Scott Peterson's playbook—the marriage to the girl with the perfect smile, giving the perception of an ideal marriage to the outside world. Then when she disappeared, Peterson went to the tearful public plea card. Sound familiar?"

"The plea was your idea—you said it would help find her."

"I just led the horse to water. It was your choice whether you'd drink or not, and I sure didn't have twist your arm very hard to get you to agree."

Darren didn't respond, his thoughts on Lilly. He stared blankly into the "boring" living room where he and his wife would spend "boring" nights watching TV. Even performing the most mundane tasks with Lilly was exciting for Darren—just being around her made his pulse rush like he was skydiving without a parachute—but sometimes he wondered if it was as exciting for her.

"Can I get you anything? A cold drink, or something to eat?" Darren played host, out of his ingrained obligation to please.

She thought for a second, and then said, "I need to use your bathroom to freshen up."

He led her through the main bedroom and pointed out the master bath.

"No snarky comments about being in another murderer's bedroom for a story?"

Darren had no idea what she was talking about, but was growing tired of the murderer insinuation. "Why would I say that?"

"Don't tell me you never heard of the Jane Callahan murder in New York?" she asked with a skeptical tone.

Darren tried to think, but his mind was too cluttered. "No, should I have?"

Jessi shook her head as she went into the bathroom and closed the door. She shouted through the door, "You're going to need to be a better liar than that, Darren McLaughlin."

Darren waited for her in the living room, gathering his thoughts for the important interview. When she returned, she began casing the house to determine the best spot to set up the camera. She decided on the back deck by the swimming pool with the Superstition Mountains in the background.

She instructed Darren to round up a couple of pictures of Lilly that could be displayed during the interview. He again questioned if he was making the right decision to make her name public. But after his morning interrogation, he no longer trusted the police—not that he had the utmost confidence in Jessi Stafford—but at least he was doing something. He decided it was worth the risk.

One of the photos was the formal wedding picture that sat on the mantel above their fireplace. A ceremony that took place four years ago last October at a resort in Scottsdale. The other was a picture of Lilly and him on vacation. A trip to Acapulco where she actually convinced him to go cliff diving. Both photos portrayed the smiles of happier times.

As they moved out by the pool, Darren focused on the interview that he hoped would propel his wife back into his arms. But the sound of footsteps inside the house jarred him out of thought.

Jessi looked at her watch in a scolding manner. "Nice of you to show up, Byung. What part of 'leading the morning rush show with exclusive interview' did you not understand?"

Byung shook his head as he set up the camera for the interview. "Sorry, I didn't believe you. I thought you were one of those vampires who only comes out at night."

Jessi appeared too involved in her extensive primping to reply. Darren did have to admit she was quite a sight. But she quickly turned from beauty to the beast, barking orders and last minute instructions—she was much better on the eyes than the ears.

Sounding like Treadwell, she declared that people trust a man in uniform, and insisted that Darren keep on his pilot uniform. Jessi applied make-up to his face like a professional, then dashed into the kitchen and returned with an onion, which she advised he use to help him cry to evoke sympathy.

He didn't want sympathy—he just wanted Lilly back.

Chapter 14

US Attorney Eicher walked to the window of his office and peered out. It was a peaceful morning outside, at least for Manhattan, featuring a pleasant spring sun. Part of him wanted to just jump out of his window onto the busy street below and get it over with. Career suicide was a much more torturous way to go.

Dava Lazinski barged into his office without a knock, carrying two Styrofoam cups. The aroma of coffee perked him up, at least temporarily.

Dava—short for Davnieska—was the Assistant US Attorney on this case that nobody wanted, and that was before last night's debacle. But while Eicher had a bad habit of becoming too personally involved in his cases, Dava was a rock. It didn't matter if it was just another Monday, or a day like today when Nick Zellen put them on Defcom-5.

"After last night's news, I figured you didn't sleep a wink, so I ordered you the ginormous," she said pleasantly and handed him the oversized cup of coffee.

He took a long look at Dava, who was dressed in her usual power suit. She was only in her early thirties, but always seemed an old soul. There was something different about her today. Something he couldn't put his finger on.

"You have a good weekend?" he asked.

"Pretty boring. Check that—the Rangers lost both their playoff games, so it was boring *and* crappy."

She was born in New York, but her formative years were spent in Lithuania, where to quote Dava, hockey gets in the blood. Eicher knew this because after spending the past year trapped under the Sarvydas case, they knew way too much about each other, including that neither, sadly, had much of a life.

"No hot date?" Eicher pushed on between sips of coffee. He was a prosecutor by trade.

"Just my usual—picked up a couple of strangers in a bar," she kidded. "How 'bout yourself?"

"I'm married to my job and it wouldn't be right to cheat on it. Although, my ex-wife's lawyer did call me a couple times, does that count?

He continued to stare vacantly at her, trying to figure out what he was missing.

She let out a heavy sigh. "It's the hair, Eicher! I had like six inches cut off—real observant, counselor."

He pointed at her with a rare smile. "I knew it was something."

Compared to his life, getting a few inches chopped off the locks and watching a hockey game was practically a bachelor party that got out of hand. But their lack of lives was no doubt factored in when it came to being assigned this case. Usually high profile trials were earmarked for the budding stars of the office—the ones with political aspirations—but nobody with long-term plans raised their hand when the US vs. Alexei Sarvydas hit the docket.

Prosecuting the Russians was a lot lower on the glamour-scale than taking on the Italian Mafia. The Sarvydas' were a different animal. They had a reputation of being ruthless and crazy, and wouldn't blink an eyelash at ordering a hit on a federal prosecutor in broad daylight. Every time Eicher had stepped onto the street this past year he had checked over his shoulder for the Moziafs.

They also lacked the ammo to make it a fair fight. While too busy chasing the more glamorous Michael Corleone wannabes, the FBI didn't even notice the red tide sweeping ashore in the 1970s, circumventing numerous new US laws that had been created to promote Jewish refuge. Upon arrival, the Russians started stealing everything that wasn't nailed down. But it was limited to low-level stuff like Medicare fraud, counterfeiting, and extortion. That changed when Viktor Sarvydas rose to power, and built a sophisticated, worldwide crime network. By the time they realized what was happening, it was too late.

So they had to look for other advantages, which was one reason why Dava was chosen for the case. The hope was that her background would provide some credibility with a jury that Sarvydas' lawyers would surely try to fill with Russians—a group that sticks together and distrusts authority. It was a very sensitive topic with Dava. She was a good prosecutor, and any notion that she was chosen for any other reason than her abilities was the one thing that could ruffle her cool demeanor.

So with all this working against them, Nick Zellen became their lifeline. He had accidentally stumbled upon Alexei Sarvydas, Viktor's son, gunning down Nick's father. And unlike those who witnessed the recent Moziaf shootings, he was willing and able to testify.

The murder had the one trademark of most killings by the Russian Mafiya—brazenness. Although, it was unusual in its sloppiness and loose ends. Even without Nick's eyewitness account, Alexei had incriminated himself, leaving fingerprints everywhere.

Nick was still the key eyewitness to tie it together for a distrusting jury. But they needed to find him, and soon, to make sure he was in one piece for the trial.

Eicher looked at Dava. "Well?"

"Well what?"

"Come on, Dava, we've been doing this for a year. You only bring me coffee when you have bad news."

Dava took a deep breath. It was similar to the one Eicher's wife gave him before she told him she was leaving.

"Lilly McLaughlin's husband just went on a local Phoenix news station and made a plea for his wife's safe return."

"LaPoint said he didn't know anything, what did he say?"

She held up a disc. "It wasn't so much what he said."

Chapter 15

Eicher watched intently as Darren McLaughlin appeared on the screen. He looked like he hadn't slept all night—*join the club!*—and he was still wearing his pilot uniform.

He sat poolside with the reporter on a sunny Arizona morning, which reminded Eicher that he could really use a vacation. He glanced out the window, and as if a mood ring was controlling it, the Monday morning in New York had changed to typical April gloomy.

Eicher recognized the reporter. "Isn't that the news anchor who got fired for inappropriate behavior in the Jane Callahan murder case?"

Dava nodded. "And by inappropriate, I think you mean was sleeping with the murder suspect in exchange for an exclusive interview."

"That's right—*Killer Sex*."

"Maybe I should try that method to get some of these Russian thugs to talk," Dava made a rare joke.

Eicher knew that a lifetime supply of sex and vodka couldn't get the Russian mobsters they dealt with to talk. "I'm just worried that history is repeating itself—missing wife, interview by a pool, Jessi Stafford..."

"You think the husband could be involved?"

"When it comes to Viktor Sarvydas, I don't rule anything or anyone out, especially the most unlikely scenario."

Dava refocused on the screen. "It must be nice to go through life looking like a Barbie doll—no lack of second chances—I would have thought the Callahan thing would be a career killer."

"Kind of like ours if we don't find Nick real soon."

Lilly McLaughlin's husband, who according to LaPoint was either sadly naïve or the greatest actor of his generation, looked solemnly into the camera. "My name is Darren McLaughlin. Last night, my wife Lilly was abducted while pumping gas at a station here in Chandler."

Jessi cued the video. And for maybe the thousandth time since last night, Eicher watched Nick roll out from under the SUV and force Lilly McLaughlin into the back at knifepoint. The only positive was that he had worn his bank-robber chic outfit—a black Under Armour body suit and stocking over his head—so he couldn't be identified, even when Eicher used advanced FBI technology to zoom in close enough to see if he had a zit on his nose. But Eicher could spot Nick's movements three-thousand-miles away. He had no doubts it was him. And worried that Sarvydas could do the same.

The camera zeroed in on two framed photos that Darren held up for the world to see. Eicher winced at the happy wedding photo. He could almost picture a Sarvydas bull's-eye on the bride. The other photo was a vacation shot. Once again, they looked happy. Of course, so did Eicher and his wife at one time.

Darren's voice cracked again as he spoke, "Lilly is five-foot-four with dark hair and brown eyes and was last seen in a silver Lexus SUV. She teaches English at South Chandler High. We have been married for four-and-a-half years and hope to start a family some day. If you have seen her, or even think you might have, please, I beg you, please call the number listed on the screen below. Your call will be anonymous."

"Lilly is my life..." he continued, before breaking down, blubbering his words as tears streamed down his face.

While it seemed sincere to Eicher, he doubted it would have a happy ending, no matter how it turned out.

As McLaughlin wiped his tears and tried to gather himself, Jessi jolted him, "That is a great story, Mr. McLaughlin, and your tears are impressive, but as a journalist I can't ignore the facts.

"My sources have told me that your wife's abduction was not gang-related, as previously reported. All indications are that it was an elaborate copycat crime, and the police believe the motive is related to a domestic issue between you and your wife. And the timing is suspicious, with you conveniently being out of town, perhaps trying to establish an alibi."

By the husband's unnerved look, Eicher was pretty sure she was improvising. He doubted McLaughlin would have agreed to go on television to be accused of kidnapping, murder, or whatever exactly she was accusing him of.

"I don't know what you are talking about. I was out of town because I am a pilot—it's my job. I would never harm Lilly. I just want her back!"

Jessi continued on, unabashed, "But you haven't been completely honest with me. You told me earlier that the police suspected one of your wife's students as being the man in the video, but you withheld the fact that there is indeed a lead suspect. Did you withhold this because it would connect you to the kidnapper?"

"Of course not, the police warned me that Lilly could be in even more serious danger if her captor felt trapped, and I shouldn't reveal his identity."

"If publicity really would put your wife in dire circumstances, then why did you agree to do this interview?"

"Because you told me you thought it would help Lilly."

"While it's very trendy to blame the media, Mr. McLaughlin, was I not completely straight with you prior, when I expressed my suspicion of your possible involvement in this crime?"

McLaughlin said nothing, which made him look guilty. Eicher figured he was probably just guilty of having poor taste in reporters, and seemingly in women in general.

"I think it's time to stop the lies and withholding of information."

He stared ahead in a trance, unresponsive.

"The only way to set Lilly free is by telling the truth, so I am now going to reveal the identity of her abductor."

"Please no, please no," Eicher began mumbling over and over.

"It could put Lilly's life in danger," Darren desperately tried to stop her.

She didn't appear to be listening. She held up an odd-shaped photograph trimmed with scissors.

When Eicher saw who it was of, he bent over in pain. Jessi smiled proudly onscreen. Maybe it was the glare of the sun, but it was one of the most beautiful smiles Eicher had ever seen. She was like the angel of death.

"This is Brett Buckley, a seventeen-year-old student at South Chandler High, and not surprisingly a student in Lilly McLaughlin's class. I have confirmed that he was the one who drove off with your wife, but I suspect you already know this."

Darren's tears turned to anger. "If anything happens to Lilly, I will personally hold you responsible."

"Brett Buckley is the name the police and FBI gave you as the name of their lead suspect, isn't it?" Jessi pushed on.

"I never told you any name."

"If you must know how I discovered his identity—I did a search of your room and found a picture of your wife's tutoring group. While you were in the living room preparing your story for the interview, I made a quick call to the school to see which of her students called in absent today, and the only one was Brett Buckley. I searched the yearbook I found on Lilly's dresser, and Buckley wasn't in it. So I matched the other kids in the tutoring photo to their yearbook pictures, and by process of elimination I discovered which one was Brett Buckley. I took the liberty of cutting the other students out to protect their identities." The proud smile grew wider.

Eicher felt like he needed to sit down, but discerned that he already was, so he stood. Nick's picture was now splashed on the screen for the entire world to see, including Viktor Sarvydas. She had exposed his Brett Buckley alias and placed him in Arizona, not to mention, ID'ing their vehicle and providing a full bio on his traveling companion.

Jessi's satisfied look told Eicher that she likely didn't understand what she'd done. Darren didn't look like he understood the full ramifications either, but he seemed to realize that Jessi had just put his wife in greater danger.

That was, if Lilly McLaughlin wasn't the one inflicting the harm on Nick. Her sudden presence in Nick's life was still gnawing at Eicher. He mocked Fitzpatrick's famous last words: *We have it all under control. The teacher won't be a problem.*

Dava patted Eicher on his slumping shoulder. "We'll get him back," she said, as if Nick was their child, and not a witness they failed to protect. "He's a levelheaded kid. There must have been a perfectly good reason for him to leave, and now he has an even better reason to let us know where he is, so we can pick him up."

"We can't wait for him to call," Eicher declared, thinking of the gruesome package he received this morning from Ivan. He turned to the eternal optimist, hoping for some positive reinforcement. "Any glass half full ideas, or at least can you get me a glass half full with a stiff drink?"

"Lilly McLaughlin is originally from Mexico, so a run to the border would make sense. She probably has contacts or extended family there that she thinks can hide her out. It's been like eight hours, they might already be there."

"They're not in Mexico."

"How can you be sure? It makes complete sense."

"That's exactly why—because nothing in this case makes sense."

Chapter 16

Lilly McLaughlin's head pounded against the wall. She saw stars, although at this point, she really wasn't sure what she was seeing. All she knew is that she never felt anything like this.

She moved away from him, but he stalked her, waiting to make his move. And he had that intense look in his eyes—the one that told her she could do nothing to stop this. He came up against her again, and she could feel his hot breath on her neck.

She let out a desperate yelp and slithered away. She took three sprinter steps across the room, but he caught her by the hair and threw her naked body onto the bed.

He grabbed her by the feet and yanked her to the edge of the bed. He then split her legs like he was breaking a wishbone.

She shut her eyes as he climbed on top of her and began thrusting like a wild animal. She couldn't believe this was happening. *It shouldn't be happening,* she thought.

When his energy vanished, he fell on top of her breathless body. Lilly held him as close to her as she could. She couldn't imagine something so wrong could ever feel so right. It had been this way ever since that first dangerous kiss in her classroom.

They'd checked into the Mirage at around three in the morning. Only in Vegas would their entrance not even stir a suspicion. Once in their room, they'd spent the rest of the night making love like there was no tomorrow. Knowing that if they were caught, there might not be.

"You were amazing, *Mrs. McLaughlin,*" he exclaimed.

"I'll do anything for my favorite student, *Brett Buckley,*" she purred back at him. "I give you an 'A' for your performance."

The role-playing was a staple of their brief relationship—the innocent student being seduced by his experienced teacher. Playing a role made it easier for Lilly to delude herself. Nobody was innocent in this scenario and the payment for their actions was almost due. She really did love Darren and the suburban fantasy they lived. But that was part of the problem—it was just that, a fantasy.

She was born to a father who was a lieutenant in a Mexican drug cartel. Following her father's murder by a rival cartel, her mother took Lilly and her brothers to the United States. They found refuge, but no relief from danger, as her brothers became heavily involved in gangs in South Phoenix. Lilly always fought against this life, seeking to put herself through school to become a teacher, and eventually finding her prince who would build her a white picket fence. *The American Dream*. But she was inherently attracted to danger and chaos—a life that never had a happy ending. She had tried to run from it, but when Brett Buckley walked into her classroom, she realized it had come for her like the Grim Reaper.

Despite the instant attraction, Lilly had no plans to cheat on Darren—*with a student no less!* She wanted no part of hurting a man who loved her like no one ever had. But Lilly underestimated the pull of the danger. And she made the mistake of keeping it close by, building an intense teacher/student relationship with Brett. It was the equivalent of a recovering alcoholic spending time in bars—eventually the temptation will win. She wondered now if maybe that's what she wanted all along.

From the first time she met Brett, Lilly could tell he was pained by something—something dark—and she could relate. They formed a bond, to the point that he entrusted her with his dangerous secret. A secret that changed everything.

His real name was Nick Zellen and he was from New York. His life was changed dramatically when he witnessed his father's murder, and was forced into the Witness Protection Program.

She understood how it felt to have a parent murdered—the intense pain of loss. And Nick's confession removed the imaginary hurdle that Lilly had put between them. He wasn't an underage high school student—Nick Zellen was a twenty-four-year-old NYU law student. It might still be immoral, but it was no longer illegal.

She told herself that their kiss was a one-time thing, but she couldn't stop, and kept pushing the stakes higher. It all came to a head last week when she showed up at a post prom party on a jealous rampage and they put on a public display in front of many of her students.

She had pushed the danger too far, and rumors started flying like wildfire through the halls of South Chandler High. When her boss grilled her, Lilly admitted she used bad judgment in attending the party, but denied any inappropriate behavior with a student.

The police weren't so understanding. When pictures taken from camera phones started showing up on Facebook pages, they had their evidence—a lot of it—and Lilly's arrest was imminent on charges of statutory rape and the endangerment of a minor. The FBI saved the day, not allowing an arrest to happen and risk exposing Nick's secret identity. They forced the local police to initially back off, without explanation. The plan was to move Nick into protective custody at an undisclosed location until the trial.

But Nick didn't trust them, believing someone in the US Attorney's Office was leaking information to those who were after him. If so, he was a dead man. These people had already killed his parents and girlfriend, and with the trial only a week away, they were probably more desperate than ever. Lilly knew that both their lives in Chandler were over, whether it be by an arrest or a bullet. So they ran. Lilly came up with the plan to make it look like the gang violence that had been prevalent in the area.

Lilly also had another reason for leaving—a more selfish one. It was that she couldn't stand the thought of being separated from Nick.

Nick seemed ready for another go at it, but there was no time to lose. After taking a quick shower, Lilly towel-dried her wet hair and slipped back into her dress. She then sat on the bed, strapped on a pair of heels, and clicked on the television.

Darren was on the television begging someone to find his "abducted" wife. He looked so tired and she wanted to make it all right for him. She wished she could love him like he loved her.

Nick stepped out of the bathroom, wearing one of Darren's suits that Lilly took from his closet in preparation for their escape. Darren was taller, but they had similar builds, and the suit fit nicely. Nick's thick, dark hair was post-shower slicked back. His features were dark, much like pictures she'd seen of his Ukrainian born father. But he had intense blue eyes from his blonde-haired, blue-eyed mother. The eyes got Lilly every time.

He clicked off the television in the middle of the interview, and wrapped her in an embrace.

"Darren is a good man—the last thing I wanted was for him to get hurt," she said.

He pulled her tighter. "It's not your fault that we fell in love."

"I made a big mistake. I should have never let it get this far."

"We try to control things, but in the end you can't protect those you love. All you can do is follow your heart."

She nodded that she understood, the pain once again bonding them. Then like a junkie who continued to hurt whoever was in the way of the next fix, the craving for danger overtook her. She needed to up the ante. And nothing would be more dangerous right now than for the two of them to be seen in public.

She helped Nick to his feet and meticulously tied the silk tie she'd bought for Darren last Christmas. "Let's go to the casino," she said.

Nick looked shocked. "The casino is loaded with cameras."

Lilly ran her hand down the length of the tie, pressing against his chest, and then kissed him. "If we're going to be on the run, then we're going to need money."

Nick broke away from the kiss, looking unsure.

"Do you trust me, Nick?"

"You saved my life by getting me out of there. I trust you."

Lilly smiled at the answer, then grabbed him by the hand and dragged him toward the danger zone.

Chapter 17

Lilly led Nick into the main lobby of the Mirage. Nick looked hesitant, but not scared—she'd yet to see fear in his eyes. She was confident that he trusted her and would follow her into battle. It remained to be seen if that was a wise choice.

The room was a tropical oasis, filled with palm trees and the sounds of waterfalls. Lilly breathed in the smell of exotic flowers as they passed over a bridge that sat beneath a ninety-foot high glass atrium. They momentarily stopped and kissed, while taking in the surroundings like a newlywed couple. Thoughts of the FBI and Russian gangsters briefly washed away into the numerous fountains.

Their next stop was the grand casino. The tropical aromas morphed into the smell of money. And Lilly loved the sound of slot machines in the morning. She felt at home.

The first time she ever played cards was with her older brothers in their tiny Phoenix apartment. They always tried to get rid of her, but being the nosy little sister, she was determined to stay. And the only way for her to stay was to be better than the boys. And soon she was.

She earned the right to tag along when her brothers made trips to Vegas. She knew they were gambling in casinos to launder their drug money, but Lilly had a protective nature, and she always believed that if she could stay near them she could keep them safe. But Nick was right about not being able to protect those you love in the end. She couldn't protect her brothers from the bullets, anymore than she could protect Darren from her addiction.

And her return to Vegas reminded her of the old adage: once an addict, always an addict. She wasn't drawn to gambling per se—it was just a symptom—she was really attracted to the high stakes. Her life with Darren had served to cover up the problem. Now her actions were about to rip his life apart—if they hadn't already—and she was knowingly putting Nick's life in jeopardy.

As if in a trance, she moved to a blackjack table and entered a double deck game. Since making the decision to leave last week, she had drained a couple thousand dollars from their joint bank account. Darren wouldn't know it was missing until they were long gone, since she handled the finances. It was the only money that she and Nick had to survive on.

The dealer was a good-looking thirty-something with a shiny shaved head. His bulky chest was busting out of his tuxedo. He read down the rules—players could double down on any two cards, when splitting aces players receive one card on each ace, and late surrender was offered. Lilly never surrendered in anything.

From the card games with her brothers, and on their Vegas trips, she had picked up the ability to effectively count cards. In fact, she had become so good that she had been banned from this very casino. So she took her act to the Gila River Casino on an Indian reservation south of Phoenix. They eventually cut their losses, and instead of banning her, offered her a job as a blackjack dealer. It was the first step toward her new life. The one that wasn't real. She used the job to put herself through school, and toward her teaching degree. It was also where she met Darren. She thought of his devastated face on TV this morning and wished she'd never agreed to go on that date with him. She knew she'd eventually hurt him.

Lilly won the first game when the dealer "busted a stiff." He wasn't as good as he looked. On the next hand, she doubled down with a ten and a three and won again. The dealer then made a brief comeback, winning the next three hands.

Lilly's card-counting abilities were rusty at first, but as the hands progressed, she regained her confidence. She didn't use a particularly sophisticated method—typical high low—but methods were overrated. She'd found it to be a myth that you have to be some math-whiz savant like Rainman to count cards. It was all based on concentration. Casinos are strategically built to distract—constant noise, free drinks, and perhaps the stress of knowing you'd just wagered your kids' college fund—but Lilly had been conditioned her whole life to deal with chaos, so casino conditions never fazed her.

The other key component was to make sure the casino surveillance didn't know you were counting. This was always her downfall, hence, her banishment. But she'd become a good actor the last few years—she convinced the world that she was Lilly McLaughlin, perfect wife, when deep down she was always Liliana Rojas, danger junkie.

On the next hand, Lilly was sitting pretty on an eighteen, while the dealer had a soft seventeen. But then the lucky bastard hit a three to go to twenty. She should have surrendered and cut their losses. But she did the opposite, betting the remainder of their savings.

The dealer gave her an "it's your funeral" look. Nick grabbed her hand and said, "That's all we got, Lilly." Still no hint of fear, but she had him concerned.

"Nick—you either trust me or you don't."

"I trust you, Lilly."

She grabbed his tie and drew him close. Then she kissed him. She couldn't help herself—he looked so good in that suit. But the risky bet was still not enough. She smiled devilishly. "You're too trusting."

"What's that supposed to mean?"

"Would you trust me if I raised the stakes higher?"

"I don't know how you could—that's all the money we've got."

"I'm not talking money, Nick."

"Then what do you mean?"

"If I win, we get married today."

He looked flabbergasted. So did the dealer, who said, "Lose all your money or get hitched? Sounds like a lose-lose proposition to me."

Lilly turned to the dealer. "You're our witness."

He looked at his twenty. "I'd hold off on booking a band if I were you, sweetheart."

The moment of truth came quick. The dealer slapped the card down. A two! She had tied the house, a miracle in itself. But Lilly wasn't done. "Hit me again," she instructed.

Nick looked like he wanted to get off the suicide train. "Lilly, c'mon."

The dealer obliged. It was an ace—the only card that could win. She had hit blackjack! The winnings for hitting blackjack were three to two, so they had significantly added to their travel chest. Now it was time to collect, before the casino figured out who they were.

She looked into the camera and winked. Then she kissed Nick again for the world to see—the FBI, the Russian mob, whoever. She was so filled with the drug that she couldn't see straight. She craved the dangerous chase they were on, and couldn't help but to smile.

It was her wedding day.

Chapter 18

Jessi Stafford knocked on the weathered door of the apartment in Mesa. No answer. She took a baby wipe out of her purse and wiped any residue from the door off her hands and then repeated the process.

As she impatiently waited, she glanced at the peeling paint on the sun-beaten door, wondering again how Brandon could live in such a dump. But it wouldn't be her concern for much longer. With her Darren McLaughlin interview having gone national on TV, and viral on the Internet, she was confident she wouldn't need Brandon Longa to be feeding her stories much longer.

On the twelfth knock, Brandon finally answered. He was wearing just a towel—his abs much more impressive than his apartment—and he looked annoyed. "If you came by for a nooner, I think you're still on New York time because it's only ten in the morning."

She held up two bags filled with food and smiled. "I brought you breakfast, even though you don't deserve it."

"Would this food be to say you're sorry for screwing up my case, or a ploy to obtain more information?"

"You should be thanking me."

"For trying to punch me in the balls, or stealing evidence?"

"After what you pulled in that bathroom last night, you deserve whatever you get. The credit card might have helped, but let's be honest, I got more out of McLaughlin in my short interview than you guys did in an hour of grilling, and I didn't need the FBI to burst in like the cavalry to bail me out."

"Darren McLaughlin doesn't have a clue what's going on, so I have no idea what you think you got out of him."

"And how would you know that?"

"I don't know, I'm only the lead investigator in the case."

Jessi pushed past him into the apartment. The place looked like a bomb had gone off, as it always did.

Brandon reached into the bag and removed some green frilly looking items. "What the hell is this?"

"Bean sprouts. I think it's time for you to start eating healthier."

He tossed the bag in the garbage. "That's not breakfast—pancakes is breakfast. Now I gotta take a shower and meet up with Gutierrez, so make yourself at home." He thought about what he said. "By make yourself at home, I mean don't touch anything."

She wouldn't touch anything in this place if he paid her. She stood in the middle of the room, afraid to sit on any of the furniture, when she heard the shower start. Then she heard a beeping sound. It was coming from Brandon's cell phone that sat on the kitchen counter. It was an incoming text message.

Maybe she'd make an exception to her "no touch" rule this one time.

Jessi moved to the bathroom door and listened. She could hear the water splashing off him, and his off-key singing—she had some time. She picked up the phone and read the message. It was from Gutierrez, Brandon's partner—a reply to Brandon's last message, which read: *Gotta go Goot ~ someone's here~ prob JS.*

On the incoming text, Gutierrez wrote: *Is she gone yet?*

Jessi had a brief moral dilemma, but after last night she could have rationalized dropping a lethal dose of arsenic in his food. She typed: *JS all gone ~ free 2 talk*

Been a change in plans, amigo

Change?

Coo Coo Cachoo Mrs. Robinson, she's on the move

Jessi had no idea what he meant, but played along: *Where she headed?*

LML & BB spotted in Vegas

What r they doing in LV?

Haha can only imagine! But LML used a credit card at mirage. I guess what happens in LV doesn't always stay in LV

LOL. Whats our next move?

I say meet me in an hour at Sky Harbor ~ catch next flight and bring em home.

See ya there, Goot

The shower water turned off, causing Jessi to jump. But then Brandon started blow-drying the hair he loved so much, which bought her some time. She scrambled, needing to check the past conversations with Gutierrez where they discussed the case in detail, but Brandon had deleted all of his past messages.

She reached into her purse and took out a small device called the SimSpy, better known as the UR Busted Machine. A palm-size gadget that could read a phone's SIM card.

She popped the SIM card from the back of the phone and placed it into the SimSpy. She then hooked the gadget up to Brandon's computer, to transfer the information. She quickly found his conversation with Gutierrez and tracked back to the beginning where Gutierrez typed: *There gotta be more to it*

I'm thinking same way

Y wld the feds jump on ths? Shouldn't they b looking 4 terrorists or something?

Maybe they wanted the publicity

My gut says its something more. Esp how secretive thr being

Wht abt drugs? Kid at Chandler High last yr busted 4 running ecstasy ring ovr state lines. Drug traffiking wld outweigh r case and crossing state lines

By all accounts BB a gd kid w/ no record & diligent. May b we shld b looking more at LML

Her parents wr members of a drug cartel in Mexico. I've hrd abt cases whr the teacher used students 2 b the runner. The kid could b the victim

LOL ~ I wish sum1 wldve victimized me lk that in high skool

Strange that the feebies wld b interested in teacher/student sex scandal, even if she took him ovr state lines

In my day you'd get a high 5 & a raise in allowance. 2day the FBI is after u!

LOL

Shit

What is it?

Gotta go Goot ~ someone's here ~ prob JS

Jessi couldn't stop smiling as she placed Brandon's SIM card back in his phone—he shouldn't have left out his cell phone if he was going to invite a reporter in.

Just when she didn't think this story could get better, she had hit the jackpot. Now she understood what Mrs. Robinson meant—older woman and young student from *The Graduate*. Lilly McLaughlin was having an affair with her student—Brett Buckley—and they ran off together! While abductions of attractive white women were ratings booms, and the "did he or didn't he do it" husband angle was intriguing, viewers could not get enough of these scandalous affairs between good looking female teachers and their male students, that had practically become an epidemic over the last decade in the US. The story had all the elements of the modern day trashy novel—and it was going to be a bestseller!

The way things were trending, Jessi figured she might as well book her flight back to New York and remember to pack her "I told you so." But first she had business in Las Vegas.

Chapter 19

Darren wandered around his empty home like a man lost. It was his first time alone since he saw the news about Lilly.

Once he rid himself of Jessi Stafford, the FBI showed up at his house. His supposed new best friend, Agent LaPoint, didn't act too friendly, giving Darren a tongue-lashing over his television interview, which according to LaPoint: "*Might very well cost your wife her life.*"

Those words turned him into a zombie. He just sat quietly on the living room couch, while the FBI searched through Lilly's things like she was some sort of criminal. They even took her computer and journal. He didn't ask them what they were looking for, convinced that they wouldn't have told him.

The FBI stayed about an hour, before leaving him alone with a stomach tied in painful knots. He couldn't believe he was actually wishing it were a gang initiation. Who knew what this Brett Buckley psycho would do?

The house was too quiet and Darren desperately needed to drown out the morbid thoughts shooting through his mind. So he turned on the television. The first thing he saw was Jessi Stafford. She was the last thing he wanted to see, but before he could turn the channel, she froze him with her words.

"This is Jessi Stafford reporting live from outside the Mirage Hotel and Casino in Las Vegas. The very place where wanted fugitive Lilly McLaughlin spent the night."

Fugitive? Las Vegas? Darren had no idea what she was talking about. The Mirage's fountains exploded into the air behind Jessi like they were competing with her for attention. He turned up the volume.

"Earlier this morning, I broke the story that Lilly McLaughlin, a teacher at South Chandler High, was not abducted by a gang, as our so-called competitors reported, but was taken by one of her students, named Brett Buckley."

Darren watched as the pictures of Lilly and Buckley flashed on the screen, side-by-side. Then Jessi reappeared—she wore the same revealing top and ditzy smile from their interview this morning.

"But while Buckley's motive was thought to be related to a teenage crush gone wrong, through my sources deep within the Chandler Police Department, I have learned that Lilly McLaughlin, thirty-two, and her student Brett Buckley, seventeen, were having an illicit affair. It was being investigated by the local police, with charges pending."

Darren couldn't believe what he just heard. All his senses froze.

"And while our competitors suggested that the couple most likely had traveled to Mexico, I have acquired Mrs. McLaughlin's credit card activity, which led me to the Mirage for this exclusive report. I have also talked to witnesses that spotted the cozy couple in the casino."

Darren tried to reach for the remote to turn off this horror movie, but he couldn't. His arm wouldn't move.

"This case is very fluid, and I will continue to break news from Las Vegas all day."

The screen split, and a blow-dried looking anchor now took up the other half.

Darren's lungs felt like he was trying to breathe under water, and his chest burned—his life was being ripped apart in crystal clear HD. The room began to spin and he no longer could fight off the images. He had visualized the boy with the intense eyes threatening his wife with a knife … but the two of them together? It couldn't be!

The anchor spoke in a deep voice, "Jessi, you have been on top of this story for Channel-6 all day and night, including your exclusive interview with Lilly McLaughlin's husband this morning. Knowing what we know now about the motive for her disappearance, it seems as if this is just another in what has become a national epidemic of teacher/student scandals, and it appears that Arizona is not immune from such predators."

"That's correct, Gil. My research has found that there have been well over a hundred arrests in the last decade in situations like this, and no telling how many that were never reported."

"It sounds like Lilly McLaughlin could be in big trouble when she is apprehended. Arizona law prohibits sexual conduct, intentionally or knowingly, with someone under the age of eighteen. Since Mr. Buckley was only seventeen, this would be a class-six felony that could result in five to fourteen years in prison for her."

"It might be a sad commentary on our society, Gil, but female teacher predators convicted over the past decade have done very little prison time, while their male counterparts convicted of similar crimes have received more severe sentences."

The anchor added, "I was working in the Seattle area at the time when Mary Kay Letourneau was convicted of multiple liaisons with her underage lover, Vili Fualaau. If I remember correctly, she did prison time."

"That is true, but she also was reported to have received a half million dollars from a national publication for rights to her wedding photos when she married Mr. Fualaau, following her release. The amount she actually suffered for her crime is very much up for debate"

"Prison time or not, I assume Lilly McLaughlin has put both her career and marriage in jeopardy. What could she possibly have been thinking?"

"What drives these woman is a mystery, Gil—is it lust, the thrill of the forbidden, or perhaps a form of mental illness? Nobody really knows. While cases like Letourneau and Debra Lafave have made national headlines, there have been hundreds of other cases ranging from a mother of four and wife of a prominent Albany, New York banker, who taught English at Christian Brothers Academy, to a twenty-nine-year-old Social Studies teacher from Colorado who had sex with one of her students on a field trip she chaperoned, the topper being that she was also the principal's wife."

"Thank you for the informative report, Jessi, and I'm sure if anyone will get to the bottom of Lilly McLaughlin's motives, it will be you. But one last question about the husband you interviewed this morning, and who might be learning this about his wife right along with the rest of us—how do you think he's feeling right now?"

Darren concluded that if you are dead you have no emotions. To answer the anchor's question, he felt nothing.

As they mercifully went to commercial, Darren saw his life floating away. He tried to get up and chase it, but he was paralyzed.

Chapter 20

Darren finally found the strength to turn off the television. He sat in silence for a few moments, and he started to put the pieces together. And his conclusion was that Jessi Stafford was an opportunist, and none of her sensationalism should be taken seriously. She had practically accused him of killing Lilly for God's sake!

But while the report couldn't possibly be accurate, he would concede that this was the theory being put forward by the police. And Jessi was their unofficial mouthpiece, which is how she got Lilly's credit card in the first place. Longa also likely provided her the "affair with a student" theory.

Now the strange interrogation made more sense. The reason they weren't in a hurry to find Lilly was because they didn't believe she was in danger. It's what Longa was going to tell him when the FBI burst in, guns blazing. But Darren was convinced they were wrong.

So he ignored the television report and returned to his original plan, which was to conduct his own investigation. His first thought was to confront Buckley's parents. They would likely know if their son showed signs of being infatuated with Lilly. They also might be able to shed some light on where he might have taken her—if Jessi Stafford said they were in Las Vegas, then Darren was convinced that they were anywhere but there—and perhaps Brett had contacted them. Either way, two heads were better than one, and they had the same goal, which was to get Brett and Lilly safely home. The rest could be sorted out later.

Darren changed out of his uniform, and into a golf shirt and khakis. Lilly had kept a list of addresses and phone numbers of all the students involved in her weekend tutoring sessions. The address took him to an upscale gated community off Queen Creek Road.

He piggybacked another vehicle through the electronic gates, and quickly found the Buckleys' impressive home. He parked Lilly's Jetta on the curb and headed for the front door, noticing a Jeep Wrangler parked in the driveway next to a Ford Taurus. Out of the corner of his eye, he noticed a young girl getting into the Jeep. She had a pretty face, except for the deep teenage scowl on it, and her hair was a rebellious combo of pink and blonde. She wore denim shorts with a pair of tattered flip-flops, and a T-shirt that read *What Are You Looking At?* The minute their eyes met she made an angry beeline for him.

"Are you Mrs. McLaughlin's husband?"

When he replied that he was, she punched him in the jaw with a surprising right hook. And with their vast height difference, she had to work to do it. It confused him more than it hurt.

"That's for your slut wife ruining my life!" she shouted, and then bolted for her Jeep.

Before Darren could even grasp what just happened, the wheels of the Jeep were laying rubber on the hot asphalt. He didn't have time to analyze the strange incident—the only thing he could think about right now was Lilly, and getting her back. He marched to the front door with purpose. He was about to ring the bell when he noticed the door was cracked open. He walked in to find a surprise.

"What are you doing here?" he asked Agent LaPoint, who was meandering through the living room. The place looked like the model house for the planned community, and had a coldness to it.

"You might want to put some ice on your jaw," LaPoint greeted him.

Darren felt his throbbing chin and realized she hit him harder than he thought. "Who was that?"

"That's Rebecca, Brett Buckley's girlfriend. She's a feisty one—doesn't take rejection well."

"Where are Buckley's parents? I want to speak to them."

"On vacation in Hawaii. Second honeymoon or some shit like that."

Darren could tell he was full of it—his eyes betrayed him.

Suddenly it hit Darren like another punch to the jaw. The FBI didn't believe that Brett Buckley abducted Lilly any more than the local cops did. They viewed Lilly as a predator who ran off with a student, and took him over state lines, which was probably why the FBI was involved in the first place. This was a dirty trick—the FBI was supposed to be the hope he was clinging to.

"Lilly didn't do what they say she did on television!"

"If you let me do my job, we can get your wife back in one piece and then the two of you can talk over whatever issues you have."

Darren angered to tears. "I want the truth—was my wife having an affair with that student!?"

"Go home, Mr. McLaughlin—there's nothing you can do here."

Darren didn't move.

LaPoint took a deep breath and slowly blew it out. "I'm sorry, Mr. McLaughlin. I really am."

Chapter 21

Lilly led Nick by the hand out of the casino and into the lobby, where a twenty-thousand-gallon saltwater-aquarium was built into the wall behind the front desk. Lilly noticed that it contained sharks, but at the moment she was more worried about the sharks on dry ground.

They exited into the fresh air and speed-walked down a path that was lined with lush vegetation and exotic sculptures, arriving at the Bare Pool Lounge. It was aptly named, as it was a place known for its topless sunbathing. Even in the morning, a party was in full swing by the pool, DJ included.

Lilly never drank alcohol or took drugs, but she was still completely intoxicated. She stripped off her dress, casually tossed her heels onto a chaise lounge, and dove into the pool. Nick showed no fear, following her in au naturel.

They resurfaced in each other's arms and kissed passionately. Nick pried his lips away and announced to the party, "We're getting married!"

The drunken crowd cheered them wildly as they kissed some more. The crowd had no idea they were cheering a couple of fugitives.

The Mirage didn't have an in-house wedding chapel, but offered a tram to Treasure Island, located at their sister hotel, the MGM Grand. The clerk warned them of a long waiting list, so they decided to hoof it down Las Vegas Boulevard, better known as the Strip.

They were doing everything fugitives shouldn't do, with maybe the lone exception of painting a target on their backs. They stopped at the Little

Church of the West at the south end of the Strip. The Little Church was a diminutive wooden chapel that was considered an antique by Vegas standards. It promoted its many celebrity weddings, including Britney Spears' infamous drunken weekend that ended in an annulment.

Before entering, Lilly turned to Nick and said, "Any last secrets you want to let me in on before we become man and wife?"

He deflected, "You first—beauty before age."

"I thought it was age before beauty?"

"You win on both counts."

That scored him a couple of points. Lilly intended this exercise to be playful, but when she started to answer, things turned serious. "My secret is that even though I denied it to myself, the minute you walked into my classroom I knew our destiny was to be together." Her face sunk. "But I also knew people would get hurt, and I did it anyway."

Nick showed little emotion. He was still hurting too much from his own losses to worry about others. "That's a little heavy. I thought you were going to tell me you listen to Neil Diamond or you fart in bed."

She hit him playfully on the arm. "Stop stalling—your turn."

His face turned solemn. "You know how I told you my parents were mega rich and all that?"

"They're not?"

"Well, they were. The feds froze my father's assets and took control of his bank accounts. Sasha and I will probably never see it again and will be lucky to pay off all the lawyer fees."

"Why are you telling me this?"

"C'mon, Lilly, I'm not one of those stupid kids from your class. I know a sophisticated woman like you is looking for a successful man. Not some law school dropout who lives in a one room apartment, struggling to pay the minimum balance on his student loans each month."

She tapped him on the head. About a sixty-forty split between playfulness and annoyance. "For someone so smart, you can be pretty stupid sometimes. The only reason I want to marry you is because I'm in love with you."

A relieved smile spread across his face, and she kissed him once again.

With their pre-wedding jitters out of the way, they entered the chapel. Lilly wondered how far she was really going to take this. The foyer was full of tube tops and leather skirts—not exactly the traditional wedding garb that she wore when she and Darren got married. They were met by a woman who actually looked more like Elvis than the many impersonators who were milling around the chapel.

"Can I help you?" she asked. Lilly was expecting a little more on the friendly side.

"I think we're looking to get married," Nick quipped.

The woman extended her arm, palm up. "Marriage license?"

Lilly and Nick exchanged glances. They hadn't thought that part through. Lilly was sure they weren't the first to come here unprepared. Britney came to mind.

The woman read their looks, sighed, and then instructed, "Clark County Municipal Building. It's on the corner of Third and Clark in downtown Las Vegas. The Strip claims to be in Las Vegas, but this is really the town of Paradise, Nevada. If you're not from around here, you can purchase a map in the gift shop."

They left the chapel unhitched. Lilly struggled to breathe in the dry desert air. She was coming down off her high—all of a sudden danger didn't seem so much like her friend. The wedding fantasy, despite being an act of insanity, had shielded her from their precarious reality.

Lilly looked down the Strip, feeling like each neon light was pointing danger in their direction. Whoever named this place Paradise sure didn't have the Russian mob chasing them.

Chapter 22

Lilly knew it was time to get off the ledge. "We can't get married today, Nick."

"What are you talking about?"

"For starters, I'm already married. And besides, the minute we enter that office and apply for our license, the place will be surrounded by the FBI…or worse."

Nick looked like he got punched in the face and stormed away from her. "That's not it and you know it, Lilly!"

He sat down curbside, seemingly oblivious of the morning traffic that was streaming by. Lilly followed and sat beside him. "What is it Nick—why don't you think I want to marry you?"

He stared down at the street like he didn't even want to look at her. "I tell you I have no money and now you have no interest in marrying me. One minute you're willing to risk your life to get to the altar, and now you're preaching patience. Suddenly I'm not such a good trade up."

She wanted to slap him, but the caretaker in her took over. "I do want to marry you—I just want to be alive to enjoy the honeymoon," she said, forcing a smile.

She nudged closer to him and draped her arm around his broad shoulders.

"You were right about one thing, Nick. I did risk everything to be with you. My marriage—my career—and perhaps my life. I risked it all to be with *you*, not to become some rich heiress. But if you don't trust me, then we might as well go our separate ways."

Nick looked like a lost child. "I'm sorry, Lilly. I guess I was just a little jealous."

"Jealous of what?"

"I'm afraid that you'll eventually find someone more successful than me, and want to be with him."

She leaned her head on his shoulder. "I'm the one who should be jealous. I see how all those girls at school look at you."

Lilly had never been the jealous type until she met Nick. From that moment on, every look in his direction from a flirty girl at school foreshadowed the day when he would kick her to the curb for a sleeker, younger model. And it drove her especially nuts when he was with his girlfriend Rebecca. That's what led her to risk everything to crash that prom party.

But that didn't even compare to her straightjacket moment the night she caught him embracing a girl in a local park. After Nick physically restrained her from scratching the mystery girl's eyes out, he explained that it was his sister, Sasha, who had risked a dangerous visit. Lilly still believed that Sasha had been followed that night, which is what put Zubov on his trail—not a leak in the US Attorney's office like Nick claimed.

But Lilly was most insecure when it came to his former girlfriend, Audrey, who had been murdered. Lilly saw the look in his eyes when he talked about her. He still loved her. Lilly could never compete with that.

He laid his head next to hers. "You're the one I want, Lilly. And for the record, I do trust you."

"I thought I warned you about that."

"I'll take my chances."

"Even if I don't marry you today?"

"It will just give me something to look forward to."

"I was thinking St. Patrick's Cathedral with the reception at the Waldorf," she said with a smile. "But now that we're poor, I guess we'll have to come back to Vegas so I can win us some more money."

They embraced and kissed deeply. When Nick came up for air, a mischievous smile appeared on his face. "I wasn't talking about the wedding. I meant I was looking forward to the honeymoon."

They kissed again, ignoring the noose tightening around them. Lilly eventually pulled Nick to his feet and they walked slowly back to the Mirage, holding hands as they whistled past the graveyard. They entered the lobby, almost expecting an army to be waiting for them—they'd certainly left them enough clues. Lilly just wasn't sure what uniform they'd be wearing.

The instant that their feet touched in the lobby, Nick stuck out his arm to hold her back.

"Oh shit, oh shit," he rambled.

"What is it?" Lilly whispered.

He pointed at a middle-aged man in a tidy gray suit. The man had a short-cropped haircut and a fluffy salt and pepper mustache. He didn't stand out from the many others who were scurrying through the lobby, except for a tattoo that colored the back of his neck.

"That's Zubov," Nick whispered.

Lilly felt fear shoot through her, even though the man's look didn't match the monster that Nick had described to her.

"Are you sure?" Lilly replied, feeling her stomach in her mouth.

"Of course I am," Nick said with a sharp glare.

They turned and began jogging away, not even risking a backward glance. Their wedding day was officially ruined. When they got outside, they desperately hailed a cab.

"Where to?" the cab driver asked.

Lilly knew they were no longer safe here. "To the airport," she said urgently.

"No," Nick said. "There's some place I need to go before we leave."

Chapter 23

Viktor Sarvydas' ponytail bounced behind him as he ushered his guest down the long corridor that led to the lavish dining room in his Netanya mansion. Although, 'mansion' might not be doing the place justice.

The decor of the hallway was similar to that in the Manhattan headquarters of Sarvy Music. It was lined with the trophies of his music career—gold records, mounted Grammy awards, and framed magazine covers that featured the many artists he had brought to life over the years. The latest was Natalie Gold, posing provocatively on this month's edition of *Rolling Stone*.

Viktor loved giving tours of his estate. And the grander the guest, the more he took pride in their dropped-jaw looks. Tonight was no different. They entered the expansive dining room that was constructed of Italian marble. The back wall was a hand-painted mural of the skyline of the Russian city of St. Petersburg, making it feel like you were there. Not almost feel like you were there—actually seem like you were overlooking the city.

They were seated at an immense dining table that was prepared with caviar and vodka—two Sarvydas essentials. The view opposite the St. Petersburg skyline was of the Mediterranean Sea, a spectacular sight from the mansion's perch on the cliffs of Netanya. This was no mural—it was very real, as was the bulletproof glass of the window they peered through. The glass could stop a heat-seeking missile, but didn't diminish the view of the sun beginning to sink into the sea. While night was approaching in Israel,

Viktor's mind was on events unfolding in the States, where it was just midday.

A less attractive sight was the presence of his protectors, caressing their trusty machine-guns. They were a necessary evil. He had many enemies who aspired to knock off the don of the Russian Mafiya. Sarvydas knew this from experience. The reason he was here was because he took out his predecessor—Vladimir Miklacz—who also happened to be his father-in-law. The lesson was to never trust anyone, especially friends and family.

His guest sent his guards away so the two men could discuss their business alone. They joined Viktor's guards on the balcony. It was an awkward mix. Viktor's group was a collection of renegades, while his guest's team was made up of elite sharpshooters provided by the state. Still, if forced to choose, Viktor would take his men every time.

Viktor raised a goblet of vodka to his guest and toasted, "To friendship and business. A combination that has brought us together again."

The man smiled. It was a smile that, along with his constant tan and perfectly groomed silver hair, made him a friend of the camera. And while he and Viktor were approximately the same age, there was no competition when it came to their physical vitality. The man across from him still ran marathons and was fitter than accomplished athletes half his age.

"I blame you for every gray hair on my head, Viktor," the Israeli prime minister Ati Kessler said in jest, although Viktor knew it was no joke. But there was really little he could do—he was only a prime minister, not the head of the Russian Mafiya. "Your display at the Wall today has many of my constituents upset with you, if they weren't already."

"In America there is a saying—that's show business."

Kessler's face tightened. "I've done all I can to protect our friendship, but you've been pushing the limits since Israel opened its arms to you."

"If I've offended them with my public posture, then I can only imagine the reaction if they knew my private business affairs," he paused for a moment, before adding, "*Our* business affairs."

Kessler understood the implication. “Please don’t take what I say as a threat, Viktor. I just have concerns, which I think we can come to agreement on. You know I love you like a brother.”

“But you love my campaign contributions like a wife. Although, the other money we’ve made acts like your mistress—secret and satisfying.”

“Thanks to our business arrangements, finances are not a problem for me,” he admitted with another thin grin. His eyes swept the room, before adding, “Although finances seem to be even less of a problem for you, my friend.”

“There would be many questions asked if you used the money we earned together. Where would such a modest man who dedicated his life to service of his country, get such a personal fortune?”

“I save it for a rainy day,” he said, his face turning serious. “Your money helped me gain office, Viktor, but now I pay for it every day.”

The perception within Israel was that Kessler was willing to harbor a fugitive like Sarvydas because of his large campaign contributions. Despite Israel’s long history of not extraditing citizens, the polls indicated that the overwhelming majority wanted to make an exception for Viktor Sarvydas. And that was before today’s video-shoot at the Western Wall had infuriated the largest religious sect in the country.

But what they didn’t know was that Kessler’s support went far beyond money. Their bond was more than brothers—they were vors.

Viktor’s black market business that arose from his work on the cruise ship as a teen, eventually ticketed him to a Siberian gulag, when he refused to give the Soviets their cut. His time in the gulag was a dehumanizing experience, but also the most important event of his life. It was there he met his future partners in crime, Ati Kessler and Karl Zellen. They were anointed as vors—thieves-in-law—an elite group of Russian criminals whose bond would never be broken, even by bloodshed.

Zellen was a fervent anti-communist journalist and writer, beaten and thrown into the gulag for his views. He was also a man of rarely matched intelligence. Years later, when Viktor gained power in Brighton Beach, he brought Zellen to the United States. With Viktor's street-smarts and visionary business savvy, combined with Zellen's behind-the-scenes strategic plotting, they took the Russian Mafiya from a bunch of local extortionists to an unmatched worldwide syndicate. This included the infiltration into Wall Street, and the legendary gas tax scam in which they controlled most of the flow of gasoline throughout the northeast corridor of North America. And while Viktor was the flamboyant face of the organization, Zellen lived below the radar in Long Island with his wife Paula, and his children. He was known as a quiet businessman and respected member of the community who avoided headlines. That was, until he was murdered.

Kessler was born in the Soviet Union, but his family moved to Israel when he was a small child. His Russian heritage, and great distaste for communism, made him the perfect recruit for Mossad, who sent him to spy behind the Iron Curtain. A dangerous choice of profession that landed him in the harshest gulag in Siberia, upon his capture. His well-publicized plight made him a national hero in his home country, where he returned upon his release. On the surface, he dedicated himself to the Israeli intelligence agency and eventually became its leader.

But as he moved up the ranks of Israeli intelligence, he never forgot his fellow vors. Using Kessler's underworld contacts and influence, Sarvydas was able to infiltrate everything from diamond mining in Sierra Leone to black market weapons sales throughout Russia and Asia. A very profitable business, to say the least, and Kessler took his share of the pie. Now, decades later, the national hero had been elected prime minister, and a very popular one, at least before Viktor took up residence.

Viktor never understood why people claimed to want honest politicians, and yet were willing to vote for an intelligence agent as prime minister. They were liars by nature.

Kessler took a large gulp of the vodka, and said, "Alexei's trial is only a week away. Is there anything I can do to help expedite his freedom?"

"You mean so that you can get me out of your country sooner."

"That is exactly what I mean."

Viktor shook his head. "The trial shouldn't be a problem. I have it all under control," he said, thinking of Nick.

Kessler looked at him searchingly. Viktor knew he needed to address the subject that was hanging over them. They had never discussed it. "I promise you that Alexei did not murder Karl, nor did I order him to do it. Karl and I had our differences the last few years, but I can assure you what the American FBI tells you about Alexei is false. We are vors—that bond can't be broken."

Kessler nodded, accepting the answer. But Viktor felt a certain underlying distrust he'd never felt before. It reminded him once again that he should never trust anyone—family, friends, *or vors*.

They quietly ate their meal. When they finished, it was time for dessert.

Chapter 24

The lights dimmed and the world's hottest pop star began her personal concert for two of the most powerful men in the world. She wore the glamorous sequined evening gown that Viktor had provided her.

She didn't sing the youthful pop songs she'd become famous for. The prime minister was a much more mature audience. She started with a beautiful rendition of *Yerushalayim Shel Zahav*—Jerusalem is Gold. Many have sung it since Naomi Shemer penned the song in 1967 just prior to the Six Day War, but Viktor was sure that it had never been done better than it was tonight. Natalie then performed a litany of Israeli favorites. They all captured the raw emotions of the daily struggles of the country and all were built on a patriotic foundation. Kessler was always a sucker for nationalism, while Viktor saw countries as nothing but an impediment to his domination of world markets.

Natalie's encore was the David Broza ballad "Yihyeh Tov"—It will be good. A politically charged song that paints an optimistic future. Kessler looked mesmerized. He and Natalie made intense eye contact as she sung the final lyrics about staying with you tonight.

The song might have been about politics, but by the look in Natalie's eyes, she had a different interpretation. And the prime minister seemed to embrace her version. All was going as planned.

Natalie's voice took Viktor back to the first time he heard Paula sing at Sarvy's. But even though she wore a replica of the dress Paula wore that night, and despite the eerie similarities in voice, Viktor realized that his powers didn't extend to being able to recreate the love of his life. Paula was irreplaceable.

So why would he kill her, like some people believe he did? And when he was on the verge of getting her back? It made no sense. He'd always respected Paula's marriage to Karl. In fact, it was his idea.

Viktor was married to Trina Miklacz, the daughter of the don of Brighton Beach, with a son named Alexei, when he first saw Paula Branche sing that night. It wasn't long before they started singing a different kind of music with each other. It was about that same time when Viktor made his move to gain control of Brighton Beach. He organized an ambush of his father-in-law as they entered a Brooklyn restaurant one night. In the hail of bullets, Viktor got enough lead pumped in him that he still can't go through an airport metal detector, while Trina and her father were killed.

When rumors began to creep out that Viktor might have been the facilitator of the assault, and not a victim, he knew he couldn't let Paula be caught in a retaliatory crossfire. He loved her too much, and knew their love was without a future. He also couldn't risk Alexei growing up knowing his father had his mother killed. So he pushed Paula to marry Karl. The perfect solution to end the speculation

Karl provided Paula something Viktor never could—a perfect family life. Karl and Paula raised two children, Nick and Sasha, and lived the suburban dream in a large mansion in Long Island. Viktor never interfered.

It was Karl's idea that Viktor help to restart the music career that Paula had given up to raise their children. He agreed to help out his best friend, but soon an innocent decision turned into anything but. As they spent time in the studio, Viktor concluded that as much as people try to control their feelings and concoct their own reality, what is meant to be would always win out. That is how Paula Zellen ended up back in his life. She was going to leave Karl to be with him, but he felt it was still too dangerous. And he proved correct.

Things quickly turned complicated after Karl was arrested. Paula's children were always the priority in her life, and the arrest had turned their lives upside down. Nick was considering dropping out of NYU law school and Sasha, a junior figure skating champion, and the unbalanced diva of the family on her best day, had stopped eating.

So Paula flew to Viktor's Florida mansion, just as she had numerous times the past year to lay down tracks for her album in his massive recording studio, but this trip wasn't about music or sex—it was about ending their affair to protect her family.

Hours later, Paula was murdered in his house. Viktor was also shot—it was done in a way to strategically inflict maximum pain, yet keeping him alive. His unconscious body was placed in the bed beside Paula's. It was the same ambush method he used to eliminate Miklacz. An obvious message. He had spent his life protecting her, but in the end all he did was delay her fate. Victor's revenge would soon be complete, but with the sad understanding that it would never bring Paula back.

He watched as Natalie belted out a rendition of "Hatikva," the Israeli national anthem. Her eyes were as beautiful as her voice, but lacked Paula's warmth.

After her performance, Natalie joined the two men for the actual dessert—pashka—a traditional Russian cheesecake shaped like a pyramid. With a smile, Viktor indicated to the prime minister that it was okay to inspect the merchandise.

Trying to banish thoughts of Paula from his mind, Viktor returned to his drug of choice—power. It was exhilarating to know that he took this woman off the street and turned her into the world's hottest star. Yet with the snap of his fingers, he could make the clock strike midnight and take it all away. *What other man could turn the world's biggest star into his personal whore?* That was power.

With a nod from Viktor, Natalie took Kessler's hand and led him to one of the many bedrooms in the house.

Viktor retired to his office. There, he watched another Natalie performance on a secure video feed. This one even more impressive than her earlier concert. When she and the prime minister finished, he took the tape out and put it into his safe for insurance purposes.

Kessler might have been a fellow vor, but he was a politician now. And Viktor knew politicians were like Russians—they will always lie to get what they want.

Chapter 25

Darren didn't know what to do. He got into his car and began driving aimlessly. He was no longer in control of his thought process.

His first stop was the scene of the crime. The gas station was back in business like nothing happened. Then, as if in a trance, he drove to South Chandler High, where his wife should have been teaching fifth period English.

South Chandler High looked nothing like the high school he attended back in Framingham, a blue-collar suburb of Boston. South Chandler was made up of modern buildings built in Spanish Hacienda style. Tanned students mingled around the palm tree lined campus, chatting on the latest-greatest cell phones.

But upon entering the school, he realized that some things don't change. It was the smell. The universal smell of all high schools throughout time. A mix of must and memories. Just for a moment, he was taken back twenty years to the delusional idealism of those days. He wondered if maybe that's what Lilly did. His stomach tightened, and his thoughts returning to the murky present.

He went directly to the office of Principal Mara Garcia. A secretary tried to stop him, but he had dealt with the FBI this morning, along with that crazy Jessi Stafford, so the secretary was no match.

Mara was busily working the phones when he barged in. She looked flustered by his presence.

Lilly had formed a close bond with Mara—they were both educators with a Mexican heritage and a passion for literature, so they had much in common. Mara and her husband, Carlos, had often socialized with Lilly and Darren. The last time they had gotten together was last February when they attended a Phoenix Suns game and then went to a wine tasting bar. That seemed like lifetimes ago, back before Lilly started acting distant. As Darren examined Mara's face, he understood that there would be no more social outings.

Mara hung up and coldly stated, "You shouldn't be here, Darren."

He couldn't tell if there was contempt or pity in her voice. "I need answers."

"Then you should have been here last period when I had to hold a full school assembly to discuss the situation regarding Mrs. McLaughlin."

Mrs. McLaughlin. Situation. Her terminology was formal, alarming coming from a woman who helped him plan Lilly's birthday party last year. "I need to know what's going on."

"It's a police matter now, Darren. Perhaps they can give you the answers you need. My first concern has to be with my school, and I must consider the ramifications of talking to you."

The tone remained clinical, but the words cut him. Just like LaPoint, she left no smidgen of hope that it was a misunderstanding. His wife had run off with a student. Fact.

Mara's look softened as their eyes met. He must have looked as pathetic as he felt, and being awake for two days straight was not helping his situation.

She got up and softly shut her door. She returned to the chair behind her desk and faced him. He was expecting a look of sympathy, but he got anger. "I put myself on the line for Lilly. There were others with much more experience, and I knew I would take heat for hiring her. But I didn't think twice about it because I knew she would be an excellent teacher. And I was right—she was damn good. That's what makes what she did even worse. Not only did she let me down, she let down every teacher in this building."

When Mara was done reading him the riot act, she started in on the gory details.

"The rumors started about a month ago. They began as the typical high school whispers that nobody takes seriously, but when they turned to shouts, I called Lilly in. She looked me right in the eyes and lied."

The betrayal in Mara's voice was unmistakable. Darren wondered why he couldn't find that same anger to direct toward his wife. He was the one who was truly betrayed. The only emotions he was able to conjure up were disbelief and sadness.

"Then a few weeks back," Mara continued, "I asked Lilly to chaperone the senior prom, which she accepted."

This was not news to Darren. He remembered how endearing he found it that Lilly was so excited about attending. She never got to attend her own prom and she even bought a new dress for the occasion. He planned to go with her, but a last minute switch of his flight schedule took him away. He offered to tell the airline he couldn't switch, but Lilly encouraged him to go, and joked that she might take old Mr. Fischer, a science teacher at the school, as her date. But before he left for his flight, Darren bought her a corsage that he pinned on her dress like he was her prom date. He couldn't get that image out of his mind.

"The prom took place Saturday night. On Monday morning, I had the police waiting for me in my office. They were investigating a complaint that Lilly had attended one of the post prom parties—not affiliated with the school—and she put on quite a show with a student from this school who was underage."

"Brett Buckley," he uttered in a defeated voice, barely audible.

Mara nodded with a touch of sadness. "I told them that rumors are as big a part of high school as algebra. I called Lilly in again. She admitted attending the party—called it bad judgment—but denied any inappropriate behavior."

"Maybe she was telling the truth," Darren said. He knew he was grasping at straws.

Mara shook her head. "The police returned later that week with physical evidence—pictures taken of Lilly at the party." She then added real slowly so he wouldn't miss the point. "Pictures of Lilly and Brett Buckley. *Together.* They planned to arrest her when she arrived this morning. I don't think it's a coincidence she failed to show today."

Darren couldn't shake the image of the mature looking kid with the intense eyes. He had to know about this boy who Lilly ripped their life apart for.

"Tell me about Brett Buckley."

Mara looked pained for him. He hated that look of pity. "Don't make this worse, Darren. Besides, he is the victim, and a minor. I could be fired for even revealing the name to you, whether that reporter beat me to it or not. Go home. The police should have them in custody soon. Then you can talk to Lilly about whatever you need to talk to her about."

"I need to know, please," he pleaded.

Mara sighed. "Not much to tell. He moved here around Christmas time from the Seattle area. I think his parents own some sort of software company. He was a good student, no doubt, but like a lot of students who come in the middle of the year, he was sort of detached. No clubs, no sports, not many friends. Seemed like kind of a loner type."

Darren thanked Mara for providing him the information, even if he didn't like the answers, and wandered into the hallway. As he did, a bell sounded and students began pouring out of the classrooms. The students whizzed past him as if he wasn't there.

A girl bumped into him, almost knocking him over. Only his sheer size enabled him to withstand the teenage kamikaze pilot, but he lost his balance and was about to fall to the floor. She grabbed him by the arm and steadied him.

"Hey, watch where you're going," she responded angrily.

"I'm sorry, I've got a lot on my mind today," Darren replied, not even looking at her.

"Are you subbing for Mrs. McLaughlin's class today?" she asked.

The mention of Lilly triggered Darren's alertness and he looked at the girl. "Excuse me?"

"You look a little old to be a student, so I figured you might be subbing for Mrs. McLaughlin. She's out today."

"So I've heard."

"I hope she's not sick. I'm worried that she might have caught something when she was screwing my boyfriend."

Chapter 26

Darren recognized the pink streaks mixed into the girl's blonde hair. "You're not going to hit me again, are you?"

"I'd like to, but I'm one suspension away from not graduating. And then I'll never get out of this shit-hole."

Darren took his first real look at the girl. She had a natural pretty face and wore little make-up. Her skin was fair with a cluster of freckles around her nose. He didn't understand why such an attractive girl would choose such a severe look, with the pink streaks and the wire fence of earrings on the top part of her ear.

Darren searched for the name LaPoint gave him, and then remembered, "Rebecca, right?"

"Rebecca Ryan, but everybody calls me Becks," she said and simultaneously handed him the pile of textbooks she was hugging close to her chest. "My boyfriend used to carry my books for me—very 1950s, I know—but he ran off with your wife, so I figure you owe me one."

Darren instinctively defended, "We need to reserve judgment until we hear her side of the story."

"I have some prom photos that show her side of the story, if you'd like to take a look at them some time."

That one hurt. Becks began walking swiftly down the hallway like the rest of the students. Darren followed her closely, carrying her books, and he wasn't sure why.

"All I'm concerned about right now is her safety. Once she's safe, then we'll figure out the rest," he said robotically.

Becks sarcastically rolled her eyes. "And by safe, do you mean did Brett wear a condom?"

If she weren't a teenage girl, he would've punched her. But he could tell she was equally hurt, and just displaying it in a different way. "Don't you have a class to get to?"

"I have senior English next period, but no worries, I got a sub. My teacher got abducted by a gang member or something like that."

She kept digging in the knife and Darren kept taking it. It was like she was providing the anger and hatred he couldn't summon for Lilly. In a strange way, it felt cathartic. Maybe that's why he kept following her through the hallway and out the double-doors into the glare of the bright morning sun.

Becks arrived at her outdoor locker. Her progress was impeded by a couple intertwined in a make-out session. The looks, fashion, and technology had changed since Darren was in school, but some things remained a constant.

"Will you two get a room," Becks shot angrily at the couple and physically shoved them away from her locker.

The girl, the attractive blonde cheerleader type, shot Becks a look to kill. "Maybe we can share a room with Mrs. McLaughlin and *Brett*."

The boyfriend, the stereotypical jock from pick-your-movie, laughed. "Better be nice, Tara, or she'll have her dad beat you up."

They both looked at Darren and laughed the cruel, mocking laughs of teenagers. He got it—he was the dad in their scenario. But the good news was they didn't recognize him.

"I was thinking about rebounding with you, Evan, but then I remembered I'm not a lesbian," Becks fired back at the boyfriend. The other locker minglers didn't even give a second glance. Darren got the idea that these types of outbursts weren't unusual for her.

"Sorry, I don't go for the clown hair," he got the last word as the couple sashayed away.

Without missing a beat, Becks demanded her textbooks. When he handed them to her, she flung them into her open locker to the sound of twanging metal. "That bitch ruined my life," she screamed.

Darren knew she meant Lilly, not the cheerleader. He again started to defend her and was met by an angry jab of Becks' finger.

"Don't you dare stick up for that slut," she screeched.

"Stop calling her that."

"You're right—by running off across state lines with an underage student, that would make her a pedophile and a kidnapper. Sorry for my poor choice of terms, but my English teacher has been a little distracted the last month, so my language skills are a little off."

Becks tossed a backpack over her shoulder and began stomping away in her flip-flops. Darren stood in stunned silence, watching her pink and blonde hair bounce like a pompom.

She turned back to him with an annoyed look. "What are you waiting for? Let's blow this joint."

"Don't you have to get to class?" Darren asked, as he trailed her toward the student parking lot. "I'd hate to see you get that suspension."

"I told you, I have a sub. Besides, book learning is overrated. I'm going to incorporate what I learned in your wife's class into the real world."

"What do you mean?"

"She's been teaching us Shakespeare. You know what Billy Shakespeare was into?"

He said nothing, afraid to ask.

"Revenge. Do you know what the best revenge is, Darren?"

"Living well, I think," he said hesitantly.

"Wrong. It's going to Vegas and killing my cheating boyfriend and your slut wife."

Chapter 27

Lilly rarely met a risk she didn't like. But they were really pushing things with this side trip. All Nick would tell her was that he had "something to take care of." The intensity in his face deterred all further inquiries.

Nick drove the SUV into Henderson, a suburb of Vegas that advertised itself as the fastest growing city in the US. Lilly had no idea where he was headed, but a city of exploding population didn't seem like the best place to find anonymity.

They entered a sprawling suburban neighborhood that looked very similar to the one she and Darren lived in back in Chandler. Nick appeared to know exactly where he was going, and drove into a driveway of one of the homes. He hopped out of the vehicle with a purpose and Lilly followed him to the front door, where Nick impatiently rang the bell.

A mustached man answered the door, and Lilly could tell that he knew Nick. He didn't look thrilled by their unannounced visit. The man was rail-thin with unhealthy looking pale skin, probably in his fifties. He wore a pair of swimming trucks with a towel slung around his neck.

He ran his bony hand through his wet hair. "You shouldn't be here, Nick," he warned. His tone seemed more worried than angry. "You and your teacher friend are all over the news."

Nick made the introduction, "Lilly McLaughlin, this is Detective Tony Dantelli. He is the lead investigator in the murders. And the one who arrested Alexei Sarvydas."

Dantelli ushered them into the house and shut the door. The interior was very "Vegas," draped in gold and leather, while the walls were covered in plasma TVs as if they were paintings. "Nick, I'm just a lowly cop, and no trial expert, but this can't be helping our case."

"I'll take my chances," Nick said coldly.

Dantelli picked up a phone and began to dial. "I'm going to call Eicher and have his men pick you up. We need you in one piece for next week."

Nick took the phone from his hand. "I'm not going anywhere until we talk."

Dantelli looked perturbed, but escorted them through a set of French doors into a backyard with a desert landscape motif. A large swimming pool took up most of the real estate. He led them to a glass table, where a breakfast spread was set up.

He smirked. "I love Vegas. Back in New York I'd be sitting in my closet-size apartment trying to decide if the day was more cloudy or overcast. And I don't need to tell you about the women, Nick." His eyes roamed over Lilly's body, making her feel uncomfortable. His vibe was creepy.

As Dantelli dug into a fruit salad, Nick viewed the yard and its trimmings. "I like it—although, I must say the feds put me up in a nice place, the Buckleys own a very lucrative software company."

"But I'm sure it's nothing like that castle you grew up in back in Long Island."

"I'm surprised you chose not to go into protection. Testifying against Sarvydas doesn't sound like it's good for the health."

"Don't get me wrong, I wasn't sticking around New York with all his thugs there. So I took early retirement and moved west. No way was I putting my life in the hands of a bunch of federal bureaucrats who can't stand the NYPD. I'll take my chances with my own protection. I've been known to be a pretty good shot."

"Yeah, you sure are," Nick continued calmly, "especially when you did all those hits for Sarvydas. I'll bet being on his payroll is the best protection a man can have. Who needs the feds when you have Viktor Sarvydas watching over you."

Dantelli almost choked on a slice of melon. He looked up, startled. But before he could even respond, Nick leaped off his seat and picked up a pair of hedge-clippers. He pounded the handle into Dantelli's forehead, knocking him to the ground.

Lilly was astounded by the turn of events. Nick turned to her, his face on fire. "What Detective Dantelli failed to mention, was that he worked with Sarvydas to set up Karl's murder. Then, after the deed was done, he returned as the first officer on the scene and acted like a hero."

"Is the heat getting to you, Nick?" Dantelli asked angrily. "I'm the lead investigator in this case. I'm going to be testifying against Alexei Sarvydas next week. Now why would I do that if I was working for him?"

Nick walked up to him like a lion stalking prey. "Are you saying you didn't do jobs for Viktor Sarvydas!?"

Dantelli hesitated. Big mistake. Nick dragged him to the pool and dunked his head. After about fifteen seconds, he pulled him up.

"We both want the same thing, Nick. We both want Alexei put away," he said in between gasps for air.

"Sure—until you magically change your testimony at trial and he walks. I can assure you we're not on the same side, you dirty cop."

This time Nick dunked him scary-long.

"No, Nick!" Lilly screamed out.

But he wasn't listening. He jerked Dantelli's head out from under the water. The cop's cocky smirk was gone, replaced with fear. "You haven't answered my question—do you work for Viktor Sarvydas?" Nick shouted.

"C'mon, Nick."

"Answer the question!"

Dantelli was boiling with anger. Lilly could tell he was used to doing the pushing around. "Hell yeah I did, and I can only hope he lets me be the one to cut you into pieces when he finds you!"

His head disappeared under water again. When Lilly looked into Nick's distant eyes, she was sure he was going to kill him.

Chapter 28

"Why didn't you go to the police if you knew this?" Lilly desperately asked Nick, as he continued to hold Dantelli's head under the water.

"He is the police, Lilly! They all work for Sarvydas. I don't know who I can trust—I have to take care of this my way."

Lilly didn't like the sound of that. "Please, Nick—don't do it. You're better than him."

He lifted Dantelli out of the water and belted him in the face.

"So how many innocent people did you kill while pretending to protect and serve?" the former law student sounded like a prosecutor. He also appeared to be the judge and jury.

Dantelli desperately sucked air into his lungs. "Sarvydas called the shots, but nobody was more ruthless than Karl Zellen. And I did so much work for your father that I'm practically part of your family, Nicky."

This sent Nick into another rage. He began pounding Dantelli unmercifully.

"No, Nick!" Lilly shouted.

He turned to her. "I thought you of all people would understand, Lilly."

"I do understand, Nick. That is why you can't do this. You can't let the anger beat you."

For a brief moment, he appeared to be accepting her words. But the anger won out. He grabbed a handful of Dantelli's slick hair and dragged him along the poolside deck, scraping his skeletal knees and leaving a trail of blood. Nick picked up the hedge-clippers in his free hand and a chill came over Lilly. She tried to scream again, but this time nothing came out. She resigned herself to the fact that Nick was going to kill him.

Nick tossed Dantelli on the diving board. He didn't try to run away or fight. Perhaps he was just hoping to die at this point. Nick raised the hedge-clippers and Lilly prayed to any god who would listen.

And her prayers were answered, at least momentarily. Nick walked to the side of the pool and fished out a couple of life preservers. He used the clippers to cut the ropes away from the preservers, before returning to Dantelli, who appeared only semi conscious. Nick tied him tightly to the diving board with the rope.

Dantelli's body was limp, but his beady eyes were no longer glassed over by shock. It was like he had stored one last reserve tank of energy to fight. "Go ahead and kill me, Nicky. Killing was always your destiny. You're the son of a killer and now you've grown up to be just like him."

"Shut your mouth!"

"It's in your DNA—there's no turning back now. Your father tried to hide his murderous ways, but he was more depraved than any of them."

Nick punched him again—he was going to make this long and painful. More blood trickled into the pool.

Lilly made one last attempt. After betraying her husband, she wasn't exactly on the moral high ground. But she never did the deeds of her own father. She never murdered or sold drugs to children. Nick didn't have to be like his father. "Nick, please let's just get out of here. It's our life—it doesn't matter what our parents did."

Another cocky laugh from Dantelli recaptured Nick's focus. "Killing me is the smart move, Nicky. The last thing you want to do is go to trial, and without you or me, there is no case. A trial would bring out all that dirty laundry of the Sarvydas and Zellen families that led up to your parents' murders. You've got to kill me to save your myth, Nicky, so go ahead and kill me!"

Nick turned to Lilly. "Give me your panties."

The request caught her off guard. “What?”

“I said give me your panties!”

He was in a rage and in no position to be argued with. She reached under her short skirt and removed them.

Nick grabbed the underwear out of her hands and shoved it into Dantelli’s mouth. He then raised the hedge clippers to Dantelli’s throat.

As he did, he looked at Lilly. She felt the same powerful connection as on the day he first walked into her classroom. The same class where she had taught him *Frost,* the poet whose most famous work ends by choosing to take the road less traveled. Her eyes implored Nick to do the same—revenge was the easy path.

After a tense moment, he dropped the clippers and tears began to roll down his face. Lilly ran to him and hugged him tightly. She could have stayed there in that embrace forever. But time was getting short.

She took his hand and led him to the SUV. They headed for the airport.

Chapter 29

Zubov eased his rental car to a stop beside the curb in a quaint neighborhood in Henderson, Nevada. Mothers pushed strollers, and joggers—one American custom he would never understand—ran by in the heat. It seemed like your typical boring suburban neighborhood. But he had arrived to add a little excitement, at least for this day.

He checked himself in the car's mirror and came away impressed. Not bad for a man in his fifties who had been in the killing business for over forty years. It was a business that aged many, and those were the lucky ones. He ran his stubby fingers through his short-cropped hair and fluffed his salt and pepper mustache. Satisfied, he stepped out of the rental car and adjusted his Armani suit. He was on a business call, and believed one should always be well presented when conducting business.

His enemies liked to say he had contempt for all things living. But that wasn't completely true. He admittedly did remove emotion from the equation—the way business should be conducted—but he took great pride in that he'd never harmed an innocent person. That wasn't to say he didn't like his image, or use it to his advantage to inject fear into his opponent.

It was a myth that began in Chernivtsi, a small city in western Ukraine. By age nine, he was known throughout the country as one of its best pickpockets—a tremendous honor in Ukrainian society. He made his first kill at age eleven, and didn't stop until he was incarcerated in the most inhumane of all the Siberian gulags.

It was there he met Viktor Sarvydas. They formed a bond of vors, and Zubov later followed him to Brighton Beach in the early eighties.

Zubov and Sarvydas worked for "Psyk" Miklacz, the don of Brighton Beach, a man Zubov thought had no honor because he would harm and torture the innocent. Their big break came when Sarvydas married Miklacz's daughter, Trina, making him royalty. And soon after, the opportunity to seize control presented itself.

From that time on, Zubov became Sarvydas' top soldier as they set out on a quest for world domination, often fighting off their arch-rivals, Stevanro Parmalov and the Moziafs. That was, until those bastards finally grasped that joining Team Sarvydas would increase their life expectancy. A merger that Zubov was against from the outset.

Zubov casually strolled toward the house, smiling at a young girl riding her bike. He chuckled at how soft American kids were raised to be—*helmets to ride a bike!?* The desert sun scorched his face. He had detested the desert ever since spending time in a stifling Israeli prison, but he didn't plan to be here long.

He found the door unlocked and walked in. It looked like he wasn't the first guest to arrive at the party. He wandered through the house, impressed by the plasma TVs, while the smell of cigarettes gave him a craving. He quit six months ago and it was the hardest thing he ever had done in his life.

He found Dantelli by the pool, tied to a diving board. He couldn't help but laugh at the pathetic sight before him. He walked up to him and removed the panties from Dantelli's mouth. He assumed they belonged to Lilly McLaughlin. He'd developed a fondness for her from afar, and not just for her beauty—he respected her fearlessness. He looked forward to meeting her.

"What the hell are you doing here?" Dantelli greeted him rudely.

"Is that any way to talk to an old friend," Zubov said, still admiring the underwear. "I was trailing Nick and his lady friend. According to my information, they were here."

"Your information always seems to be a day late and a dollar short. Now untie me so I can go kill that little punk."

Zubov reached down and scooped up a pair of hedge-clippers. He performed a couple of quick chops like a batter in baseball taking warm-up swings, and then snipped away the ropes.

As Dantelli shook the circulation back into his limbs, Zubov laughed again. A deep hearty one—his trademark. "You better watch yourself. It looks like that little punk almost killed *you*. Maybe next time he'll do better."

He took note of the anger simmering within Dantelli and laughed. The guineas were always so emotional. No matter what that line in the movie said, it was always personal with them. It was their weakness, and the reason that the Russians had passed them by.

"That kid disrespected me in my home and now I'm going to kill him."

Zubov began clapping. "Bravo, bravo."

Dantelli looked frustrated. "You don't think I'll do it?"

"I think you are doing a great acting job, because the last thing you really want to do is kill Nick."

Dantelli appeared to gather himself. "You're right. Mr. Sarvydas has said he wants to deal with Nick personally. His word is the only word."

Zubov laughed again. "More acting—I love it! It's like I'm talking to fucken DeNiro! I think the reason you don't want to kill Nick is that his testimony can put Alexei away for a long time, and with Viktor in exile, your new boss, Parmalov, can take over the Organizatsiya."

A moment of terror came over Dantelli's face. This was Zubov's favorite part.

Dantelli didn't crumble, as expected. "I work for Viktor Sarvydas and only him. I have always been loyal to him."

Zubov shook his head. The guineas were always talking about loyalty. When will they learn—the only loyalty is to one's self. Zubov shrugged. "I hear things—it's my job to check them out."

"If you checked things out, then you'd know that I followed Mr. Sarvydas' orders. I set up the Zellen meeting, tied him to a chair in the kitchen, and then left the place wide-open for whoever was going to do the job. I had no idea Alexei was to be the one. I returned as the first officer on the scene, just as I was ordered. I did my job. Everything went as planned."

Zubov knew exactly why Alexei was the one. It all went back to that night Zubov ambushed Miklacz and Alexei's mother. And that was just the beginning—the secrets went much deeper. Family was always the ugliest of businesses.

"I don't remember the part of the plan where Nick shows up."

"We figured he must have arrived in between our leaving and Alexei arriving, because he didn't know anything about Bachynsky and me. And he claimed to come in through the back entrance, so he didn't see Karl in the kitchen until he heard Alexei doing the job. So someone must be talking to him."

"Or Nick is a smart kid, and he figured things out."

"Whatever happened, if he isn't stopped, he's going to keep messing things up."

"Don't worry—Nick will be taken care of," Zubov said with a crooked smile. "I'm more concerned that you are scheduled to testify against Alexei next week. With what you know, that could be very damaging testimony."

"I am just following my orders."

"Yet Parmalov is the only one who benefits from this trial continuing."

"I told you—I only follow Mr. Sarvydas' orders! I don't know why he wants me to testify against his son, but he ordered me to work with the prosecution, so that's what I'm going to do."

"Well, I'm here to inform you that there's been a change in plans. Alexei has learned his lesson, and suffered enough. A trial is good for nobody, except Parmalov. Secrets could come out that should stay hidden."

"So what are you saying?"

"To make long story short, you won't be testifying, and I can assure you Nick Zellen won't be either. There will be no trial."

Dantelli remained defiant. "Why should I listen to some washed-up hitman?"

Zubov smiled. "You see, Viktor Sarvydas is not calling the shots right now. I'm here representing the don's son. And his son doesn't want a trial. We both agree that the secrets of that day need to stay buried."

"I have always kept Mr. Sarvydas' secrets and I can be trusted with his son's," Dantelli saw which way the winds were blowing on this one. He hadn't lasted this long by not being flexible.

So much for the loyalty thing. Zubov was a little disappointed—people always seemed to disappoint him in the end. "His son is confident you take your secrets to grave."

Dantelli's face filled with fear and he began to tremble. He then dove head first into the pool. Moments later, after Zubov finished his work with the hedge-clippers, the rest of his body followed.

Chapter 30

Eicher hit the pause button and stared at the blonde reporter in disbelief. He was watching a video of a report on a local Phoenix TV station, which exposed the teacher/student sex scandal at South Chandler High. After earlier revealing Nick's identity, she was now pinpointing his location.

As much as he detested this Stafford woman, he understood she was doing her job … maybe a little too well. Unlike Fitzpatrick, who claimed that it would be safer to "integrate" Nick into society, in this case a school setting, rather than lock him away from the world. Eicher couldn't believe he signed off on that, and he should have been more forceful in demanding that they got Nick out of there at the first hint of trouble.

"All taken care of," he mocked Fitzpatrick's false confidence. He then started in on Nick and the reckless act that had put everything at risk.

"I think we need to cut the kid a break," Dava said calmly.

"We can *cut* him all the breaks we want, but Zubov is going to *cut* his head off. How could he be so damn stupid?"

"Put yourself in his shoes for a minute. The kid is in a foreign place, not knowing who to trust, and has all this pressure building on him with the trial coming up. His parents and girlfriend were murdered. He was looking for something to cling to, and Lilly McLaughlin was there for him."

"A tantalizingly attractive female just happened to be there to seduce him," he wondered aloud, still staring at the frozen screen. His phone rang, waking him from the nightmare. It was LaPoint.

Eicher didn't even give him a chance to speak. "Have you seen this damn report?"

"It's like watching Nick's funeral," LaPoint said soberly.

"Can't we get this bimbo off the air?"

"The cat's out of the bag now, so what's the point? And besides…"

"Besides what?"

LaPoint sighed. "She's the most accurate source we have on Nick's whereabouts. Nobody had them in Vegas—we were thinking Mexico or somewhere out in the middle of the desert. But somehow this Jessi Stafford found them."

"You've confirmed her report?"

"Yes, they were spotted on the casino cameras, and she's paying with the husband's credit card. One way or another, they'll be captured within an hour. It just depends on who gets there first."

"Maybe we can hire Stafford to replace Fitzpatrick's sorry ass."

"There will be plenty of blame to go around on this one. But a lot less shit will hit the fan if we can get Nick back in one piece."

Eicher agreed. "Where do we go from here?"

"Did you check out the videos I emailed you?"

"Not yet. If you haven't noticed, it's been kind of a busy morning."

"Check them out—I'll mobilize here—and let's reconvene in an hour."

Eicher hung up and scrambled to his computer. Dava followed close behind and asked, "What is it?"

Eicher played the videos, recognizing them as a feed from a casino. Lilly and Nick were at the blackjack table. The next video featured them strolling hand-in-hand past rows of slot machines like a honeymooning couple. Lilly was in the same miniscule dress she wore for her abduction, while Nick was dressed in a suit, looking much older than normal. It confirmed that they were there, but Eicher wasn't sure why LaPoint was so eager for him to look at the video.

Then he saw it.

His heart sank. Dava spoke for him, "Oh God—it's Zubov."

Eicher spilled his cold coffee. The brown puddle expanded over his desk without an attempt to stop it. He just stared ahead, as it began dripping off the desk onto his lap like a waterfall.

As Eicher slumped in his chair, the phone rang again. But this time it was Dava's.

"Hello," she answered pleasantly, but her face quickly dropped. She muttered something in Lithuanian, but the term "uh-oh" crossed all language barriers.

She hung up and turned to Eicher. "That was Fitzpatrick."

"Don't tell me—Fitzpatrick is arranging a FBI escort for Sarvydas from Israel to Vegas?"

"No—Dantelli's dead."

That was a big uh-oh.

Sarvydas seemed pretty determined that there would be no trial. Eicher begged Dantelli numerous times to go into protective custody, but he wouldn't listen—still fighting his childish FBI/NYPD turf wars.

Dava pushed the dazed Eicher away from his computer, and signed in to her email. "They sent me the video from Dantelli's security system," she explained.

The first video stunned them. It was Nick and Lilly being invited in by Dantelli. The next video was of them leaving about twenty minutes later. The cameras covered the exterior, but they had no shots of what happened during those twenty minutes inside the house.

Dava appeared befuddled. "Why would Nick go there?"

Eicher shrugged. "Dantelli was the lead investigator in his father's case. Maybe he was looking for some protection."

"Do you think they killed him? That makes no sense."

"They didn't," Eicher proclaimed, his concentration on the next video. This one showing Zubov entering the house through an unlocked door. "But I know who did."

"Zubov makes much more sense," Dava remarked. "Fitzpatrick said that Dantelli was decapitated."

Predictable—the removal of body parts was Zubov's M.O. What more interested Eicher was that everywhere Nick went, Zubov seemed to follow. Eicher didn't believe this was a coincidence any more than he thought Lilly McLaughlin coming into Nick's life was.

Chapter 31

A knock rattled Eicher and Dava to attention. A bespectacled man in a white lab coat entered the office, carrying a manila folder. It was Kurt Wilson.

"I got your results," he stated proudly, as he barged into the office.

Dava looked stumped. "Results for what?"

"From the hands they found during the raid in Brooklyn. The ones you guys asked me to ID."

Dava looked annoyed that she wasn't in the loop.

Eicher tried to explain, "They are Audrey Mays' hands. They were discovered in a freezer at the Moziafs' butcher shop. The tattoo is identical to Audrey's. I just wanted to send it to the lab to make it official before I told you."

Judging from her icy stare, Dava accepted the apology, but had put him on probation.

"That's why I ran up here so fast," Wilson said excitedly. "Those hands don't belong to Audrey Mays."

Eicher was stumped. "But they're a match."

"If you are speaking some alternate language in which match means they *don't* match, then I would have to agree with you."

"Are you sure you're not mistaken. What are the odds of another female hand with an identical tattoo being found in the Moziafs' freezer?"

Wilson shrugged—he was about the science, not speculation. "In this specific case, 100%. With the low temps in that meat locker, it is possible that the hand shrunk, distorting the ink, so perhaps it wasn't the same tattoo. But the fingerprint science doesn't lie—it definitely isn't Audrey Mays."

Dava looked at the report, her normally placid expression turning agitated. "Then whose hands are they?"

Wilson smiled. "That I do know. Her name is Rachel Grant. Ms. Grant was a 'professional' dancer here in the city who used the stage name Carrie Grant. Her prints were in the system because she was arrested on a couple of occasions for prostitution, a few years back. Her parents, who are from Wyoming, reported her missing about a year ago."

"Is it possible," Dava asked, still studying the report, "that this Grant woman is the one who is buried in Oklahoma?"

It was connected somehow. It had to be. "If the girl who was slaughtered in that apartment was Rachel Grant, what was she doing in Audrey's apartment? And what the hell happened to Audrey Mays?" Eicher asked.

"Maybe somebody is trying to throw us off. I think we need to exhume the body in Oklahoma and do a DNA match to the hands," Dava thought out loud.

When Wilson left, Eicher instructed Dava to work on getting information on Rachel Grant. And most importantly, anything that would connect her to Audrey Mays.

Eicher cleaned the coffee off his pants, and then reviewed the case in his head. He felt like he was missing something.

It all began with Karl Zellen's arrest on money laundering charges, and things went downhill from there. On the surface, what followed was both logical and primal—Zellen was going to take down Sarvydas, who responded to the threat by having the wife of his longtime business associate killed. Karl sought revenge for Paula's murder, and he ended up dead.

All of this would have landed in the large pile of lore and myth about the Russian mob—just as it did years ago with the ambush that brought Viktor to power—but Nick happened to make an unscheduled visit home that day, and witnessed his father's murder.

But with the events of the last twenty-four hours, Eicher was now starting to wonder about how easily the case came together. Especially how Karl Zellen, with little persuasion, was willing to turn evidence against his longtime business associate.

Zellen was also known as the brains behind the Sarvydas Empire, who knew the monster better than anyone. And while Alexei was no genius by any stretch, he was brilliant when it came to murder, and Eicher wondered about all those clues he left behind. As he stared at a pair of hands that didn't belong to Audrey Mays, he wondered if it fit too well.

Was it possible that he was so intent on finally catching a break against Sarvydas that he overlooked all the coincidences and questions about the case, Lilly McLaughlin included?

Eicher's phone rang again, knocking him out of his distressing thoughts. He was expecting LaPoint, but it wasn't.

"You lied to me, Eicher. You said you'd protect me, but you didn't keep your promise."

He immediately recognized Nick's voice. "You are not safe out there. Tell me where you are, so we can pick you up."

"I'm safer than I'd be with your people guarding me. You have a leak in your office, Eicher. They found me. If I stayed I'd be as dead as my parents and Audrey."

Eicher kept the part about Rachel Grant to himself, until he had more answers than questions on that subject. "I admit we made mistakes, Nick. But whoever you're trusting now is leading you toward danger."

"Maybe I don't have a choice," he paused to let the statement hang in the dead air. "Maybe the decision was made for me. Like I said, if I stayed I was a dead man."

He again thought of Lilly McLaughlin. "What are you trying to tell me, Nick?"

"Remember what you told me about not believing in coincidences?" he said and hung up.

Chapter 32

"The gas pedal is the vertical one on the right," Becks snipped.

She hadn't been a ray of sunshine since they met, but ever since Darren took away her driving privileges on account of her crazed tantrum at her school locker, she'd been downright surly.

"Turn here," she demanded. Darren continued to follow her orders.

But he wasn't a total pushover—he had changed the original plan. Darren knew nothing good could come of going to Las Vegas and confronting Lilly. Or as Becks preferred—kill her. It was best to allow the professionals to bring her into custody and then they could figure out what happened together. And if it was some sort of mental illness, he wanted to make sure Lilly got the best medical care.

They arrived at Brett Buckley's house. The place Darren had met Becks—fist to face—just hours ago. She hopped out of the car and jogged toward the house, craning her neck back at Darren and blazing a "what's taking you so long" look.

Becks ran around to the backyard and began scaling a cedar fence. The Buckley house was impressive, built on the shore of a man-made lake. He remembered Mara Garcia saying something about the parents owning a software company.

"I don't think this is a good idea," he shouted to Becks, as she scooted over the wall like a cat. Or a cat burglar.

"What, don't you think you can get over, old man?" her muffled shout came from the other side of the fence.

He couldn't believe that he let a teenage girl talk him into breaking and entering. A long jail term seemed like the one thing that could actually make this day worse. "Let's take a moment and really think this through."

"No wonder your wife left you for a younger man."

A cheap shot, no doubt, but motivational. He aggressively scaled the wall and leaped into the lushest backyard he'd ever seen in Arizona. Not the usual sand and cactus design. The yard sloped down to a lakeside dock.

Becks was busy working on a fuse-box at the back of the house. She smiled like a Cheshire cat. "You would think that since the Buckley's business is to make security software, that their own house would be better protected."

"We are compounding the problem by being here," Darren proclaimed.

"No, your wife is com-*pounding* my boyfriend, that's why we're here. Don't worry, Brett gave me the code so I could sneak in at night when his parents were sleeping. Shoulda been my first clue that he had honesty issues."

Once the alarm was deactivated, Becks found a ladder and set it up against the house. She scooted up to the second floor and pried open a window with a gardening tool, before disappearing inside.

Darren continued to follow the juvenile delinquent. Probably straight to prison. But something told him that she was the one who could lead him to the truth.

He landed in a 21st-century teenage room. It wasn't much different from Darren's day—just the Heather Thomas poster was replaced with Brooklyn Decker, and Darren's boom box and television with rabbit ears was now a shiny Mac computer and an iPod docking station.

"The FBI was just here an hour ago, they could come back," Darren warned.

"The FBI?" she scoffed. "They couldn't even figure out that a bunch of guys on terrorist watch lists signing up for flight school was a bad idea."

"What about his parents? The authorities probably called them."

"Trust me, the Buckleys are not going to cut a Hawaiian vacation short because Brett skipped town with some chick. Those stuck-up sons of bitches never liked me anyway."

"I can't imagine why."

Becks feigned laughter. "Good one," she said and picked up a picture and handed it to him. It was a prom photo of her and Brett. Darren had to admit she cleaned up well. The form-fitting gown matched the streaks in her hair. With the Arizona sun setting in the background, they looked like a striking couple.

"Look at me—I'm damn cute. You'd do me, right?"

"Um…what?"

"I mean if you weren't married and I weren't in high school. If we met at some bar, you'd find me attractive, no?"

"Sure, I guess," Darren stuttered uncomfortably, expecting that *Catch a Predator* guy from Dateline NBC to jump out at any moment and slap the cuffs on him.

"But obviously not as hot as our chaperone—the lovely and talented Lilly McLaughlin. Wearing her skanky dress and prancing around in her stripper kicks. Always bending over so all the boys can see her tramp stamp right above her ass. And I'm not talking about the prom—I mean everyday at school when she was trying to steal my boyfriend!"

Becks grabbed the picture from Darren and launched it into the wall. The frame shattered off of Brooklyn's nose.

"Lilly's not like that—there has to be an explanation," Darren stated.

"Oh, she's not?" Becks replied, her eyes now burning with a competitive fire. She hurried to the computer stand where a laptop was plugged in. "We'll just see about that."

Chapter 33

Becks booted up the computer and began furiously typing.

"What are you doing?" Darren asked.

"Breaking into Brett's computer," she said coldly. "I want to show you something."

She filled in all the appropriate passwords and was logged on.

"You stole your boyfriend's passwords?" he asked.

"What can I say—I was a dedicated girlfriend. I wanted to know what was going on in my man's life."

"Relationships are built on trust," he lectured.

She looked at him incredulously. "You *can't* be serious. Maybe you shoulda done a little more checking up on your wife."

The comment, besides angering him, turned his thoughts to the computer. "Don't you find it odd that that the FBI confiscated Lilly's computer when they searched our house, but they left Brett's computer. I know they were here because I talked to Agent LaPoint when I came by."

"Maybe because she's the one who committed the felony."

She had an answer for everything. She was also making the proverbial woman scorned look contented.

She pulled up the Internet and called Darren over. What she showed him made him understand her hurt. He viewed endless blogs, Facebook pages, and random websites created in honor of his wife. The most creative was called *Pictures of Lilly* based on The Who song of the same name—actually an updated techno version of the song made by some hip-hop artist that

Darren had never heard of. The song played over and over, as the photos from the infamous post-prom party looped endlessly in slide-show format.

The majority featured Lilly and Brett Buckley nestled on a couch, her arms and legs wrapped around him like she didn't want to let go. When Darren saw that she was still wearing the corsage he bought for her, his heart broke.

The pictures were bad enough, but one site had an amateur video taken on a student's phone. It followed a kissing Lilly and Brett into a bedroom. The giggling couple finally shooed away the cameraman so they could have some "privacy." His mind kept trying to make up excuses—maybe someone gave her that date rape drug—but it was obvious that at the very least, Lilly was a willing partner, if not the aggressor. He felt sick.

The blogs and chat rooms were even worse. He was amazed how vicious the kids on these sites were. The names they called Lilly were far worse than anything Becks said about her. Becks referred to them as "keyboard commandos," who were only tough when they could hide behind an online alias. She didn't seem to be a fan.

Becks was determined to keep his nightmare going. "And if you think she just had a bad night, maybe you should take a look at this."

She displayed an archive of text messages sent between Brett and Lilly over the past month. Darren didn't even want to ask how she got access to them.

As painful as the Internet photos were, the correspondence between them hurt even more. Words are by far the most intimate stimulus.

Lilly expressed how she felt their relationship was "wrong," but she "couldn't stop." How Brett took over her mind, body, and soul. How she craved him when they weren't together, and how she never wanted to return home when they were together. He realized why she was distracted—she was thinking of him.

It also detailed the places where they'd been intimate. Different classrooms in the school and parks around the Chandler area. Darren felt most betrayed when they plotted a rendezvous at their home while he was out of town on a flight. The thought of this boy in his bed made him nauseous.

As time went on, their actions grew riskier. Brett wrote of avoiding his "rents," which Becks explained was the millennium generation's term for parents.

But after that infamous prom party, the tone of the messages turned to damage control, discussing the importance of getting their stories straight, and even plotting their escape in general terms. The messages came to an abrupt end, likely because they suspected the authorities were onto them.

Darren's head began to spin so fast that he thought it was going to fly off his neck. He wandered out of Brett's room like a drunk looking for his keys and bumped his way down a staircase. He found the front door and rushed into the Arizona sun, needing air. The picture of Lilly and Brett Buckley together was the last thing he saw in his mind just before everything went black.

Chapter 34

Darren felt a sharp slap across his face. And then another. He heard a faint voice. It seemed to be coming from far away. "Wake up."

He opened his eyes just in time to see the hand once again headed for his face. His reflexes responded in time to grab it before another slap connected with his throbbing cheek. He found himself in the passenger seat of his Jetta. They were no longer at the Buckley's house.

"Any chance the last twenty-four hours was a really bad dream?" he asked in a hoarse voice.

"That's what all the guys say when they wake up next to me," Becks replied with a smile.

"What happened?"

"You passed out, so I dragged you to the car and brought you for help. BTW—you're waaay heavier than you look!"

He looked around, unsure of his surroundings. "This sure doesn't look like the hospital."

"The hospital will kill you. Do you know how many germs and bacteria are in that place?"

"Where are we, Becks?"

"I brought you to Cholla's. I figure a Cholla Burger and curly fries can cure any ailment."

Now the neighborhood came into focus. They were in the parking lot of the popular hamburger stand on Chandler Boulevard, not far from Darren's home. "How long was I out?"

"About twenty minutes, I guess. I really didn't keep track. I thought you were trying to scam me into giving you CPR—that so wasn't happening. Now let's go," she ordered. Darren wasn't going anywhere.

Becks walked around to the passenger side and unhooked him out of his seat-belt. She then yanked him to his feet.

"I'm not really hungry," Darren groaned.

"It's a Cholla Burger and curly fries. What does hunger have to do with anything?"

He hesitantly followed her to one of the outdoor patio tables. Once he was seated, she took out a tube of 30-block and began smudging it on his scalp. "Don't want you to be sorry in the morning—did you know the sun is the leading cause of sunburn?"

"You must have Mr. Fischer for science."

"I was thinking about running away with him to get back at Brett."

He smiled—he'd almost forgotten what it felt like. "He's pretty spry for his age, you think you can keep up?"

"Tell me about it. Instead of teaching physics, physics should be teaching him," she replied with a grin.

But the nice moment quickly waned. Darren figured that's how things would be from now on. After ordering, they fell into silence. Lilly and Brett was their only common conversation piece, and neither of them wanted to discuss it anymore.

"Shouldn't you be back in school?" he finally asked.

She looked at him like he'd said the most absurd thing ever. "Let me see—school—Cholla Burger—school—Cholla Burger. It was a tough choice, but I went with Cholla Burger," she mocked.

"Be careful or they'll send the truant officer after you."

"The wha...?"

"Truant officers were a volunteer section of the local police force that rounded up kids who were cutting school—what they called truancy. My grandfather was a truant officer."

Becks snorted a laugh. "I think they need to send one of those dudes after Brett and your wife. They are the ones cutting school today. Or maybe we should declare ourselves honorary truant officers for the day and drag their asses back here."

He was impressed by her sharp wit, even if most of the humor was at his expense. But her face soured, and even the arrival of their food didn't remove her frown. She sighed heavily. "I really thought it was meant to be."

"What was?" Darren asked, confused.

"Brett and I. All the Barbies in school wanted him, and would always trash me behind my back or in those stupid chat rooms, but I was convinced they were just jealous of what we had."

Darren nodded as he bit into his burger. Becks was right—it hit the spot. He couldn't remember the last time he ate, which probably played a role in his passing out.

"We were inseparable," Becks continued, still not touching her food. "People eventually accepted us. They called us Posh and Becks—how cute is that?"

"Posh and Becks?'

You know, like Victoria and David Beckham—the British supercouple. Brett was actually Posh because he was so pretty, and I was Becks, because, well, I'm Becks. But we were more than cute, we had a lot in common. We both moved here in the middle of our senior year, which BTW, really sucks."

He continued to devour his burger, half-listening to her teenage tangent.

"And Chandler is like totally the worst place. The guys are a bunch of suburban wangsters and the girls are all tanorexic backstabbers."

"Where did you move here from?" Darren asked as he whisked a curly fry through a mound of ketchup and slung it into his mouth.

"Boston. My father got a job out here and chose the scrilla over his daughter's sanity."

Darren perked up, feeling the connection. "I'm from Framingham."

"Wicked awesam," she replied, displaying a heavy Boston accent. "I guess we have more in common than our sig-ohs being a couple of cheating louses. I got accepted to BC, so hopefully I'll be heading back in the fall…if I graduate, that is."

"I left when I was eighteen and don't get back much, unless I'm flying into Logan. My parents both passed about ten years ago and I lost track of most of my childhood buddies. But I do miss the old neighborhood."

"That Paul Revere thing musta been pretty cool," Becks said with a smirk that resuscitated him.

"I'm not quite *that* old, but I lived there when the Red Sox were the cursed team that lost every year."

"That was way before my time, but I've read about those teams," she said. Her smile faded and she stared forlornly at the traffic on Chandler Boulevard. "Do you think we are just setting ourselves up for failure?"

"What do you mean?" Darren asked, washing down his burger with his diet soda.

"No offense to us, but we're playing OOOL here."

"OOOL?"

"Out of our league. My boyfriend and your wife are serious hotties. I'm nerd-sexy enough to be a rock star at a Harry Potter convention, but I can't compete with your flirt-in-a-skirt wife."

Darren took a close look at her. And despite the ketchup dripping from the side of her lip and her light skin losing the battle against the sun, he thought she was selling herself short.

"And you…" she continued.

"And me, what?"

"You're not exactly a lollipop. There's a reason it's Angelina and Brad, and not Angelina and some follicley-challenged boring guy from Arizona."

"When you get older you'll learn that it's not all about looks. It's what's on the inside that counts."

"Thanks for the backseat mothering, but I'll take that a little more seriously when Tom Brady dumps Giselle for Madam Curie."

"I heard Mr. Fischer and Madam Curie once had a steamy affair," Darren tried to joke a subject change.

Becks didn't laugh, but seemed in favor of the shift in topics. "So what's your deal?" she asked.

"My deal?"

"I told you my sad tale, and my parents taught me not to eat Cholla Burgers with strangers. Tell me about yourself and then you won't be a stranger anymore. So far, all I know is that you're boring, your baseball team never won, your grandfather arrested kids for not going to school, and you have bad taste in women. The story has nowhere to go but up."

Darren shrugged. "Not much to tell. Grew up in the Boston area, Irish Catholic, so I have lots of guilt to go with my boringness and bad taste. I went to the Air Force Academy in Colorado Springs, and was an officer for ten years before joining civilian life. Flying planes is what I did, so flying commercial seemed like the logical step. And that's when I met Lilly."

Becks burst into laughter.

"What's so funny?" Darren asked, rankled.

"It's so ironic," she said through chokes of laughter, "our lives are exactly like those Greek tragedies we studied in your wife's class. Things are going along and then one wrong turn and things come crashing down. *And then I met Lilly,* cue the horror-film music."

She shook her head in disbelief, unable to stop laughing. "I guess ya gotta either laugh or cry."

So Darren cried.

Chapter 35

The red light flashed on and Jessi Stafford sprung into action. She was about to deliver another in her exclusive reports on the teacher/student scandal.

The case was already a screenwriters dream. It included: the abduction of an attractive woman, forbidden romance, and a tear-jerking plea by a distraught husband to strum the heartstrings. But it now added a few more elements that made America weak in the knees—weddings, gambling, and Elvis. And the best part for Jessi was that since Channel-6 was an unaffiliated station, they were able to syndicate her reports to the national outlets. She was getting nationwide coverage!

"I am reporting to you live from the Little Church of the West in Las Vegas. Where, after a night of reckless gambling, fugitive couple Lilly McLaughlin and Brett Buckley were last seen trying to get married without a proper marriage license."

Jessi smiled into the camera. It wasn't one of the smiles she'd had to fake this past year—this one was full of joy. The joy of a possible return to New York and spreading the gospel of kiss my ass.

"Since Lilly McLaughlin is already married, we can add bigamy to the laundry list of charges," she continued.

She sneaked a smirk at her cameraman, Byung. Always the skeptic, he actually thought coming to Vegas was a bad idea. Another reason why he would spend his whole career behind the camera in that Arizona cowtown.

She turned to a man who had witnessed Lilly and Brett in the chapel, and had agreed to go on the air with her. He featured a large pompadour haircut, and wore a sequined jumpsuit unbuttoned to his navel, oversized sunglasses, and disco boots. As if this wasn't enough of a circus already, her eyewitness was an Elvis impersonator.

Interviewing Elvis was actually more along the lines of the career she thought she'd have while growing up in Kissimmee, Florida. She wasn't sure exactly what she would do with her life, but knew it would take place in front of a camera. She never thought about the news, and frankly the idea bored her—if you've witnessed one crime or political scandal, you've seen them all—entertainment was where the real stars were made.

Following the interview with Elvis, Jessi received a phone call. More good news. Her source informed her that Lilly McLaughlin was spotted at McCarran International, and had purchased a ticket on a flight to Mexico City.

She practically dragged Byung to their rental car and made a dash for the airport. Not wanting to take time to park, she told Byung to drop her off at the terminal. But she had a hunch, and changed her mind. Instead, she directed him to go to long-term parking.

And sure enough it was there. The McLaughlins' Lexus SUV. She had Byung film a shot of it for her next report, and then they returned to the terminal.

Jessi hightailed it into the airport, but when she did, the winning streak came to an end. She learned that the flight to Mexico City had already taken off.

Byung was much less devastated. "We gave it our best shot. But since they're no longer here in Vegas, and we don't have the travel budget for Mexico City, I'm going to hop the next flight back to Phoenix."

For once, Jessi agreed with him. But something was bugging her, and she said, "Go ahead—I'll catch up with you later. I just need to take care of something."

He looked strangely at her for a second, and then headed toward the domestic flights.

Mexico was too obvious, Jessi thought. Using the credit card, being seen at the wedding chapel, and now leaving the car in plain sight. If they were actually this stupid, they wouldn't have gotten this far. Something was fishy.

She went to the Air Mexico counter and demanded the flight manifest, along with any security video of the passengers getting on the plane.

"And you are?" the attendant asked.

"I'm Jessi Stafford from Channel-6 News in Phoenix, and this is related to an important story I'm covering."

"Sorry, we are not allowed to give that type of information to reporters."

"Are you aware of the Freedom of Information Act?"

"I am, and it is not related to your request."

Jessi figured that this was above the attendant's pay grade, so she requested to see her supervisor. When she refused, Jessi began to make a loud scene. Squeaky wheel gets the grease. But all she got was an escort out of the terminal.

A cab driver came up to her as she stood curbside. "You need a ride?"

Jessi shook her head without looking at the man, pondering her next move.

"You were right, you know."

This got her attention. "Right about what?"

"The runaway teacher and her student. They didn't get on that flight."

"You saw them?"

"I gave them a ride out of here."

Jessi could feel a rush of excitement as the man handed her his card. Then he took out a piece of paper and wrote something on it.

He handed the paper to her. "Here are my rates for the ride you want to go on."

She looked at it—it wasn't even close to being within their budget. And how did she know he wasn't lying? She was just about to make a counter offer, when her phone rang. She hoped it was more good news from her source.

It was Brandon Longa. Uh-oh.

"Hey, baby, funny thing happened when I got out of the shower. You were gone. I was worried sick that you were taken in one of those gang abductions."

"I'm sorry, Brandon, I was called into an emergency at work."

"Yeah, I saw your reports from Vegas. You must have been in a hurry because you forgot to shut off my computer, and hide the fact that you broke into my phone to steal police evidence with intent to broadcast it."

"I don't know what you're talking about, Brandon," she said as if mortally wounded by the accusation.

"I must be mistaken. Because you wouldn't do anything like that, since it's a felony, and we already went over the whole you're not a prison kinda girl thing."

"Apology accepted. Can we talk later, sweetie, I have a big interview lined up."

The moment the words left her mouth, she felt her arms being ripped behind her. She looked to see Brandon with his cell phone still resting on his ear, as he handcuffed her. "You wouldn't lie to me, would you … sweetie?"

She struggled to get out of the handcuffs, but it was no use. So she attempted charm—she flipped her blonde mane and batted her eyelashes at him. "I did it for us."

"Don't worry, I heard Las Vegas jails are nice—slot machines, showgirls—you're going to have a blast."

She began swearing like a sailor at him. He laughed, infuriating her more. Once he made his point, he unlatched the handcuffs.

She turned indignant. "How did you find me, anyway?"

A sly grin appeared. "How do you think your source got that information about the flight to Mexico?"

She swung her fist at his most sensitive area, and this time didn't miss.

He bent over in pain. "Assaulting an officer twice in one day? The next story you break is going to be about Jessi Stafford doing hard time."

"Tell it to the judge, Longa," she fired back, imitating his Brooklyn accent.

He quickly recovered. "I'll tell ya what—I'm willing to look past the assault charges in exchange for you buying me lunch. I'm starving."

Jessi hadn't eaten all day, and it would buy her time to plot her next move. So she agreed to the terms. They took a cab to the New York-New York Hotel & Casino. Jessi wanted to go to Chin-Chin, the trendy eatery to the stars, but Brandon decided on an Italian place.

As Jessi picked at her salad, she concluded that this was as close to New York as she would get until she was able to rid herself of Brandon Longa.

He looked across the table at her, and said, "I have to pick up Goot at the airport, but after that I'm free for the rest of the night—why don't you and I hit the town?"

She faked a smile. "I'd love that Brandon."

But she already had plans.

Chapter 36

Jessi stepped up to the dilapidated-looking warehouse on Balazar Avenue, took a deep breath, and then knocked.

There was no response, but she remained undeterred, and knocked again. This time the loud salsa music stopped and she heard footsteps heading toward the door. "Who's there?" demanded a voice.

"I'm here to see Ramiro Cortez."

"Name your business."

"I'm here for our date."

A sliding peephole abruptly opened and two beady eyes were staring at her. She could feel their eyes on her fire engine red halter dress with mini sarong skirt. It was the most revealing outfit she could find at a trendy shop in New York-New York.

The door slid open, and now she faced three gangster-looking Mexicans with guns pointed at her. The lead guy smiled at her devilishly. "Where have you been all my life, senorita?"

"Is Ramiro here or not? I don't have all day."

"Time is money, and I'll bet Ramiro is paying you mucho dinero."

Jessi would have loved to recoup some of the cost of the dress, and the king's ransom she had to pay the driver to deliver her here, but that wasn't going to happen. The only thing that was going to be exchanged was information.

They marched her into an open area filled with cars, being worked on by grease-stained men. But she knew these weren't typical auto mechanics.

They brought her to a shirtless man who was supervising the work on a souped-up Mustang. His hair was cut short to the scalp and his muscular body was colored with tattoos like graffiti on a building.

"This chica says she's with you, Miro."

He looked her up and down, then reached into the waistband of his jeans and drew a pistol. "I'm going to check my calendar, and if you're name isn't on it, blondie, then we're going to have big problems," Ramiro stated, his voice guttural.

"I have some questions for you about Lilly McLaughlin."

"I don't know any Lilly. I think you got lost on your way to the Cirque du Soleil show, and this is not a neighborhood you wanna get lost in."

"Perhaps if you answer my questions, I won't have a talk with the police about the obvious chop shop you're running here. And I'm sure when they take a look at these cars, they'll find some interesting hiding places that would be advantageous in drug running or taking illegals over the border."

The men around him tensed and raised their weapons, but Ramiro just laughed. "The 5-0 don't even come around Balazar Avenue no more—too dangerous."

He then sent the men away, including the ones settled on a nearby couch watching a soccer game on a TV. "Vamos!" They hurried out of the room—Ramiro Cortez appeared to be a powerful man.

"I'm a reporter, Ramiro" Jessi said. "Can I call you Ramiro?"

He looked her up and down. "You can call me whatever you want."

She smiled at him. "You're sweet. I just have a few questions, and then I'll be on my way."

"How do I know you're not a cop?"

"You just said that the police no longer patrol Balazar."

His look wandered to her legs. "I'm still going to have to check you for a wire, just to be sure. And I know you chicas like to hide them in the most private of places."

"Then the next thing you'll be checking, is yourself into a hospital."

He laughed. "You're feisty, and very brave to come down here. I like that in my women."

"I'm not one of your women. But I get the feeling that Lilly is. Now tell me why she came to see you today." She held up the picture of her and handed it to him.

He observed the photo, and remarked, "Her name is Liliana Rojas, the Lilly stuff is just a character she's playing."

He motioned her to join him on the couch. It made Jessi uncomfortable, but she knew it was imperative that she appear confident, and she took a seat next to him.

"Liliana is an old friend who was in town, and dropped by—she used to come up here with her brothers back in the day."

"She just dropped by to say hello?" Jessi asked skeptically.

"She was going on a trip, so I loaned her a car."

"Funny thing is, she had bought plane tickets to go on a trip. And she already had a car, which she left at McCarran. Seems like she had a sudden change of plans."

"Flying can be very dangerous with all these terrorists running around."

"I've learned a lot about Liliana today, and she doesn't seem like someone who is scared of danger."

A proud smile encompassed his face. "Liliana always likes to live on the edge, and she likes her men just as edgy."

"Is that why she came to see you—because you were one of these dangerous guys?"

"No, I was never her type."

"Your rap sheet tells a different story."

"I might meet her danger fix, but she's also attracted to those who could help her climb the ladder, if you know what I mean. I'm just a lowly mechanic."

Jessi agreed that Lilly's history did show that the men in her life helped her achieve upward mobility. "What about the guy she was with—Brett Buckley—did he seem like her type?"

He shrugged. "I could tell that he came from money. And since he was on the run from the law, yeah, I'd say she liked that he was living on the edge."

"You mentioned that you're old friends. I'm guessing you didn't meet Liliana at a Chandler PTA meeting."

"Her brothers and I fought together in the war. She used to tag along with them when they came to Vegas to do their laundry."

"The war we're talking about is not in Iraq or Afghanistan, correct? It's the kind of war where they abduct innocent women as an initiation."

"That was a long time ago. Now I'm just a small business owner trying to make ends meet."

"A couple of Liliana's brothers were killed in this war, isn't that right?"

His face turned distressed. "She was closest with her brother Manuel. It changed Liliana when he was killed. It was like she began to create a new life—went back to school, married some white bread Mr. Suburbia type, never visited the old neighborhood. I guess that's when she became this Lilly character, but the thing is, you can never run from your past."

"Sounds like you resent her for it."

"It doesn't matter what I think of her—Manuel was like a brother to me." He pointed to a portrait tattoo of him on his chest. "I promised him if Liliana ever needed help, I'd be there for her."

"And the help she needed was to get out of town before the authorities put a stop to her joyride with her underage boyfriend. So they bought airline tickets to leave the country. They even checked their bags, which likely contained their cell phones, so the police will follow the GPS all the way to Mexico. That means they were in the market for new cell phones, preferably the untraceable kind that Ramiro Cortez's drug-dealing clients often purchased from him. So now that I know why they came to see you, the remaining question is, where did they go?"

He picked up a remote and changed the soccer game to a newscast. It was reporting from the home of a Tony Dantelli in Henderson, a former New

York police officer who was murdered earlier in the day. "It's not where they are going that should interest you. It's where they were before they came to see me."

Jessi looked at the TV screen with amazement. "Are you saying that Brett and Lilly had something to do with that murder?"

"Sorry, lady—it's time for me to get paid for my information."

"I don't know who you think you're dealing with, but I'm not one of those tabloid journalists who pays for a story."

"Like when you paid someone to deliver you to me?" His grin turned evil. "I mean that you owe me for the information I already gave you. It's time to pay your debt."

He forcefully climbed on top of her, and moved his hand under her skirt. She tried to fight back, but it was no use. She screamed, but the only ones that might hear her were Ramiro Cortez's men.

"Freeze, scum bag!" a shout echoed throughout the spacious room.

Jessi looked up to see Brandon Longa holding a gun on them. Ramiro made a move for his gun, but an arm came seemingly out of nowhere and chopped it out of his hand.

It was Brandon's partner, Gutierrez. "You give us Mexicans a bad name, amigo," he said and punched him in the ribs. "It's time for you to grow up and get a real job."

Brandon checked that Jessi was all right, and then walked her out of the warehouse with no response from Ramiro or his men. Once outside, she asked, "How did you find me?"

"You were late for our date, so I came looking for you."

She looked skeptically at him. "Were you following me?"

"Is that as close to a 'thank you' as I'm gonna get?"

"Brandon?"

He shrugged. "We thought it might be our best chance of solving the case."

Jessi begrudgingly smiled. "Thank you."

Chapter 37

Agent LaPoint drove his government-issued Taurus up to the house that was serving as his makeshift office in Chandler. He hurried inside as fast as his cranky knees would allow. He couldn't believe people chose to live in the god-forsaken heat—and it was only April!

The protection of Nick Zellen was a joint operation between Special Agents of the FBI and the US Federal Marshals, causing numerous turf wars. The Marshals ran the Federal Witness Protection Program, so they took the lead in the day-to-day logistics. But when Deputy Marshal Fitzpatrick began to lose control, Eicher flew him in to oversee the moving of Nick to a new locale. Unfortunately it was too late, and was now a recovery mission.

He'd gone for a drive to try to compose himself after watching another Jessi Stafford report on the whereabouts of Nick and Lilly, from a wedding chapel of all places. He hoped they enjoyed their nuptials, because he was pretty certain that death would be parting them very soon.

He was about to grab a bite to eat—cleaning up Fitzpatrick's messes had left him famished—when the phone rang. It was Eicher with more bad news. Seems Dantelli had lost his head—literally—which frankly wasn't that surprising. Sarvydas seemed pretty determined to put an end to Alexei's trial before it started. The more interesting aspect was that Nick and Lilly had showed up at Dantelli's prior to Zubov's visit.

Eicher also informed him about a pair of hands found during a raid, which belonged to a stripper named Rachel Grant. This one left LaPoint perplexed.

"I might need you to go to Oklahoma tomorrow morning to exhume Audrey Mays' body … if it is her body," Eicher suggested.

Not exactly the south of France, but better than this oven. "Not a problem. Any news that doesn't involve limbs being chopped off?"

"Nick called me."

"When?"

"Twenty minutes ago."

"Did you run a trace?"

"Came up empty. The phone was blocked—total professional job. Now where would a kid like Nick get something like that?"

"I'm guessing Dantelli, which would explain their visit. But sounds like you are skeptical of his travel companion."

"Too many coincidences. She shows up in his life out of the blue, and now he's taking these crazy risks. And Zubov keeps appearing wherever they show up. First the casino and then Dantelli's house."

LaPoint was skeptical. "I think you're selling the kid short. He lost confidence in us, which I don't blame him for, and he believes the woman is the only person he can trust."

"He's also convinced there's a leak in my office, and that's how they found him."

"Your office is too busy blaming the FBI for everything to be leaking information," he replied with a laugh.

"Would you consider it 'blaming you' if I ask you to keep an eye out for any of your people in the field who might be acting suspiciously?"

"No, but it would prove you have no sense of humor. I think we need to be more worried about Zubov, than leaks, or Nick's putting too much trust in his teacher."

"Based on what he told me, I'm not sure Nick still trusts her."

"We all wise up at some point in life, but the question always is: did you figure it out in time to save yourself."

After hanging up with Eicher, LaPoint returned to the kitchen and found a carton of leftover PF Chang's in the refrigerator. But before he could indulge himself, LaPoint heard the front door open. He pulled his gun.

Chapter 38

"Where have you been?" LaPoint barked at Fitzpatrick, and put his gun away.

"Since you're the one who demoted me to stakeout duty, I think you know the answer. If I die of boredom, would that be considered being killed in the line of duty?"

"I'm glad you can find humor in this fiasco."

"Don't worry, I don't charge extra for the comedy."

LaPoint sighed. "I can't believe Eicher let you talk him into this high school nonsense."

"It's called Integration Theory, and I have safely incorporated numerous witnesses into communities, schools, etc. Last I checked, you have never been in charge of the safety of a witness. And if you were, you would know that it only works if the witness doesn't break the rule—make no contact with anyone from the outside. There is no second rule, because if they break the first one they will end up dead. Nick was busted because he contacted his sister."

"Barricading him was the right move, not integration. You should have learned from Osama. If he'd stayed in his cave he wouldn't be fish food right now. But he must have read your book, because he decided to move the family to the suburbs."

"Wrong again. He got caught because he chose to hide out in that fortress, instead of blending into society. It raised suspicion, and once they figured out his location, he was trapped. And the same thing would have happened to Nick."

LaPoint could never win with Fitzpatrick, so he changed the subject. "So what's Mr. McLaughlin up to?"

"After you delivered him the truth about his wife, he went to the high school to talk to Principal Garcia. He also made a new friend named Rebecca Ryan. Quite a cutie, I must say. They left the school and came here."

"Here?"

"Yeah, he and his new friend broke in. May I suggest a better security system with that crazy Zubov on the loose?"

"What did McLaughlin do here?"

"Broke into Brett's computer. Saw some racy photos of his wife partying like a rock star at the prom."

"Then what?"

"He actually passed out. Once he was revived, he and Rebecca went out for a burger. He did prove himself to be a gentleman, returning the girl to school so she could pick up her vehicle."

"So what's your take on McLaughlin?"

"I agree with your initial analysis. He had no clue about his wife's extracurricular activities. And as far as I know, he hasn't made contact with the Mrs. since she left town."

"Speaking of the wife, Eicher thinks she might be working with Sarvydas."

"If she was, we'd be packing up our things and heading home. It would be over."

"Rumor has it that Nick left because he thinks there is a leak in the US Attorney's Office, but Eicher thinks it might be coming from the field," LaPoint stated firmly, his eyes fixed on the young marshal.

Fitzpatrick looked annoyed. "You think I'm the leak? Do you really believe I would've screwed up this much if I was on the take? It would be too obvious."

He couldn't argue with that one. A double-agent would at least offer an attempt at deception.

Despite this debacle, Fitzpatrick was a talented young marshal who had a bright future. But all young law enforcement officials—no matter if they're in the FBI, USFM, CIA, or a local agency—learn lessons the hard way. And when you mess up in this job, people usually die. The good ones come back from that, but some don't.

"Congratulations, you've almost made it through an entire afternoon without effing anything else up."

"I think I'm in line for a promotion," Fitzpatrick replied with the breezy smile that always worried LaPoint. "Any word on Nick?"

"He called Eicher."

"Called? Is he okay?"

"Doing better than Dantelli."

Fitzpatrick looked baffled. "What happened to Dantelli?"

Now it was LaPoint's turn to look surprised. "Eicher said you emailed the video to them. Had a run-in with Zubov that turned out like most run-ins with Zubov."

"This is the first I've heard of it—can I see the video?"

"I thought he said it was you, but maybe I misunderstood. I have bigger things to think about than who sent who what." He took out a hand-held device and showed Fitzpatrick the video of Zubov entering Dantelli's home. The results of his visit were documented in the gory crime scene photos that followed.

LaPoint backed off, knowing Fitzpatrick's failure to protect Nick caused a chain reaction that ended with Dantelli floating dead in a pool.

He changed the subject, offering up the information about Audrey Mays' hands, which actually weren't her hands, and his scheduled trip to Oklahoma in the morning.

"I'm coming with you," Fitzpatrick stated, still showing an idealistic vigor. A good sign.

"I don't think so."

"C'mon, there's nothing left for me to do here."

He shook his head. "You're grounded, Fitzpatrick."

After the yelling stopped, Fitzpatrick marched into the bedroom where Brett Buckley once resided, and slammed the door in anger.

Chapter 39

Natalie Gold sprawled naked across the elegant bed, her gaze fixed on the prime minister as he finished dressing. The room was fit for royalty, filled with rose petals and expensive aromas. But despite what the cover of *Rolling Stone* said, Natalie knew she was nothing more than a well paid prostitute, and Viktor was her pimp. But it was a means to an end, or in this case, a surprise ending.

He met her look. His eyes then wandered down her body. “You were amazing, Natalie.”

To go through with Viktor’s requests, she had to transform into the ice princess called Natalie Gold. It was as if she was having an out-of-body experience. She smiled. “You weren’t so bad yourself.”

“I can only hope that Viktor and I do more business while he’s in Israel.”

“I’d like that,” she said, holding the smile.

He ran the tips of his fingers over her naked body from toes to nose, then softly rubbed her cheek with the back of his hand. It was like he wanted one last touch to store in his mind.

When Kessler departed, Natalie moved into a grand bathroom. She stared into the mirror, no longer recognizing herself. She still hadn’t got used to the look of the voluptuous pop star. After being murdered, she really had no other choice.

Natalie cupped her large breasts as if to make sure they were actually attached to her body. They acted like an elaborate costume she couldn’t remove. When she looked in the mirror she still saw her once lithe body. She pulled off her blonde wig, the tape scraping at her shaved scalp. She longed for her natural brown, straight hair that once hung below her shoulders. *Viktor probably had the same problem,* she thought with a laugh. She didn't know who he thought he was fooling with the wig he wore so proudly. And he caked-on more make-up than she ever did

The plastic surgery that changed her into Natalie Gold was all about making her dream come true. And Natalie would go to any lengths to make it happen. But her dream wasn't to be a pop star.

That didn't mean that her first great love wasn't singing. Her first public performance was in a small church in Oklahoma where her father was the minister. By the time she was ten, she was a showstopper, with people coming from hundreds of miles to see the neophyte with the angelic voice. No wedding or funeral in Cotton County was official until it was marked by her voice.

Her small town of Devol even raised money to send her to perform on *Star Search* when she was eleven. She lost out to a nine-year-old rapper who got three-and-a-half stars, while all she got was a goodbye wish from Ed McMahon. But it was on a church trip to New York to see *The Nutcracker*, when she knew where her destiny lay. Following graduation from high school, she was accepted to the Juilliard School, arguably the most prestigious performing arts school in the nation.

Once in New York, she took jobs singing in clubs to make rent on her closet-sized apartment in Brooklyn Heights. And then one day she found her second love. He was a tall and handsome law student who came up to her after a performance to compliment her. He did make an odd statement, telling her that she reminded him of his mother. She had met some weirdos during her time in New York, and initially shied away. But he explained that his mother also was a singer with a beautiful voice.

They became inseparable. And she discovered that while singing was her passion, it was not her dream. Her dream was to spend the rest of her life with him. But when Nick's world came crashing down, and she was "murdered," Audrey Mays realized that she'd have to become someone else to make her dream come true.

Her new dream was to kill Viktor Sarvydas.

Chapter 40

Natalie changed into a baggy T-shirt and shorts. More along the lines of something Audrey would wear to bed than how Viktor normally had her dress for him. She moved down the quiet hallway and slipped into the master bedroom.

Viktor was propped on top of the bed, wearing purple satin pajamas, and still had on his wig and make-up. The television was on, but Viktor was engrossed in his Russian crime novel. He took off his reading glasses and looked at her like the cat that ate the canary. "Did the prime minister enjoy his stay?"

Audrey found her brash Natalie Gold persona, and her veins filled with ice. "They are going to have to surgically remove the smile from his face."

He looked pleased. "I aptly named you—you are worth your weight in gold."

She crawled up next to him and ran her hand over his satin-covered chest. "It's not the same as being with you, Viktor."

When he gently nudged her away, she disguised her relief. She curled up beside him as if she were disappointed.

"You should save your strength for tomorrow. You have a long flight and a full day of promotion. Then the premiere party for your video in the evening."

"I'm so excited, I've never been to New York," she exclaimed. Technically, Natalie Gold never had, even if the late Audrey Mays once lived there.

"It's the greatest city in the world," Viktor gushed. "Far greater than any so-called city you'll find in Israel. One day when this mess with Alexei is cleared up, I will show you around the city as a princess should see it."

She rubbed her hand over his chest once more, this time more comforting than seductive. "It's terrible how they are treating him like some animal. Your family has done so much for that country."

He patted her hand and held it close to where his heart would be if he had one. "Speaking of Alexei, I have a favor to ask of you when you arrive in the States."

"Let me guess, you want me to work my charm on the prison guards and break him out," she chortled coyly.

Viktor remained serious. This trial was no joke to him. "Alexei will need no help getting out of prison, but he will need a ride when he is released tomorrow. I want you to pick him up. Buy him a decent outfit and bring him as your date to the party. After his ordeal, he deserves a good night out on the town."

"They are releasing him?" she asked, caught unaware.

"By tomorrow they will be left with no other choice."

She didn't doubt him. What Viktor wanted, he got. He didn't clarify why his son would be released in the face of the overwhelming evidence against him. Viktor bookmarked his page in the novel and turned his focus to the television. Their nightly ritual was to watch the news and then fall asleep. But in actuality, Viktor slept, while Natalie lay awake and cursed each breath he took.

He always watched GNZ cable news, refusing to acknowledge the local Tel Aviv networks that he thought portrayed him as a Russian criminal who'd bought off the prime minister. He didn't dispute it—he just didn't like it.

The first story was about political primaries set for the following day in the States, where it was still Monday afternoon. The second was about the aftermath of an earthquake in India that had killed over a hundred. The controversy they created at the Wailing Wall—timed perfectly to coincide with her much anticipated US arrival—was the third.

Three stories later came a detailed report about Alexei's upcoming trial. One of the key witnesses, a retired NYPD detective named Dantelli, had been murdered in his suburban Las Vegas home. Viktor avoided any eye contact with her as the story unfolded, but she now had a better idea of why he was so confident of Alexei's release.

The news reports started to run together, until one stood out to her about a high school teacher who ran away with her underage student. A photo of the teacher was displayed on the screen, along with the student, named Brett Buckley. Audrey froze.

It was Nick!

She gathered herself. When she got her bearings, she sneaked a peek at Viktor to see if he recognized him, but thankfully he had slipped off to sleep. This allowed Audrey to safely view the report. She hadn't seen Nick in a year, and felt a pang of relief that he was healthy and alive. But filled with jealousy when the reporter called Nick and his teacher "lovers." She could only hope it was the same means-to-an-end strategy she was using.

Things fell apart so fast in New York that Audrey never had time to really review the demise. It started when Nick's mother was killed, followed shortly thereafter by his father, a murder that Nick witnessed. What Audrey didn't know was the next person to be killed was her.

Nick came to her with the news that he was going to testify against Alexei Sarvydas and had to go into the Witness Protection Program. It was staggering news that tossed their lives upside down, but Nick seemed more concerned with her safety than his own. He implored her to get out of New York immediately and to change her identity. He warned her not to even contact her parents in Oklahoma. His trembling words still rang in her ears: *"These people will do anything to keep me from testifying. And they will come after you to get to me."*

She was a strong independent woman from Oklahoma. Nobody told her what to do, not even the man she loved. But when she returned to her

Brooklyn Heights apartment, she found it draped in yellow police tape. It was like a scene from a movie as they carried a body out.

Her body!

Audrey Mays, twenty-three years old of Brooklyn, was murdered by an intruder in her apartment. It also crassly mentioned that her body was mutilated beyond recognition. At least according to the newspaper articles she read online at the Montreal train station, where she fled.

It was so hard not to contact her parents. She thought about how devastating it must have been for them to bury their daughter. She visualized her father being strong and philosophical, comforting her mother, who surely was an emotional wreck. She read about her own funeral in an Oklahoma paper online. The townsfolk seemed to blame the big bad, morally bankrupt city of New York, but Audrey knew who was behind her murder.

Viktor Sarvydas

And it was at that train station in Montreal where her new dream materialized. She knew that only then could they be together again.

In their last meeting, Nick had provided her with money to run—actually, it was enough money to live comfortably in her old life back in Oklahoma—she used it on a flight to Paris and a plastic surgeon who completely altered her look, turning the fresh-faced All-American girl into a sultry bombshell. She started singing for her supper in seedy bars, where she met the type of people who could provide her with a new identity.

She became an Israeli named Daria Scheffer, and while the surgeon's knife had changed her look, she still had the same voice that brought the house down back in Devol. She made her way to Tel Aviv, where she purposely began singing outside the bookstore that Viktor frequented. She knew he had a great eye for talent.

She took another look at the television and stared at the photo labeled Brett Buckley.

"What are you up to, Nick?" she mumbled to herself.

Chapter 41

Rob Bachynsky eyed the woman across the bar. She was just his type. Actually most women were his type, which had always been his downfall.

He pulled his stare away and scolded himself for succumbing to his vice. It's what got him in this mess, and made him drive the two hours from his mountain hideaway in Vail to the Denver suburb of Aurora. Dantelli was dead and Zubov was the lead suspect! It didn't make sense—Rob had thought they were all on the same side.

He sipped his drink and thought of the marriages, the alimony, the daughters in private school. It all stretched his police check very thin. As his beloved mother had told him, "Robby, you live a champagne lifestyle on a beer paycheck." As usual, Mom was right, which was why he was open to the offer from his partner, Tony Dantelli, to do some side jobs.

He was promoted to the organized crime unit in his Brooklyn precinct a few years back. His bosses sold him on the fact that his Eastern European heritage would be an advantage in dealing with the rising threat of the Russian Mafiya, and it was also a great opportunity to move quickly up the ranks. Rob was a self-proclaimed dumb Pollack, but was smart enough to know that the real reason for his "promotion" was because the Russians were a bunch of lunatics who would shoot you in the middle of Times Square because they didn't like the way you looked at them. In other words, nobody else volunteered. Rob Bachynsky was expendable and he knew it.

At first, the side jobs consisted of him roughing up some guys—bad guys, drug runners—for Dantelli's contact. But then it changed from rough-up to rub-out. When Rob drew the line, Dantelli revealed that his source was Viktor Sarvydas, and that his leaving would become an issue, as in a dead issue. He had no choice but to continue.

The Karl Zellen job itself was quite simple. Their instructions were to set up a meeting with Zellen under the pretext that they had found new information on his wife's murder. Once inside, Rob tied Zellen to a chair in the kitchen, while Dantelli dismantled the alarm, did a sweep of the mansion, and made sure there was easy entrance for Zellen's executioner, probably Zubov. Ten minutes in and out, and since Zellen greeted them as friends, there was no forced entry. Basically their job was to use their badges to clear a neat path. They would later return as the first officers on the scene and make the arrest for the murder of Karl Zellen. It wouldn't be a difficult case to crack, since prints would be left of the man Sarvydas wanted arrested.

But when they returned, they found that Zellen's son, Nick, had somehow witnessed his father's murder, and claimed the killer was none other than Alexei Sarvydas. Worse yet, the prints matched Alexei's, leaving them no choice but to arrest him.

When Viktor Sarvydas arranged a secret meeting with him and Dantelli, Rob thought they were dead men walking. They must have missed Nick when they did the sweep of the house, and someone must have screwed up on the prints, how else would they be plastered all over the crime scene? But surprisingly, Viktor praised their work. He instructed them, as the lead investigators, to work with the prosecution in its case against Alexei, until further notice. He said he would take care of everything else.

Dantelli advised Rob not to go into any federal protection programs, probably afraid that the feds could trick him into spilling the truth. So he took early retirement and moved to Vail, where Pavel Kovalenko would protect him. So when he received the news about Dantelli, he hightailed it to the Red Menace, a club owned by Kovalenko.

A large hand gripped Rob's shoulder. He practically jumped out of his skin. He had been like a cat on a hot tin roof since that phone call.

"I know how you love those dark skinned beauties, Rob," Kovalenko said in his thick Russian accent, noticing his stare at the woman.

It wasn't too hard to figure out who he was looking at—the place was practically deserted, which was not unusual. Kovalenko owned two Red Menaces, one located in downtown Denver on Blake Street, which was usually jammed wall-to-wall, often with fans from Rockies or Colorado Avalanche games, many wearing the jersey of their hero, Pavel Kovalenko. But this one in suburban Aurora usually just had a few "regulars" on a typical night. The feds were always interested how a seventeen-thousand-square-foot club could stay in business with the only customers being a couple of mobbed-up Russians drinking for free every night. They knew it was a money laundromat for Sarvydas, but could never prove it.

"She is beautiful," Rob conceded, avoiding eye contact with Kovalenko. Just the sight of his scar-lined face usually filled him with fear.

Pavel Kovalenko was a physical defenseman, nicknamed The Red Menace, who had a distinguished career in professional hockey. But in Russian Mafiya circles, he was known as an important Sarvydas lieutenant.

As legend had it, Kovalenko came to the US from Russia at the age of seventeen, signing a contract with the New York Islanders. His interests expanded beyond hockey, which led him to the Russian World Art Gallery on Fifth Street in Manhattan. It was there that he met a fellow Russian art buff named Karl Zellen. At the time, like many Russian hockey players in the States, Kovalenko was being extorted by Moscow thugs, who were demanding a piece of his salary in exchange for his family's safety back in Russia. They even kidnapped his mother one time to prove they were serious about a late payment. But Zellen and his business partner, Viktor Sarvydas, cleared up that problem. It was the first step in what would be a bond of vors.

After retiring from hockey, he took over the western wing of the Russian Mafiya, headquartered in Denver. With over eighty thousand Russian immigrants residing in the area, it was the perfect place to blend into. And the affluent suburbs of Glendale, Englewood, and Aurora allowed them to open legitimate businesses as a cover. Unlike the flashy styles of Brighton Beach and Miami, Kovalenko conditioned his men to not draw attention to themselves, most living in modest homes and driving Hondas.

Rob looked up at Kovalenko. He had diagonal scars on his furrowed brow, perhaps from hockey, but more likely from other activities. Rob had heard many stories about him that he hoped were just urban myths, but he wasn't taking any chances.

"No worries, Rob. Mr. Sarvydas left me in charge of your safety, so you have nothing to fear."

"Maybe I panicked—I shouldn't have come and bothered you like this. I know you're a busy man."

The grip on his shoulder tightened. "You made the right decision. If it's true that Zubov killed your partner, then you also could be in danger."

"I don't understand, I thought Zubov was Mr. Sarvydas' most loyal soldier," Rob began, then stopped abruptly. The less he knew the better.

Kovalenko chuckled. "Zubov is as loyal as an alley cat. And I can assure you he didn't get his orders from Mr. Sarvydas to harm your partner. You are safe here."

Rob wasn't sure what to believe. His glance again wandered to the woman.

Kovalenko followed his eyes to the sparkling creature. "Let me talk to her and see if I can arrange a meeting with you. She seems alone, and I think you could use a friend tonight."

Women were always his downfall.

Chapter 42

Lilly kissed him deeply on the lips. She then clasped his hand and led him to the dark room. The second they moved past the curtain, out of sight, she released his hand.

On cue, the lights came on and the clenched fist headed for Rob Bachynsky's nose. Before he could figure out what was happening to him, Nick hit him with another punch. And then another.

Lilly had no remorse for luring the dirty cop into the backroom. A broken nose was the least this Bachynsky character deserved for being involved in the killing of Nick's father.

After leaving Dantelli's home in the late morning, they first headed to McCarran Airport, before stopping by to see an old friend. He provided Lilly with a Thunderbird convertible, along with a pair of "scrambled" cell phones.

Lilly did most of the driving, averaging over eighty on the desolate highways I-15 North and I-70 East. They filled up the tank in St George, Utah, where Nick walked off, saying he needed to make a call to soothe his sister's fears, after she likely saw their faces splashed all over the television.

While Nick was on the phone, Lilly purchased a bottled water and a couple of magazines, including the latest *Rolling Stone* with Natalie Gold on the cover. Just another in a line of young girls she had become jealous of since her first kiss with Nick.

They rolled into the Denver area around ten, Colorado time. By 10:30, they had slipped into the Red Menace.

"You killed him, you son of a bitch," Nick continued to pound away.

Bachynsky was now huddled on the floor in a pool of blood, unsuccessfully trying to stop the attack.

"I don't understand, Nick. I thought we were on the same side."

"Same side? That's a good one. I guess we are until you get into court and start playing dumb on the stand. Although, I don't know how much acting you have to do to appear dumb."

"I didn't kill him," Bachynsky pleaded.

"Don't bullshit me—Dantelli already sold you out. Just because you didn't pull the trigger doesn't mean you didn't kill him. That's even worse...and gutless!"

Lilly felt like she was watching a replay from earlier. "I was just following orders," Bachynsky said between blows.

"Viktor Sarvydas' orders?"

He said nothing, which served as an admission. His eyes began shifting around the room like he was looking for help that wasn't coming.

Lilly stood by the door, keeping a watch on the scary-looking guy named Kovalenko. Just her brief conversation with him at the bar had sent chills down her spine. For the moment, he appeared too busy running his restaurant to be concerned about the action in the backroom.

As Nick's punches intensified, Lilly was sure that he was going to kill him, sensing he was having second thoughts about letting Dantelli off the hook. She vacated her post by the door and tried to intervene. "C'mon, Nick—you promised that you just wanted to scare him. Now you're scaring me."

"Sometimes plans get changed," he replied coldly.

A voice abruptly stopped the onslaught. "That is so very true. Sometimes plans do get changed. And you can think of me as a plan-changer."

Lilly looked at the man in a suit with a neatly groomed mustache. He looked calm and composed.

Nick whispered into Lilly's ear, "Zubov."

Just the name made Lilly shudder.

Chapter 43

"I figured you'd be here, Rob. But Nick … what a surprise. It'll save me a trip. And with the price of gas these days, that's quite a blessing."

Nick said nothing, as they watched Zubov take out a gun and twist on a silencer. Zubov's calm, almost ho-hum demeanor scared Lilly.

Bachynsky struggled to his feet, but still looked wobbly. "We just followed Mr. Sarvydas' orders. I don't understand why you killed Dantelli."

Lilly traded glances with Nick, who looked just as floored as she was. *Dantelli was dead?*

Zubov chuckled. "People always want to know why, why, why. Why are we here? Why me? Things happen or they don't—it don't matter why."

Nobody said anything, so Zubov continued, "Getting back to the change of plans, there was once going to be a trial and now there won't be one. Rob, Nick, and our late friend, Detective Dantelli, all have decided not to testify against Alexei."

"I don't understand—we followed orders," Bachynsky blubbered.

"Let me put it so even you can understand, Rob. I used to take orders directly from the don, Viktor Sarvydas—that was good for you. But with him out of the country, I now take my orders from the don's son. Not so good for you."

He smiled again, and it was scary.

Another Russian accent filled the room, this one a deep baritone, "The only thing that will be good for you, Zubov, is to put down that gun and move away from Mr. Bachynsky. I still take my orders from the don."

Pavel Kovalenko held a gun at them.

Lilly wasn't sure who to root for. The killer taking orders from Viktor Sarvydas, or the killer taking orders from his son. Bachynsky appeared to be off the hook, but she and Nick were in trouble either way. Pick your poison.

Zubov surprisingly dropped his gun without a fight.

Kovalenko backed Zubov toward a pool table with a wave of his gun. He then indicated for Nick and Lilly to join him. Standing beside Zubov was as comfortable as laying on a bed of nails.

Still holding his gun on them, Kovalenko walked to Bachynsky and checked on his physical well-being. He was a sniveling mess. Kovalenko showed little sympathy, ordering him to stop or he would shoot him just like "the rest of them," as if they were already past tense. He complied.

Kovalenko turned to Zubov. "Nobody crosses Viktor Sarvydas and lives to tell about it. Not even the great Zubov."

Zubov laughed. "You are an excellent actor. You don't work for Viktor Sarvydas any more than I do, so let's stop the charade."

"Charade?"

"Let me spell it out for you, Pavel. You are now working for Parmalov, as part of a coalition to take power from the Sarvydas family. I understand how system works. And with Viktor exiled, and Alexei in jail, you are making the prudent move. I have no hard feelings toward you, but that don't mean I'm not going to kill you."

"Do the math, Zubov. I have the gun."

"You no deny my accusation. Viktor was teaching Alexei a lesson, and now that he has, he sees no need for trial. But he left it up to his son to make final decision, and I'm here to enforce those wishes. My condolences to you and Parmalov, maybe next time your wishes come true." Zubov laughed again. "Oops, I forgot, there will be no next time." The more dire his situation, the more confidence he seemed to gain.

Lilly gauged Nick, who looked unsure. But nothing compared to Bachynsky, whose darting eyes said he didn't know who to trust. Kovalenko was his best shot to get out of here alive, but he seemed to be questioning the trust-level of that relationship.

"Don't worry, Rob, you did everything asked of you," Zubov read his confusion. "But I'm still going to kill you."

Then with lightning precision, Zubov grabbed a pool cue and ripped it across Kovalenko's face. He followed up the slash with a poke to the eyes, temporarily blinding his adversary. He crashed to the ground and Zubov pounced. He used the stick to keep Kovalenko on the defensive. Zubov then broke the stick on the floor creating a jagged edge.

Lilly knew she had to do something. "Freeze, or I'll shoot," she yelled out, but wasn't sure who to shoot or who to save.

Zubov turned and looked at Lilly, who was holding the gun that Kovalenko had dropped to the floor. He exploded into laughter. "Can you imagine after all my battles, if I would die at the hands of a *woman?*"

Even Kovalenko found that one a little funny. The Russians didn't lack for chauvinism. Lilly hated guns, a reaction to growing up around violence. But her father had taught her how to use one, and it felt comfortable in her hands.

Zubov's smirk never left his face as he lunged at her with the jagged pool cue. He missed and she fired. It hit him in the shoulder and blood began to spill through his suit.

He lunged at her again. She was momentarily paralyzed, before remembering something that Nick told her about Zubov back when he was just an imaginary figure of horror. He had both his knees tattooed to tell the world that he wouldn't kneel to anyone. It triggered her to action. Lilly fired at his knees.

He fell in a heap on the floor, writhing in pain.

There was no time to dwell on what she had just done. *They had to get out of here!* But there was a big problem—Bachynsky had picked up Zubov's gun and was holding Nick hostage.

"I don't know what's going on here, but I'm leaving this place alive," he yelled out.

"Let him go," Lilly sternly warned, riding the wave of confidence from her stunning take-down of Zubov.

"Drop the gun!" Bachynsky yelled back at her. "Drop the gun or Nick dies!"

Lilly began to lower her gun.

Nick shouted, "Don't do it, Lilly! You drop that gun and he kills me."

Lilly overloaded with doubts. Bachynsky raised his gun to Nick's temple and repeated, "Put the gun down or he dies."

"Shoot him, Lilly," Nick countered.

Lilly couldn't lose Nick—not now. She showed her gun to indicate that she was going to slowly lower it to the ground.

As she lowered the gun, she made eye contact with Nick. "I trust you, Lilly," he said.

"I told you never to do that," she replied back.

Bachynsky should have taken the same advice. He momentarily let down his guard.

Just before laying the gun on the cold linoleum, Lilly quickly raised it and fired. Now she was the plan changer.

Chapter 44

After ridding himself of Becks—dropping the teenager from hell back at her school—Darren returned home. He planned on a quiet evening of wallowing in self-pity, hoping to wake tomorrow to find that this whole thing was just a cruel nightmare.

But like a masochist, he couldn't resist turning on the television. And as was true to his luck, he was just in time to hear Jessi Stafford reporting that Lilly and Brett Buckley had been spotted at a Las Vegas wedding chapel.

He angrily shut the TV off, and sat in silence. At just before nine, Treadwell dropped by. He came straight from the airport, returning on the route they were supposed to have piloted together.

He first complained that Darren's emergency exit had caused a chain reaction in the scheduling that resulted in him having to fly back to New York tomorrow, and throwing a wet blanket on a night of club-hopping he had planned.

Darren filled him in on the details as best he knew them. Starting with Lilly's abduction and taking him up to his trip to South Chandler High.

"Then what are you doing here?" Treadwell asked, sounding baffled.

"What am I supposed to do—drag her back here like I'm her dad, and send her to her room?"

"You need to track Lilly down so you can tell her that you're sorry."

"I should apologize to *her?*"

"It's your fault. She gave you like five years to grow a pair, how long did you expect her to wait?"

"What are you talking about?"

"Come to think of it, you also owe me one."

"You?"

"I could have taken Lilly home that night, but I sacrificed my own pleasure for my friend. And how do you repay me—by screwing the whole thing up."

"You must be kidding me. You and Lilly?"

"I don't have looks, wealth, or even one of those senses of humor that women are always claiming they want. Yet I'm always flying first class with the ladies. You wanna know why?"

"We're talking about marriage, not picking up some girl in a bar."

"It all comes down to the same thing—what women really want is a man. And not the modern day sissified types like yourself, who are masquerading as men. They want a cave man. So if I were you, I'd be on the next flight to Vegas. I'd track her down, club her over the head and drag her back home. Show her who the man is. That punk high school boy wouldn't know what hit him!"

Treadwell made himself a sandwich like this was a normal night, and watched the Diamondbacks game to its conclusion. When he eventually left, the words began to soak in for Darren. While most of it was the typical over-the-top Treadwell, he did make one point that was indisputable—he had to get to Lilly as soon as possible.

Darren had his keys in his hand ready to head to the airport when a knock on the front door stopped him. He checked his watch—it was quarter to eleven. Who could be here at this hour.

Chapter 45

In stumbled Becks, carrying a twelve pack of Corona.

"What are you doing here?" Darren asked with chagrin.

"I hate drinking alone," she said, and plopped down at his kitchen table like it was a bar stool. She was wearing the same pair of shorts and flip-flops from earlier, but had on a different T-shirt, this one read: *I Caught Senioritis From Your Boyfriend.*

"How did you get beer, you're not twenty-one?"

Her words slurred, "When you think about it, it's kinda ironic that teenagers can't drink. We're the ones who need a drink the most … since we have to deal with you adults!"

"Do your parents know you're out drinking?"

She snorted a laugh. "My parents are so clueless they should be in the FBI. It takes more than a depressed and humiliated daughter to keep them from their important lives." She patted the seat beside her. "Now get over here and drink with me."

"You will not drink in my house—you're underage!"

She chugged the remainder of the bottle and tossed it toward an imaginary garbage can, shattering glass across the kitchen floor. "Maybe you should save that lecture for your wife."

"Did you drive here? I can't even begin to tell you how dangerous that is, or how a DUI could affect your admission to BC."

"What can I say, I'm just a crunk. No wonder my boyfriend ran off with his teacher. Can you blame him?"

"I don't have time for this—I gotta get to Lilly."

Becks hit her palm to her forehead. "You must be kidding! Are you planning on joining them on their honeymoon?"

She sat glued to the chair, sipping on another beer, and not giving any sign that she was going to be moving any time soon.

"So you haven't told me why you are really here," he said.

She stood and stumbled toward him. She wrapped her arms around his neck like they were slow dancing. "There is nothing better than revenge sex."

It took Darren a moment to figure out she was talking about him. "I'm married," he replied in an embarrassed high-pitch. He lightly pushed her away and she almost fell over.

Becks fumbled through her purse until she found her cell phone. She pretended to take a call. "The gander just called and said if it's good with the goose then she's cool with it."

She reached in her purse again and pulled out her wallet, removing her driver's license. "And for your information, I turned eighteen last month—so I'm no longer jailbait. So let's go hook your line, sailor!"

She tried to hand him the license, but he rebuffed her. "I'm calling your parents."

Becks shrugged. "Whatever floats your boat. Tell them I'm going to a party and if I had a curfew I'd be breaking it."

Darren took out the phone directory, but found twenty-four Ryans listed in Chandler alone. Becks wasn't about to offer a hint. He grew frustrated and snapped, "How can you go to a party on a school night?"

She laughed like he just told the funniest joke ever. "Were you born this boring, or is there something in the water out here in Suburbia? Now please point me in the direction of the changing room so I can get ready for the party."

"The only place you're going is home, and I'm driving you."

"Ooh, I'm scared—please have mercy on me, Mr. Truant Officer."

"Let's go."

"Fine, then I'll change right here," she announced. Before Darren could stop her, she had begun a striptease that included slurred singing and tipsy dancing. She lifted her shirt over her head, exposing a lacy bra and tight abs. Darren looked away.

He grabbed her by the arm, still looking away, and directed her into the master bedroom. "You can change in here," he stated tersely.

"I thought you'd see it my way," she replied with a beer-buzzed grin and hopped on his bed.

Darren shut the door. "Just hurry it up, I don't have all night."

"You're missing out," she shouted.

Darren had no intention of letting her go to any party. He grabbed her keys off the table. He would drive her home and explain to her parents why their teenage daughter was drinking at his house while his wife was away. On second thought, he would just drop her at the door and drive off. He would then head to Sky Harbor and catch the next flight to Las Vegas to deal with the nuclear fallout of his marriage.

A minute turned into ten. He was just about to check on her—fearing she might have passed out from the alcohol—when a loud crash sent him into action. Darren dashed into the room to find Becks sitting in the walk-in closet, surrounded by fallen boxes.

"What are you doing?" he asked angrily, viewing the items the nosy teenager had taken down from their perch on the shelf.

Sporting a wide grin, she held up his dust-covered high school yearbook. "You weren't born boring—I knew it!"

The picture she held up was of Darren McLaughlin the all-state wide receiver they nicknamed Run DMC after the popular rap group, which coincided with the initials of his name. And run is what he did really well on the field. But he no longer recognized that person.

"And how rock star were you? Look at your long hair!" Becks gushed, turning to a picture of Darren's band, The Flying Aces, performing at the homecoming dance. He and a couple of friends started the band in his garage, hoping to be the next Aerosmith to come out of Boston.

Becks began sifting through a box of ancient pictures. She held up a photo of Lilly and Darren kissing at a sidewalk café.

Looking at the picture seemed to slightly sober her. "It's your honeymoon, isn't it?"

He nodded, his heart bouncing in his throat.

"I know honeymoons aren't the best subject right now, but where is this? It's beautiful."

"The French Riviera."

"Impressive—not a bad deal for a poor girl from a Mexican ghetto."

Darren was offended by the insinuation. "What's that supposed to mean?"

"All I'm saying is that your wife seems to have a trend of trading up. From daughter of illegal-alien drug-dealer to marrying a pilot and having her first honeymoon on the French Riviera, and now upgrading to the heir to the Buckley software company? What's next, Lilly Rockefeller-Gates?"

Darren angrily pulled her to her feet, refusing to dignify that with an answer. "Let's go," he commanded.

"But I haven't even changed yet."

"You had your chance."

She smiled at him. "Cheer up, Run DMC. We're going to a party."

Chapter 46

The party was at the Questa Vida Golf Course. Darren had played there a couple of times with Treadwell, or as Mark Twain noted, spoiled a few good walks. When he asked Becks what kind of party it was, she shrugged and replied, "Typical high school."

If there was any lesson learned today, it was that adults and high school parties don't mix. But on the ride over, Darren saw it as a chance to put together the puzzle of what happened. People like LaPoint and Mara Garcia thought they knew what went down, but these kids had firsthand knowledge. Going to this party was like infiltrating the enemy on an intelligence-gathering mission.

The party centered around a beer keg that was planted in a sandy bunker on the eighteenth hole. The night was lit by a full moon that reflected off the dewy emerald lawns. Teenagers huddled in circular groups, sucking beer from plastic cups, their voices bouncing off the desert night.

Becks explained that a classmate of hers, Kevin Chambers, was the son of the club pro, which unofficially allowed them after-hours access. Darren studied the attendees and recognized a few of them from Lilly's tutoring sessions. He got stares, but was convinced they were related to his age. He had changed into an Air Force Academy sweatshirt and jeans. He also wore a faded Red Sox cap that he pulled down as far as possible.

"They think you're the bacon," Becks informed him, noticing the stares. Because he didn't speak teenager, she translated—'bacon' meant police.

Their attention was diverted by a screech. All heads turned to witness two speeding golf carts crash into the bunker and roll over, just missing the precious keg.

"Total morons," Becks said with a sad shake of her head. She explained that it was the Meyer brothers, who would always play "drunken crash up derby" with the golf carts, despite having ended up in the emergency room on several occasions.

"What kind of parents let their kids go to a beer bash on a school night? Darren asked. He couldn't get past it.

"Pretty much everyone here has been accepted to college. That's all parents around here care about, so they can brag to the neighbors and return to their Oxycontin. Any excuse to get rid of the kids is a good excuse."

Becks led him into the bunker. Darren didn't think drinking alcohol with minors seemed like a good idea, but wanted to make it look good to help him fit in, or at least not be seen as the bacon.

A surfer-looking kid wearing a Steve Nash basketball jersey was manning the keg like a bartender. Becks gave Darren the impression of being the high school outcast, but she seemed to have a bond with the surfer guy, whom she greeted with a complicated handshake. "Good seein' ya here, Becks. Totally whack what Brett did to you. You're way better than that beggar."

"Thanks, dude," Becks replied, as he filled her cup with beer, expertly removing all foam.

"You're looking butter tonight. If you're looking to rebound like Rodman, I'm your man."

"You know I'm always a sucker for an old-school NBA reference, but I already got me a new guy," she said and introduced Darren as Run DMC.

The surfer looked at him with a spacey grin, "I like your look, dude—you got that creepy molester thing going on." Darren didn't know how to take that, but the tone was complimentary, so he just nodded his head and accepted his cup of beer.

As they ventured into the fairway, their path was cut off by a pack of scowling teenage girls wearing revealing outfits. Becks didn't look particularly happy to see them, referring to them as her frenemies.

"Where's Brett?" the first girl asked. Her friend than added, "Oh yeah, he married Mrs. McLaughlin." The first girl laughed and followed up with, "An F in the bedroom equals an A in the classroom."

Becks faked a laugh back in their direction. "You look great, Kristi—glad to see the bulimia is really working out for ya."

Without warning, one girl began sizing-up Darren. An uncomfortable feeling came over him and he inched backward. He recognized her. She was the cheerleader-type that Becks got into the shouting match with at her locker earlier in the day. Her gawk continued to bore a hole in him, but it wasn't because she recognized him as the husband of the aforementioned Mrs. McLaughlin.

Cheerleader turned to her friend and said, "Looks like Becks found a daddy of her own for a little payback."

"Maybe she like joined the Cougar Hunt," the other girl added. "Only in reverse."

"She has a long way to go to catch Brett. I hear Mrs. McLaughlin was a ten pointer."

They both looked at Darren. "What do you think this one's worth?"

Cheerleader snickered. "Maybe like negative-two points."

The girls mocked him with another laugh. Then after volleying a few more insults back-and-forth with Becks, they headed off to join the rest of the pack.

When the coast was clear, Darren asked Becks, "Cougar Hunt?"

"Cougar is a term for attractive older women who seek younger men."

"I know that, what does it have to do with Lilly?"

"My bad—didn't think you were up on anything that occurred after 1988. Basically, the immature guys at school have bets going on who can hook up with the most cougars. And they use a point system based on hotness level, as determined by the village idiots themselves. You should be proud, your wife is a ten-pointer," Becks explained in her heaviest sarcasm. "And they get double points for a cougar cub."

"Cougar cub?"

"If they get her pregnant."

What was wrong with these kids? He thought of his wife being part of some sick game. The taste of vomit filled his mouth. "This stuff really goes on?"

"Welcome to sex-ed, Millennium Generation style," Becks said with a shrug.

It seemed that English wasn't the only class Lilly taught. And with that realization, Darren puked his guts out.

Chapter 47

With an assist from Becks, Darren steadied himself. The spinning slowed, and he regained his bearings.

The good news, according to Becks, was that many of the partygoers witnessed him unload his Cholla Burger onto the fairway, and they no longer believed he was the police. Sadly, it was the best news Darren had heard in the last twenty-four hours.

Becks moved toward a group of boys who were huddled on the green, and Darren followed.

She gave him the lowdown on the group as they approached. The Meyer brothers were there, still quarreling with each other over their crash. Kevin Chambers was the preppy leader with a sense of entitlement as big as the Grand Canyon. He was headed to Arizona State next year on a golf scholarship, hyped to be the next Mickelson.

Chris Westmoreland was the quarterback of the football team and was strangely proud that his mother had been the highest rated "prize" before Lilly joined the "hunt." He greeted Becks with, "Too bad Brett couldn't make it, I hear he's on a hunting trip in Vegas."

Inebriated laughs filled the air, and one of the Meyer brothers added, "Ten pointer, bro," and imitated shooting a basketball.

Becks was not one to back down. "If Meyer knocked-up your mother, what would you two be, like, jackasses once removed?"

"My mom is divorced, her business is her business," Westmoreland responded to the laughs.

Becks wouldn't let up, "So Westmoreland, how many points did you get for playing hide the jockstrap with Coach Jenks? He's quite a lollipop—I'm especially attracted to his stylish ear-hair."

"How do you think he got the starting position," Kevin Chambers chimed in with an arrogant laugh.

Westmoreland shrugged, "Hey, I'd be bitter too if my boyfriend climbed up Mount McLaughlin and planted his flag. I've got to give it up to Brett on that one."

Becks looked ready to fight him. "Spare me the details of your man-crush. How long was it going on?"

"You're just pissed that your teacher beat you out for prom queen."

"I'm serious."

"About a month ago I got a call from Chambers, informing me that Brett asked him to open up the course. He needed a place to do some hunting. So we met up here, and Brett was already waiting for us. We waited for like an hour until an SUV pulled into the parking lot. I didn't know what I was expecting, but it sure wasn't that hottie English teacher, dressed totally stripper. When I see her, it blows my mind."

"That's not hard to do," Becks sniped.

Westmoreland ignored her. "At first she's totally pissed that me and Kevin are there, especially since we have her for class. She started yelling at Brett—thought I could trust you and shit like that, said you wouldn't tell anyone. She stormed off. Brett followed and they got into this intense conversation for like fifteen minutes. But then they came back. We opened the equipment shed just off the sixteenth, and let nature take its course."

Chambers eagerly jumped into the conversation, "There's a window in the back where if you climb up on the garbage dumpster, you can see into shed." He smiled coyly. "And of course, we did this to make sure the points were gained within the rules of the game."

"Of course," Westmoreland seconded with a big grin.

Darren's anger intensified as he viewed this evil circle of laughter before him. He wondered how many points someone would get to mutilate these punks and use them to fertilize the golf course, but he felt Becks subtly hold him back. If Becks had become the voice of reason, then they might be in real trouble.

At the same time, Kevin Chambers began staring at Darren. Before that, it was like he wasn't even there. When Chambers whispered to the Meyer brothers and they exchanged knowing laughter, Darren knew he was busted.

Westmoreland was not in on their discovery, and continued. "Brett said they had been flirting for a while and that Mrs. McLaughlin's husband was a total tool who couldn't satisfy her." As the laughing intensified, Westmoreland flashed a stupefied look. "What?"

They looked at Darren and laughed.

"He's the husband, isn't he?"

Their laughter turned hysterical.

Darren was about to explode, but Becks stepped in. "You're an asshole, Westmoreland," she shouted as she dragged Darren from the group. She turned to Darren and said, "The problem with high school is that it's so high school."

If her aim was to comfort him, she failed. And strangely, Darren's resolve to get to Lilly grew even stronger after what he'd heard. The sordid tale actually alleviated his biggest fear—that his wife and Brett Buckley were in love—she was just a physical object to him. A ten-pointer. He needed to get to her and let her know that she was part of some twisted game and the rest he was willing to work through. He would believe even the lamest of excuses—that she was drugged, that the students threatened her if she didn't go through with it, or that she was depressed from their failure to conceive and sought the arms of another, with Darren gone all the time—he didn't care, as long as they could be together again.

"I'm going to drop you off, and then I need to get to Lilly," he said.

Becks said nothing this time, but instead put her hands on his chest like she was some sort of healer. She pulled them away and acted like they were covered with a sticky substance.

"What are you doing?" he asked.

"Seeing how much sap you actually have. Those guys might be embellishing, but they aren't smart enough to keep a story straight. They weren't making it up."

"Thanks for your backseat mothering," he turned it around on her, "but last I checked, marriage is for better or *worse*. When you become an adult, then maybe you'll understand that type of commitment."

She put her hands together and dramatically acted like she couldn't get them apart. "So much sap!"

He ignored her theatrics and walked briskly to the car. But like a flash of lightning, she snuck behind him and grabbed the keys away. "I might be a little buzzed, but you are legally insane, so I'm the lesser of the evils to drive."

Before he could even argue, she was behind the wheel and had started the car. He wasn't planning on being stranded at a high school beer-bash and hopped in the passenger side. As they moved down Riggs Road, Darren became overwhelmed by what he just witnessed. "I can't believe those kids are involved in something as sick as that."

"Teenagers are just as horny and mixed-up as they've always been. It's just that the parents suck a lot more than they used to, so they're allowed to act on it."

"God, when I was in school you just hoped to get to second base before you graduated. And I'm not *that* old."

"Well, these days second base is hooking up with your teacher and taking her on a road trip to Vegas. You should see what third base is."

"I'm not sure I want to know."

"Third base is when the jilted girlfriend takes the teacher's husband back to his place and gives him the best revenge he ever had."

She beamed an impish smile and hit the accelerator.

Chapter 48

Eicher was quickly running out of time and witnesses, so he decided to head directly to the source.

Alexei Sarvydas was housed in a collection of cinder blocks in Lower Manhattan called MCC. Even as a US Attorney, he had to maneuver through the heavy checkpoints of prison security. He was forced to leave all his belongings with a guard and had his hands coded with incandescent ink. But before he left his cell phone behind, he received a call from Dava.

In a rare moment of good fortune for them, Rachel Grant's mother had traveled to Manhattan in her quest to find her daughter. Dava was also able to determine that Alexei owned the strip club where Rachel had worked.

They needed to be working on two fronts to try to plug this dam. Eicher would conduct the questioning of Alexei, while Dava handled the situation with Mrs. Grant. He instructed Dava not to reveal the details of her daughter's death until she drained all the information she could out of her. It sounded callous, but Eicher thought she might shut down emotionally once she knew her daughter was gone. He'd seen it before. There was nothing they could do now to bring Rachel back, but it was possible that Mrs. Grant might unknowingly have useful information for their case.

Eicher was ushered into a tomb-like room. Moments later, Alexei was brought in, his hands and feet chained. He looked nothing like the man who entered MCC almost a year ago. His tanned face was now gaunt and pale. His flashy Versace clothing was replaced by a drab prison-issued jumpsuit. His once flowing rocker-hair was now shaved to the scalp.

Alexei was seated across from Eicher at a steel table. He showed that he still possessed one thing he entered MCC with—his cocky smile, which he displayed as he lit a cigarette with jittery fingers.

The book on Alexei had always been that he had the "Killer B's." Big mouthed, brash, and a set of big balls. His hobbies were extortion and abusing women, and like his father, he had a passion for music—his band Acid Bath was often a headliner at Sarvy's prior to his arrest. But Alexei lacked an important B—brains—and that's what got him locked up. And it's what Eicher hoped would lead him to the information he needed.

Alexei originally left New York to get away from his father's wide shadow. He made his mark in Miami—often referred to as the second city of Russian mob activity—starting up a line of high-end strip clubs, which served as a cover for a prostitution ring. He gained stature in his father's business by brokering deals with the Columbian drug cartels, but found his true niche in arms sales. He would secure automatic weapons from the Columbians, and sell them back in Russia, where such weapons were in high demand.

"I'm glad you're here, Eicher," Alexei began.

"And why is that?"

"I needed to get laid tonight. And I've already had every ass in this place, so I was looking for some fresh meat. Why don't you bend over so we can get this show on the road."

"You're not really my type. You remind me too much of my ex-wife."

"Why do you hurt me like that, Eicher? I was going to be gentle with you, but when you say things like that it makes me want to rip you apart."

Eicher didn't take the bait. "We've had some developments in your case."

Alexei faked a stunned look. "You don't say."

"The two lead investigators, Dantelli and Bachynsky, are dead, and Nick Zellen is missing."

"If you're looking for Nick, a little birdie told me he was getting married in Vegas."

"And by little birdie, are you referring to your father?"

"I was invited, but unable to attend. If you talk to Nick, please assure him that the next time I see him I will give him the most memorable wedding gift ever."

"Answer the question!" Eicher demanded.

Alexei shrugged. "Maybe you have a leak in your office."

He had heard that one before. "So you're telling me that you and your father had nothing to do with any of this … Dantelli? Nick? Leaks?"

"What could I do from in here? And my father and I aren't exactly on speaking terms since he let me rot in prison for a year on these trumped up charges."

"If you don't stop trying to play me, you'll be rotting in here for a lot longer."

The statement carried no weight. After today's events, Alexei and his father were way ahead on the scoreboard, and they both knew it.

Eicher was expecting smugness, but got anger. "People say I'm dumb, people say I'm a killer, people say I beat the shit out of women. I have no problem with that, but don't ever call me a liar!"

Eicher took a deep breath. He needed answers more than he needed a fight. "But you must admit that these events do benefit your case."

Sarcasm replaced his anger. "Now that you mention it, I recognize that they do benefit my case."

"You had nothing to do with this?" Eicher pushed.

"I told you since day one that I was set up."

It was true that he'd maintained that stance since his arrest, but for the first time Eicher was starting to wonder if there was some truth behind the bluster. So he took a chance. He laid out his theory about Alexei being set up to take the fall for Karl Zellen's murder, paving the way for Parmalov to gain control of the Russian Mafiya. He left out the part about how he still believed Alexei killed Karl.

"What's a Parmalov?" Alexei asked with a hearty chuckle. "I'll take a roast beef with Parmalov on rye."

"You don't know the man who is second in command at Sarvy Music?" Eicher asked with a raised eyebrow, holding up a photo of Parmalov and Alexei looking chummy during an all-night card game at a cabaret.

"Oh, that guy. I've been in here so long my memory is not so good."

"Then let me refresh it. Parmalov's closest confidantes are two killers named Oleg and Vana Moziaf. They own a butcher shop in Brighton Beach where we found the hands of a murdered stripper, who worked in a club you own. In fact, we have witnesses that say you and the girl had more than an employer/employee relationship," Eicher made up the next part on a hunch. "Parmalov wants me to think you killed her, making sure you grow old in here. That's why he planted the hands for us to find."

Eicher slid the "before" photos of the girl across the table. Followed by the photos of her mutilated body and hands. "Do you know her?"

Alexei studied them coldly, and answered, "I don't know. I screwed most of the whores there, but I never looked at their faces. And I was usually too messed up on coke to remember."

It wasn't George Washington chopping down the cherry tree, but it was likely a candid admission. Eicher didn't want to admit it, but there was a trend of truthfulness in Alexei's statements since the arrest.

"I'm on your side here, Alexei. But I need to know who set you up, so I can work to bring them to justice."

Alexei wasn't biting. He trusted no one, especially the government. He shook his head and confidently stated, "Don't worry your pretty little head, Eicher. I will take care of it myself."

"That might be a little hard to do from prison."

Alexei's laugh echoed throughout the chamber. "We both know I'm not going to be in prison much longer."

"No matter how many witnesses you knock off, you left your prints all over Zellen's house, and you still have a lot of motive, but no alibi. And Nick just called me—we're picking him up as we speak—so your ass is going to be sore for a long-long time."

"A little birdie told me that Zubov is on Nick's trail. That doesn't sound too promising for you. And even if he is safe, I hope you haven't hinged your whole case on the word of Nick Zellen. Your ass is going to be the one that's sore if you have."

"And why is that?"

He gleamed an evil grin. "Because then I'm guaranteed of getting out of this place. And when I do, I'm going to show you and that pretty assistant of yours some of the tricks I've learned in here."

Chapter 49

Dava watched the Rangers game at Nellie's sports bar on the Upper West Side, waiting to meet Wendy Grant. While the Rangers uninspired play was pinching at her nerves, she still couldn't help but to smile at her good fortune.

The first thing Dava did was pay a visit to the strip joint where Rachel had worked. The husky Russian manager didn't want to talk to her at first, but when she began to question the age of a couple of dancers he employed, Sergei suddenly turned chatty. But she learned nothing new—Rachel Grant was a wannabe actress who danced at a couple of clubs to make ends meet, rented a small apartment in Brooklyn, and was officially declared missing about a year ago.

Her father was a professor of political science at the University of Wyoming. When she put in a call to Dr. Grant, he informed her that his wife was currently in New York, following up a new tip on their daughter, and provided her cell phone number. From his tone, Dava could tell he was skeptical of a happy ending and sought to move on with their lives, while his wife needed some sense of closure. For better or worse, they would soon have it.

Upon contacting Wendy Grant, Dava took Eicher's advice and didn't mention anything about the grizzly discovery. Dava told her that Rachel's name had come up in a case the US Attorney's Office was investigating. Wendy said the name 'Sarvydas' meant nothing to her, but was still willing to meet. There was desperation in her voice that said she would grasp at any straw.

Wendy Grant was a thin, attractive woman in her late-forties. Her auburn hair was tied in a no-frills ponytail and she wore a pair of glasses. She appeared more sophisticated than Dava expected.

But what stood out was her worn, defeated look. Her head and eyes moved constantly, as if she was looking for Rachel with every twitch. Dava approached her and introduced herself. She reached out to shake Wendy's hand, even though a hug seemed more appropriate.

Wendy Grant had no time for small talk. It was as if any moment that wasn't spent searching for Rachel was wasted time. "You say that Rachel might have some information about a case you're working on?"

Dava nodded. "That's correct."

"What kind of case?"

Dava needed to do a little fishing to see what Mom knew about Rachel's work in New York. "It was connected to her job."

Wendy didn't flinch. "You mean the dancing?"

"I mean the activities that the dancing led to," Dava said as gently as possible.

"I know about the prostitution arrests, Ms. Lazinski."

Instead of adding anything, Dava used a technique that Eicher taught her. Just let the witness talk. And Wendy Grant did just that.

"Rachel was always a bit of a rebel. With Paul's job we moved around a lot from place to place. So I thought it was an army brat type situation. By the time she became a teenager, we had settled in Laramie. Raising a rebellious teenage daughter in a college-town wasn't always the easiest thing—there was a lot of drinking and parties that anyone with a decent fake ID could get into, and there were a couple of arrests. But at least in Laramie I felt like we could keep her in our sights and have some sense of control over her well-being. But things changed when she moved to New York."

"How so?"

"She turned distant, and rarely called. Paul thought it was because of the fights we had about her choosing not to go to college. But I knew there was something more to it—call it mother's intuition, but I could feel it. When she came home for Thanksgiving it was like she was a different person."

"Any idea what caused this change?"

"There was a boyfriend. She was so mysterious about him and she didn't even introduce us when we came to New York to visit her. The whole time we were here, it was like she was putting on a show for us and couldn't wait to get us out of town. I think this boyfriend was the reason for the change in her, but I have no proof."

"A mother's intuition is often correct. What was her boyfriend's name?"

"She called him Alex, but never provided a last name. And for all I know, it could have been a made up name. I have tried to locate him, but I've come up empty. He's what this case of yours is about, isn't it?"

"What do you mean?"

"Please don't treat me like a fragile flower, Ms. Lazinski. When your daughter goes missing you find strength you never thought you had. This Alex was her pimp, wasn't he? And you think it's possible that he ran off with Rachel, or that," she gulped her tears back, before finding resolve. "Or that he killed her."

Wendy had given her an opening, and Dava took it. "We are investigating a prostitution ring run by an Alexei Sarvydas. He is currently in prison and awaiting trial. I am just trying to interview all the girls who might have worked for him to help build our case. I think he might be the Alex that Rachel referred to."

Wendy Grant's face said she had no sympathy for the man she felt led her daughter down a dark path. She would likely have even less when she found out where that path led.

Chapter 50

"When I spoke to your husband, he mentioned something about following up a new lead," Dava said.

"I had vowed to move on. Logic says that Rachel is either dead or wants us to think she is. But last week I received a call from a woman named Justina, who shared an apartment in Brooklyn with Rachel."

This perked Dava's interest. "Was she a…"

"Another working girl that you might want to talk to…yes," Wendy said, tears trickling down her face. "She might have been the last person to have seen my daughter. She told me that Rachel had left to go on a date, and she never returned."

"And by date, you don't mean with her boyfriend, this Alex?"

Wendy shook her head. "It was for her job."

"So this roommate just got in touch with you out of the blue?"

"According to Justina, when Rachel went missing she hightailed it out of New York. She had assumed that Rachel had been busted, and feared that she might give up the other girls. So she grabbed everything she could and was on the next bus to Reno."

"And you met with this Justina?"

"Yes—she came to meet with us in Laramie. She was going through the things she took from the apartment, which she'd stashed away in storage. She found unsent letters from Rachel that she must have accidentally grabbed in her haste to leave. They were very personal in nature and Justina thought we would want them. She was as surprised as anyone that we hadn't heard from Rachel."

"These letters are why you returned to New York?"

"No, the reason I came back to New York was that Justina also found a key to a self-storage space that Rachel had rented. I think I might be able to find some clues there, and I know that Rachel had kept a journal her whole life, which was nowhere to be found when we cleaned out her apartment. That is where I was headed when you called."

Dava felt an excitement shoot through her. Although it was tempered every time she looked at Wendy Grant, the image of her daughter's severed hands etched in her mind. Rachel Grant was caught up in something dangerous and now her mother was going to have to bear the brunt of the pain from that perilous liaison. But there was no time for sentiment. Dava had a job to do—she needed to get that journal.

They took the subway. Rachel did not rent the storage near her apartment or place of work, both in Brooklyn, giving Dava the impression she might be using it to hide something. It was located on the southern tip of Manhattan on South Street at Catherine Slip.

With midnight approaching, the place was practically deserted. They were met by the night manager. When he located Rachel Grant's storage area on a computer, he mentioned that she hadn't paid her bill in about a year, which meant her stuff had been put up for blind auction. He explained that this was company policy, as stated in Rachel's rental agreement.

Dava felt like a deflated balloon, and Wendy's shoulders sagged. But after further research, he informed them that nobody had bid on Rachel's stuff, so it would remain stored until it was thrown out, which it hadn't been yet.

The night manager led them to a storage area that he claimed could hold about fifteen to twenty boxes, along with a half closet of clothes. He then tried to sell them on an upgrade, forcing Dava to flash her badge. He got the hint and scurried away.

Rachel had gotten the most out of her space. It was filled with taped-up boxes. A bike hung on one wall. A rack of clothing was beside the other.

Wendy looked overwhelmed. She touched any object she could, and even smelled them as if she were checking for Rachel's scent. As Dava looked at the desperate mother, she pitied her, knowing this wasn't going to turn out well.

Wendy continued to search through the clutter, before suddenly breaking into tears. "She was always such a mess. I would tell her to clean her room and she would just make it messier to spite me. God, what I'd give to have another one of our fights."

It was another moment that called for a hug, but Dava decided against it. She needed to distance herself from Wendy Grant, cognizant of what she was going to have to reveal to her very soon.

Wendy continued to sift through the rubble until she found what she was looking for. It was a leather bound journal. She opened it, but it was like she didn't want to know about the life Rachel lived in New York. Not wanting to risk forever losing the image of that rebellious but innocent girl from Laramie. She shut the journal and handed it to Dava.

Dava knew the journal was the key. As she read Rachel's words, it contained all the elements she'd expected. Dangerous associations, fears of a scared girl who was in over her head, and it fingered the most likely suspect in her brutal murder. It had the potential to blow the whole case wide open.

"Why do you think she used the name Carrie Grant? Dava asked.

"I've thought about that," Wendy said. "Her father was a big fan of the actor. She was always a daddy's girl, and when Paul gave her a puppy when she was about six or seven she named it Carrie Grant to impress her father. It was an innocent time. Maybe this is just the naïve mother in me talking, but I think it was a way for her to keep some of her innocence when she was up on that stage."

Dava nodded. "I sometimes use a different name, but it has nothing to do with innocence."

Wendy looked at her from across the room with a mystified look. But then her mind retreated to her own world where she was still tracking her daughter.

"My name is Davnieska. At my summer job in college, I had a boss who would refer to me as 'that stupid communist girl'. I stood up to him—told him that my name was Davnieska and that is what he should call me. I lived for a time in Lithuania as a child, but I was born in New York, and was just as much an American citizen as he was. He told me that he wouldn't call me no 'commi name,' and from now on he'd refer to me as Kelli. With an 'i' on the end because he said it would always remind him that I was a 'commi'."

Wendy looked back at her, probably wondering if this had any connection to finding Rachel. Her daughter consumed her mind. So much so that she almost missed that the gun was already pointing at her, with silencer attached. Dava then continued to help Wendy Grant find her daughter. In fact, with three soft tugs on the trigger, she sent her to be with her.

Dava locked the dead woman in the storage area, and casually walked away, gripping the journal close to her. She crossed paths with the night manager on her way out. He asked if there was anything else he could do for her. She displayed her badge and ordered that he turn over the surveillance tapes to her for a highly sensitive case she was working on, including the ones that taped her entering the facility. The scared clerk obediently followed orders, and Dava rewarded him with a bullet to the head. She then took a few moments to make it look like a robbery.

When she got outside, she walked down to the pier and stared out at the lights of Brooklyn in the distance. She waited ten minutes and then called the don's son. "It's Kelli. Just wanted you to know that Rachel Grant kept a journal."

He said nothing, but there was awe in his silence.

"Don't worry. It's all taken care of. And tomorrow morning I'm being sent to Oklahoma to exhume Rachel's body. I'll take care of that too."

She could almost hear him smile through the phone.

"Sounds like there might be a leak in the US Attorney's Office," he replied.

Chapter 51

With morning rapidly marching toward them, Lilly still clutched the gun she had shot Rob Bachynsky with. She hadn't let it go since they departed Colorado.

They beat great odds in getting out of Red Menace alive, but were faced with the reality of trying to find refuge. Lilly wanted to jump in the Thunderbird and head as fast as they could to nowhere.

But Nick had a place in mind where they would be welcome to spend the night. Lilly knew it was the right decision, but that didn't mean that jealousy wasn't gnawing at her like termites.

As soon as the bullet whistled through Bachynsky's skull, the other men in the room treated Lilly with a different respect level. And she used it to her advantage. At gunpoint, she ordered Kovalenko to tie Zubov up. Even though Zubov didn't show any signs of being able to walk on his wounded knees, she still wasn't going near that venomous snake.

Nick had picked up Bachynsky's gun and used it to force Kovalenko to prepare his private jet for them. To be sure that there was no trickery, they brought him along as an insurance policy.

Following Nick's orders, they flew from Denver to Dallas. During the two-hour flight, Nick interrogated Kovalenko with the same rage as he did Dantelli and Bachynsky, but this time his questions centered on what he knew about any potential leak in the US Attorney's Office. Kovalenko didn't budge.

When they arrived in Dallas during the predawn hours, they left Kovalenko and his pilot securely fastened in the baggage area of the plane. By the time they were able to free themselves, Nick and Lilly would be long gone. Or at least that would be the perception. Lilly rented a car in her name with Darren's credit card. On the surface, it didn't sound like a smart move, but they wanted those after them to know their location. Dallas is the central hub of the US, which meant they could be anywhere—Mexico to the south, the Great Plains to the north, New Orleans to the east, or possibly westward.

They drove to Devol, Oklahoma—a town of a hundred and fifty people, about a two-hour drive from Dallas. There were more tornadoes in Devol than people.

As they drove across the deserted Oklahoma prairie, Lilly flipped on the radio. She picked up a station coming from Wichita Falls, Texas that was playing pop hits. Natalie Gold's latest single "Vengeance" took them into Cotton County.

Nick appeared to know exactly where he was going, as he turned down a dusty road. When they arrived at their destination, they were surprised that the lights were on in the brick ranch house.

Lilly's first thought was that the Russian army was waiting for them. She wasn't going to argue if Nick wanted to drive right past and head back to I-36. And even if it was a safe haven, part of her didn't want to step inside the home where Audrey Mays grew up.

Reverend Carter Mays answered the door in his bathrobe. He was a tall, slender man with patches of gray mixed into his dark hair. His face was handsome, but the lines were deeply engraved—Lilly remembered similar lines appearing on her mother's face after her brother was killed. What Lilly noticed most was that he didn't look as surprised as he should have that his dead daughter's boyfriend showed up at his door at three in the morning.

One of the advantages that Nick saw in coming here was that the Mays' didn't own a television, computer, or radio. So it was doubtful they'd heard the news of Lilly and Nick's plight.

Lilly searched Reverend Mays' eyes for trepidation or suspicion, but found none. In fact, he looked at Nick like his own son had returned home from battle. The two men embraced. Nick introduced Lilly as a "business associate" from the law firm that he worked for.

After a pleasant greeting for Lilly, the reverend turned his attention back to Nick. "You must have heard the news about Audrey. That's why you're here, isn't it?" he asked in a polished Oklahoma drawl.

Lilly's eyes met Nick's. He had no idea what the reverend was talking about any more than she did. But Nick's look said to play along.

"Yes, I came as soon as I heard," he replied.

Reverend Mays nodded. "We got the call a couple hours ago. We haven't been able to go back to sleep since we heard."

"Who called you?" Nick asked, still fishing for information.

"The FBI. And imagine my reaction when they told me that Audrey might not have been the girl in the apartment that night. And it might not be Audrey buried in the cemetery here. They are coming in the morning to exhume the body. Cassie and I have to go to court to give our approval."

Chapter 52

Nick played it cool. "That's why I thought it was important that I come, being that I'm a lawyer. Was it a Fitzpatrick who called?"

Reverend Mays thought for a moment, and then replied, "No, his name was LaPoint. He and some gal from the US Attorney's Office are coming out in the morning. She had a funny name."

"Dava Lazinski?"

He nodded as if to say the name sounded familiar, and then invited them into his neat and orderly home. Just as Nick mentioned, no sign of any TV or radio.

"Cassie is in the living room," he said, lowering his voice. "On the surface this sounds like great news, but the likelihood is still that Audrey is gone and this is nothing but false hope. We haven't heard from her in a year—something terrible has happened to our daughter, regardless of tomorrow's outcome. So that call shredded all the work we've done to try to move on with our lives. Cassie has been up looking at old photographs all night."

He led them into the living room where Cassie Mays was huddled on a couch, cradling a photo album. Lilly had seen photos of Audrey, and she saw the same shoulder-length brunette hair and apple pie features in her mother. But like Reverend Mays, her brow was furrowed with the scars of loss.

Cassie was surrounded by used tissues and her eyes were worn from crying, but she rose up and hugged Nick.

When they broke the embrace, Nick again introduced Lilly as a lawyer in his firm. The story had expanded. He and Lilly had been in Houston working on a case for a large energy company and drove to Devol immediately after hearing the news. But unlike her husband, Cassie Mays looked suspiciously at Lilly. Her intent was obvious—she wouldn't accept that her daughter had been replaced.

Lilly just wanted to find a warm bed. She hadn't slept since Sunday morning. But Cassie Mays insisted on making them a meal. She brought out some leftover ham and cornbread, which Lilly washed down with a glass of pulpy lemonade. It hit the spot. She had eaten as little as she'd slept in the last forty-eight hours.

They returned to the living room to eulogize Audrey some more. It was a shrine—her photos practically wallpapered the room, including merry group shots taken during Nick's last visit to Oklahoma, two Christmases ago. The Audrey photos outnumbered ten to one those of her brother Scott, a marine stationed in Afghanistan. Lilly didn't want to despise a dead woman, but she was growing tired of Saint Audrey, and the more Nick lit up at each nostalgic memory, the more pain she felt.

There was even a photo album of her funeral, where according to Cassie Mays, people came from all over Cotton County and as far as Tulsa to attend. A recording of Audrey singing "Amazing Grace" was played at the funeral. Lilly thought singing at your own funeral was a little on the macabre side, to say the least.

While Lilly's snippy thoughts couldn't even dent Audrey's angelic aura, the more Cassie Mays went on, the more Lilly understood what a good choice it was by Nick to come here. There would be no questions asked. They didn't even seem to have knowledge that he was in witness protection, or of his potential testimony. The only time they even looked remotely puzzled was when Nick mentioned that it was important not to tell the FBI that they were here, and that they wouldn't be able to be present for the exhumation, due to a key deposition tomorrow in the energy case. The Mays' soon returned to drinking their Nick Zellen Kool Aid, and any suspicions fluttered away.

After the tribute to Audrey mercifully ended, Lilly finally got that warm bed she craved. She was given Scott's room. Lilly slept with her gun, while Nick was in Audrey's old room, sharing the bed with her ghost.

Chapter 53

Nick couldn't sleep. He felt Audrey's presence everywhere.

The news that the girl in Audrey's grave might be someone else should have been shocking. But since Karl's arrest, and the events that followed, he'd lost all ability to be shocked. Up until that moment when he was removed from his torts class at NYU Law School and told of the arrest, his life had been idyllic. But there was no point in looking back—he was a new person now.

He took out the photos he always carried with him, even when his witness protection guardians like Fitzpatrick disallowed it. The first was of the man who raised him. He stood with his arm around a cap-and-gowned Nick at his college graduation, Karl looking as he always had with his neatly trimmed goatee and horn-rimmed glasses.

Like most moments between them, it wasn't devoid of love, but was businesslike in nature. That's how Karl always was with Nick and Sasha. He wouldn't even let them call him Dad. He was always Karl. But no matter how laborious his business schedule was he found time for Nick and his sister, whether it was sharing a passion for skating and hockey, or passing on his love of art.

The next picture was of his mother, Paula. Her blonde-haired, blue-eyed features were the direct opposite of Karl's, as was her personality, which was all fire and brimstone. The photo was from her fiftieth birthday party with her arms wrapped around her two most precious jewels—Nick and Sasha—whom she gave up her music career to raise. He could still hear her voice at his hockey games, *C'mon Zellen, skate, don't give up, skate Zellen!* Even her yelling was melodic.

Sasha was alone in the picture he had of her, just as the little diva would want it. She was never one to share the spotlight, but she never had trouble sharing how she felt. And since their mother died, her emotions turned into a Category-5 hurricane. And that's why it was so hard for Nick to leave her.

Sasha predictably refused to go into protective custody. She had inherited their mother's stubbornness. Nick did risk his cover to meet her when she was at a skating competition in Phoenix—the only danger turned out to be when Lilly thought she was a girl he was seeing behind her back—but now he needed to get back to New York to protect her.

The last photo was of Audrey—not that he needed one in this room. Although, the woman he fell in love with in New York was different from the Devol version. She could meld into the city and be herself. She was able to live, instead of having people living vicariously through her. The Audrey he knew had a sarcastic wit and was quite a spectacle when she got a few drinks in her. She was also tough, as the guy who tried to steal her purse on the subway found out the hard way. She wasn't a sinner, but she wasn't the saint they made her out to be here in Devol. When he came back here that Christmas, it was like she was putting on a Broadway play for the people, reprising a role she thought they wanted her to play. He thought it was too bad they never got to see the real Audrey.

Their last conversation was so rushed that he didn't get to tell her everything he wanted. He instructed her to get out of the country, and made it clear that it would be too dangerous to return to her apartment, or here to Oklahoma. The next thing he knew he was at her funeral. His lasting memory was of the disguised federal agents whisking him away, back into protection, before her body was even in the ground.

Unable to sleep, he wandered into the hallway. The door to the Mays' room was ajar, and he slipped inside. He stared at them like a parent might at a newborn. They were sleeping, but not soundly. He spent an hour in their room. Before he left, he whispered how sorry he was that he failed to protect their daughter. They didn't wake, but he felt like they had heard him.

When he returned to Audrey's room, he skimmed through some old yearbooks, getting a particular kick out of some of her historical hairstyles. He found prom photos that she attended with a boy named Luke, whom she posed with next to his pickup truck. She couldn't have looked more beautiful.

There were no posters of pop stars, or teenybopper magazines. And with her father being the reverend, she had no shortage of bibles and crucifixes. But most of the room was dedicated to the great love of Audrey's life—her music.

He browsed through a pile of demo tapes that she had compiled over the years. Many featured Audrey singing at her father's church, while others were auditions for Juilliard, but some were pop songs that she probably hid away from her parents.

Nick took one of the "pop" tapes and slid it into an old Walkman that he found on her nightstand. He put the headphones on and let Audrey's powerful voice overtake his senses. He could listen to that voice all night.

One song sounded familiar to him. He rewound the tape and played it again. At first he thought Audrey had her music stolen from her, but then he realized it was her. He had heard the song numerous times on the radio, but hadn't really listened to it before.

He picked up the *Rolling Stone* magazine that he had borrowed from Lilly. He studied the picture of Natalie Gold that graced the cover. He mentally dissected the image, removing the top layer. First the hair, then the enhanced breasts, and finally the trashy clothes. What was left took his breath away.

Nick played the demo song again. The lyrics had been altered, but it was the same song. It was "Vengeance," the smash hit by Israeli pop star Natalie Gold.

Who was being managed by Viktor Sarvydas!

Nick was wrong—he could be shocked again.

"What are you up to, Audrey?" he said to himself.

Chapter 54

Darren couldn't stop the banging in his head. It was like two lead pipes rhythmically clanging together.

He woke up in fear, finding himself on the couch in the same clothes as last night and smelling like a fraternity party. As yesterday came back into focus, he remembered it was actually a high school party.

He realized the banging sound was coming from the front door. He struggled off the couch and found his way to the door, shielding his eyes from the Tuesday morning sun that was flooding through the windows. Despite the bright light, Darren felt like he was trapped in a dark room. He looked through the peephole and groaned. The nightmare just wouldn't stop.

Agent LaPoint burst in without even a hello. "We need to talk."

"Do you have new information on my wife?"

"We tracked them from Las Vegas to Colorado, and now Dallas. But they continue to be one step ahead of us."

"Why would they be going to all these places?"

"If I knew I wouldn't be here talking to you, now would I?"

"Since I don't know anything, I guess we have nothing to talk about. So if you'll excuse me, I need to go find my wife. Dallas, you say?"

"You have travel plans today, Mr. McLaughlin, but you're not going to Dallas."

Darren looked defiantly at LaPoint. He wanted to give him a piece of his mind, order him to get a warrant or some other line he'd heard on *Law & Order*, and toss him out of his house. But as he weighed his best course of action, Becks wandered out of the master bedroom, her hair a tangled nest of pink and blonde. She wore the same T-shirt she had on last night, barely covering a skimpy pair of panties.

"What's with the tension convention?" she asked with an annoyed look, like she'd been awoken from a perfect sleep.

"Well, well, what do we have here?" LaPoint responded.

Becks sneered at him. "I don't know what you're looking at. I don't do threesomes, so maybe go take your horn dog for a walk in a different neighborhood, pervert."

Darren didn't know what she was implying, but nothing like that happened last night. Not only weren't there any threesomes going on here, there weren't any twosomes, or onesomes, for that matter.

He turned to LaPoint, "This isn't what you think."

"You don't even want to know what I'm thinking, Mr. McLaughlin."

"She just came over last night and…" Darren started, causing LaPoint's eyebrows to rise. "What I mean is that we went to a party and…"

Darren kept digging a bigger hole, so he decided he would choose not to further incriminate himself.

"What you're telling me is that you attended a party with an underage girl, then you brought her back to your place for an innocent little sleepover while your wife is away."

"Not that it's any of your business," Becks snarled, "but I'm eighteen, so I can bang anyone I want."

Darren wanted to sink into the floor. He held up a stop sign and said, "Nothing was banged, or even lightly tapped." He then tried to set the story straight. "Listen, I let her stay here last night. Maybe it wasn't the smartest move, but nothing happened, so can we just move on?"

"Seems like you and your wife make similar choices."

Darren wasn't going to take the bait. "I'm responsible for her being here, so now I'm going to make sure she gets to school on time."

"Who do you think you are, a truant officer?" LaPoint asked with a grin.

Becks sighed loudly. "What, did you two take some sort of old people bad joke class?"

LaPoint ignored her, turning serious. "Nobody is going anywhere without my say so. Mr. McLaughlin has a date in New York, and I will be escorting him to the airport to make sure he is on his flight. But first I will drop Miss Ryan at school, so she can further her education, and hopefully one day make a positive contribution to society, although I'm not holding my breath on that one."

"So after you finish carpooling, will you have that surgery to loosen up your tight ass?" Becks wasn't done fighting. Her hangover had made her even more cantankerous and confrontational, if that were possible.

LaPoint smiled back at her, as if she'd met her match. "I will be headed to spend my day in Oklahoma, so consider yourself lucky."

"I'm going with you," Becks stated to befuddled looks.

"Going with me where?"

"To Oklahoma. Obviously that's where you think Brett is. Why else would anyone go to Oklahoma? We have a big chemistry test today and I wouldn't want Brett to miss it. Think of me as a truant officer, just like you two. Only cuter."

"May I remind you, Miss Ryan, that Brett Buckley is the victim in this case," LaPoint said calmly.

"The problem is, he's been putting his victim where it don't belong, so I'm going to turn him into a victimless crime. And then we all live happily ever after."

Darren was starting to get the feeling that would never be the case ever again.

Chapter 55

Darren was instructed to prepare like he was going to be on his normal flight schedule. That would be his cover. Why a cover was needed, he had no idea, but he didn't have time to think about it. LaPoint gave him five minutes to dress into his pilot uniform and prepare for his trip.

Becks went over the allotted time. But nobody could argue with the results. Darren barely recognized the sophisticated woman before him—she looked like she had aged ten years, in a good way. She wore one of Lilly's business suits with mid-thigh skirt, and her hair was stylishly tied up.

She smiled at the stares and did a pirouette. "I figured since your wife stole my boyfriend, the least she could do was let me borrow her clothes.

Just the mention of Lilly sent Darren crashing back to reality.

They drove in LaPoint's car. The first stop was South Chandler High. Becks might have looked classier, but it hadn't yet carried over to her actions. She slammed the door upon arrival and gave them the finger. She disappeared between a couple of school buses, walking awkwardly in Lilly's heels.

LaPoint then escorted Darren to Sky Harbor Airport. With Becks' impressionable ears out of the way, he explained the day's itinerary. Upon arrival in New York, Darren would be met by a team of federal agents who would escort him to the office of US Attorney Aaron Eicher, where he would be briefed on the details of Lilly's case. LaPoint refused to answer any further questions.

Before they parted ways, Darren again assured LaPoint that nothing had gone on with Becks at his house last night. "I'm an honorable man, Agent LaPoint, and I would never take advantage of a young girl like that."

"I know, Mr. McLaughlin. But unfortunately people take advantage of the honorable in this world."

He knew he meant Lilly. And he couldn't blame him for thinking that. But LaPoint didn't know her like he did.

Darren walked to his normal sign-in for his flight, and then to his gate. The federal agents weren't surrounding him like a pack of Secret Service around the president. They were spread out in tactical positions disguised as airport officials.

His comfort level rose when he met the flight crew. Especially the familiar face of Ron Treadwell. He looked pleasantly surprised to see Darren, and greeted him with, "And here I thought Sunday was our last flight. The things you'll do for a free night out in Manhattan."

Darren actually came close to a smile. He was thankful for Treadwell's presence, as he was the one person who could possibly take his mind off what awaited him in New York.

According to LaPoint, nobody knew the reason for his trip, including the flight crew. No explanation was given for Darren's riding in the cockpit, other than it was approved by the airline. Treadwell didn't question it, but his newbie first officer appeared concerned that Darren was doing an evaluation of him, and was on his best behavior.

As they took off, Treadwell began giddily singing "New York, New York". "Start spreading the news … I'm leaving today..."

"What's got you in such a good mood?" Darren asked as they hit their cruising altitude.

"That Kelli chick from the other night emailed me. Said she wants to meet up next time I'm in New York, which thanks to you messing up my schedule, my friend, is today." A big grin formed on his face. "I guess my charm outweighed my complicated nature."

He handed Darren his phone with instructions to check out the pictures she had sent him. The first one was that group shot from Sunday night in which Darren served as the third wheel. He couldn't believe today was only Tuesday. It was like the world had slowed to a painful crawl. The next pictures were the ones Darren believed Treadwell wanted him to see. Suggestive photos of Kelli with an attached message.

"She says she can't stop thinking of you. I wonder if there's a vaccine for that," Darren said, and this time did smile.

Treadwell laughed.

Their moment was broken up by the intercom—the flight attendant requesting access to the cockpit, which Treadwell granted. But when the door opened, a girl burst in, almost knocking the flight attendant over in the process.

"Wow, what a big cockpit you boys have," the intruder exclaimed.

Darren looked back to see a smiling Becks.

Chapter 56

Darren stepped into John F. Kennedy Airport, just as he'd done on hundreds of occasions. But this time was different—each step he took through the crowded airport was a step further into the unknown.

He was still surrounded by his invisible net of federal agents. During the flight, he tried to come up with reasons as to why his wife's case attracted this much priority. But came up empty.

He felt a jab in the ribs. His whole body tightened. He turned sharply, not knowing what to expect.

"So what's with all the VIP treatment, Run DMC? Are they protecting you from all your groupies?"

"What do you think you're doing here?"

"Just chillaxin in the NYC."

After bursting into the cabin, the federal air marshals had immediately removed Becks and sequestered her in her seat. He hadn't spoken to her since, and had no plans to do so while in New York. "You said you had a test today."

"C'mon, DMC, I told you that life experience is always better than book-learning. You and I have way more chemistry than some periodic table."

"You didn't answer my question—what are you doing here?

"Did you drink too much Hatorade on the flight? I bought a ticket like everyone else. You should thank me—I'm helping to pay your salary. Maybe if you make enough, your wife will drop Mr. Software Heir and come crawling back."

His skin had thickened. Her daggers now bounced off. "You shouldn't be here. It could be dangerous."

"Nothing is more dangerous than chemistry class. Those Bunsen burners are an accident waiting to happen." She flashed her usual smart-ass smile, before turning serious. "And besides, I'm in this thing as much as you are. I got screwed over just as much."

Darren strained to remember what it was like to be a teenager. Every relationship was Romeo & Juliet to the nth degree. She'd learn soon enough that the puppy love could never compare to a committed marriage. But he also remembered that it was impossible to argue with a teenager. So he didn't.

"What do you plan to accomplish by this stunt? I don't even know what's going on here."

The fierceness in her eyes remained. "Just remember that when someone screws me over, I won't stop until justice is served."

Darren didn't doubt that. They headed toward the baggage claim, where he was supposed to meet the FBI agents. He wheeled his travel bag behind him and looked the part of the arriving pilot. And despite the pink streaks in the hair, Becks could pass for a business traveler. Darren couldn't get over how different she appeared from the extreme teenager he'd met just yesterday.

As instructed, he marched past the rental car counters and out the sliding glass doors that led to the pickup area, congested with hotel transportation vans and honking cabs. Darren could wake from a Rip Van Winkle sleep and immediately know he was in New York—it had a different intensity.

A black SUV pulled curbside, muscling between a couple of gridlocked cabbies. Darren was supposed to head toward it. He kept waiting for the federal agents to remove Becks from his side, but figured that they probably didn't want to make a scene.

The moment Darren's foot stepped off the curb, a screech of tires grabbed his attention. A van was hurtling toward the sidewalk as if it had no brakes. People screamed as they scattered, leaving their luggage behind. The van shot up onto the sidewalk right in front of Darren and Becks. It buckled to a stop, cutting them off at the pass.

Out of the vehicle leaped two of the largest creatures Darren had ever seen. The first one was at least three hundred pounds, and that was a conservative estimate. He was holding an Uzi, which looked like a toy gun in his enormous arms.

The second one was not as big, but equally scary. He let out a primal scream and began randomly firing a pistol. When Darren took a closer look, he discerned that the second creature was actually a female.

The bravest of their protectors identified himself as FBI, and demanded that the assailants drop their weapons.

The woman laughed and sliced the agent's arm with a bullet, causing his weapon to drop to the ground. A satisfied look spread across her face.

The male began spraying machine-gun fire, pelting cars and shattering glass. Darren tackled Becks and tried to cover her. But there was no place to hide from these maniacs. And their FBI protectors were no match for them.

The woman picked up Darren and Becks, one in each arm like they were a light dumbbell workout at the gym. She then shot-putted them into the back of the van, one at a time. The male slammed the door shut.

Darren's dark room just got darker.

Chapter 57

The male was pacing in the back of the van. Darren wasn't sure how the creaky floorboards were holding him.

The male had the biggest neck Darren had ever seen. It was like the trunk of an oak tree and it took a forest of a beard to cover it.

Darren was too stunned to speak. But Becks was never at a loss for words, "Who the hell are you, and where are you taking us?"

The male answered, "I'm Oleg Moziaf and this is my wife, Vana."

Darren wasn't sure which one was the chip and which one was the salsa, but he did know that Vana was the driver. And it felt like she was doing about 100 mph through the city streets.

"I don't know who you think we are, but you got the wrong people," Becks shouted.

He flipped Darren over like a pancake and removed his wallet. He looked at his license and said in a thick accent, "Nope—Darren McLaughlin—he's the right guy."

Darren felt a shiver down his spine—not only was he their focal point, but they were willing to risk a shootout with federal agents to capture him!

"What do you want with us?' Becks asked again, this time in a more civilized tone.

"That depends—who are you?"

"My name is Rebecca Ryan. I am a high school student from Arizona. And I'm late for my chemistry test."

"Do you get good grades in school?"

"All A's."

"Then you probably figure out we have no need for you. So I'm going to kill you."

Darren was struck by the excitement in his voice when he talked of killing her. He was sickened that he might be responsible for this innocent girl's death.

"Oh no you don't, Oleg," Vana's husky voice echoed to the back of the van.

Darren felt relief for a moment, but then she uttered, "We kill together, or we don't kill at all."

"You know I've never killed without you since we've been married, Vana. I wait for you, of course."

She shook her large head. "Our orders are no killing."

"But the girl is an extra."

"I said no, Oleg!" she shouted.

He first looked disappointed, but then found a compromise plan. "I promise not to kill her. But she talks too much, so I will cut her tongue out!"

Becks began inching toward the back door. Diving out onto a busy street at high speed seemed like her best option.

Darren had to do something—and fast. "Let her go. She has nothing to do with this! This is about me—you got me, so leave her be."

"Only God can save her now, and even God's scared of the Moziafs," Oleg replied with a laugh.

Becks had moved as far back against the door as she could. When the van swerved sharply, almost tipping, Darren made his move. He tried to tackle Oleg like he was back playing high school football. But it was like hitting a brick wall, and he tossed him to the ground without a reaction. All he could do is watch as the behemoth headed for Becks.

"No!" Darren shouted out.

Becks had run out of wiggle room. "You two are crazy mofos!" she yelled out.

Oleg seemed to take it as a compliment. He moved closer, his hand clenched around a knife handle. Darren expected to see fear in Becks' eyes, but what he saw was fight.

"You better kill me, because if you leave me alive, I will hunt you down and make you wish you were dead!"

The threat didn't deter him, but then Vana shouted out, "I like her sassy mouth—don't touch her tongue. We'll let the Rabbi decide what to do with her."

Oleg looked disappointed, but Darren got the idea he didn't cross his wife.

Moments later, they skidded to a stop. Oleg forcefully picked Darren and Becks up by the collars, kicked open the back doors, and dragged them out into the gray afternoon.

"Time to go see the Rabbi," he announced.

Chapter 58

They would meet the Rabbi in a sparkling oasis built within a rundown urban area. To Darren, it looked more like a nightclub than a synagogue.

Oleg carried Darren and Becks under a striped awning that declared the place as Sarvy's. Before entering, they were frisked by two barrel-chested bouncer types. One let his hands roam underneath Becks' skirt with a grin "Just looking for a gun. People have been known to hide them there."

"If you ever put your hand there again the only thing I'm going to hide is my foot in your ass," Becks fired back.

The bouncer kept grinning, seemingly not taking her seriously.

The Moziafs physically ushered them inside. "Welcome to Sarvy's," Oleg announced.

Walking into the cavernous room was like walking into a domed football stadium. And it wasn't just impressive in its size. The place oozed money, from the art deco columns to the chrome and parquet fixtures. But it also appeared to be in the middle of a reconstruction project. Beefy men in sharp suits supervised. Tables were being set up, hammers pounded, and drills bored into walls. Carts filled with Smirnoff bottles whizzed past them. Microphone sound checks deafened.

"This place is totally off-the-chain. What is it?" Becks asked.

"You not know Sarvy's?" Oleg asked, sounding dumbfounded.

"Only the hottest nightclub in the world," Vana added as if she was Paris Hilton.

"And this is where we're supposed to meet this Rabbi dude, or will he be too busy DJ'ing?" Becks continued with the sassy tongue that Vana seemed to like.

"He upstairs," Oleg responded mechanically.

"We apologize for noise, but they preparing for Natalie Gold video premiere party tonight," Vana informed.

Darren remembered her as the Israeli pop star that Treadwell's kids were fans of. It was also very evident that he was out of his element, so he let Becks lead the dialogue.

"Natalie Gold—that's fly. And the Rabbi still had time to give his blessing to lil' ole us."

"More like circumcise you," Oleg replied with a laugh.

As they moved toward a marble staircase, Vana pointed out that Viktor Sarvydas, the owner, had shelled out over four million dollars for the party, including half a million on the bathroom alone. They made it clear that he would do whatever it takes to get what he wanted. And right now it appeared what he wanted was Darren.

Oleg pushed them up the staircase and into a windowless, but otherwise exquisite office.

The Rabbi did not have a long Hasidic beard or wear the traditional garb of an Orthodox. He was a trim man, dressed in a simple sweater with khakis. If Darren had to guess, he would say he was in his early sixties. His face was littered with red splotches on his otherwise pale skin.

He rose from behind his desk and greeted them as if they were foreign dignitaries. Unlike the Moziafs, his English was polished, with only a slight accent.

He turned to Becks, appearing curious by her presence. "And who would you be, young lady?"

She said nothing, stubbornly pressing her lips together.

"I'm talking to you," the Rabbi raised his voice.

Becks looked at the Moziafs, who stood behind the desk with their enormous arms crossed across their heaving chests. “My B, I guess your cats got my tongue.”

“Cats can be quite dangerous when you don’t give them what they want.”

“The name is Ryan. Rebecca Ryan. Who wants to know?”

The name seemed to trigger his memory. “Ah, the girlfriend.”

The Rabbi sat back down behind his desk. With a nod, the Moziafs prepared chairs for the guests, before returning to their station.

“My name is Steve Parmalov,” the Rabbi said in a calm tone, “and I’m the deputy lieutenant of Sarvy Music and the many other assorted businesses of Viktor Sarvydas.”

It was like he expected the name Sarvydas to send them into cartwheels.

“The music mogul dude?” Becks asked with surprise.

Darren had heard of Sarvy Music, of course, but the name didn’t ring a bell until Becks’ last statement. Now he remembered the flamboyant Sarvydas, who was most famous for cultivating the career of pop star Maria DeMaio and marrying her when she was only nineteen. What this had to do with Lilly, Darren had no idea.

Parmalov smiled thinly. “He’s a music mogul like I’m a rabbi, and the Moziafs are butchers.” He chuckled to himself. “Well, actually the Moziafs are very much butchers.”

They found humor in their boss’s words.

Becks remained feisty. “So did you bring us here to see your standup act?”

Parmalov turned his beady eyes toward Darren. “No, you’re here because Mr. Sarvydas is very interested in finding your wife, Mr. McLaughlin. He has business with her travel companion.”

Becks looked like she was putting something together in her mind. “I’ve been following his story on the news. He fled the country after his son was arrested on murder charges. His son killed his business partner, or something like that."

"The trial starts next week," Parmalov replied.

"I don't understand what that has to do with us," Darren said again.

Parmalov leaned back in his chair, and ran his hand through his thinning hair. "Viktor doesn't like the way things are going and would like to sit down with Nick Zellen and have a heart-to-heart about the direction of the trial. But unfortunately, your wife has gotten in the way."

"Who is Nick Zellen?" Becks asked.

Chapter 59

Parmalov began to answer, before stopping in mid-sentence. He gauged their blank looks and a smile crept from his thin lips. “You don’t know, do you?”

“Know what?” Darren asked.

“That the name of your wife’s boyfriend is Nick Zellen, not Brett Buckley.”

Their looks turned puzzled. “What are you talking about?

“Nick Zellen was in the Witness Protection Program. He claims to have witnessed Alexei Sarvydas murder his father, and plans to testify against him in the trial. Viktor thinks that Nick might be mistaken in what he saw, so he plans on speaking with him.”

Becks lashed back at him, “That’s a total load of crap!”

“Oh, it is?” Parmalov replied with a scary calmness, and then tossed a folder in Becks’ direction. It contained pictures of Nick Zellen from a boy to the young man she knew as Brett Buckley. His identity might have changed, but his dark features and intense eyes hadn’t. It was undeniably the same person.

Darren read through the file. Nick Zellen was a twenty-four-year-old law student at NYU. He grew up in Sands Point, Long Island, the son of Karl and Paula Zellen. He had a sister named Sasha, who was a junior figure skating champion. Nick attended high school at the Taft School in Connecticut, where he was a hockey star. He did his undergrad at Cornell, before entering law school at NYU. He took a leave of absence last spring after his father's murder.

Darren sat in a state of shock, now keenly aware of the danger Lilly was in, and why the FBI was so interested in this case.

Becks appeared more angry than stunned. "Let me guess, you and Uncle Viktor want us to help you find Lilly to lead you to Brett … Nick … or whatever his name is, so you can kill him. Then Alexei goes free."

Parmalov shook his head. "I hope you take solace, Rebecca, in the knowledge that a relationship built on lies is not a relationship at all. You can do better than a boy who wouldn't even tell you his real name."

Becks didn't appear comforted.

Parmalov continued, "Honesty is everything in a relationship. Look no further than Oleg and Vana—as sick and twisted as they are, they never break their bond of trust. And that's why they've had such a successful union."

Darren sat in a catatonic state. *Could this be real?* It was like something out of a movie—murder trials and Russian mobsters. And when they caught Lilly … he couldn't let that happen.

"I look in your troubled eyes, Mr. McLaughlin and I don't understand your worry," Parmalov addressed him. "The reason I want to find them is to make sure Nick will be safe to testify. Viktor has complete confidence that Alexei will be exonerated at trial, but is concerned that if anything happens to Nick, it will confirm many of the wrongful myths about the Sarvydas family, and harm Alexei in the jury's eyes."

Even Darren, the sap, wasn't buying that one.

A point echoed by Becks, "If you're on our team, then why'd you send Tweedle Dumb and Tweedle Dumber after us?" She pointed at the Moziafs, still stationed behind the desk.

"I apologize. We had to get to you before the feds did. They would poison your minds against the Sarvydas family. If I wanted you harmed, the Moziafs would have gladly helped me with that endeavor."

"Why should we believe you?" Becks snapped back.

"I believe in the justice system, as does Viktor. When we first came here many years ago, Viktor and I worked for a man named Vladimir Miklacz. He put us in charge of what we called the People's Court. It began in a back room of a small restaurant on Brighton Beach Avenue, and later moved to this very room.

"The people of the neighborhood accused of a crime came before our panel. It had been a violent area where it was cheaper to hire a hitman for two grand than to pay off your debts. But we cleaned it up in a way the police could never have done. Alexei deserves the same right to face his accuser."

Darren had an idea that this People's Court was more about thugs torturing and extorting the community members, than Judge Wapner rendering an impartial decision based on the facts.

"So what do you want us to do?" Darren got to the point.

"You are going to be my main contact in getting your wife back. I predict her guilt will eventually get the best of her, and she will contact you. When she does, you will come directly to me with this information."

"What if we refuse?" Becks interjected.

"Then Mr. McLaughlin will get to watch the Moziafs cut you to pieces."

The Moziafs appeared to be slobbering at the possibilities.

Parmalov's final words were, "And you are not to talk to the FBI or the US Attorney's Office under any circumstances."

The meeting was over.

The Moziafs literally carried them out of Sarvy's and tossed them onto the pavement.

"Enjoy New York," Vana said.

"We'll be watching," Oleg ominously added.

Chapter 60

Becks helped Darren up off of the cement sidewalk.

"You look like you're going to pass out again," she said with a concerned look. "Let's get you some food."

She walked him away from Sarvy's toward a nearby street vendor—a bearded man in a fur cap, manning a pushcart. He was selling some sort of spicy pork and Darren wasn't sure if it would be more help or hindrance to his queasy stomach.

Like most on the Brighton streets, the man spoke in a deep Russian accent. Becks ordered two dishes of pork and a couple cans of soda. They bartered on money—the man didn't seem to have any set prices. Becks haggled him down, showing tough negotiating skills, before handing him a crisp twenty. She told him to keep the change with a grin, as if to remind him that she won the battle of wills.

As they walked away, the man began shouting out, "Help, police! Thieves!"

Darren looked back, concerned that the vendor was being robbed, but it became clear that he was referring to them. Before he could protest, two black SUVs with tinted windows skidded to the street corner. A couple of men jumped out and dragged Becks and Darren into the vehicle, then sped off.

Darren struggled to make out where they were taking them—he recognized the Brooklyn Bridge as they passed over it into Manhattan—skyscrapers whizzed by as they powered through the busy traffic.

They veered into the underground garage of a building. Then were whisked out of the vehicle and up a maze of stairwells and elevators. They landed in what looked like a typical business setting, and were led through busy cube farm into a cluttered office.

It was very different from Parmalov's. There was no marble or mahogany, and the steel desk was piled with paperwork and half-full mugs of coffee.

A man entered the room. This time there were no fake greetings and handshakes. Just a no-nonsense instruction to take a seat in the chairs facing his desk. He dismissed their captors, ordering them to close the door on their way out.

He sat behind his desk and swallowed some coffee. "I'm US Attorney Eicher. We were supposed to meet an hour ago, and you're late."

"We sort of ran into a couple of roadblocks," Darren said.

"About seven-hundred-pounds of roadblocks named Moziaf," Eicher replied.

"Next time you wanna use us as bait for the skeepy mahnstas, how 'bout gettin' some rent-a-cops who know how to use their heaters. You almost got us killed!" Becks snapped.

Eicher's face contorted in annoyance. "I don't remember inviting you here, Miss Ryan. And for the record, not following directions is what almost got you killed."

"You didn't invite me, just like you didn't warn me that my boyfriend was wanted by the Russian mob. Or that he wasn't who he said he was. What is this witness protection bullshit?"

"You, along with the rest of the world now know that Brett Buckley is actually Nick Zellen. It's very important that we find Nick before others do."

Becks didn't look impressed. "The bottom line is, you put people like me at risk, and people got hurt."

Eicher and Becks traded angry glances. They seemed to be made from the same cloth. "As long as Nick's identity was a secret, then nobody was in harm's way. But the federal marshal in charge didn't do a very good job of keeping tabs on Nick, resulting in our current mess."

Becks stewed, while Eicher focused on Darren.

"I'm sure Parmalov filled you in on the fact that Nick is a very important witness in an upcoming trial. We feel you, as Lilly's husband, are our best chance to find her, and that she will lead us to Nick. So we are going to need your cooperation."

Darren thought of Parmalov's threats. *Do not talk to the feds or the US Attorney's Office.* The Moziafs popped into his head.

"I have nothing to say," he announced.

Eicher leaned back in his chair. "My agent on the scene in Arizona, LaPoint, thinks you are a dumbass who has no idea what is going on. He's half right—you are a dumbass. But if you don't talk to me, I'm going to be forced to believe you and your wife are working with Viktor Sarvydas."

Becks took up his fight, "Darren has nothing to do with it!"

"And how would you know this?"

"Because I went through all of Brett's emails. And while his wife might be a cheating skank, her emails read like a lovesick teenager, not some mobbed-up chick—and if you can't see that, then I think you are the dumbass. Maybe you should stop looking for others to blame and acknowledge that you effed up this case all on your own."

Becks rose up like she wanted to fight. Eicher did the same.

But before a confrontation ensued, Darren uttered, "Fine, if you think it'll get Lilly back safely, then I'll help you."

Chapter 61

Eicher gathered them around his computer. "If you are as ignorant of the facts as you claim, Mr. McLaughlin, then I think you need to know who you're dealing with here."

He played the video of the airport shootout. He froze it just as the Moziafs leaped out of the van.

"Oleg and Vana Moziaf are Olympic champion weightlifters turned ruthless killers. They are also an unintended consequence of 1970s amendments that were supposed to assist the religiously persecuted, but also opened our shores to numerous gangsters and gulag-hardened thugs from Russia. What we call the Red Tide."

"The Moziafs are more like a tsunami," Becks commented.

"Trust me, you saw their softer side," Eicher remarked. "But they're not the only ones you need to worry about. They learned their craft from the original don of Brighton Beach, Vladimir Miklacz—also known as Psyk, Russian for psycho. He was a cruel man who ruled with fear, until he and his daughter were gunned down in cold blood. His son-in-law, Viktor Sarvydas survived the shooting, and upon recovering from his wounds, was elevated to don. Most believe that Viktor was the one who set up the hit in the first place. This includes your new friend, Parmalov, who has always thought of himself as the rightful heir to the throne."

"What's with the Rabbi stuff?" Becks asked. "The guy was anything but kosher."

"Back in the 1980s, Parmalov and Viktor were known for running scams in the Diamond District. At least until Viktor double-crossed him, setting Parmalov up to take the fall for their operation. With the authorities closing in, Parmalov went on the run. The FBI eventually found him hiding in a synagogue in California, posing as a rabbi, which was how the name came about. It also sent him to prison, which cleared a path for Sarvydas to put into motion his plan to rise to power.

"Upon his release, Parmalov declared war on Sarvydas. With the Moziafs acting as his chief soldiers, the bloody battle lasted for ten years, and left bodies from Brooklyn to Moscow. That was, until they agreed to join forces with Sarvydas. It made good business sense for all parties—there was just too much money to be lost on both sides by that time to continue waging a war that was draining treasure and assets—but we have remained skeptical of this merger."

A slide show of photos passed over the screen—one grisly murder scene after another. According to Eicher, all the work of the Moziafs. Darren felt ill—these were the people after Lilly!

Eicher continued, "Viktor Sarvydas has gotten the lion's share of credit for taking the Russian Mafiya from local extortionists to a worldwide financial empire. But this man was equally important."

An image of a bookish looking, bespectacled man with a neatly trimmed goatee appeared on the screen. "This is Sarvydas' business partner, Karl Zellen—the undisputed smarts of the operation. He was a prominent Jewish dissident, a writer who had penned anti-Soviet articles for *The New Yorker* and *Jewish Digest*, and was a champion of the arts—often found hanging out with the literary elite at Elaine's or at jazz clubs in Greenwich Village. But he was also a cold, efficient killer. He was the antithesis of Sarvydas, preferring a low-profile life with his family in Long Island."

Becks looked long and hard at the photo. "Sounds a lot like his son, living a double life. Difference is that Karl got the easy way out, compared to what I'm going to do to Nick."

Eicher ignored her. "About eighteen months ago, we arrested Karl Zellen on money laundering charges. Not even the tip of the iceberg when it comes to the crimes he committed, but enough to send him away for the next twenty years. Facing this long stint in federal prison, he agreed to cooperate with us, and spill the beans on Sarvydas—our top target. To make a long story short, word of this got out to Sarvydas, and Zellen's wife ended up dead."

Eicher turned his chair back to his desk and pushed photos across the desk. It was of Paula Zellen, her naked body riddled with bullets. Her eyes were open, staring straight ahead with the blank look of death.

Darren turned away, worried about a similar ending for Lilly.

Having made his point, Eicher put the photo away. "She was killed at Sarvydas' mansion in Florida. Done in the same manner that Vladimir and Trina Miklacz were killed. Viktor was present, and took a bullet to the face, but he pulled through. Funny how that always happens."

Darren was feeling too sick to respond, but Becks looked inspired. "Whoa, horsee … if Karl Zellen was going to turn evidence against Sarvydas, then why is his wife allowed anywhere near him, much less his house!?"

"Zellen and Sarvydas were longtime business associates and friends—Paula had been working with Sarvydas to revive her music career, and had been flying down every weekend to work on an album. The Zellens believed that it was important to maintain their normal schedule after the arrest, not wanting to alarm Viktor of Karl's intentions."

"Can't see how that could possibly have gone wrong," she quipped sarcastically. "And it sounds to me like she was working on more than an album. What did Karl think about his wife playing hide the Sputnik with his old buddy Viktor?"

"He wouldn't even consider the possibility—lashed out at any talk of an affair. But he had no such reservations when it came to his belief that Viktor was the one behind her murder. It came to a head at Paula's funeral, where they had a confrontation in front of about a hundred witnesses. Karl had to be physically restrained by his children—Nick and Sasha. Challenging Sarvydas in that manner was as good as a death sentence. Last April, Karl Zellen was found murdered at his Long Island mansion."

"Sounds like you did a bang up job of protecting him. You knew Sarvydas would come after him, but did nothing. Are you also going to blame that one on the marshal?" Becks fired away.

Eicher looked irritated. He was getting taken to task by a stowaway teenager. "He declined our protection—I've never met a Russian who trusted the feds. There will be plenty of time to assess blame when the trial is over, right now my only concern is getting Nick back in one piece."

Darren noticed that there was no mention of Lilly.

"The only way he's going to testify, is if we get to him before Sarvydas does. But we have a big problem."

"Parmalov? He claimed that he was trying to help Nick. Yeah right."

"I actually don't doubt that he is. With the don and his son incapacitated, it would be the perfect time for him to gain control of the operation, and in that regard, it's to his advantage if Nick helped put Alexei away. I'm certain that Alexei killed Zellen, but I also think someone wanted to make sure that he was caught. But Nick has a much more pressing problem than Parmalov."

He clicked a button on his computer, and a photo of Nick and Lilly entering a suburban looking home shot to the screen. Seeing them together felt like a gut punch for Darren.

"This is from a security camera at Tony Dantelli's home in Henderson, Nevada yesterday. Tony was the lead investigator in the Karl Zellen case and scheduled to testify against Alexei. I'm not sure why Nick and Lilly went there, but I do know that Dantelli ended up dead shortly thereafter."

A picture of Dantelli's body floating in the pool came on the screen.

"She didn't kill him," Darren blindly defended.

The picture changed to a middle aged man in a business suit entering the same house.

"I know, Mr. McLaughlin—the man you're looking at did. His name is Zubov and he is a killing machine. Problem is, everywhere Nick goes, Zubov is right behind. Someone is tipping Zubov off, and it will be your job to prove to me that it isn't you or your wife providing those tips."

"And how do you expect me to do that?"

Eicher glared at Darren. "You will be escorted back to Arizona by a team of federal agents. As we speak, your phones, email, and anything else we can think of in your home is being tapped so we can monitor your every move. Your life is now mine—when we find your wife, hopefully alive, then you can have it back. If you have any contact with your wife, we will be listening. It might be our only chance of getting her back alive."

He then addressed Becks, "You, Miss Ryan, are getting on the next flight back to Phoenix. You will forget any of this ever happened and return to the life of a normal teenage girl—if there is such a thing. If you need a note from the Attorney General to make up your chemistry test, let me know."

Eicher got up and headed for the door.

"Where do you think you're going?" Becks asked.

"I'm going to court, where I can only pray that the judge doesn't throw out my case on the grounds that all my witnesses are dead. You two have an hour to kill before heading back to the airport. If you want to grab some food, an agent will take you down to the cafeteria. I recommend the Caesar salad, but I might avoid the Russian dressing."

Chapter 62

Dava arrived in Oklahoma City on Tuesday morning, met by Agent LaPoint of the FBI. He drove her the ninety miles west to Devol in his rented Chevy Blazer.

"I sent Darren McLaughlin to New York to meet with Eicher, so he can take over the babysitting duties," LaPoint said.

"Do you think he'll be safe there?"

"Eicher or McLaughlin?"

She shot him an annoyed look. "McLaughlin."

"I sent a team of federal marshals with him, headed by Fitzpatrick, and he'll be met by a team of FBI agents in New York."

"Somehow the presence of Fitzpatrick doesn't make me feel any better about the situation."

"Everybody makes mistakes," LaPoint replied, a little too defensively.

"Eicher has a theory that both the McLaughlins are in on Nick's disappearance."

He shrugged. "The woman is a possibility, but I'm not buying the husband."

"I do see the logic in Eicher's point. She just happens to drop into his life and all hell breaks loose? She had access to Nick every day, and her husband's job made him the perfect courier to New York and Brighton. Of course, this is all predicated on Sarvydas having found out Nick's location."

"You've seen how the Russians operate—they don't tend to get cute with double-agent high school teachers. They usually just roll the heavy artillery in and start shooting."

"Nick called Eicher. He thinks there's a leak in our office, which he blames for Sarvydas locating him."

"Like I said, if there was, Nick wouldn't be calling anyone. I just think your case is shot to hell and he's looking for excuses … no offense."

"Then how do you explain Zubov's presence? And if we want to play the blame game, we could start with the FBI and the US Marshals Office, who botched Nick's protection."

"Since you seem to be the all-knowing one, maybe you can enlighten me as to what happened."

"I think Nick contacted his sister. Sarvydas was probably tracking her every move, but whatever the reason—sister, the potential arrest of his teacher, or a leak—the bottom line is that Nick felt the heat and ran. I really can't blame him, and unlike my boss, I don't believe that Lilly McLaughlin's presence is sinister. In fact, I'm fairly certain that she had no idea what she got herself involved in."

LaPoint nodded. "I don't know what I believe anymore. But if we don't come up with some good news today, then Alexei Sarvydas is going to be a free man very soon."

"No kidding. He'll be back running prostitution rings out of his strip clubs by sunset."

"Speaking of which, what happened with the stripper's mother last night?"

"No idea."

LaPoint looked surprised. "I thought you had a meeting with her?"

"We were supposed to meet, but she never showed. I waited until well past midnight, before calling her husband in Wyoming. He hadn't heard from her either. He said she usually called in from New York when she's on one of her searches, so it was a little strange not to hear from her. I hope nothing happened to her."

"With our luck, Sarvydas' people probably got to her."

"If he got to Wendy Grant, then I'm going to start to believe those leak theories."

The hot midday sun hung over the Oklahoma Plains. Devol was so small that they almost missed it. There wasn't much sightseeing to do—a diminutive main street with a local diner, a post office, and a movie theater that featured an old time marquee. They passed a one-room red schoolhouse that looked like something from the nineteenth century. It sat beside the church where Audrey Mays' father preached. At the rear of the church, on farmland that stretched to the horizon, was the cemetery where today's action would take place.

"So who do you think is buried in Grant's tomb?" LaPoint asked.

"Do you mean who is buried in Audrey Mays' grave?"

"I was just trying to add some morbid humor to the situation. You Russians are always so literal."

"My heritage is Lithuanian, not Russian."

"I rest my case. Besides, it's just a matter of time until they invade you just like they did with Georgia and Chechnya. Then you'll be Russian again."

"Last I checked, I'm an American citizen, no different from yourself."

"Again, literal."

She sneered at him. He had no idea how lucky he was that she would let him live. Unfortunately, she needed him to pull this off.

LaPoint dropped her at the Mays' home. Dava's job was to get the family's permission to exhume the body. LaPoint would head to the Cotton County courthouse in Walters, to lay the groundwork. He didn't want any part of dealing with the grieving family. People relations weren't his thing, especially when crying might be involved.

Dava walked into the home through an open door. Devol didn't look like a place of high crime, but she got the idea that the door wasn't left open due to the peaceful nature of the area. Or Reverend Mays' faith in his fellow human beings. Someone had been here.

She immediately knew it was Nick—she could smell him. It made her think about the finish line. They would cross paths soon enough.

She did a sweep of the house, taking care of the business she came for. Then she called Eicher.

"It's me, Dava. I've got some bad news—Reverend Mays and his wife are dead."

Chapter 63

Jessi Stafford's journalistic instincts had been screaming at her, telling her to get to New York. It would be the place where this all would come to a climax—both the story and her career.

The goodwill with Brandon ended about a half hour after the incident with Cortez, when he tried to leverage his hero status to get her back to his room for a "thank you." She told him she was tired from the ordeal, but agreed to meet him later on at The Palms to have a drink at Ghost Bar. In the meantime, she planned her escape.

She caught a break when Gutierrez dragged Brandon to the casino. She figured they'd lose what little money they had, and hit on cocktail waitresses they had no chance with, until the wee morning hours. It gave Jessi the opening she needed.

Before the sun rose above the Nevada desert, she was on her way to McCarran. All the non-stops were booked, so she had to settle for changing planes in Chicago O'Hare with a ninety-minute layover. But the ninety minutes turned into three hours, when the connecting flight arriving from Dallas had been delayed.

After the flight finally took off, rising over Lake Michigan, Jessi's attention gravitated to the laughter of an affectionate couple. They were seated three rows in front of her, on the opposite side of the aisle. The woman was beautiful and appeared to be in her thirties, while her boyfriend looked much younger, maybe early to mid twenties.

The woman abruptly got up and began walking to the back of the plane. Jessi couldn't believe her eyes! She did a double-take just to be sure, but she had seen that face so much in the last thirty-six hours that it was engraved on her brain.

When Lilly McLaughlin disappeared into the lavatory, Jessi returned her scrutiny to the boyfriend. He rose to his feet and headed down the aisle, repeating the same path as Lilly. Sure enough, it was Brett Buckley.

They made eye contact as he strolled by, but luckily he didn't recognize her. He followed Lilly into the lavatory. Jessi decided it would be a good time to freshen up. She would act like she was waiting in line for the restroom and then cut them off at the pass.

She put her ear up to the door, which was marked *Occupied.* She heard crashing sounds and muffled screams that she doubted were related to turbulence. The sound was familiar, but it had been so long she didn't recognize it immediately. To be specific, it was her last boyfriend in New York—an actor named Jeremy, who decided to take the word of tabloid newspapers over her own in the Callahan scandal—over two years ago.

After about ten minutes, the door folded open, almost tearing off Jessi's earring in the process. Nobody ever said journalism wasn't a rough business. Out came Lilly McLaughlin, walking gingerly, a pleased smile on her face. Her hair was a mess and her T-shirt, that she wore casually with painted-on jeans, was on inside out, the tag exposed. *There must be a strong turbulence in the bathroom,* Jessi thought to herself with a smile.

She politely apologized to Jessi for almost bumping into her and returned to her seat. Jessi turned back to the lavatory door and watched as the sign clicked back to *Occupied.*

She thought to follow Lilly back to her seat and confront her. But she decided to wait for Brett. She had always done much better with men, and couldn't remember ever having a female friend. Either way, nobody was getting off this plane without giving her an interview.

The door flashed *Vacant* and whipped open. With blinding speed, a hand reached out and grabbed her by her blonde mane and forcefully snatched her into the lavatory.

Jessi was staring straight into Brett Buckley's intense eyes, their bodies pushed together and their faces just inches apart. He pulled the door shut.

Occupied.

Chapter 64

"Are you following us?" Brett asked sternly.

They were inches from each other in the crammed bathroom. For once, she was speechless, unprepared for the sneak attack.

"You're that reporter, right? The one who outed Lilly and me."

She extended her hand the best she could in such close quarters, and introduced herself, "Jessi Stafford—Channel-6 News—and yes, I am the one who broke the story about you and your teacher."

A smile came over his face. "I can't be this lucky."

Jessi threw up her hands. "I don't know what rumors you've been reading about me, but I don't make a habit of making it with wanted fugitives." Although, with his looks, she figured she could do much worse.

"The only thing I want to give you is the story of a lifetime."

Jessi's ears perked up. He really knew how to sweet-talk a girl. "I'm listening."

His voice lowered to a whisper, "We have to be very careful because if she finds out that I know…"

"Who finds out what?"

Brett took a couple deep breaths as if he wasn't sure he should continue. Jessi radiated her most comforting look, and urged, "Go on."

He nodded. "Let me start from the beginning. My name isn't Brett Buckley, it's Nick Zellen. The reason for the name change was that I witnessed the murder of Karl Zellen."

Now it was Jessi's turn to count her blessings. The Alexei Sarvydas case had made national headlines. "He was murdered by the son of the famous record producer," she clarified.

"Viktor Sarvydas is a lot more than a record producer. He is one of the most dangerous organized crime figures in the world. That's why I was in Arizona as part of the Witness Protection Program."

"But if you were being protected, I don't understand why you felt compelled to run."

"In recent weeks my cover was blown. I had no choice."

"How was it blown?"

"There's a leak in the US Attorney's Office. Someone who works for Sarvydas. And now I have proof."

He took out a cell phone and handed it to Jessi. "Her name is Dava Lazinski, and she goes by the codename of Kelli. She is the one who coordinated with the McLaughlins to lure me to Sarvydas."

"When you say McLaughlins, plural, are you saying that Darren McLaughlin is involved in this, too?"

"Take a look at this." Nick showed her his evidence—photos on the phone of the Dava/Kelli woman he believed to be leaking information. The picture was a group photo in a bar with her arms wrapped around Darren and another man, also wearing a pilot uniform.

"Who is the other guy?" Jessi asked.

"I'm not sure. It's Lilly's cell phone. I was just able to snatch it from her purse while I had her distracted. What other reason would she have a picture like that? Plus, she claimed she got rid of the phone in the bags we checked at the airport. I also found a bunch of text messages between Dava and Lilly. I couldn't figure out how they tracked us everywhere we went—Dantelli's house, Red Menace, and then to Oklahoma."

Jessi slipped the phone into her purse. "So what now—do you want me to go live with the story?"

"They'll kill my sister if this gets exposed—I need to get to New York to secure her safety before you can report any of this. But I want you to keep the phone as insurance. Hopefully Lilly won't notice it's gone until we're off the plane."

"Tell me how I can help you."

"Lilly is using my need to get back to my sister against me. She's acting like I'm leading the way to New York, but I'm really playing into her hands. That's where Sarvydas' home base is—Brighton Beach. According to the dialogue between Lilly and Dava, they're planning to lure me to Natalie Gold's premiere party at Sarvy's tonight."

"That is one of the hottest parties of the year—the place will be crawling with celebrities and media. Not exactly a smart place to harm you."

"It's actually the perfect place. They're going to use my sister as bait, and then make it look like I'm a renegade fugitive looking to avenge the murder of my family. It will look like self-defense on their part, on camera in front of a large group of people, so that there are no accusations leveled at Sarvydas. Read the texts in the phone, they should tell you everything else you need to know—I don't have time to go into all the details right now."

Jessi smiled. She saw where this was going. "So you want me to cover the premiere party, to make sure that the real story is told."

"Exactly. And for your trouble you'll get an exclusive interview with Nick Zellen/Brett Buckley right on the red carpet, where I will expose their contemptible plan on live TV. And by making myself so visible, I will create insurance for my sister and myself. Consider the cell phone a down payment, and if I don't show up alive at the premiere, then I want you to run with the information I provided you."

Holding onto a story like this was against Jessi's journalistic DNA, but an exclusive interview with the famed fugitive would be worth it.

Nick grabbed her tightly by the shoulders. "I have to get back to Lilly before she suspects anything. Do you understand what I just told you?"

Jessi nodded her head, more excited than scared.

"Good," he said, "because my life depends on you."

Chapter 65

Darren joined Becks in the cafeteria of the headquarters of the US Attorney's Office for the Southern District of New York. He had no appetite, and wondered if he ever would again, unable to get the gruesome photos out of his head. Becks, on the other hand, ate for the two of them.

It was early afternoon on Tuesday. Just thirty-six hours since Darren was in this same city, three thousand miles from home, watching his wife be abducted in what he thought was a local gang initiation. And now such a scenario would be inviting. The women abducted by the gangs were beaten and raped, but with the Russian mob, it seemed like that would just be the appetizer.

He had to save Lilly. She had betrayed him, he had come to grips with that, but she didn't deserve to be murdered. And if for no other reason, he had taken vows to protect in good times and bad. Taking a vow still meant something to him, and he planned to live up to his part, no matter the cost.

He had no idea how he would accomplish this, but two things were clear. First off, Becks mustn't be involved. He needed to get her home while she still had her sharp tongue. The other was that if he was going to find Lilly, he was going to have to do it himself. After this morning's events, he had even less faith in the authorities. And frankly, they seemed a little scared of this Sarvydas character.

After lunch, they were driven back to the airport in a parade of black SUVs, manned by federal marshals. It had the feel of a funeral procession, which perfectly captured the mood, and fit with the gray New York skies.

Darren and Becks were led into the airport, this time closely surrounded by the FBI agents, avoiding another shootout at the OK Corral.

As they moved to the gate area, Becks grabbed Darren's hand. "Thanks for sticking up for me. It's nice to know there's at least one honorable man left in the world."

"I wouldn't want you to lose that tongue. The world would miss your insightful comments," he said with a grin. She was starting to rub off on him, and he didn't know if that was good or bad.

She smiled back at him. "You mean like *incite* a riot?"

Darren returned to his serious nature. "You shouldn't have come. This is dangerous stuff, not a game. To use your term, we are really OOOL here. You have your whole life in front of you, and you're also too young to be as cynical as you are. I think you'll find that there are a lot of honorable guys in the world. This Nick … Brett … or whatever his name is, doesn't deserve you."

"I say we combine the names and call him Brick Zuckley, just for clarity," she said with a chuckle. She then matched his serious demeanor. "And I'm sorry about all the skank and slut comments I made. I was frustrated with the situation and I took it out on her. My emotions get the best of me sometimes."

The mention of Lilly glummed Darren's face.

Becks took notice. "Don't you do that."

"Do what?"

"Buy into those amateur scare tactics that Eicher dude tried to use on you."

"But those killers were on their tail. That's a fact—he didn't make up those pictures. And just the thought of that Zubov character near Lilly gives me chills."

"Think about it. If Lilly and Brick Zuckley were already caught, why was the Rabbi willing to have a shootout with a bunch of federal agents in front of JFK Airport, and threatening us if we don't help him out? Brick is an ass, but he's also smart and savvy, and has these Russian mobsters scared. I can tell by their faces."

It was a good pep talk, but it didn't allay Darren's fears as they boarded the plane. "Eicher thinks Lilly might be involved."

"Eicher was totally CYA'ing, and if you haven't forgot, he also thought you were involved. He couldn't even figure out if the Rabbi was working with Sarvydas, or if he set up his son, yet he had the gall to blame the federal marshal who was in charge of Brick."

Darren nodded. "You're pretty smart for a high school kid."

"I have good instincts when it comes to people. I sat in your wife's class every day for three months and I got to observe her. I know her better than Eicher ever will. And while she might not be an innocent victim, she isn't working with the Russian mob."

"I hope your instincts are right."

"I was right about you," she said with a smile. She then gave him a glomp, which she explained was a non-sexual hug, but more for a friend than a hug with your grandparents, and veered toward her seat in coach.

Darren was escorted to the cockpit. He was looking forward to returning home, where he would figure out a strategy to find Lilly.

The entire flight crew was present, except for one—Treadwell. Darren figured that he was still out with Kelli, and would soon return to regale them with tales of how he "buzzed her tower."

Darren almost smiled to himself—who would've ever thought he would have a more eventful day than Treadwell? Who was the boring one now? A secret meeting with the FBI, a shootout in front of the airport, and a van ride from hell with a couple of psychotic Russian mobsters. And Treadwell could never again say that Darren never went to any of the hip clubs—he couldn't wait to tell him of his VIP trip to Sarvy's.

Minutes turned into a half-hour, and Treadwell was still AWOL. Darren grew apprehensive, as did the passengers. Tensions grew to the point that a fight was about to break out because someone had occupied the bathroom for the duration of the delay.

Screams suddenly filled the cabin. They were the type of primal screams usually reserved for strong turbulence or when the plane experienced a sharp drop in altitude. Darren ran to the back, pushing through the crowded aisle. The passengers were evacuating toward the front of the plane like a hurricane warning had been issued for the rear.

Darren fought his way through the crowd to the lavatory. The door had been wedged open, allowing him a perfect view of what was inside.

Ron Treadwell's lifeless body was propped onto the toilet with a butcher knife jammed between his eyes. Connected to the knife handle was a note that read:

I thought I told you not to talk to the feds, McLaughlin.

Chapter 66

Dava got off the plane in New York, non-stop from Oklahoma City. With the Mays' untimely passing, they were unable to sign-off on the exhumation. The US Attorney's Office was sending a team of lawyers to Oklahoma, but it would take weeks to get through the red tape. So on orders from Eicher, Dava returned home.

LaPoint stayed behind to head the murder investigation of Reverend Mays and his wife. The initial analysis of the coroner was that they were suffocated to death. Dantelli and Bachynsky were dead, Nick was on the run, and now they wouldn't be able to get to the mystery of Rachel Grant's hands. For Dava, it was a job well done.

The moment her plane touched down on the tarmac, she checked her messages. The first one was from Eicher. Alexei's lawyers had filed a motion to have his case thrown out of court and he didn't sound hopeful.

LaPoint had sent her numerous messages from Oklahoma. He had gotten a search warrant for Kovalenko's plane that was parked overnight in Dallas—the same airport Nick and Lilly had been traced to. They found him and his pilot tied-up and gagged in the luggage compartment.

Kovalenko didn't claim to be simply traveling on business, or play the ignorance card, as he normally did when questioned by the feds. According to LaPoint, he concocted a story that Lilly McLaughlin and Nick had come to his restaurant in Denver, seeking him out. He claimed that Lilly shot Bachynsky and forced him at gunpoint to fly them to Dallas. LaPoint was skeptical, to say the least.

Dava wanted to blow off his messages, but it was a crucial time for her—nothing could seem out of the norm. Dava always promptly returned messages. So she called him, planning to play to his ego by agreeing with his theory. But he blindsided her with a new twist.

"We just got word of two airline tickets purchased with a credit card we've connected to Rob Bachynsky. The flight originated in Dallas, stopped for a brief layover in Chicago, and should be arriving at JFK any minute. I have confirmed that a couple matching the description of Nick and Lilly is on the flight—it sure as hell isn't Bachynsky. I think it's time we had a little talk with our favorite runaways."

Before signing off, LaPoint provided her their gate information. Nick would be arriving any minute—at the very airport she stood in. *Could this day fall into place any better?* She would have him on a plane heading for a meeting with Viktor by the end of the day.

She tried to reach Eicher, but he was still hung up in court. So she took matters into her own hands, hurrying toward Nick's gate, flashing her US Attorney's badge to clear the way. She pictured the look on his face when he saw her waiting for him.

But as she neared the gate, an NYPD captain, flanked by a posse of airport security, approached her. She was surrounded. *Had something gone wrong? Was LaPoint onto her and sent her to the gate to set her up?*

"Attorney Lazinski?" the police captain named Ziegler addressed her.

"Yes," she answered, heart racing. She was carrying a weapon, but she would never get out of the airport alive. And being arrested would be a worse option than dying in a hail of bullets—Viktor and his son couldn't afford to risk her talking, so it would be a death sentence. Just more painful.

"Could you come with us? We have an important matter we need your assistance on," Ziegler said, a hint of urgency in his voice. The whole place seemed on edge.

Assistance sounded non-threatening, but they could be deceiving her to avoid a public conflict. "What does this matter pertain to?" she asked, holding her voice steady.

"There has been a murder on an airliner. A pilot. Your office believes it might be connected to a trial you are working and gave us a heads-up that you had just arrived."

"Why do they think it's related to my case?"

"If you come with us, we think it will be very clear to you."

Dava let out a sigh of relief as she trailed the men to the crime scene. She couldn't risk turning them down, but she had one eye locked on the gate where Nick would be arriving shortly. She needed to make this fast and get back to him.

The plane had been evacuated. The authorities in the gate area were questioning the passengers. Ziegler led her back to the rear lavatory and showed her Ron Treadwell—Darren McLaughlin's best friend—who had a butcher knife lodged in his head.

They handed her the note: I thought I told you not to talk to the feds, McLaughlin.

Dava moved to the body and appeared to be examining it. "Looks like the work of the Russians, no doubt."

"Ron Treadwell, forty years old from Chandler, Arizona. He was the pilot. No criminal record. Not sure how he relates to the Russian mob," Ziegler stated curiously.

"There are confidential items I can't discuss, due to witness protection," Dava deflected, but she was concentrating more on the pocket of Treadwell's jacket. She removed his cell phone and stealthily slipped it into her jacket pocket. The phone contained the pictures and messages from Kelli. She couldn't help but to feel like someone was watching over her today.

Now she needed to get to Nick. She complimented Ziegler on how he had things so fabulously under control, and explained that she needed to leave for important business, but they would touch base later in the afternoon. They shook hands and she was off.

The place was now swarming with federal agents—many were Dava's colleagues. She greeted a few of them as she tried to pass through the gate area, but while getting to Nick and Lilly was top priority, it was more important not to arouse suspicion. She would catch up with them soon enough, and she was confident she would beat Parmalov to them. Although, she had to admit that this strike on Treadwell was an impressive move by Parmalov and his people. It was acting as the perfect distraction, throwing her off the main goal—to get to Nick.

Suddenly phones began ringing and beepers started going off. It was an emergency of some sort. She couldn't help but wonder if the commotion was because they had learned of a double-agent named Dava Lazinski, who worked for the Sarvydas family.

Chapter 67

"It's Zubov," shouted an FBI agent. "He's in the airport."

Dava held back a sigh of relief.

They now had their number one suspect in Treadwell's murder. But once again, they were thinking on the surface, in direct contrast to the Russian Mafiya. Viktor had often told her that the FBI was playing checkers, while the Russians were mastering chess. They had the wrong guy … again.

Dava followed. Not doing so would be deemed peculiar behavior, especially since this was obviously connected to her case. She took one last look at Nick's empty gate, feeling conflicted.

They spotted Zubov just outside of a Hudson News in a wheelchair, wearing a wig of long hair and the look of a homeless man. "Freeze," yelled the FBI leader.

Zubov, always the contrarian, began wheeling away with impressive speed. Dava assumed the wheelchair was a prop, but she couldn't imagine him going any faster on foot. He bowled over travelers and cut corners like a speed skater. He expertly maneuvered the chair down an escalator, and wheeled toward the baggage claim. Where he was headed was anybody's guess.

Crowds continued to clear. Taking a shot at him was a near impossibility. He was swerving left and right at high speed and used the crowds as cover. The FBI looked like bullies chasing a handicapped man.

Zubov plowed past security. He was heading toward international flights. Dava now understood. It was brilliant.

Zubov continued toward an Air Israel flight that was deplaning. This plane carried Israeli pop star Natalie Gold—the latest protégée of Viktor Sarvydas.

They all came to a stop at the ropes that were set up to wall off the slobbering media, along with clashing fans and protestors. Zubov was able to use the mob of spectators as a blocker to move safely to the gate area.

Natalie Gold exited her plane, surrounded by a halo of charisma. She was also encircled by a cluster of men wearing military fatigues, and carrying assault rifles—not something normally seen in the United States. If Zubov planned to harm the pop star then it was up to these sharpshooters to protect her. The FBI could do nothing now.

But there would be no confrontation. Natalie headed right toward Zubov. She bent down and hugged him as he remained in his chair, a large smile on her face. *She sings, she dances, she hugs the handicapped!*

Their joyful reunion was short-lived. The FBI moved in and took Zubov into custody. Dava would join the federal team in interrogating Zubov.

Nick and Lilly would have to wait. She would catch up with them later.

Chapter 68

Eicher met Dava outside the interrogation room deep beneath JFK Airport. Even though their case was looking hopeless, it was still nice to see a friendly face. He hadn't seen her since yesterday afternoon, and since they had spent practically every working day together for the past year, he was feeling a little separation anxiety.

He'd come straight from court. The defense made a motion to drop the case, based on the whole rigmarole of the last couple of days. The judge said he would take the motion under advisement and have a ruling in the near future. Based on the stern lecture Eicher received about the "reckless circus atmosphere" the judge believed he was responsible for, he wasn't feeling confident.

After he informed Dava of the latest undoing, she filled him in on everything from Oklahoma to Ron Treadwell's murder, and the Zubov wheelchair race through the airport.

Eicher bounced his theory off Dava, the one about Parmalov trying to take control of the Sarvydas Empire.

Dava didn't seem so sure. "Then Zubov wouldn't be a suspect in the Treadwell murder, unless he swapped sides. And if he did, it wouldn't make sense for him to kill Dantelli, because Parmalov would want a trial to put Alexei away, and Dantelli would need to be alive to testify at it. Plus, Zubov picked up Natalie Gold, who is Sarvydas' latest protégé, and word would have trickled back to Sarvydas by now if he'd switched teams. So the only possibility with your theory is that Zubov didn't kill Treadwell, and that doesn't seem to add up."

Eicher nodded, soaking in her words. He hated it when she was so logical. *And right!*

They walked into the interrogation room and were greeted by Ziegler from the NYPD. A couple of FBI agents were also present.

Eicher scanned the room. He first noticed Natalie Gold, who lived up to expectations, at least physically. Even the long flight from Israel didn't diminish her beauty or wrinkle her miniscule dress. A singer must have good lungs, and she sure had those too.

He didn't want to take his eyes off her. Not because of her beauty—it was a ploy to avoid having to look into Zubov's soulless eyes. Just being in the same room with him made Eicher's skin crawl.

Natalie Gold spoke first, "My lawyer is on his way. If this is what America is all about, then no wonder people around the world are always burning your flag."

"Mr. Zubov is a lead suspect in a murder case, which makes you an accessory," Eicher fired back.

"I know nothing of any murder. But I do know that Zubov was sent to pick me up by Viktor Sarvydas, a man you Americans have treated with utter disrespect, despite all he's done for your country."

"Yeah, he's some hero," Eicher quipped, then found the courage to face the man in the suit. He looked like your average business traveler—having shed his disguise—but Eicher had seen his type of business in many gruesome crime scene photos. It was the work of the devil.

"So what are you really doing here, Zubov?" Eicher asked in his most forceful voice, fighting off any signs of weakness.

"How many times do I have to tell you? You think if you keep telling a rabbit he's a pig he will oink."

"Just humor me, Bugs."

Zubov dramatically sighed. "I arrive on flight from Denver. My job is to pick up Natalie at gate. I arrive early because your friends come after me."

"Denver? That's an interesting coincidence, because Rob Bachynsky was murdered in Denver last night."

"That's too bad. But you know how Rob liked to play the ladies, especially the married ones. I knew eventually one of those angry husbands would get him."

"I think you killed him."

"How could I kill anyone in my position. I'm handicapped."

"Why are you in a wheelchair?"

"Skiing accident—was on vacation in Colorado. I wasn't there to kill some dumb cop."

The comment sent the normally cool Dava over the edge. "You're lying, you son of a bitch!"

He laughed, further infuriating her.

Eicher gave her a calming look. No good could come of fighting this monster.

"Show me your knees," Eicher demanded.

"I don't give it up on the first date," Zubov replied with a grin.

"Our lawyer is going to have a field day with you, Eicher. And then I'm going to trash you in the press tonight for your police brutality," Natalie snarled. "Your ignorance will be headlines around the world tomorrow."

He ignored her. Although, he did notice that her accent had transformed since she arrived. She had been in America for less than an hour, but had picked up a slight twang that might be found in the Great Plains or Northern Texas. Interesting, but he moved on. This was about Zubov, not Natalie Gold.

"Skiing in Colorado after spending your morning in Las Vegas? I'm jealous. Sarvydas must take good care of you—what's your position again?" Eicher knew Zubov was too smart to deny being in Vegas, aware that the casino cameras picked up his every move.

"I am Director of Human Resources at Sarvy Music," he said with a grin—he was enjoying this, no doubt. He pushed a business card across the table, which Eicher examined.

"Director of Human Resources, that's a good one," Eicher mocked. "Did you know that while you were in Vegas, Officer Dantelli had an unfortunate accident in his pool?"

"Perhaps he don't wait hour to swim after eating. My mother always told me that."

Eicher pushed a couple photos back at him. They were of Dantelli's decapitated body.

Zubov admired his work. Then bellowed, "How do you get a guinea out of the pool?"

Receiving no response, he answered his own joke, "Throw in bar of soap." He laughed so hard he almost tipped his wheelchair over.

Eicher calmly pushed more photos across the table. "It seems you were his last visitor."

The smile wiped from his face as he looked at the photo of him entering. "Right after Nick Zellen and Lilly McLaughlin were there. No wonder I couldn't find Dantelli to say hello. They must have killed him before I got there."

Eicher rose to his feet and began pacing. "I understand why you killed Dantelli and Bachynsky, but I'm confused by Ron Treadwell, the pilot."

"I don't know what you speak of, but I do admit my doctor tell me to lose a couple pounds. He said maybe I should ron on a treadwell."

"Tell us why you killed him!" Dava jumped back into the tiger cage.

"Check the surveillance videos, lady" he sneered. "I got off my plane and went right to Natalie's gate. I have no time for other things. Everybody knows I have killed a lot of people," he wagged his finger, "but I have *never* killed an innocent person! This Ron Treadwell you speak of sounds like an innocent person."

Eicher was about to follow up about the note left in Treadwell's skull, when the doors swung open and a portly man in a rumpled suit barged in like he owned the place. His balding head glared from the sharp lighting of the interrogation room.

Eicher groaned.

Chapter 69

"Don't answer that question!" famed trial lawyer Barney Cook shouted out.

Zubov didn't seem happy that someone was raining on his parade. "Go fuck yourself, Barney. I'll answer any question I want."

"Like it or not, Zubov, I'm your lawyer. And Mr. Sarvydas says you won't answer that question."

"I only take orders from the don's son these days."

"I'm hired by the entire Sarvydas estate, and you will not answer."

Zubov quieted. Even he didn't cross Sarvydas.

Cook supplied airport surveillance tapes, which confirmed that Zubov was never near the airline in which Treadwell was murdered. He laughed off Eicher's assertion that wearing a disguise indicated flight, and therefore, guilt.

Zubov butted in, "I'm a celebrity. I need to wear disguise for privacy. People are always bugging me, please sign an autograph, Zubov—please kill my wife for me, Zubov—it gets very tiring."

Natalie stood, and moved to a pushing position behind Zubov. They were walking out of here and they knew it, even if one of them would do it in a wheelchair. But before they did, Cook and Eicher's cell phones simultaneously rang. Eicher listened to the news and his face sunk. He avoided any eye contact with Dava, who appeared eager to hear the news. He couldn't bring himself to tell her.

Cook spoke for him, "That was the judge. Alexei Sarvydas is being released—the case has been dismissed."

Natalie immediately began wheeling Zubov toward the door. "We have to go pick up Alexei. He is going to be my date to my party tonight."

Zubov craned his head back toward Eicher and Dava. "I just want to remind you one more time. I have never killed an innocent person."

"What do you want, a medal?" Dava fired back at him. "Now get out of my face!"

When they were gone, Dava marched toward the door.

"Where are you going?" Eicher asked.

"I'm going to find Nick. This thing isn't over yet!"

Chapter 70

In the midst of the chaos, Darren and Becks were able to slip out of the plane unnoticed. But the gate area was overcrowding with police and airport security—there was no way to avoid them. Darren knew he didn't have time for their inquiries about Treadwell's death—he needed to get to Lilly before she ended up with a similar fate.

As if repulsed by the sight of him, the authorities began running in the opposite direction. Darren had no idea where they were headed, but wasn't complaining. It was the small miracle that he needed.

He wasn't sure of his next move, but Becks was decisive. She declared airport security to be the dumbest organism on the planet, and began marching their way out of the airport, pretending her South Chandler High ID was the badge of a federal air marshal. They were let through, without even a request to look at the credentials.

They ran out of the airport and hopped into a cab at almost the same spot where the earlier shootout took place. When the cabbie asked them where to, Darren replied, "Brighton Beach." He knew that's where this whole thing was headed. Where everything would be decided, one way or another. He knew he had to plant his feet and fight back. There was no other choice.

"Moscow on the Hudson, here we come," the driver replied. "Any place in particular?"

"Sarvy's," Becks said, catching on.

"That's the place to be tonight. You big Natalie Gold fans?" the driver asked.

"I love her song 'Vengeance'," Becks replied. "We're all about vengeance today. It's kind of our theme."

They couldn't get within five blocks of Sarvy's—the area had been secured for the Natalie Gold's arrival. The driver dropped them under an elevated subway track, near an enormous housing project. He provided them with directions, and they headed toward Sarvy's on foot. A light rain began to fall.

Brighton Beach, or Little Odessa as the driver called it, was a place of great highs and lows. The oceanfront of the Atlantic was lined with gaudy art deco apartments. Flashy Mercedes sped the streets, and Armani-clad men shopped the boardwalk with gold-draped women. But a block later, it turned into infested crack houses and decaying clapboard homes.

There was one consistent theme—*Russian, Russian, Russian.* Darren was convinced that Moscow was less Russian than Brighton Beach. The storefronts were labeled in Russian, and it was the preferred language of the street. Darren thought there were a lot of guns in Arizona, but in Brighton they seemed as common as wearing a watch.

They passed the pushcart vendor who was responsible for their "arrest." He winked at them. Darren felt another attack of paranoia coming on—nobody was who they seemed.

They arrived at Sarvy's, which already had a parade of limos out front, despite the party being hours away. The men were dressed in tuxedos, accompanied by plastic blondes in low-cut evening gowns. And of course, gold was everywhere. This was not the trendy/celebrity crowd that would show up later, this was standard Brighton Beach.

Darren realized that they weren't getting in to the club with their current outfits. The pilot uniform wasn't going to cut it. So when in Russia, do as the Russians do. They found a nearby high-end clothing store where Darren purchased a tuxedo, while Becks was fitted for a silk chiffon dress that cascaded to the floor. When Darren met her yesterday she was a high school kid trudging around in flip-flops, and a day later it looked like it was her wedding day. They grow up so fast.

They came across a street vendor selling gold, and they strung all they could afford around themselves. The vendor proudly told them the jewelry was stolen. Thievery seemed to be a source of pride in these parts.

Looking the part, they were able to gain entrance into the club. The same bouncers frisked them as earlier, yet they went unrecognized in their new duds. They passed the weapons inspection, but Darren got the idea that maybe they should have thought twice about not being armed.

They walked inside to find the reconstruction project complete. The cavernous room had been transformed into a laser-light-show extravaganza with elaborate stage and video screen. There was no shortage of food, drink, or drug.

Becks went right to a beefy guard and demanded to see Parmalov. He claimed not to know of any such person, and walked away.

She would not be so easily deterred. She shot up onto the stage where Natalie Gold would perform later, and grabbed the microphone. "The Russian mob is red, the police are blue, and Parmalov I've come for you!" she shouted into the PA system, before the guards could even figure out their response.

Becks wasn't done. She showed off impressive karaoke abilities, belting out The Beatles classic "Back in the USSR" without any accompanying music. It seemed an appropriate choice.

Darren thought she was either the gutsiest or craziest person he'd ever met. Maybe both. He was initially frozen by fear, but a vision of Treadwell popped into his head. He remembered his words about being a caveman, which inspired him to make a mad dash for the stage in an attempt to save her. But a group of Parmalov's men met him there, and put an end to his heroism.

"You're going to get your wish. Mr. Parmalov will see you now," one guard said.

"I thought you didn't know who he was," Becks shot back.

The guard smiled fiendishly. "When he gets done with you, you're going to wish I was right."

Chapter 71

Lilly held Nick's hand as they deplaned in New York. It was a cross-country chase that had taken them from Arizona to Las Vegas to Denver, with a stopover in Dallas/Oklahoma, and would end with a headfirst dive into the Sarvydas' shark tank in Brighton Beach.

But Lilly knew that she couldn't have talked Nick out of it even if she'd wanted to. He was desperate to get home to try to protect Sasha.

Lilly stepped into the gate area, still clutching onto Nick. The first thing she noticed was the chaos—something was going on in the airport. A tension hung in the air, and a large police presence was detectable.

It was too late to turn around, so they confidently stepped forward. Lilly straightened her posture, and walked confidently into the unknown.

The chaotic scene seemed to slightly unnerve Nick, but he calmly asked a security guard, "What's all the commotion?"

The large man replied in a robust whisper. "Found a pilot dead on one of the planes."

"Dead?" Lilly inquired further.

The guard shrugged. "There are rumors that he was murdered, but you didn't hear that from me. My guess is he killed himself. These pilots sometimes live some lonely lives. If he was suicidal, I'm just glad he wasn't flying my plane."

As they spoke with the guard, something caught her eye. A tall blonde woman strolling carelessly through the terminal.

She whispered, “Isn’t that the reporter who put our picture on the TV, Jessi something-or-other?”

Nick said nothing, but his startled look confirmed her thoughts. He tightened the grip on her hand and pulled her out of the gate area, almost pulling her shoulder out of the socket in the process.

Lilly didn’t think it was by chance that a reporter who’d been tracking them across the country ended up in the same airport terminal. But the woman took a turn in the opposite direction without even a glance their way. Lilly watched as she disappeared into the crowd.

There was no time for relief. Around the next corner, both she and Nick recognized the man in the wheelchair. He wore a wig like he was some mustached cross-dresser. When you stand close enough to the Grim Reaper, you never forget his face. Lilly also knew the wheelchair wasn’t a total disguise. She had shot this man’s knees out.

“Zubov,” she whispered.

But he had other issues to deal with—the authorities began heading toward him, his disguise transparent. Despite the overwhelming numbers against him, Lilly still thought Zubov was the safe bet to prevail.

They weren’t going to hang around to find out. They exited the airport, passing mobs of screaming teenagers who had come to greet the arrival of their hero, Natalie Gold.

Nick found a limo service driver whose client failed to show, and he agreed to take them to the Zellen estate in Sands Point, Long Island.

Once settled in the vehicle, the first thing Lilly noticed was that her cell phone was missing. She went over in her mind where she could have left it—the most likely scenario was that it had fallen out of her pocket in her haste. And one particular instance came to mind. “I think I dropped my cell phone in the bathroom when we were…”

Nick grinned. “And they say phone sex isn’t as good as the real thing.”

Lilly bristled. “That’s not funny.”

“What’s the big deal? It’s just one of the throwaways you got in Vegas.”

Lilly bit her lip, mulling over the consequences of losing her phone.

As they hit the Long Island Expressway, passing over the Throgs Neck Bridge, they morphed into the doldrums. After all the excitement of the last forty hours, sitting in New York traffic just wasn't feeding the monster.

Through the intercom, Lilly asked the driver to turn on the radio. He put on the all-news station *1010 WINS* just in time for a breaking news story that a pilot named Ron Treadwell had been found dead at JFK Airport. No details had been released at this point, but there was speculation that it was linked to the airport shooting earlier in the day.

Lilly felt sick. She thought of Darren's kooky but loyal friend—the one responsible for bringing them together. She prayed silently for Darren's safety. She knew she could do nothing to stop the pain she had already caused him, but she couldn't live with herself if he suffered a similar fate as Ron.

"Are you okay?" Nick asked with a concerned look, drawing her close.

She told him that she was. What was another lie at this point?

The other breaking news from JFK was that pop star Natalie Gold had arrived on American soil. Her high-profile arrival was complicating an already turbulent scene at the airport.

Nick's thoughts seemed to go to a faraway place. But the next news item snapped him back to reality.

Alexei Sarvydas had been released from prison.

Chapter 72

Nick put his phone away, looking disgusted. "She's still not answering!"

Lilly attempted to put her arm around him, but he rebuffed her.

"Sasha has been able to survive this year without protection, and she even worked out that secret meeting with you in Arizona. She's tough, gutsy, and I'm sure, safe."

"She needs protection from herself."

"What do you mean by that?"

"She's going to the Natalie Gold premiere party tonight at Sarvy's. When I called her from the road last night, she told me what she planned to do. She is so damn stubborn—once she sets her mind on something, it's impossible to talk her out of it."

Lilly's look turned inquisitive. "Why would she do that? She knows what Sarvydas did to your parents, and that his people will be there, right?"

"I'm afraid she's going to go after Sarvydas' people."

"But wouldn't that be suicidal?"

His face turned determined. "That's why I need to get to her ASAP, to put a stop to it. There will only be one Zellen representing my family at that party, and it will be me."

"Are you sure?"

"I'm tired of running and hiding. I need to face them head on. If they want to kill me, then so be it, but I will not run. I'm not a coward."

Lilly ran her hand over his arm. "Running hasn't been all bad, has it?"

He kissed her deeply, then smiled. "If I die, I will die a happy man."

She hugged him as tight to her body as she could.

They sat in silence for moments, before Nick said, "You didn't try to talk me out of it."

"I know you need to do this."

"Really?" he replied with a half smile. "I was kind of hoping you'd try to talk me out of it."

She returned the smile. "I think you just want to see that Natalie Gold chick. So being the jealous girlfriend that I am, I'm going with you."

He tried to dissuade her, but Lilly would have none of it, "Just like you need to do this, so do I. We are in this together."

Nick nodded, his face grim.

"What's wrong?" Lilly asked, feeling it went beyond his inability to contact Sasha.

"It's Audrey."

Just the name filled Lilly with mixed emotions. "What about her?"

"I think she's alive."

"Because they are digging up her grave? Remember what her father said—even if that isn't her in the cemetery, they still haven't seen or heard from her in a year. Something happened to her."

"It wasn't that."

"Then what?" Lilly asked intently.

"Just a feeling I got when I was in her room."

Lilly could tell he was holding something back, but she didn't push the issue.

They drove through heavy gates and up the long driveway of the Zellen estate. Nick ordered the driver to drop them off at a cobblestone courtyard, in front of the largest house Lilly had ever seen. With its thickly mortared brick walls and steeply pitched roofs, it had a medieval feel to it. To add to the wow factor, it was built right on the cliffs of Long Island Sound.

"I should have held out for a better deal," the driver said with a smile, observing the compound. Nick wasn't listening—he was already running toward the mansion. Lilly paid the driver with the rest of their traveling money and ran after him.

Nick dashed inside, yelling "Sasha!" at the top of his lungs.

Lilly followed him into the house. The interior was equally spectacular—she passed through an indoor garden, before entering an opulent hall that had a Gatsbyian feel to it. It was filled with expensive woodcarvings and lined with paintings from the 16th and 17th centuries. Lilly remembered that Karl Zellen was an art connoisseur.

But the room also was filled with the trappings of a teenager living there alone. Sasha's ice skates were scattered on the floor, along with numerous fast food wrappers and DVD cases.

Nick ran up a spiral staircase. "Sasha!" he yelled again.

He burst into a room, practically breaking down the door. Lilly followed close behind.

The scene before them was not pretty. Sasha was lying naked on the bed, her wrists tied with rope and her mouth gagged with a scarf.

Nick ran to her and removed the gag. He covered her body with a comforter. "Who did this to you?" he demanded.

Before Sasha could answer, a voice rang out, "Hello, Nick. I've been looking all over for you."

A woman appeared from the shadows, holding a gun.

She smirked at Lilly, then formally introduced herself, "My name is Dava Lazinski and I am working on the Karl Zellen murder case for the US Attorney's Office."

Lilly guessed that Nick had found the leak. She was reminded of a lesson she'd learned from playing cards—the dealer always wins in the end.

Chapter 73

Darren and Becks were again in the Rabbi's office.

Parmalov was seated at his desk, the Moziafs standing behind him like two stuffed bears.

Just looking at them filled Darren with rage. Everything happened so fast at the airport that Treadwell's murder hadn't fully sunk in until now. But all he could do was to quietly stew. Any attempt at retribution would be hopeless.

Parmalov ordered the Moziafs into action, "Frisk them."

By frisk, he meant a full body search. Its uncomfortable nature was only eclipsed by the embarrassment. After they were re-dressed—Darren in his tux and Becks in her wedding-ish gown—Parmalov stood before them. "You didn't listen to me and it got your friend killed."

Darren just had to stand there and take it.

"One thing you'll learn about me, is that when I say something I mean it. Next time you'll remember that."

The Moziafs looked like they were betting against there being a next time.

"But because I'm such a nice guy, I'll give you one more chance," Parmalov continued. "Why have you returned? I don't remember inviting you to tonight's party."

Darren gulped. "I love my wife, no matter what she might have done. And I will do anything to bring her home safe. Eicher believes that you are secretly at war with Viktor Sarvydas, and trying to provide a safe journey for Nick so that he can testify against his son. I am here to help."

Parmalov tapped Darren lightly on the cheek and then returned to his position behind the desk. "Because you're being honest with me, I will return the favor. What Eicher says is true, but if you had listened to me the first time, we could have avoided that ugliness on the airplane."

Darren felt his blood boil, but remained silent.

"You are too late, I'm sorry. I am no longer motivated to find her, or her lover. I just learned that Alexei has been released from prison. We are now re-mobilizing our troops."

Darren knew that made them expendable. He only had one bargaining chip left. "I can offer information."

Parmalov looked interested. "In Russian we call you a *musor,* a snitch. The lowest form of life. What do you want in return?"

"I want my wife to be safe."

Parmalov nodded for Darren to continue.

"Eicher thinks you planted evidence at Karl Zellen's home. He theorized that the plan was for Alexei to kill Zellen, in which he succeeded, but you planted evidence to make sure he was caught."

Parmalov scoffed, "I did nothing of the sort. What I did was show Alexei the truth about what happened to his mother. Then I just sat back and enjoyed the show—Alexei's hotheaded nature was always his downfall. Yes, I was thrilled to see him rotting in prison, while his father was exiled to Israel. But I planted nothing!"

He sat back in his chair, displaying a poker face—*was he their executioner or savior?*

After a long silence, he offered, "I think I have figured out a way to save your wife."

Darren was all ears.

"My people will get to her and Nick first. The feds can't get out of their own way, and with Alexei freed, Viktor no longer has an urgency to find them. So when we do, I will allow your wife to live in exchange for you eliminating Nick."

That wasn't what Darren had in mind. Becks looked at him in horror. She might have talked tough about her high school boyfriend, but she really didn't want Nick to be killed.

"Why would you want Nick dead? He was on your side, trying to take down Alexei," Darren inquired.

"Nick is a Zellen. The Sarvydas and Zellen partnership killed my mentor, Vladimir Miklacz, and his daughter. Then they took what was rightfully mine. So now I'm going to eliminate both their families from the face of the earth."

Darren felt like he couldn't breathe, but he still found words, "So how do you want to do this?"

"A good old-fashioned duel in your wife's honor. Lilly will back up your story that it was self-defense, I can guarantee you that. Nick's sister will also be caught in the crossfire and tragically perish. It's a win-win—the last remaining Zellens are scrubbed from the face of the earth, and you get your wife back."

"You said nothing about the sister. If I take her out, then you must guarantee that nothing happens to Rebecca."

He nodded. "Then I believe we have a deal."

Becks didn't exactly look thrilled that Darren had bargained for her life. In fact, she looked like she wanted to kill Darren for even thinking about committing murder, no matter how dire the circumstances. A trip to the dark side was not one you come back from.

Without warning, a knock rattled the door. "US Attorney—open up now!"

Parmalov shot an accusatory look at Darren and Becks.

"I had nothing to do with this," Darren proclaimed.

"Your word is good with me, Mr. McLaughlin, but now you must prove your loyalty. You will stand in front of me for protection while Oleg blows the head off this fed."

It wasn't a request—Vana placed him in front of Parmalov, as he rose from his seat.

Oleg aimed at the door, looking excited.

Becks was forced to open the door. She had no choice. She turned the door handle.

Darren braced.

Chapter 74

In barged a woman holding up a gun and badge.

Shots were fired. But it wasn't the woman falling to the ground. It was Oleg Moziaf. He crashed to the floor with a perfectly placed bullet in his heart.

"I'm Dava Lazinski from the US Attorney's Office. And Stevanro Parmalov—you are under arrest."

"What charge?" he demanded, pushing Darren away.

"You have committed the worst possible crime—a crime against Viktor Sarvydas."

Darren felt a punch to the gut. He thought the woman was on their side, but she was working for Sarvydas.

Vana Moziaf tried to get to her dead husband, but Dava fired two shots into her chest. It didn't even seem to faze Vana, so Dava shot another one into her head and she crashed to the floor like a redwood.

Dava addressed Parmalov, "Now that I've got your attention—I have something you've been looking for."

She momentarily left the room, before returning with two prisoners that she held at gunpoint. They were chained together by their ankles and wrists. Dava slammed the door shut.

Darren's jaw dropped and the blood drained from his face.

He looked past Brick Zuckley—he meant nothing to him—and his gaze fell on his wife. He searched for something in her eyes—anything—that would explain what had happened. But while he saw regret, he couldn't find sorrow.

"Oh, Darren," she mumbled. It could have meant a million different things.

Parmalov interrupted the moment, "I must congratulate you on the Alexei Sarvydas case, Attorney Lazinski. I see you got the result you were looking for."

Darren's eyes never left Lilly. He noticed Zellen reaching out his hand to comfort her. She subtly looked away from Darren. It felt like a sledgehammer had slammed into his ribs.

His eyes moved to the woman from the US Attorney's Office. And suddenly he recognized her. It was Kelli—Treadwell's Kelli—and Darren grew aware that they'd been pawns from the beginning. It wasn't a matter of wrong place/wrong time, or just dumb luck. But what was he being set up for?

"What do you want?" Parmalov barked at her. His voice was confident, despite his lack of leverage.

"I'm here for Darren McLaughlin—he's coming with me."

Darren knew he needed to stand firm. These people thrived on weakness. "What if I refuse?"

"Then I will kill your wife right in front of you."

Darren's knees buckled. His stand had lasted a matter of seconds.

"Fine—take the three of them and get out of here," Parmalov cut his losses. "I don't ever want to see your face in this office ever again."

"You forget that you are a guest in Viktor Sarvydas' home. The man you are attempting to overthrow. Before I go, I must relieve you of your duties."

She raised her gun at Parmalov and was about to fire.

Darren looked at his wife, but for the first time his mind wasn't on her. It was on another female. *What happened to Becks?*

As if she had read his mind, she emerged from behind Parmalov's desk. She was holding one of the guns that the Moziafs had dropped, and looked like a deranged bride in her white dress.

Becks' reappearance momentarily diverted Dava's attention. It was like she noticed her for the first time.

"Federal Marshal, freeze!" Becks shouted.

Darren thought she was trying to pull the same stunt she performed successfully at the airport. A dangerous game to play with these killers.

Dava turned her gun toward Becks. "Hello, Fitzpatrick. Nice of you to join us."

"Drop the gun, Dava."

"You first, Fitzpatrick."

Darren was floored. He looked at Lilly once more, huddled close to Zellen. He no longer recognized her. Then at Becks, who wasn't really Becks. And finally at Kelli, who he thought he'd met by chance. Nothing was real anymore. *Or was it ever?*

The stare-down gained intensity, until Dava changed course. She made a swift ninety-degree turn and fired a shot into Parmalov's head. He slumped to the ground.

Before anyone could respond, Dava placed her gun on Lilly's temple.

Becks raised her gun.

"No Becks, don't," Darren shrieked.

"They're going to kill you, Darren, if you go with them. She's not worth it—she wouldn't do the same for you. I don't want anyone else to die here, but if I have to choose who lives, I'll choose you every time."

Darren couldn't let her do it. He moved in front of Lilly to act as a shield.

"Move out of the way, Darren. It's my job. I can't let her walk out of here without handcuffs. I'm gonna do what I have to do."

Darren stood firm, all six-foot-three of him. "Then you're going to have to shoot me."

She sighed. "Now you decide to stand up for yourself?"

Darren stood his ground.

Becks looked at him, and then at Dava. She shook her head in disgust and dropped her gun.

Dava took advantage. She raised the gun and pierced Becks' shoulder with a shot, staining her white dress red.

Becks grabbed her shoulder and cursed loudly.

"You're lucky, Fitzpatrick, that I don't kill federal agents," Dava hissed. "This mess is now yours to clean up. It will be my word against your disastrous record, and unfortunately for you, there will be no witnesses to back up your story—*ya nectevo ne znago.*"

Dava jabbed Darren in the ribs with her gun and angled him toward the door. She marched him, along with his wife and her lover, out of Sarvy's and into the unknown, leaving Becks at the altar.

Chapter 75

Eicher circled the witness like a shark. But this wasn't a courtroom. He was back in his office at Foley Square. He had three more dead bodies—Parmalov and the Moziafs—and he was now grilling the lead suspect.

"Can you drop the tough guy act? It's totally fugazy," the witness snapped. "You don't seem to understand—they're in danger!"

He glared at Fitzpatrick. "What I do understand is that any danger is the result of you not listening. You were told to remove the McLaughlin woman from Nick's life, and look how that ended up. I personally instructed you to grab some lunch and then to escort the husband back to Arizona. I didn't think it was too complicated a request, yet you ended up in a shootout in Brighton Beach. That's quite a detour."

"I planned on going back, but things changed."

"Things always change with you, Fitzpatrick, but never for the better."

"Parmalov's people had gotten past airport security and killed Ron Treadwell, who oh by the way, was Darren's best friend. He was at risk, so I made a call. And I stand by it."

"And your call was to go right to Parmalov without backup? Witnesses said you entered Sarvy's with McLaughlin, acting erratically, then publicly taunted Parmalov until you were granted a meeting. You were the aggressor and out of control. We found the cab driver that picked you up at the airport. He said you told him, and I quote, 'We are all about vengeance today.'"

"Oh c'mon, Eicher. I'd love to stake a claim to killing those murderers, but you *really* think I shot them?"

"The initial ballistics testing has come back, and surprise-surprise, the bullets found in the victims matched your gun."

"And I shot myself? I told you why the guns match—because the person who did the shooting was issued the same type of weapon!"

Eicher looked at Fitzpatrick's shoulder, heavily wrapped from the gunshot wound. She had removed her "wedding dress" and now wore a plain T-shirt and jeans, her pink-striped hair in a ponytail. He conceded that she was right on one thing—whoever shot her was the same person who shot Parmalov. But he refused to buy her story about Dava being involved, no matter how convincing she sounded.

"I worked with Dava Lazinski every day for a year. I know her better than I knew my ex-wife."

"Hence the ex part. I'm telling you the truth, and every second you continue to bury your head in the sand it increases the odds that there will be a sale on Nick at the Moziaf Butcher Shop."

"It would have to be a going-out-of-business sale, since they're dead."

"And I'll bet you think I killed them, also."

"No witness inside of Sarvy's saw anyone matching the description of Dava. And someone certainly would've noticed if a federal agent marched in there with Nick and Lilly chained like a couple of POWs. The Russians can spot a federal agent three continents away."

Fitzpatrick sighed. "Newsflash, Eicher, the Russians don't talk. *Ya nectevo ne znago.* And when they do, they lie!"

Eicher respected her passion—he was the same way when he started out as a prosecutor in his twenties. And the sad thing was, those days weren't that long ago, even if they seemed like a different lifetime. While he refused to consider the possibility of Dava's involvement, and thought Fitzpatrick had continued her trend of poor judgment, he didn't think she went on some vigilante murder spree. Nor did he think she was a liar.

There must have been something that would explain what Fitzpatrick thought she saw. He sought to shut down Sarvy's—Natalie Gold or no

Natalie Gold—to find the answer. But he had no influence. And that was before more dead bodies accumulated, with a rogue federal marshal playing the role of lead suspect.

"Maybe you should take a cue from the Russians—you talk way too much. And you also get too close to those you protect. Nick is exhibit-A, and now you're too close to this Darren McLaughlin."

"I was supposed to be Nick's girlfriend, it was part of the gig. And I happen to be worried about Darren because he's in real danger," she said, "but maybe I should become cold and detached like my father."

"Your father is a good man who wants the best for you. And besides, this has nothing to do with him—this is about you."

A light bulb seemed to go on. She snapped her fingers a couple times. "No, this is totally about parents."

Before Eicher could inquire into the meaning of her cryptic statement, a guest walked into his office. It was Ivan. Eicher was relieved he carried no ice chest this time.

"I talk to sources. The ones I most trust. A woman flashed the badge of Dava Lazinski, demanding to see Parmalov. She had two hostages who met description of Nick and his lady friend. They were chained like prisoners."

Eicher sat down slowly in his seat, stricken by Ivan's words. "Are you sure it wasn't someone who had gotten hold of her badge?"

Ivan shook his head. "They remember her from Brooklyn DA's Office, when she tried to take down a Sarvydas prostitution ring."

Dava had come to the US Attorney's office from the Brooklyn DA's Office, true, but the idea that she could be working for Sarvydas just wasn't computing.

Fitzpatrick didn't look especially relieved to hear the news, even if it backed her story. She appeared to be stuck on the eureka moment she had before Ivan arrived.

"I was wrong," she muttered. "I told Darren that parents suck more these days. But parents have always sucked."

Chapter 76

"Ivan, tell me about Nick's mother. You knew her, correct?" Fitzpatrick asked, as if an energy bolt had shot through her.

Ivan smiled. It was the same way Nick smiled when he talked about his mother. Paula Zellen had a way of eliciting that reaction.

"Her beauty was only eclipsed by her voice," he began. "She came to Brooklyn as a young girl from Canada. She was Paula Branche then. She would sing at local clubs as teenager. That's when Viktor Sarvydas discover her, and made her headline act at Sarvy's."

"She also began headlining in his bedroom, right?"

"Yes, but Viktor's bedroom wasn't most exclusive club, especially when it came to his protégés. That's what made Paula different."

"How so?"

"He was in love. He'd practically skip down Brighton Beach Avenue. But it had to remain hush-hush because of Trina and their child, Alexei."

Fitzpatrick looked mystified. "I don't get it. Sarvydas is one of the world's greatest plotters and strategists. Yet his ambush on Miklacz and his wife was a failure. It doesn't add up."

"What do you mean failure?" Eicher interjected. "He ended up becoming the don of the Russian Mafiya and one of the most powerful men in the world. And nobody could ever prove he was behind it."

Fitzpatrick shook her head. "I just spent six months in high school. And you know what I learned—it has the same dynamics as the Russian Mafiya. Both have certain codes that must be adhered to, to maintain the balance in the society. One common code is that the star quarterback always gets the prettiest cheerleader. Paula was the cheerleader, but she didn't end up with the quarterback—she ended up with his nerdy sidekick, Karl Zellen. It goes against the laws of high school, and the Russian mob."

"Most believe he have Trina killed to be with Paula. Sometimes man don't think straight when in love," Ivan said. "But then rumors began."

"They're not rumors when they're true," Fitzpatrick asserted.

Ivan nodded. "They were started by a Parmalov—he thought he should be king. Viktor wasn't untouchable like today—his power was fragile, at best, and wouldn't survive full-scale war. He needed to immediately squash rumors. That's why I think he push Paula to marry Zellen and have child. It put him in clear."

"But Sarvydas is a cake-and-eat-it-too kinda guy. And while he's always been brazen, he is never stupid. Taking out her father made sense, but killing Trina was stupid. Why not just maintain the affair with Paula? Mistresses for powerful Russian mobsters are as common as vodka and extortion. Trina was no threat to his power, even though she was a blood Miklacz. The Russians are chauvinists by nature, a woman would never become the don. Killing her made no sense, except…"

"I don't see where you're going with this, Fitzpatrick," Eicher said.

She ignored him. "She wouldn't have been a threat to his power once he got it, but what if she was a threat to him ever gaining power? What if she was about to kick Viktor to the curb at the time of the ambush? If he got booted out of the Miklacz family, he would lose his place in the succession line."

Eicher took the bait, "You think she was going to divorce him because she found out about the affair with Paula?"

"Affairs were accepted for Russian men of stature," Ivan agreed with Becks. "It would have to be something more. Some secret he need Trina to take to grave, before her father found out."

"Any ideas what that might be?" Eicher asked with exasperation.

"No—but I know who might," Fitzpatrick said.

"And who would that be?"

"Parmalov told Darren and me that he set things in motion by revealing the truth to Alexei about his mother's death, and then just sat back and watched the Sarvydases tear each other apart. I think Alexei was the one responsible for killing Paula Zellen. Who else would have access to that fortress of a mansion, where she was supposedly working on her music? And I don't think it was a coinkidink that it was done in the same manner that Viktor used to kill Alexei's mother."

Eicher never truly believed that Viktor was behind Paula's murder. If Viktor was going to take bullets for the show, they wouldn't be directed at his face. He was too vain.

He tried to piece Fitzpatrick's ramblings together. "So you're saying that after Parmalov confirmed Alexei's suspicions that Viktor murdered his mother, Alexei killed Paula for revenge—hitting Viktor where it hurts most. But Karl believed that Viktor was the one responsible for his wife's death, in response to his potential testimony, and was going to go after him. But Viktor beat him to the punch, by putting a hit on Karl before he could act. And for such a special job, he called on his son, and future heir, Alexei."

Fitzpatrick nodded. "But once again, Viktor was a step ahead. He secretly knew Alexei had betrayed him by killing Paula. So when Alexei did the deed on Zellen, his fingerprints were planted at the crime scene. My guess is Dantelli, Bachynsky, or both, were dirty, which is probably why they're dead. Alexei was set up to take the fall, and with a lot of time on his hands to think, even a simpleton like Alexei was able to figure out who set him up—his own father."

"He's getting set up again," Ivan said, catching on. "Viktor is returning favor of fake loyalty, just like Alexei did by accepting to do hit on Karl. By killing all evidence, it looks like Viktor freed him from prison—but it was all for show."

"They got him out of jail to kill him," Fitzpatrick stated emphatically.

Eicher cringed. “And he’ll go right to them. Alexei has said repeatedly that he knows who set him up and he’ll ‘take care of it.’ They’ll use his aggression against him. But what I don’t understand is why didn’t Viktor just have him killed when he learned about the betrayal. Why jump through all the hoops for the same result?”

A look came over Fitzpatrick’s face like she just solved the whole thing. She mumbled that she now knew why Viktor killed Trina, but provided no details. “Family is complicated,” she stated with a look of wonderment. She grabbed her jacket and headed for the door.

“Where do you think you’re going?” Eicher demanded, she was technically still in custody.

“I’m going to the Natalie Gold video premiere party. That’s where they plan to kill Alexei.”

Eicher grabbed his coat and followed. Ivan wished them well—he couldn’t afford to risk his cover. Then Eicher remembered something. “Zubov went with Natalie Gold to pick up Alexei. He is going to be her date tonight.”

“Zubov isn’t going to kill him,” Fitzpatrick said.

“Then who is?”

“Darren McLaughlin.”

Chapter 77

Jessi Stafford stood outside the club where the Natalie Gold premiere party was about to commence.

The GNZ cable news network had negotiated a deal with Channel-6 for exclusive rights to her reports on the case. What this deal did for Jessi was provide a car and cameraman upon her arrival in New York, along with a press pass for the party. And best of all, a budget to purchase a designer dress for the event and use of the best hair and make-up people in Manhattan.

She anchored the prime position right in front of the Sarvy's entrance, under its famed awning. She would have the last word with the glamorous celebrities before they entered the party. Not only had she clawed her way back to the top of the mountain, but she'd finally exchanged a monotonous news career for the exciting world of entertainment.

She could feel the buzz of energy as the stars rolled in—the streets had been blocked off, but that didn't stop the fans from showing up to display their love for Natalie Gold. Jessi was more interested in seeing someone else—Nick Zellen.

She nervously checked her watch, beginning to grow anxious about his arrival. But when she looked up, he appeared out of the blue like a superhero to save the day. He sure did clean up well, looking dapper in a black Hugo Boss suit. He was alone, which surprised her. The way he talked, she expected him to be surrounded by a posse of gun toting grease-balls ready to shoot him on command. The McLaughlins were nowhere to be seen, nor was the leaker, Dava Lazinski.

Jessi knew there was no time to lose. "I'm standing here with Nick Zellen, a man we've learned also goes by the name Brett Buckley."

Nick said nothing, appearing agitated.

Jessi pushed, "Are you ready to tell your story to the world, Nick?"

"There's been a change of plans, I need to get inside," he said, his eyes fixed on an enormous Hummer limo that had just arrived.

The comment threw her for a loop—she had withheld the information in exchange for this interview, and he'd made it sound like his life depended on it. But before she could lash out, he whispered in her ear, "I will provide you what I promised, but I just can't at the moment. I was able to escape my captors, but I need to get inside before they track me." He slipped her an object. He explained, still whispering, "It's a secure cell phone—I will call you as soon as I can for our interview. But if I don't make it out of here in one piece, run with the photos and text messages I gave you."

Nick bolted into Sarvy's. Before Jessi could even process what just happened, all eyes returned to the limo that Nick was so fascinated by.

Chapter 78

Natalie Gold stepped out of the limo to the screams of adoring fans, while camera-wielding paparazzi snapped photos. She looked stunning in a gold gown.

Her date was none other than Alexei Sarvydas, the rebellious son of music mogul Viktor Sarvydas, who was sporting a prison-chic hairstyle. Jessi understood that the bad-boy always attracted attention—and ratings. Alexei was as bad as they came, having just beaten a murder rap.

A third man was helped out of the vehicle and settled into a wheelchair. With his ill-fitting suit and out-of-date mustache, he didn't seem to fit with the star-studded couple and their entourage. The cynic in Jessi figured he was a handicapped war veteran that celebrities would exploit in exchange for some good PR. He wasn't stylish enough to be an agent or publicist.

He led them down the red carpet, shoving away any reporters who sought a word with Natalie. This didn't discourage Jessi, who had blockaded the Sarvy's doorway.

"Get out of the way or I'll slit your throat," the man in the wheelchair threatened. "That face of yours won't look so pretty if I slice it up."

"And you would be?"

"My name is Zubov, but most people call me their worst nightmare."

"Were you wounded in the war? Speaking as a proud American, I thank you for your service."

He smiled smugly. "Yeah, I was wounded in a war, but I don't think it's any war you're talking about. Now get out of our way!"

Hero or no hero, he wasn't going to keep Jessi from getting a few words with the world's biggest pop star. "So how does it feel to be in America?" she asked Natalie Gold.

"It has already been a memorable experience. Just at the airport alone."

"Tell me about the song from the video tonight—'Vengeance.' I think any woman who has had their heart broken can relate to this song."

"The song is actually about a dream I had. I was standing outside my apartment building and watching as my own body was carried out. And I vowed to get vengeance on those who murdered me."

"Well, many would say your rise is the thing of dreams. Just six months ago you were living on the streets of Tel Aviv and singing for your supper, but now you are the biggest star in the world."

After performing the prerequisite duties of an entertainment reporter—discussing Natalie's dress, shoes, hair, and every other accessory she wore, while giving proper credit to those responsible for her look—Jessi asked about the accessory on her arm. "And who is this handsome man who escorted you here tonight."

"This is Alexei Sarvydas."

"The son of your manager, Viktor Sarvydas," Jessi subtly moved the microphone in front of Alexei. "How does it feel to be a free man, Alexei?"

"It's a great feeling. And I have come tonight to personally thank those who are responsible for making tonight necessary."

That was the last question she could get in before Zubov pushed them inside. Jessi returned her attention to the red carpet, and witnessed a tuxedo clad Darren McLaughlin running toward the entrance like he was trying to catch a bus.

She tried to stop him, hoping for a follow-up interview from yesterday morning, but he rudely pushed past her. She followed him, her cameraman right behind, tape rolling.

She reached out and grabbed Darren's arm, pulling him back.

He looked like a different person—gone were the puppy dog eyes of the grieving husband. His personality had transformed. He reached into the cummerbund of his tuxedo and whipped out a gun. "I've got a job to do, and if you get in my way, I'm going to shoot you on national TV."

He turned and marched into Sarvy's.

Jessi followed him. The story just kept getting better.

Chapter 79

For the third time today, Darren entered Sarvy's. But for the first time he was on offense.

The place had been transformed into a space-age dance club. The heavy bass of Natalie Gold music pounded the walls, creating the illusion that the structure was shaking. Or maybe it truly was shaking—Darren wasn't sure. He wasn't sure of anything anymore.

Natalie stood with Alexei and Zubov at her side, mingling with celebrities in the middle of the room, her gold dress practically glowing. Bodyguards surrounded her like they were protecting the president.

Right on cue, Nick Zellen moved toward the trio. Darren gripped his gun tightly. There was part of him that wanted to shoot Nick, but that wasn't his instructions—plans had changed since Dava Lazinski put that bullet through Parmalov's forehead. He was to kill only Alexei.

But his mission veered sharply off course … again. Nick and Natalie's eyes met and it was like their world had stopped. It was a strange scene—it was as if they knew each other—and Darren couldn't take his eyes off them, captured by their intense connection.

He was close enough now to overhear Nick address her. "Audrey?"

"Nick," Natalie belted over the pounding music. She ran to him as a mishmash of celebrities and bodyguards cleared out of her path. They flew into each other's arms and embraced like they would never let go. This was not part of the plan.

Darren moved closer. Her guards were too mesmerized by the couple to stop him.

"I told you to go away, Audrey," Nick said.

"I did this for you," she passionately shot back.

"I never told you to do anything for me. I told you to stay out of it—it's too dangerous. I didn't want you to get hurt."

"But Nick…"

"And to go to *him*—you have no idea what you've got yourself into. There is no way out of this for you now."

"I don't want out. I want to be where you are."

The conversation baffled Darren. But his attention was diverted by his target—Alexei Sarvydas. Perhaps not thrilled that Nick was spending time with his date, Alexei brandished a gun.

"So we meet again," Alexei announced with a menacing smile, his gun locked on Nick's temple. Part of Darren wanted to let him go through with it.

"Haven't you killed enough of my family, Alexei?"

"Because of you, I spent a year in prison. But the funny thing is, I was sent there for a murder I didn't commit."

"You killed my mother, you son of a bitch!" Nick shouted over the music. His face was filled with rage. But Alexei had something he didn't have—a gun.

"Now you and your mommy are going to get to spend a lot of time together."

Natalie screamed, but it was drowned out by her own music. Security backed off.

It was time for Darren to move in. "Drop the gun, Alexei," he yelled as loud as he could.

Alexei looked more confused than anything. As expected, Zubov offered Alexei no help. When Alexei saw that his new adversary was Darren, his smug look returned. "Nick is the one you should be aiming at—he's the one who's been banging your wife."

"I said put the gun down," Darren remained firm.

Alexei bellowed a laugh. "Why would I put the gun down if you are going to shoot me?"

"Because if you don't, then I will," rang out a familiar voice.

Darren turned to see Becks. She had changed clothing, and her left shoulder was bandaged, but he was relieved to see that she was alive and kicking. She demonstrated that her shooting arm was completely healthy, as she held her Glock on Alexei.

"You too, Darren. Drop the gun—now!"

Dropping the gun meant Lilly would die. "Get out of here, Becks. I need to take care of this."

"I can't let you do that, Darren. If you don't drop your weapon, I'm going to have to shoot you. I know I haven't been straight with you the last couple days, but I'm dead serious right now."

Darren raised his gun in defiance.

"I know why you're doing this, Darren," Becks pleaded. "Dava threatened Lilly's life if you didn't kill Alexei for them. And my guess is that Nick was used to lure Alexei, or else they'll harm his sister. Isn't that right, Nick?"

He didn't get a chance to answer.

"If you don't shut up, bitch, I'm going to make your death slow and torturous. First, I'm going to shoot your friends. And then I'm going to shoot you," Alexei stated confidently.

"This place is surrounded by FBI—that's a suicide mission, Alexei," Becks shouted.

"Then I guess we're all going to hell together," Alexei said and took aim directly at Darren.

Before Darren could even compute what was happening, a gunshot echoed throughout the club and he hit the ground with a painful thud. But he hadn't been shot. Becks had tackled him. And she returned fire at Alexei. A direct hit right through the heart.

People scattered. Celebrities, bodyguards, and Russian mobsters all stampeded. The music was drowned out by screams.

Becks pushed Darren away. "Get out of here now!"

"Not without you," he replied.

She shook her head in annoyance. "I don't like this new spine thing. Now get attah here!"

Darren knew how to take orders—it's what he was best at. He scrambled to his feet. The feds and Russian thugs began shooting at each other like they were reenacting the Cold War. The gunshots were so loud that Darren thought his ears would pop.

Darren ran like he hadn't done since he was known as Run DMC. He had one purpose—to get to Lilly and make sure she was safe.

Chapter 80

Darren knew the object being thrust into the small of his back was a gun. He turned slowly to see Zubov, sitting in his wheelchair with a smile on his face.

"You failed in your mission," he said coldly.

"Alexei is dead, that's what I was sent to do."

"Technically yes, but I don't remember anyone giving you permission to outsource the dirty work."

"I would've killed him."

A chuckling Zubov removed the gun. "Tell it to the judge."

The Hummer limo skidded to a stop just feet from them, adding to the curbside bedlam. A door flung open and Darren was shoved into the back. Zubov was helped in, leaving his wheelchair behind.

Darren was seated next to Lilly, who was shaking. He wanted to reach out to her, until he noticed Nick on her other side. He *had* reached out to her, their hands were touching. It was like salt was running through an IV into his wounds.

Dava was seated across from them, along with Nick and his sister, and a visibly shaken Natalie Gold.

"Zubov tells me the mission was completed, even if it fell far from a success," Dava said, glaring right through Darren.

"I did my part, now let Sasha go free like you promised," Nick implored.

Sasha didn't agree. "I'm not going anywhere without my brother."

But Zubov had the final word. He grabbed her, opened the door and threw her out onto the sidewalk.

Zubov limped to the front of the limo. Without warning, he put two shots through the driver's head. The gunfire sent shock waves of fear through the captives, and Lilly's scream sliced through the limo.

In an apparent justification of his actions, Zubov declared that the driver was not innocent, as he had been working for Parmalov.

Zubov took over the driving duties—not acknowledging any pain from his kneecaps—directing the limo away from the chaos outside of Sarvy's.

Darren remained seated beside Lilly, with Nick on her other side. Lilly was once again in the middle.

Dava addressed Lilly, "You are a very lucky woman to have these two men fighting over you."

Lilly said nothing, but Darren couldn't help noticing her subtle movement toward Nick. It was almost instinctive. She thought of him as the one who would protect her.

Nick didn't seem to pick up on her body language—he was too busy staring at Natalie Gold. The woman he had embraced like a long-lost lover in Sarvy's and referred to as Audrey. Darren still didn't know what to make of that.

"I think you chose the wrong man," Dava continued. "Your husband was the one who risked his life for you, willing to take another man's life to save your pathetic one."

Lilly hung her head. "Please let Darren go—he's innocent. I'm the one who deserves to die."

The look in her eyes told Darren another story. She would never put her life on the line for him, the way he did for her. And he couldn't get the woman who did risk her life for him out of his thoughts. He feared the worst for Becks and regretted leaving her in that crossfire.

"It's not up to you if you die," Dava shot back, "but you will soon go on trial, just as all of you will."

"Trial?" Nick asked.

"You will be tried in the court of Viktor Sarvydas at his estate in Netanya. I will be the prosecutor in the case."

"Netanya, as in Israel?" Darren asked. This thing got crazier by the moment.

"It's certainly not out on Long Island," Dava snapped back.

"Why did you kill Alexei?" Natalie Gold asked.

"I'm sorry about your date, Ms. Gold, and that your party didn't come off as expected. But we were ordered to bring you home," Dava informed.

"You didn't answer my question," Natalie pushed.

"All the answers you seek will come out at trial."

Darren found his inner-Becks, and proclaimed, "I have no idea who came up with this insane plan, but there is no way you will be able to get to Israel. All the airports are already on high alert. Do you really think they are just going to let you board a plane with hostages and clear you for takeoff?"

"No, I expect you to walk us onto a plane. And I expect you to fly us to Israel."

"That has a zero percent chance of working."

"Oh really," Dava responded to Darren. She took out a cell phone and made a call. "It's Kelli. We're headed for the airport … we'll see you soon." Pause. "Yes, Nick is with us. Along with the McLaughlins and Natalie Gold. Let me know when we've been cleared."

Dava smiled confidently upon hanging up. "That was Viktor—he sends his best and looks forward to your arrival. He assured me we will be cleared for takeoff. It seems the US doesn't want blood on its hands if Israel's national treasure, Natalie Gold, was to be killed on US soil. And when you have friends in the highest places, these things have a way of working themselves out so that everyone gets what they want."

All eyes went to Natalie. Except Nick's—his had never left her. Dava picked up on this, as had Lilly.

"Seems your favorite student has a wandering eye," Dava announced. She then turned to Darren.

"You are a better person than I am, Mr. McLaughlin."

"Since you are a murderer, I don't think that's saying much."

She ignored his retort. "After your wife so egregiously betrayed you, you risked your life for her, knowing that she wouldn't even piss on you if you were on fire. Your response amazes me."

"Marriage is for better or worse. Until death do us part," Darren said.

"We'll see what the judge has to say about that."

Chapter 81

Becks stood fists on hips, refusing any medical treatment for her second bullet wound of the day, which tied her personal record. This one grazed her thigh, and besides the awful pain, it ruined a good pair of jeans. Just a typical night out in Brighton Beach.

At least three medical technicians and two federal agents informed her that she was "lucky" to only have a flesh wound. She just gritted her teeth and nodded. The sting in her leg was pulsating through her entire body, but she wouldn't allow anyone to see her wince, especially the FBI agents. Or Eicher, who stood next to her outside of Sarvy's under the April moonlight.

Before he could even start in with the predictable condescending lecture, she went on the offensive, "So do you believe me now?"

"What I *believe* is that you messed up this whole case from the beginning, Fitzpatrick. From your substandard protection of Nick in Arizona, to recklessly exacerbating the situation in the club."

"He was going to shoot Darren."

"I think the judge will see it that Darren was the aggressor, especially since he threatened to shoot that TV reporter on his way in. The Sarvydas lawyers will have a field day—they already have made the case that we were on a witch hunt after their client, and now five minutes after he gets out of prison he gets shot by a rogue federal marshal."

"If it wasn't for me, Alexei Sarvydas would be dead," she paused for a moment, her face turning distressed. "Okay, he's dead anyway—but if I didn't determine that Darren would be the shooter, he would have shot him instead of me." She thought for a moment. "Yeah, I guess that's not in our favor either. If it makes you feel any better, I think they were planning to kill Lilly McLaughlin and Sasha Zellen if Alexei lived. So you could make the case that I saved lives."

Eicher sadly shook his head.

A team of FBI agents approached. "The place is secure," said the lead agent, his silver hair illuminated by the moonlight.

Becks remained on the offensive, "What are you doing here? I thought they put you out to pasture in Oklahoma."

LaPoint shook his head. It was like he and Eicher took a head-shaking class at Quantico. "When word got out that you were in New York, Chelsea, they sent me to clean up whatever mess you were going to make. And I must say, you outdid yourself this time."

"It's Fitzpatrick to you."

"Since you want to keep this professional, I think it's time to head back to Foley so we can depose you."

Becks cringed. It was standard procedure anytime a federal agent was involved in a fatal shooting, but it could be long and tedious, and sometimes took days. She didn't have that kind of time. She'd figured out what was going on here, and by their blank looks, she could see that her compadres had yet to solve the puzzle. The bottom line was that Darren was in deep trouble. She needed to think, so she headed toward a place she could better think.

"Where do you think you're going?" LaPoint's abrasive voice shot through the night air. She kept limping away. Their choice was to shoot or follow. They chose the latter, probably because they didn't want to deal with the tedious deposition.

Brighton Beach was right on the Atlantic Ocean, and Becks could feel the salty sea air in her lungs. It was hard to believe they were only a couple of subway stops from skyscraper-lined Manhattan. It was also hard to believe they were in America. The sign on the bar she walked into was written in Cyrillic, so she didn't know the name of the establishment, but could tell it was a bar by the guttural laughter of inebriation. They might have been speaking Russian, but Becks needed a drink, so they were speaking her language.

"Dos Vedanya?" a strapping brick wall of a bartender asked her, inquiring if she and her party were Russian.

Becks held up her badge. "Federal Marshals, FBI, KGB, it's all the same. Now hook me up with a stiff White Russian, and I don't mean that albino at the end of the bar."

"We don't serve cops," the bartender informed.

"They told us the same thing at Sarvy's—so I shot Alexei Sarvydas."

She reached for her gun, but realized it had been confiscated, as her badge soon would be. But she had made her point. Word of Alexei's death had spread throughout Brighton, and probably all the way to Moscow. The now agreeable bartender motioned for a waitress to take them to a table.

Becks didn't really want to share her theory with Eicher and LaPoint, but since she would probably be on unpaid vacation by the time the clock hit midnight, they might be Darren's only chance. So she laid out what she believed happened that fateful day at the Zellen estate. Alexei didn't kill Karl Zellen, in fact, he wasn't even there. And then she told them who did shoot Karl, and why.

The reaction was expected. "That's ridiculous," Eicher said. "It can't be."

LaPoint was even less gracious. "Just because you were undercover in high school didn't mean you had to start smoking pot."

They weren't buying what she was selling, but one thing they couldn't deny was the fact that what happened to Karl was linked directly to the night long ago when Viktor allegedly had his wife and father-in-law murdered.

"I was right about Dava. Has she called in yet, Eicher? Maybe she was taking a nap and missed your five gazillion calls."

Eicher looked like she'd slapped him across the face, and said nothing.

"And I was right about Darren. He was going to shoot Alexei at the party. So keep betting against me, boys, but remind me to never take you with me to Vegas."

"So what do you suggest we do?" Eicher finally gave in.

Chapter 82

Before Becks could even pretend that she had a plan, a buzz swept through the bar and the chatter surrounding them intensified. The programming on the mounted televisions had changed from Russian language shows to a voice that was way too familiar to Becks.

The view on the screen was of the back of the Hummer limo that Natalie Gold arrived in at Sarvy's. The camera angle was coming from a vehicle behind the limo, providing a perspective similar to that of an in-car camera during television coverage of auto racing. On the bottom of the screen was a banner graphic that shouted: *Sarvy's Shootout!*

"This is Jessi Stafford reporting. After escaping Sarvy's, we are now attempting to chase down the culprit in the tragic shooting, Darren McLaughlin.

"For those of you just tuning in, we will again play the video for you where the assailant came after Nick Zellen with a gun in an act of revenge. Zellen was thought to be a student named Brett Buckley, who ran off with McLaughlin's wife."

The video appeared on the screen of Darren pointing a gun at Jessi. The camera continued to roll, and moments later he would pull the same gun on Alexei Sarvydas and threaten to kill him.

That's when Becks flew in to save the day. Sort of. After that, everything went dark, as the cameraman ran for his life as screams and gunshots rang out. Becks was glad the film ended there. She had no desire to relive the agony, the gunshot she received was the least of her pain. But that didn't lessen the discomfort from the sharpest thorn in her side—Jessi Stafford.

"What Darren McLaughlin wasn't counting on was Buckley's high school girlfriend, Rebecca Ryan, also showing up looking for revenge. This toxic combination ended in deadly gunfire, and the death of Alexei Sarvydas."

The view on the screen returned to the car chase. "We are following the suspects of the *Sarvy's Shooting*, led by an armed and dangerous Darren McLaughlin. I am reporting that two partners in crime, Dava 'Kelli' Lazinski of the US Attorney's Office, and his estranged wife, Lilly McLaughlin, are assisting him. This was confirmed when I gained access to Lilly McLaughlin's cell phone, which included messages between Lilly and Lazinski. Nick Zellen has provided me information that will fully explain this situation, which I agreed to release only upon his instructions. But as a preview, we are releasing the first photo of Darren McLaughlin and Lazinski together, along with murder victim Ron Treadwell."

The photo of the three amigos appeared on the screen. It was of Darren and Treadwell, posing with Dava, and appeared to have been taken in a bar. This new development was a speed bump in Becks' theory and got her sideways looks from Eicher and LaPoint. She wasn't sure how it fit in, but it didn't cause her to waver. And it's not like Eicher could talk, since he believed Dava was an innocent bystander in all this.

"To the best of our knowledge, the other victims inside the vehicle include pop princess Natalie Gold, a war veteran who calls himself Zubov, and Nick Zellen."

Zubov a victim—really? The reporter was making Becks crave another gunshot wound—this one to her head—and she couldn't believe she was reporting that Darren was the criminal mastermind. It seemed to Becks that she was the only one who had figured out who the real villain was.

Becks was forced to give some credit to the reporter—the video was very helpful. She couldn't take her eyes off the screen as the limo cruised through the New York night. *Where were they headed?*

LaPoint answered the question, "They're going to the airport!"

"That's suicide," Eicher declared. "They will be shot on sight."

But not only did they make it safely onto the airport grounds, they drove right up to the terminal—and crashed through the glass doors like a tank. There was no resistance from security.

Becks couldn't believe what she was watching, as the news vehicle followed them in through the broken glass, allowing the show to continue. The US policy on hijackings had always been drilled into their heads, sometimes even calling for a plane to be shot out of the sky, sacrificing innocent people to halt the danger to a larger population or interest. Yet they just let a limo of Russian mobsters drive into an international airport with hostages!?

Once inside, the limo slowed to a crawl. The walkways were clear, indicating the airport had been evacuated. Becks couldn't get over how strange this was. The president of the United States wouldn't get this type of treatment.

Eicher echoed her sentiments, "I've never seen anything like this. It's like God himself cleared the way."

"It would take someone more powerful than God," LaPoint commented, "like Sarvydas."

"How do they know they don't have a bomb aboard? This is crazy," Eicher asserted.

"Maybe they do, and that was their ticket in," Becks added.

LaPoint shrugged. "It's Homeland Security's problem now."

The limo came to a halt at the Air Israel terminal. Becks figured that like many Russian mobsters who were in trouble, they were going to seek refuge in Israel. The question was—would they be allowed to leave US soil?

She couldn't imagine it, but she also would never have thought they'd get this far.

Darren got out of the vehicle first, still wearing his tux, and holding a gun. He ordered the others out. Dava pretended to be a victim, unaware that she had already been outed by the newscast. Lilly and Nick were next. Zubov limped out using a cane, clearing the way for the grand finale, which was Natalie Gold appearing with her hands raised, still looking like a star in her gold dress.

Darren ordered them to place their hands over their heads. Becks couldn't believe he was doing this for his undeserving wife.

Jessi Stafford got out of her vehicle and foolishly ran toward the hijackers in her oversized heels. Darren fired his gun in her direction, not coming close. Becks almost cheered when she dove to the ground and writhed in fear.

Darren followed his "hostages" toward the gate. Once again he displayed his gun, trying too hard to let people know he was the hijacker. He then marched them onto the airplane. When they were all aboard, he shut the door.

Chapter 83

Darren sat at the controls in the cockpit. But despite thousands of flight hours, this time was different. And not just because he had moved to the left of the control panel into the captain seat. Or because this was an Airbus A380, a double-deck, wide-body, four-engine airliner sometimes referred to as the Superjumbo. The largest plane he'd ever flown was a Boeing 747-400.

This flight was different because a couple of Russian mobsters named Dava and Zubov were holding guns to his head. But he didn't take their death threats very seriously. They needed him to fly them to safety, just as they needed him to pose as a hijacker. He had been chosen to be the fall guy.

Lilly sat in the first officer seat, handcuffed to Nick. When Darren glanced at her the tornado of emotions swirled again.

"The flight plan is set from New York to Ben Gurion in Tel Aviv. We should get clearance very soon," Dava instructed.

"I will fly the plane if you release Lilly. I am your only pilot, which makes me your lone hope to get out of here. Viktor Sarvydas will kill us anyway, so I have nothing to lose. You, on the other hand, have everything to lose."

Zubov raised his walking cane and slashed it across Lilly's knees. She cried out in pain.

Nick rose to confront Zubov, but Dava's gun settled him back into his seat. Anger flowed through Darren's veins like jet fuel, but he knew that another hotheaded reaction would only cause Lilly more pain.

Zubov turned to Lilly. "We're still not even for shooting my knees. Every time I feel pain I want to share it with you."

Lilly shot a deadly assassin? It hammered home the point that Darren really didn't know this woman at all.

"This is crazy," Darren stated. "The US doesn't negotiate with hijackers. They will blow the plane up before they let us leave."

"Not with Natalie Gold on board," Dava countered.

Darren agreed she was a game-changer, but not to the point that they would just let them fly away without repercussions. At the very least, they would storm the plane.

"You were in Air Force. You've trained your whole life for this moment," Zubov said.

"I flew cargo planes, not suicide missions."

Zubov's cane came at him so fast that Darren didn't even see it. His ear began ringing like someone was blowing a whistle inches from it. Darren reached to touch it and it felt like it had doubled in size. Blood filled his hand.

"Stop talking," Zubov said coldly.

"Leave him alone," Lilly shrieked. "He has nothing to do with this."

"He has everything to do with this now," Dava responded angrily.

Zubov actually played peacemaker, wedging himself between the two women. "I think these two lovebirds have a lot to talk about. Let's leave them alone."

Dava nodded her approval.

Zubov shrugged. "What can I say, I'm a romantic."

He unlatched Nick from his handcuffs and led him out of the cabin. Dava informed Darren that she would return when they got clearance for takeoff.

It was just the two of them. They sat in dead silence. He stared straight ahead at the dark runway. It was filled with emergency vehicles, fire trucks, and camouflaged military trucks. Hijacked airplanes always seemed to attract a lot of attention.

Finally Lilly broke the silence, "I hate when you do this."

"Do what?"

"The passive-aggressive thing where you want to scream at me, but you bottle it all up and give me the silent treatment."

"I think you've given up the right to tell me what to do."

"Just let me have it!" she shouted at him. "I betrayed you—I betrayed our marriage! Yell at me—hit me—do something!"

Darren had nothing to say. To be either passive or aggressive would require him to be alive, and she had ripped the life from him. He wasn't angry—he was lifeless. He stared back out at the runway. It was as if he was looking toward a hopeless future.

Lilly finally accepted that the patient was dying, so she stopped CPR and just tried to comfort him in his final moments. She found a First Aid kit that contained an icepack. She softly applied the ice to his ear. "You'll be better off without me," she said.

Darren didn't reply.

"You were like an angel who came into my life, but I'm too messed up. You should have run away from me. The worst part is that I always knew I'd hurt you, but I fooled myself because I wanted to live the dream."

"Do you love him?" he asked.

She paused for a long moment, and then said, "I'm not sure I know what love is, but I've never felt like this before."

There was one question he needed answered before he could completely wither away and die. "Were you really not able to get pregnant?"

She bowed her head. "I wasn't worthy of mothering your children. I would've hurt them just like I hurt you."

She reached out her hand to him, but Darren pushed it away, suddenly feeling alive again. Life flowed back through his veins. "That's a total cop-out! The reason you're messed up is because of what you did, not who you are!

She sniffled away tears. "I'm so sorry, Darren."

He finally found the rage. "I thought of not going through with it, Lilly. I would let Alexei live and let them kill you! The only reason I did was for the vows, not for you. Don't ever forget that."

As tears streamed down her face, Dava returned with a smug look. "Sorry, the counseling session is over. We've been cleared for takeoff. New York to Tel Aviv, nonstop. Seems the president of the United States agreed to our terms."

Darren felt like his mind might explode as he watched the runway vehicles clear out of the way. This was really happening. But once the awe wore off, he got down to business. He struggled to program the GPS, which he'd never done before without assistance from the tower. The gun pointed at the back of his head added to his anxiety.

But once he found his comfort zone, he got into a groove. The Airbus A380 had a different setup, but two multi-function displays provided an easy to use interface to the flight management system, making Darren's transition seamless.

He went through his checks with sweaty palms. He turned on the fuel-igniters and auxiliary power unit. He cooled the cabin and then spun the engines. There was no tower to clear him, so he pushed the throttle and pulled back the yoke.

The hijacked plane took off into the night.

Chapter 84

Nick strolled back into the plane's cabin. He could have had any seat he wanted, but he chose to sit right next to Audrey.

He wished the plane were a time-machine that could take him back to the time before Karl was arrested. Back when things were simple. There were two aspects to his life back then—his time with Audrey and the time he spent thinking about being with her. They planned on being together for the rest of their lives, but things had taken a dramatic turn, and by the looks of Audrey, so had she. He knew he was a different person now with a different destiny, so there was no use looking back.

Words wouldn't be sufficient, so they said nothing. But as the plane surged upward, Audrey began to hyperventilate. It wasn't her succumbing to the hijacking situation, Nick knew she was petrified of flying.

He instinctively reached out and grabbed her hand. He noticed that the interlocking NZ tattoo between her thumb and index finger had been converted into a Star of David. It wasn't just a reference to her new home. It also represented what she'd become since they last saw each other—a star. She looked different, she talked different, she smelled different, but her touch had the same effect on him. Nick wanted to take her into her arms and not let her go. But that wasn't possible right now.

When the plane settled into its cruising altitude, and the color began to return to her cheeks, Nick remarked, "It's amazing to see you again."

The words seemed to distress her. "I've been worried about you, Nick."

He attempted the smile that had always been able to comfort her. "It's been an interesting year, huh?"

"You could say that," she replied, emotionless.

"You certainly look…um…like you've changed a lot in the past year." It was hard not to notice her busting out of her gold gown. The dramatic blonde hair was also hard to get used to.

"I did what I had to do."

"What *did* you have to do, Audrey?"

Her eyes fearfully wandered to Dava, who was nervously pacing the aisle like a prison guard. When the coast was clear, she stated, "They can't learn who I really am. They'll kill me."

Nick's voice lowered, "Okay, *Natalie*, tell me what this is all about."

"I told you—I did what I had to do."

"If I remember correctly, you are the one who always preached about total honesty in a relationship. Viktor Sarvydas? Are you nuts!?"

"Are we still in a relationship?"

"I'm just happy to see you again."

Her face intensified. "That's not what I asked you."

"If you haven't noticed, things are a little complicated at the moment."

She peered toward the cockpit area in an accusatory manner. "Who is she?"

"Her name is Lilly—she was my teacher."

"Are you in love with her?"

"I did what I had to do."

"I gave up everything for you," her voice raised, receiving a look from Dava.

When she returned to her pacing, he said, "I never asked you to do that."

"I know, you told me to give up my life. Never see my parents again. Never see you again. I'd rather live dangerously than not live at all."

"You don't get it, Audrey. Sarvydas will kill you, and it won't be quick and easy."

"He already did kill me. And from what I read in the papers, there wasn't much left of me. Who was killed in my apartment, Nick?"

"I thought you went back there. Jesus, Audrey, I even went to your funeral. I helped identify your body. But last night at your parents' house, the FBI called and wanted to exhume you, or whoever is buried under your headstone in Devol."

She looked at him with wonder. "You saw my parents ... last night?"

"We were on the run and needed a place to stay. They will never get over your death, but they've been able to move on the best they can. I think your father's faith has really helped your mother." He attempted another smile. "She had all the photo albums out last night. I haven't seen someone so glorified in death since Elvis."

Audrey remained stoic, her eyes glued to Zubov. "We are going to need a miracle to get out of this one."

Nick again grabbed her hand, feeling more shock waves. "I have a plan, but you're going to have to trust me."

"I've always believed in you, Nick."

"It might include things I would never want you to see. You're going to have to follow me, even if you don't understand."

Audrey glanced again toward the cockpit area, as if she was debating whether she could stomach seeing him and Lilly together once more. "I've done things too that I'm not proud of."

He wanted to take her in his arms and kiss her, but that would certainly give away her cover, and he wasn't ready to do that yet.

"I've done nothing to earn your loyalty," Nick said. He then called for Dava and told her that he needed to use the bathroom. Zubov escorted him to the lavatory and waited outside.

Nick closed the door and took out the cell phone.

Chapter 85

Jessi stood outside the terminal at JFK—the once-bustling airport had turned into a giant crime scene. As she filed her latest breaking report about the hijacked plane being allowed to takeoff, a ringing sound startled her. It was coming from the phone that Nick had given her at the premiere party!

She put it on speaker, and motioned her cameraman to roll tape. She answered, "Thank God, Nick, are you okay?"

His voice was low, "I am in the bathroom of the hijacked plane. I don't have much time and must speak softly. They are waiting right outside the door."

Jessi played with the volume so that the camera microphone would pick up his words.

"Who is waiting outside the door—Darren McLaughlin?" she asked.

"McLaughlin is flying the plane."

"What about his wife?"

"Lilly is in the cockpit with him. They are working as a team."

"No wonder he was so desperate to get back to her."

"They are also working with Dava Lazinski of the US Attorney's Office, and the assassin Zubov. Dava was the key leak that allowed Viktor Sarvydas to find me when I was in witness protection."

"The only person you haven't mentioned is Natalie Gold, I don't want to speculate, but should we fear the worst?"

"Natalie is unharmed, she is their bargaining chip—it's the rest of us who are in the most immediate danger."

"Have your captors provided any details of where the plane is headed, and why?"

"They plan on taking us to Israel to meet with Sarvydas for what the hijackers are calling a 'trial'. But my guess is that the Israelis will shoot the plane down before allowing hijackers to land."

Jessi couldn't let Nick know that thoughts of a happy ending dissipated when the plane was allowed to leave New York. All the more reason to not let this moment pass—it would likely be her last chance to get the whole story.

"Take us back to the beginning, Nick."

He paused for a moment, as if collecting his thoughts, then began, "After witnessing the murder of Karl Zellen by Alexei Sarvydas, I was put into witness protection until the trial, under the name of Buckley. They moved me to Chandler last December, where I lived the life of a high school senior. My teacher, Lilly McLaughlin, took a great interest in me, and I fell for her.

"We began an affair. I knew she was married, and I tried to call it off a couple of times, but Lilly always knew the right things to say to make me stay close to her."

"What made you run?"

"I saw Zubov, a Sarvydas hitman, in a local mall. I knew my cover had been blown and I was as good as dead if I remained there. I now know it was the work of Dava Lazinski of the US Attorneys Office.

"Lilly suggested that we run, and that we make it look like a gang-style abduction. I was so stupid."

Jessi could sense that Nick was becoming overwhelmed. She needed to keep him lucid and on course. "How, and at what point did you begin to suspect that Lilly McLaughlin was working for Sarvydas?"

"Once we got on the road, there were a lot of coincidences. Everywhere we went Zubov was right on our tail. I called US Attorney Eicher, who was prosecuting the case. I thought about telling him my location, but I was worried that there was a leak in his office. Sure enough, I was able to get hold of Lilly's cell phone and it was full of messages between her and Dava. That's how they found me."

"Nick has provided me with these text messages, and I will be displaying them on both the Channel-6 and GNZ web sites as soon as we get clearance from the proper authorities. But for the audience, Nick, could you provide a brief summary of what those messages said?"

"They described how they planned to kill me at Sarvy's during the Natalie Gold party, using my sister Sasha to lure me there. So when I returned to New York, I headed straight home to check on Sasha, but Dava was there waiting for me. She first took us to the office of Stevanro Parmalov, one of Sarvydas' chief lieutenants. She shot him and his two assistants, who had been lured there by Darren McLaughlin. I was able to briefly escape, but McLaughlin was right on my tail … and you know the rest."

"My exclusive video of the shootout in Sarvy's showed Alexei Sarvydas being gunned down by a Rebecca Ryan, but my guess is that was an alias, just as Brett Buckley was not your real name?"

"That was Deputy Marshal Fitzpatrick of the US Federal Marshals. She was my guardian angel in the program. She warned me about Lilly, but I didn't listen. She had figured out that Alexei was going to shoot me as revenge for agreeing to testify against him. She saved my life."

"But the video clearly shows that she also protected Darren McLaughlin, and helped him get away. Is it possible that she is also involved in the hijacking plot?"

"I think she fell into the same trap that I did with the McLaughlins. They are very charming and charismatic people. She trusted Darren, just as I trusted Lilly."

All of a sudden Nick's voice turned panicked. "Someone's coming. I have to go."

The phone clicked off.

Chapter 86

The lavatory door swung open and Dava barged in, gun in hand.

"Times up—either shit or get off the pot," she said with a sly grin. She shut the door behind her and locked it.

Nick hid the cell phone in his pocket.

She engulfed him in a passionate embrace. "I've wanted to do that for so long."

"I couldn't have gotten this far without you," he said with a smile.

"I always take care of things. I'm just doing my job."

She moved in to kiss him. He turned his head.

He could tell his rejection hurt her. The feelings she'd expressed to him this past year seemed real, but he'd been surrounded by some of the world's greatest liars throughout his life. So he knew that the truth was a gray area.

"You said when this was over, we could be together. There are no longer any obstacles in our way."

"We have a long way to go, Dava. It would be too dangerous at this point."

"I've been completely honest with you. So don't you lie to me."

His face tensed. "This will never be over."

"This is about her, isn't it? As long as she's out there somewhere, you will still long for her. No matter what you say."

He didn't enjoy the hurt in her eyes. But when Dava spoke of Audrey, he could tell that she had no idea that she'd become Natalie Gold.

"When Audrey left, it was the same as if she had died. I knew I'd never be able to see her again. I have moved on with my life, but that doesn't mean that I won't do everything within my power to make sure nobody figures out that she isn't in that grave in Oklahoma."

Dava handed him Rachel Grant's leather-bound journal. Nick felt great relief. He had no idea that it was out there—in the wrong hands it could have ruined everything.

"I will do anything to keep you safe," she stated.

Nick first met Dava when he clerked at the Brooklyn DA's Office between his first and second years of law school. He found her unremarkable and didn't think twice about her once he returned to school in the fall. Little did he know that she would become his biggest ally following his mother's death.

While at the DA's Office, he assisted on the case of Rachel Grant, in which Dava was prosecuting. It took on a higher priority than the typical prostitution case when the investigation expanded to include the ringleader of the operation, and Rachel's boyfriend, Alexei Sarvydas. At that point, Nick was removed from the case because of the Zellen family's connection with the Sarvydases. That was the last Nick thought he would see and hear of Dava Lazinski and Rachel Grant.

What neither he or Rachel knew was that Viktor Sarvydas had set up a meeting with Dava concerning his son's case. But he didn't make the predictable power play to drop the investigation. Instead, he made a surprising offer for a "side job." He would assist Dava in her case by having Rachel Grant's apartment set up with hidden cameras.

That way, Viktor could gain valuable information about a son he didn't trust, but protect him from jail. And Rachel Grant would cleanse her soul, by cooperating with the DA's Office in the taking down of her boyfriend's ugly business. Rachel didn't know that she was really working for Viktor.

And when Dava formed this unholy alliance with Viktor, a man she had admired while growing up in Brighton Beach, Nick's life changed forever.

Nick skimmed through the journal entries. Rachel detailed her incriminating conversations with Alexei. She also mentioned the young law student with a disarming smile who had implored her to go "straight" after her arrest. And even though he was taken off her case, his words lingered, and helped her make the decision to cooperate.

Her tone turned upbeat when she had a chance meeting with that same law student, almost a year later. Or at least she believed it to be random. Nick's mother had recently been murdered, and she was able to become a sounding board for him, providing comfort in his loss.

Her words became even more optimistic when their relationship turned physical. But she also wrote of her reservations that things might be moving too fast, and her trepidation about Nick's current girlfriend, especially since they would rendezvous at her Brooklyn apartment while Audrey was away. He even provided her a key.

She knew that their "love" was likely a one-way street, the result of Nick being at his most vulnerable, yet his girlfriend was preoccupied with her career, spending her nights singing at clubs. Rachel moved ahead anyway, even describing in one entry how she got Nick's initials tattooed on her hand at his request.

Not only was Rachel the ideal inside source who would unknowingly assist his quest for justice, but also a means to keep Audrey safe—the last piece of the puzzle.

After Alexei's arrest, Rachel's writing indicated she had grown fearful. The one person she trusted was Nick, and for the first time let him in on the fact that she had been helping the DA's Office gather information against Alexei, still unaware of the true role she played. Rachel informed Nick of her plans to hightail it out of New York and return to Wyoming until things cooled down.

He convinced her that this wasn't safe, explaining that the Sarvydases would go to any length to keep either of them from testifying.

Nick's words were chronicled verbatim in the journal: It won't take them long to figure out my relationship to you, and then they will come after you, whether that's in Brooklyn or Wyoming. We have to lie low for a few days. Meet me at Audrey's apartment tonight. You will be safe there.

Dava took note of the passage he was reading—the last one in the journal. "That could have been very damaging if Eicher got his hands on those words."

Nick wondered about the expression on Rachel's face when she found Dava waiting for her at the apartment that night.

Upon first meeting her, Nick would have found it impossible to comprehend that the demure, workaholic prosecutor could also be a cold, efficient killer. But he had learned all too well how the events of life could change one's belief system. Dava was born in Brighton Beach, but when she was a small girl, her father returned to their native Lithuania to help the fight for independence against the Soviet occupation, losing his life in the process. When she returned to the United States, she knew that unlike her father, she would worry first for her own life. That was the only way to survive. The Russian way.

There was a time when Nick would find this type of thinking to be incomprehensible, but as he shut the journal, he knew his earlier words were never truer—he wouldn't have made it this far without her.

"It had to be done," she said, emotionless, as if reading his mind. "It was the only way to save Audrey."

Nick nodded, knowing that now was the time to once again do what must be done.

Chapter 87

Lilly watched Zubov limp into the cockpit. He looked at her and commanded, "You're coming with me."

Before she could protest, he grabbed her by the hair and dragged her to the back of the plane. He cursed with each step, and informed her that he couldn't wait to chop her legs off at the knees to even the score.

Zubov forced her into a conference room situated in the back of the plane. Nick stood facing her, with Dava clinging to his arm. Zubov forced Lilly into a chair beside Natalie Gold. He then joined Nick and Dava behind the table.

Lilly was disorientated. What was Nick doing standing arm-in-arm with their captors?

Nick spoke, "Now that we're all here, I have an announcement to make. This is a very special day for me and my family, a day we've waited over a year for, and at times thought might never come."

Dava moved even closer to him. *What was going on?*

Nick continued, "We are headed to Israel to pay a visit to Viktor Sarvydas. I'm sure you have many questions, but I guarantee that you will get all your answers when we arrive. So as your captain, I urge you to sit back and enjoy the trip."

He stared at Lilly as he said it. She could taste the lies and betrayal in her mouth, and it went down her throat like a shot of her own medicine. This was a worse fate than Zubov capping her knees and then firing a bullet into her skull. And she got the feeling that it was just the beginning.

Nick's charming smile faded, exposing a dark look that Lilly had never seen before. Or had she seen it, but attached her own spin to it? Was it the look he had at Dantelli's, but she misinterpreted it as him being hurt? Deep down, she knew it was what had so attracted her to him.

Dava added, "Because if you don't, then I'm going to have to put Zubov to work and nobody wants that." She was the muscle.

Lilly was an expert face-reader, whether at the casino or with her students, but Nick gave nothing away. Was he taking them to Israel to avenge his mother's death, or was he working with Sarvydas? Either scenario was too surreal to grasp.

Nick embraced Zubov. He had said he worked for Sarvydas' son, but now that Alexei was dead, it appeared that he had aligned himself with Nick—for someone who's persona was centered around death, Zubov sure seemed to have a good handle on the concept of survival.

While it wasn't clear what was happening, Lilly knew it was derived from a cold and calculated strategy. She had told Nick that they didn't have to be like their fathers, but she realized that he was a carbon copy of Karl Zellen. She thought of what Dantelli had told him about killing being his destiny. It seemed that Nick was a chip off the old block.

"You don't have to do this, Nick," Lilly pleaded.

But this time he looked at her differently—that first look in her classroom was a distant memory. Back then he looked almost apologetic when he delivered his pet line, "It wasn't your fault that you fell in love with me, Lilly."

He would always use the line as a way to ease her guilt about Darren, but now she saw a different interpretation. What he really meant was that she had been chosen to take the fall.

It also made sense why Nick never showed fear—because he was never in danger. Zubov could have killed them at any time along the way if he wanted to. The Russian mob wasn't after him—Nick *was* the Russian mob. And like Sarvydas, he'd hidden behind the veil of legitimacy, having others do his dirty work for him—Zubov killed Dantelli, Darren was sent after Alexei, Dava took out Parmalov, and he even conned Lilly into shooting Bachynsky.

Natalie Gold rose to her feet with an accusatory point of her finger. "So we were nothing but lies, Nick?"

"What did I say about trusting me, Audrey?"

Lilly felt staggered. Saint Audrey? Dava also seemed bowled over by the revelation.

"You had that girl in my apartment killed, didn't you?"

"All I ever cared about was keeping you safe, Audrey."

"I never asked you to protect me. Now you better protect yourself."

She took off her gold pumps and fired the first one at Nick's head. He coolly ducked, and it landed in the wall behind him. The next one didn't miss, striking off his chin. Natalie stormed off in the direction of the cockpit.

"Get back here, Audrey," Nick demanded.

She didn't respond.

"I said get back here," his voice was a mix of anger and desperation.

Dava displayed her gun, looking like she wanted to fire a couple of shots into Audrey's back as she walked up the aisle. Nick knocked the gun out of her hand and kicked it away.

"If you ever raise a weapon to her again, I will kill you, do you understand?"

Dava brooded, causing Zubov to break into laughter. "Looks like Nicky's got women problems. If I were you I'd find a parachute and get out of here before they eat you alive!"

Nick wasn't listening. He couldn't take his eyes off Audrey as she disappeared into the cockpit, slamming the door.

Chapter 88

Lilly watched as Nick took a seat at the conference table. He flipped on a television and a newscast appeared. It featured Jessi Stafford, and she was re-playing a phone interview she'd just done … with Nick!

Dava looked bewildered as she watched Nick throw her under the proverbial bus, exposing her as the double-agent that she was. She appeared scared and hurt. In the report, Lilly was portrayed as her partner in crime.

He noticed Dava's confused look, and explained, "If you remember, before I entered the program you bought me a phone in your name so we'd be able to communicate in case of an emergency."

He handed her the phone and then turned to Lilly. "Just like you bought a phone for me in your name, for similar purposes. You never know when one of those urgent tutoring sessions will come up. While I never used the phones to call either of you, I did create some interesting text conversations between Dava and Lilly's phones in your names, and upload that photo Kelli sent me. I think you'll be impressed in how my creative writing has improved since taking your class, Mrs. McLaughlin.

"I gave the phone you bought me to the reporter, Lilly, but just so you don't feel left out, here's the one I took from you when you were inducting me into the Mile High Club."

He took another phone from his pocket and tossed it in Lilly's direction. She made no attempt to catch it, letting it fall to the floor.

He flipped off the television and looked at the two women. "This changes things. You both have become a liability to me," he announced, as if he wasn't the one responsible for the interview.

Dava trembled as she spoke, "You know I have always been loyal to you. I will spend life in prison to protect you if I have to."

He looked to Lilly, but she wasn't going to beg for her life. She had learned enough about the Russian mob to know their distaste for living witnesses, and knew any plea would be in vain.

Nick turned to Zubov. "What do you think?"

"I say they play a game. Winner gets Nick—the loser gets tossed overboard."

Nick seemed to like the idea. "Gambling—it's the American way." He turned to Lilly. "You like games, Mrs. McLaughlin, what do you want to play?"

She said nothing.

Nick looked disappointed. "Then I say we play your game—blackjack. If you win, Lilly, then what do you say we get married?"

Zubov took out two decks of cards and began to deal. Dava looked eager to destroy her competition, but Lilly refused to participate.

He sneered at her. "If you don't play, I will carve you up in front of your husband."

She knew it wasn't just a threat. So she grudgingly agreed—best two out of three. She lost the first game on purpose, trying to speed up the inevitable. But then her competitive juices kicked in.

Lilly won the second hand. And as the game went on, she felt her dark side take over her being. This was the ultimate thrill—the highest form of risk—playing for her life. Although, deep down, she knew that it really wasn't her life that she was fighting for—she wanted to win so that she could have a life with Nick.

Her concentration turned pinpoint and she seamlessly counted the cards. She blocked out all the chaos surrounding her.

Chapter 89

It had been over five hours since Darren had heard the gunshot, followed by Lilly's scream. There had been nothing but silence since, not even the typical radio static he'd become used to over the years of flying.

He filled with worry and despair, as he flew the plane toward the horizon. The sun was reflecting off the water, thirty-five-thousand feet beneath them, blinding him. It was already afternoon in this part of the world.

Darren kept expecting the plane to be swarmed by fighter jets in a daring rescue attempt, but none came. Just more silence.

The lone bright spot of the journey was when Natalie Gold joined him in the cockpit. It was like a scene out of an old movie—the heroic pilot dressed in his tux and the beautiful damsel in distress, decked out in her golden gown.

It wasn't a movie, but Darren did learn that his co-star was acting. Natalie Gold was just her stage name. She revealed herself as an intelligent down-to-earth girl from Oklahoma named Audrey Mays, who still had both of her hands. She was much different from the narcissistic diva Darren expected. They also had something in common: she got in this mess for the same reason Darren did—a bad choice in mates.

She walked him through the whole story, as she knew it, including the drastic measures she took with the intent to kill Sarvydas. She also told him of the proclamation Nick had made in the back of the plane that changed everything.

The movie soon turned into a horror flick. The gunshot rang through the cabin. The only thing Darren could remember was Lilly's scream. Moments later, Zubov entered the cockpit and physically returned Natalie to the back of the plane. Darren was left alone.

About two hours ago, he began to go stir crazy—he never thought he would miss chatting with the tower. But the silence had left him time to think. He couldn't believe they would be allowed to just land at Ben Gurion and be shuttled to Sarvydas' home without any accountability. It went against every international hijacking law known to man. He expected the Israelis to shoot down the plane, and figured that might be the painless way to go.

The cockpit door swung open and Nick stormed in. He handed Darren a piece of paper with handwritten coordinates. "There has been a change of plans—I need you to land."

When Darren computed the coordinates, his face filled with confusion. "You want me to land on the Mediterranean Sea?"

"It's either that or strapping on parachutes."

While a water landing was unappealing, to say the least, parachuting out of a commercial airliner at this altitude was a certain death sentence, no matter what the DB Cooper enthusiasts like to think. He was certain that Nick didn't just get the sudden urge to plunge a plane into the sea. It was a calculated decision determined long before the plane lifted off the runaway in New York, just like the choice to make Darren and Lilly the scapegoats. But one that would likely end in a fiery death for all.

"That's crazy," Darren proclaimed.

"Maybe, but also plausible."

"I have been trained to 'ditch' an airline, but in the history of aviation no wide-bodied plane has ever had a successful water landing."

"Then I guess I didn't really watch the heroic Captain Sully land his plane on the Hudson River."

"I really hope you didn't base your end game on the Miracle on the Hudson. This isn't remotely the same thing—they had just taken off and he landed on a smooth river. We are at full cruising altitude, and using the Mediterranean as our runway would be like landing in a mountain range, except that the mountains would be moving."

"Please don't bullshit me, Darren. We both know that in 1996 a 767 out of Ethiopia ditched after being hijacked. Not only can it be done, it has been successfully completed."

"I'm not sure what your definition of success is. Ethiopian-961 caught its wing on the water, causing the plane to shatter into three different pieces and over a hundred people died."

"But fifty-two passengers did live, and many of the deaths were because of the failure to evacuate quickly enough. We only have five on board."

Darren was good at math. Six minus one equals five. He had seen Nick, Natalie, and Zubov since the gunshot. That would leave Dava and Lilly, and according to Natalie, Dava was working with them…

"Even in the best circumstances 'ditching' a plane is not pretty. Planes crumble like soda cans when hitting hard surfaces at high speeds. And like I said, it's not like we will be landing on a calm pond. We will have to deal with wind and high waves, and even if we live through it, and perform a flawless evacuation, we will probably end up as shark food."

Nick patted Darren on the shoulder. "I have faith in you, Darren. Even if you don't have it in yourself. Your record as a pilot is fantastic. That is one of the reasons we picked you."

"I won't do anything until I see that my wife is okay."

"I can assure you that Lilly is far better than okay. She's the best I ever had."

Darren pushed the yoke in and headed straight into a nosedive, thrashing Nick to the floor. When he felt he made his point, he straightened the plane out. Nick shoved a gun in his ear and threatened to shoot him. But despite all his bluster, he agreed to Darren's terms. As long as they remained in the air, he had some bargaining power.

Zubov brought Lilly to the cockpit and strapped her into the first officer seat. With confirmation that his wife was alive, Darren agreed to land the plane on the water, which meant that she likely wouldn't be alive much longer. He ordered them all to strap themselves into the seats in the middle of the plane—the cockpit and tail were the most dangerous areas. He should have had them all strap into straightjackets—this was certifiably nuts!

Lilly refused to go. She looked Darren in the eye, and then reached her arm across to touch his hand. "I'm staying with my husband. Until death do us part, right?"

Darren couldn't break her stare. And her touch was as dazzling as ever to his senses. But the eyes never lie. Her devotion wasn't about their marriage, it was about her attraction to danger.

And as Darren began their descent to destruction, he got the feeling that it would be a fatal attraction.

Chapter 90

Darren dropped the speed of the plane to a minimum. His one advantage was the knowledge of where and when they were landing. The other times a water-ditch had been attempted, it was a last resort emergency situation that had little planning or forethought. Even so, Darren still felt the weight of the world on his shoulders. Lilly was with him, but for the first time since he laid eyes on her in that casino, he felt all-alone in her presence.

He found a comfortable glide speed. The flaps helped slow the plane to the lowest possible speed without stalling. As they approached the water, he used the intercom to address the passengers. He had only done this in a simulator, but he knew they were going to experience a jarring impact the likes of which they probably couldn't even imagine. They also had to be prepared for flippage, fires, and explosions. Once they landed, they needed to get out of the plane as fast as possible, but he warned against inflating their life jackets prior to removing themselves from the plane—a common cause of death in small planes during water-landings. And once they escaped the wreckage, it was imperative that they stay away from the explosive engines that would be floating nearby.

Darren guided the plane over the top of the sea. He was lining up the waves for the safest landing spot when he was rocked by the loudest bang he'd ever heard. Lilly screamed at the top of her lungs, yet he could barely hear it.

Darren kept his calm—he knew what happened. The wind tilted the plane too far to the left, clipping the wing against the unforgiving water. The wing came off, as it was built to do, causing the plane to fight any attempt to control it. It was like swimming against the tide, and it was all happening too fast. To make matters worse, the left engine acted like an ice cream scoop in the water and had ripped off.

Instead of gripping tighter, Darren eased off. He tried to "horseback ride" on the yoke to keep the nose up as long as possible. He used the flaps to reduce speed, desperately trying to avoid a "slam." He raised the nose—not sufficient to climb, but enough to bleed off any air speed. Lilly's screams continued to be drowned out by the hissing sound coming from the gaping hole left by the missing engine.

Darren placed the belly down on the water as gently as possible. He thought he had lucked into finding a "meadow" between the waves, but just when he thought this might actually work, he was overwhelmed by the sound of crunching metal.

The plane shook from side to side as if it had landed on an earthquake, and he could feel the thousand pounds of thrust spraying water like a geyser. Darren was sure they were about to flip over, or worse, rip into pieces.

Just when it seemed hopeless, the plane miraculously skidded to a halt.

But there was no time to send a thank you note to the heavens. Darren un-strapped himself and tried to stand, at least as well as his wobbly legs would allow. He viewed the cockpit. It looked like a bomb had hit—the control panel was torn from the console and the windshield was shattered. Glass was everywhere.

He found Lilly curled up on the floor. She had been completely dislodged from her seat-belt.

She was barely conscious, her face leaking blood and bruised like a plum. She was still breathing, but she would not make it out on her own. He tried to pull her to her feet, but she couldn't put any weight on her leg. So Darren picked his wife up and carried her. Pain shot through his ankle, which had jammed into the console during impact.

He winced in pain, as he kicked open the door to the cockpit just wide enough so they could fit through. But then he was hit with another troubling reality. The electric had shorted and the airframe was broken. The cabin was filling with water, and there was no sign of life.

Staring to the back of the plane, Darren realized what caused that horrific sound that had stabbed his ears. He had clipped the tail off, causing a gaping hole in the back of the plane! He understood the likelihood that all passengers were sucked through the hole to an unpleasant death.

He waded through the waist-high water in the cabin—seats had been ripped right out of the floor—it was worse than any hurricane footage he'd ever seen. With Lilly still in his arms, he headed for the bright sunlight shooting through the tail.

He put Lilly onto his back and used all his remaining strength to swim from the plane. The first thing to hit him was the smell of jet fuel. He also noticed the huge engines floating nearby—a Rolls Royce Trent-900 model that was bigger than a small truck. But what most attracted his attention were the survivors floating in a life raft with dazed looks. They were alive!

Darren had been trained in water simulators, so he wasn't disorientated like the others. He swam Lilly to the life raft and handed her over to Zubov—a scary thought.

When Darren tried to climb into the raft himself, he was met by the point of Nick's gun. "You messed up and now you're going to pay for it!"

Darren was confused. He was pretty sure he'd pulled off the miracle of all miracles. He landed a wide-bodied commercial jet in the Mediterranean Sea with no loss of life. But when he did a headcount, he realized that someone was missing.

"Either you find Audrey or you will die the most painful death I can think of," he screamed at him.

Darren was in leader-mode. He remained calm, asking, "What happened to her?"

"When the tail ripped off the plane, her seat came unhinged and she was sucked out. Find her!"

Darren began to swim toward what he recognized as the tailpieces. He slogged through the cold water and sifted through the pieces of wreckage. He was skeptical that Audrey Mays had escaped death this time. Even if she survived the impact, she likely would've been badly burned.

Then he witnessed his second miracle of the day. He located her, or at least her body. She was bobbing in her seat, being held above water by her life-jacket. Her gold dress had been torn to shreds and a blonde wig ripped from her head, exposing short-cropped, brown hair.

Darren moved closer, not expecting her to be alive. But he found her semiconscious—her breathing was shallow, and she appeared dazed, but she was alive. He felt momentary relief.

He swam Audrey to a piece of the wing and lugged the groggy pop star up on it. As he did, he noticed a large speedboat slicing through the swells of water. At first, he thought it was a rescue crew who'd seen the plane go down. It came to a sweeping stop right in front of Darren and Audrey, hanging on to their wing and a prayer.

Darren implored them to radio for help, as both Lilly and Audrey would need immediate medical attention. But the only response he received was a machine-gun pointing in his direction.

"We've come to take you to Mr. Sarvydas."

Chapter 91

The boat took them to the point where the sea met the cliffs of Netanya. They were loaded into a Jeep and driven up the rugged terrain until they reached the Sarvydas mansion.

They were rushed inside and shown to separate rooms by machine-gun-toting guards. Darren's room rivaled the size of his home in Arizona. A fresh suit was laid out on the bed and he was instructed to clean himself up for dinner. The guard promised to return in half-an-hour.

Darren put on the dark suit, but wasn't sure if he was dressing for a formal dinner or his own funeral.

As nightfall crept through the large bay window of the room, the guard returned. He escorted Darren through a maze of grand rooms and staircases to a breathtaking dining room. One side of the room looked out at a beautiful city skyline. But when Darren looked closer, he realized it was a mural of St. Petersburg. The opposing wall had a cliffside view of the dark sea. This one wasn't a painting, and neither were the armed guards on the balcony. It was all too real.

A television newscast was being projected on the glass wall, making it the biggest TV Darren had ever seen. The news anchor—thankfully not Jessi Stafford—was reporting that the Israeli government had confirmed that the hijacked Air Israel flight had crashed into the Mediterranean Sea off the coast of Israel. There was no word on survivors, but the prognosis was bleak. They displayed the first photos of the mangled plane before it sunk to the bottom of the sea, the wings and tail ripped away. Divers were currently at the crash site searching for survivors, and they planned to do so through the night.

In between coverage of the many Natalie Gold vigils being held around the world was a report on the three suspected hijackers. Darren's photo was from his pilot license, and as usual, he didn't smile, making him appear menacing. Lilly's photo was from her school yearbook, while Dava's photo came courtesy of the US Attorney's Office. The photo of Darren, Dava, and Ron Treadwell together in the bar was also shown, linking the "hijackers" together in infamy. The motive of the crime had yet to be pinpointed, but it had been linked to the Sarvydas trial and the Sarvy's shootout.

The others joined Darren in the dining room. His eyes first went to Lilly. He was relieved to see that the color had returned to her bronzed skin. They were all dressed for dinner—men in dark suits and women in black evening gowns. Lilly also sported a pair of crutches, her leg set in a cast.

Her eyes appeared hazy, probably the result of pain medication. She gave him a cloudy smile. He pulled his eyes away before her look trapped him. He planned to die with his dignity intact, as best he could.

Audrey had turned back into Natalie Gold, including the blonde wig. Her fans could extinguish their candles and save their tears. It was a miracle she didn't at the least suffer severe burns or head trauma, and with the wonder of make-up, her facial abrasions could barely be detected. Darren was the only one who was informed enough to understand the odds they beat to survive the crash landing. But the group seemed to comprehend that the odds of surviving Sarvydas were much steeper.

The most surprising guest was Nick. He stood next to Natalie like they were posing for prom photos, which led Darren to again think of Becks. He was worried for her, but wherever she was, it was less precarious than being at this dinner party, especially since they'd likely be the main course.

Viktor entered the room, flanked by a limping Zubov and a handful of bodyguards. The moment called for trumpets to play, but the room was pin-drop silent. He was shorter than Darren expected and wore a flamboyant purple suit. He seemed more like an eccentric musician than a feared international gangster.

As he got closer, Sarvydas locked eyes with Nick. The intensity between them made Darren uncomfortable. They stood in silence, and then Nick rushed toward him.

Surprisingly, Zubov and the guards didn't make any move to restrain him. The two men embraced. Not a good sign.

"It's so good to see you again, my son," Sarvydas said, his words choking with emotion.

The two words hung like a dark cloud over the room—*my son.*

"Oh my god," Natalie exclaimed.

Viktor viewed the room, before resting his eyes on Darren. He felt a chill down his newly found spine.

Chapter 92

"I'd like to welcome you, Mr. McLaughlin. Your work in getting all parties safely here tonight was nothing short of heroic. But this is not surprising to me—it's why you were chosen."

Darren didn't acknowledge the words.

Sarvydas' eyes traveled down Lilly's body until they arrived at the cast. "How is your leg feeling? I employ only the best doctors, and they tell me that you'll be back to new in no time."

"What's the difference? I already died in a plane crash, or at least that is what my obituary will state," she replied with defiance.

Sarvydas didn't try to reassure her. He turned his attention to Natalie. "It appears I didn't know you as well as I thought I did, *Audrey.* A relationship can't be built on lies. Lies always get you in the end."

She fired back, "You would be speaking from experience. You tried to murder me once, and used me to lead Alexei to his death. What kind of monster murders his own son?"

"I made you a star, and this is how you repay me?"

Natalie turned to Nick, and seemed to turn back into Audrey. "I don't understand, Nick. This is the man who killed your mother."

Sarvydas boiled. "I never did anything of the sort! I have spent my life protecting Nick and his mother."

He looked deep into Nick's eyes. He might have been talking to the group, but his words were meant for Nick. "I loved your mother and I wouldn't allow her to be harmed by my enemies. And when I found out she was pregnant, it wasn't just her I had to protect, it was also you. So I encouraged Paula to pursue a relationship with Karl, which she did. When Paula informed Karl that she was pregnant, they rushed to marriage, and you were born soon after. I made sure that Paula's doctor indicated for the record that you were born prematurely. But I doubt that Karl would've questioned it, anyway." He looked at Audrey. "Sometimes we want to believe something so bad that we make ourselves believe that lies are truth.

"After the marriage and child, my enemies backed off Paula. And Karl took a more behind-the-scenes role in my organizatsiya—a role he would thrive in, resulting in our worldwide economic dominance. My enemies knew a simple fact—if Paula Branche belonged to Viktor Sarvydas, then he would never allow his subordinate to impregnate her and live. I was counting on such a response. It pained me everyday to think of Paula with another man, raising my son, but when you love someone you have to make the ultimate sacrifice."

Darren looked at Lilly. It was clear to him that making these ultimate sacrifices for the one you love is not always enough.

Audrey agreed. "A relationship can't be built on lies. They always get you in the end," she threw his words back at him.

Sarvydas didn't rage, as Darren expected. He bowed his head in shameful acceptance. "Paula and I had no apologies for taking any means to protect our son. But in the end, you are right, the kingdom that is built on lies will fall like a house of cards."

Audrey once again turned to Nick. "Did you know about this the whole time, Nick? Was *our* relationship built on lies!?"

"I had no idea of any of this until after my mother was killed. I was just waiting for the right time to tell you, Audrey, I swear."

"You've got me here now, Nick."

"Do you remember when Viktor showed up at my mother's funeral?"

"Yes, when Karl accused him of being behind your mother's murder and threatened to kill him if he didn't leave. You were the one with the calm head. You separated them and then escorted Viktor off the premises. The funeral went on without further incident."

"Before he left, Viktor gave me an item he claimed would help me to understand what happened to my mother. It was a key to a lock box in a bank. I threw the key to the ground. But my curiosity got the best of me, and I went back to pick it up after he left."

"What was in the lock box?"

"A letter from my mother, explaining that Viktor was indeed my biological father. It repeated what he just told you—basically that she and Viktor thought I was in danger, and that Karl never knew. But I still didn't believe it—I thought it was some sort of trick by Viktor, maybe to give him an alibi for her murder."

"What made you believe him?"

"I went back to Viktor, demanding answers. He offered up his DNA and I had it tested. It came back as a perfect match—I was his son. He assured me that he was not behind her death, but he knew who was."

"Who killed your mother, Nick?"

"Viktor gave me the name of someone who he claimed had the answers. That person turned out to be Dava Lazinski—she became our intermediary. She provided me with a video."

"What was on the video?"

"The moment that changed everything."

Chapter 93

Nick clicked a remote and the video projected onto the window-television.

The tape was amateurish. Its source was a camera hidden in the wall of a small New York apartment.

Onscreen, Alexei Sarvydas entered the room—he looked heavier than his post-prison look, and his hair much longer. A man followed him into the apartment. He was of average height and build and sported a casual outfit of sweater and jeans. He wore a neatly trimmed goatee on a face that was otherwise bookish-looking. It was Karl Zellen.

"What is this place?" Karl asked, seemingly annoyed to be in Alexei's presence.

"A little hiding place I use when I need to have a private conversation—I think Viktor has bugged the club. It belongs to this chick Rachel I've been seeing."

"One of your whores, I'm sure. So what is so important that requires such secrecy? I have to pick Sasha up from skating practice, so make it quick."

"My father would have told you himself, but he's too busy making music with your wife," Alexei replied with a knowing smirk.

"Is this about Paula's album? Viktor tells me it's coming along nicely. She's been very excited about it."

Alexei reached into the pocket of his leather coat and took out an object. He tossed it onto a coffee table that was cluttered with girly magazines. It was a tape recorder. Alexei indicated for Karl to click it on. The tape played the voices of Viktor and Paula.

It started with talk of recapturing their love, agreeing that they had wasted so many years by not being together. Paula stated that she feared hurting Karl, but had made up her mind to leave him for Viktor. “I can’t live a lie anymore. These last weeks in your arms have made that clear. The kids are grown now—they will be angry at first, but they will come to accept us.”

Karl slumped onto a couch as if he’d been mortally wounded. Then it got worse. Viktor protested on tape, “As much as I want to be with you, Paula, the danger is too great. I sent you to Karl, not just to protect you, but also to protect our son. If we are together again, then my enemies will re-examine the past and wonder if Nick is really Karl’s son. It could put him in danger.”

“That was a long time ago. You are Nick’s father, Viktor. Karl is a great man who did a wonderful job raising him, but a young man should know his father.”

“Time might have passed, but old grudges never die.”

“I would do anything to protect my children, and I have, which is why I’ve decided I must tell Nick the truth. Then I will do the same with Karl. The lies are more dangerous to us than your enemies.”

The tape clicked off.

Karl lashed out at Alexei, “You made this up! This can’t be true. Nick is my son, a father would know that!”

“What would I gain from making this up? I am in line to take over the business when Viktor steps aside. The last thing I want is some gold-digging stepmother to take my portion, or a bastard brother dropping in from out of the blue.”

Karl began pacing. “Don’t talk about them that way!”

“Don’t talk about who? Your cheating wife or the son you’re still pretending to be yours?”

“How did you get that tape?”

Alexei smiled wickedly. "When I moved to Florida, I lived at the family compound in Fisher Island. I didn't think the place was safe enough, so I put in a recording system. I guess I forgot to mention it to my father, must have slipped my mind. Viktor and Paula should have rented an apartment like this if they wanted privacy."

According to Eicher, Karl was a cool, efficient assassin who rarely showed emotion. But that person had been taken over by the lust for revenge. He screamed out his plans to shred Viktor's body parts, and a desire to cut out Paula's womb as a punishment for what she had done. He fired his fist into a coffee table, sending magazines and assorted knickknacks in all directions. He shouted that he would never allow them to be together, and Nick would always be his son. He wouldn't let them take his life away from him.

Karl gathered himself and morphed into his cold, calculating persona. The two men then hatched a plan. It would start by leaking enough information to the feds so that Karl would be arrested on money laundering charges. They would get word out that he planned to cooperate—make it clear that he was willing to take down Viktor to save his own hide. Viktor would predictably respond with threats, and when those failed, he would make his point in blood. Perhaps a family member of Karl's would end up dead. Viktor would be blamed when Paula Zellen was murdered.

Karl didn't waver or flinch as he signed off on the plan that would send his wife to her execution. Alexei, who had access to the mansion, would arrange her murder during one of Paula and Viktor's "music sessions" that Karl assured her were necessary to keep up for appearances' sake.

Paula would be killed in the same ambush style that Viktor had used to take power—the ultimate copycat crime. The rumors were always there that Viktor had Alexei's mother killed, and after what he heard on the tape, Alexei could no longer dismiss them. He would leave Viktor alive, to suffer the same way he did.

When the tape clicked off, Audrey looked at Nick. Her face was horrified, but filled with compassion. "So when you saw that video, you set up a plan to get revenge on the people who killed your mother—Alexei and Karl."

Viktor spoke for his son, "I had the police set up a meeting with Karl, claiming new leads on his wife's murder. Karl was very interested in them finding Paula's killer, just not the real one … himself. Officers Dantelli and Bachynsky told me that the look on Karl's face was priceless when they informed him that the apartment he and Alexei used to seek privacy, had been under surveillance."

"But the police didn't kill him, did they? And neither did Alexei," Audrey blurted, her eyes locked on Nick. She now knew who killed Karl Zellen—they all did.

Nick stated without emotion, "I didn't come home unexpectedly. I came home to get justice for my mother. But not until I made him beg for his life."

"And you also set up Alexei."

"Dantelli and Bachynsky had access to Alexei's fingerprints from the NYPD and left them behind. Alexei was on one of his coke benders, and had no alibi … at least not one he could remember. Of course my fingerprints would be there, since I lived in that house of lies most of my life."

Lilly spoke, "You played the victim and were put in witness protection, but really the person we needed to be protected from was you."

"You did this to yourself, Lilly. You are no more a victim than I am."

"You had to get out of Arizona to make sure there was no trial, while getting rid of the evidence along the way—Dantelli and Bachynsky. And your desperation to get to back to New York had nothing to do with Sasha's safety—Viktor never would have let anything happen to her—it was to finish the job by killing Alexei. But you were too much of a coward to do it yourself—you had to use Darren and I as your cover."

"You wanted this, Lilly, as much as I did. And deep down, even with what you know now, you would do the same thing again."

"So now that your revenge is complete, you can get rid of the rest of the evidence. Toss us out at sea and claim we died in the plane crash."

"This is not over," Nick shot back, glaring at her.

Viktor put his arm around him. "Your mother will never return, but she would be happy that you are home now, son."

Nick looked incredulously at his father. "Home? That's an interesting word. I lived in a great home with a loving family and a hopeful future. I had a girlfriend, whom I loved and wanted to marry. I was happy, but then you chose to re-enter my life. And you killed your own son, and I don't mean Alexei. You killed Nick Zellen. He will never be that person again."

"Everything I did was to protect you."

"Yet in the end, by engaging in an affair with my mother, you essentially destroyed my true family."

"I would never harm your mother. I loved her more than life itself."

"Good intentions never mitigate destruction. A crime was committed and there needs to be a punishment. So I find the defendant responsible for the murder of my mother."

Nick raised a gun, and gasps filled the room. Viktor was too stunned to talk. But when he found the words, he did what most bullies do when being forced to swallow their own medicine. He groveled for his pitiful life.

Nick put the gun down with a grin. "Don't worry, I would never shoot my own father."

Then an explosion filled the room. Lilly and Audrey screamed, as Darren tried to shield them from the horrific scene.

Zubov lowered his still-smoking gun to his side as he watched Viktor's body fall to the ground.

The room stood silent. Zubov looked past their fear to Nick, and declared, "He deserved his fate. Your mother was innocent. Nobody should ever kill an innocent person."

Chapter 94

Not one shot was fired by Viktor's bodyguards when their leader was gunned down. They too now worked for the don's son.

Nick ran right to Audrey and grabbed tightly to her arm. "Get away from me," she screeched, wrestling away from his grip.

He continued after her. "It's over now, Audrey. It's over."

He caught up to her, forcing her into an embrace.

Audrey thrashed with her arms, trying to break loose. Heavy tears began falling down her face. "It will never be over," she shouted. But then she gave in and accepted his arms around her.

"I can't stop thinking about Rachel—you killed that innocent girl!" she wailed through sobs.

"Dava took matters into her own hands. I swear that wasn't my idea. That is why Zubov shot her on the plane."

"I read all the reports, Nick. There was no forced entry. The intruder had used my key—that's why they were so sure it was me who'd been killed. How many times had you taken her to my apartment? You were the reason she was there that night."

Nick said nothing.

"When you were with her, did you know you were going to kill her?"

The question caused him to snap. "I would do anything to protect you. I have no apologies! We had to make people believe you were dead."

"You sound just like Viktor." She looked at his dead body on the floor, his purple suit stained red. "Look how that worked out."

"Audrey, please understand. I did this so we could be together again. My life is nothing without you."

Darren noticed Lilly out of the corner of his eye. She looked almost jealous. He didn't take satisfaction in his wife's pain, even if it was deserved. Revenge was a hollow drug. It didn't give Nick his mother back, and it wasn't going to heal their marriage.

"Together? Who would I be together with? I don't know who you are. All I know is that you're not the man I fell in love with," Audrey continued to resist.

"I'm still the same person. Only the circumstances have changed. A soldier might have to go off to war to protect his loved ones, and the experience might shape him, but that doesn't change his core," Nick was practically begging.

"You are so filled with revenge you can't even see straight. You're not the Nick I knew." She dragged him in front of one of Viktor's many vanity mirrors and made him stare at himself. "You're not him!"

He twitched, as if sickened by the sight of himself. "You came here to kill Viktor, just like me. But I never blamed you or judged you. Because I love you. I killed him so you didn't have to."

"Get away from me!" Audrey shrieked. She jerked away from his touch and turned to leave.

The guards didn't stop her, but Nick's words did. "I know you love me, because you did things for me that you wouldn't be proud of, just like I did for you."

He clicked the remote and another video displayed on the window screen. It was of Natalie Gold. Darren couldn't believe what he was watching. It was of an intimate encounter between Natalie and the prime minister of Israel!

Audrey began to cry as she watched herself in action.

"You were Viktor's whore. You did that for me. You did that to get revenge on him—to gain his trust so you could kill him. We are no different."

He paused the film, freezing Audrey in mid thrust. He walked to her and wiped the tears from her face, and then took her into his arms. "You said on the plane that you would follow me, even if you saw things you didn't understand. You pledged your loyalty, and now I'm going to pledge mine to you."

He began to kiss her, and Audrey reciprocated. But Nick unexpectedly pulled away and wiped blood from his lip. Audrey had bit him.

"I might be a whore, but I'm not a murderer."

Nick stood eerily calm, as if his metamorphosis into a Sarvydas was now complete.

"I have proven my loyalty to you, Audrey. I don't hold it against you that you shared a bed with the man responsible for my mother's death, and worked for him. I think it's time for you to return the favor and prove your loyalty to me."

She slapped him.

He rubbed his cheek, then coldly handed her his gun. "I want you take the McLaughlins out to the cliffs and shoot them."

"What will you do if I refuse—kill me?"

"No—I will send Zubov to meet with your parents. He needs to find religion, and I think he would hit it off with the Reverend."

Audrey remained defiant, but her hands were shaking. "You wouldn't."

"You're a pragmatic girl. Look how you persevered this past year. You did whatever it took. One act of loyalty is all I'm asking for. They're going to die anyway."

He held the gun out for her. She looked at him and then to Darren and Lilly. After a long moment, she accepted the gun. Darren understood her decision. She chose to make any sacrifice, no matter how vile, to protect those that she loved—her parents. They all had made a similar decision in the past few days.

She led Lilly and Darren outside with the gun pointing at their spines. Just outside the estate was a Jeep. Zubov would go as a witness to the execution.

Nick instructed Audrey to drive across the estate until she came to the cliffs. She wasn't really to shoot them—the gun was just symbolic. Nick wanted them to wash up ashore as victims of the plane crash. So Audrey was to bash their heads in with a crowbar found in the back of the Jeep, while Zubov held them down. Then toss them into the sea.

But as Audrey and the prisoners arrived at the Jeep, she turned and hit Zubov with the gun handle. His wounded knees couldn't hold him, and he fell to the ground. Nick made a move at her and she pressed the trigger, but nothing came out.

His telling look said that he knew the gun wasn't loaded. But he looked saddened by the irreconcilable wedge that she'd just driven into their relationship.

"Run!" Audrey shouted to Darren. He tossed Lilly over his shoulders and climbed into the Jeep. He found the key and started the vehicle. They sped off over the dark terrain.

Nick calmly helped Zubov up and instructed him to go after them. Zubov limped to another Jeep, and drove off after the McLaughlins.

He then grabbed Audrey by her Natalie Gold wig. "You betrayed me!" he shouted so viciously it echoed off the sea.

She again slapped him across the face. "I already know you killed my parents. I could see it in your eyes, Nick."

"Anything I did was to keep you safe."

"Spare me!" She thought for a moment and then said, "I take that back—kill me. Do it now. Then you really will be just like your father."

"I'm not going to kill you…yet. I loved Audrey Mays and she was murdered in her apartment and is buried in Oklahoma."

He returned her slap, violently knocking her head to the side. "You are Natalie Gold, nothing but a cheap whore. But a whore who makes me money. You see, Viktor left his financial empire to his living son. That makes me the head of Sarvy Music and you are my top-selling artist. As long as you make me money, you will get to live another day. And each day I let you live, I want you to remember that I own you."

Chapter 95

Darren tightly gripped the wheel. The sound of the crashing waves told him that he was heading for the cliffs.

He'd thought about this mad-dash since they arrived. And had studied the landscape from the vantage point of his room when he changed for dinner. But like most plans, it was much different in reality, and the vehicle closing quickly on his ass wasn't helping.

He had to make it to the path that led down the cliffs to the sea. He put the lights on—the chaser was on his tail, anyway—they weren't fooling anyone. Audrey had outlined the plan to him during their time in the cockpit, including where the key was hidden in the Jeep.

When she wasn't cutting albums and making controversial videos, Audrey was stuck on the Sarvydas estate like a prisoner. So to entertain herself, she had the staff take her out into the Mediterranean in one of Viktor's boats and teach her to scuba dive.

Now the scuba gear she'd kept in the Jeep had another purpose. She told Darren if he could make it to the boat, it was possible to use the scuba gear to make a swim for it. Audrey provided the contact info of a man in Tel Aviv who could change identities—or if he got to the US Embassy, he could possibly gain some protection. It was a long shot, especially since being declared an international hijacker his picture would be everywhere. But at least he'd have a fighting chance.

But Darren couldn't locate the path in the dark. And as certain death moved closer to their back bumper, he knew this wasn't going to end well.

Lilly looked at him and said, "It wasn't your fault that you fell in love with me."

Her tone said that she came to the same conclusion he had. It was over. She was saying goodbye.

Darren looked behind them, the headlights growing larger.

Lilly continued, "You tried to save me, but I was a lost cause. I wanted it so badly to work for us that I fooled myself. And one thing they said in there was right—you can't build a relationship on lies. But just because we're not going to have a fairytale ending, doesn't mean that you're not my hero. I really did love you—I need you to know that."

He looked at her with a sideways glance, momentarily taking his eyes off the fast-approaching cliff top. "I will always love you, Lilly. Marriage is for better or worse. And we had a lot more better than worse."

She stared ahead blankly at the jagged cliffs coming into view. Then solemnly added, "Until death do us part."

Darren looked ahead and knew she was right. They had two choices—be mutilated by Zubov, or go out on their own terms. He grabbed Lilly's hand and looked into her eyes. She understood what he was saying and nodded. He kissed her on the bandaged cheek and hit the gas. They headed for the end.

Just as they approached certain death, shots rang out. One pinged off the metal roll bar just above their heads. Since they just agreed to plunge to their deaths, Darren wasn't sure why they were ducking. Maybe they weren't ready to die. But when an explosion rocked their vehicle, he understood that they didn't have much of a choice in the matter.

The gunshots had ripped through their tires and caused a blowout. The Jeep teetered and tottered, then flipped onto its back. It skidded to an upside-down stop.

Darren and Lilly hung like bats as they heard the footsteps of their killer move toward them. They were trapped. They were still going to die, just not on their own terms.

Zubov bent down to look into the upturned Jeep. He chuckled. "You left so fast, I didn't get chance to say goodbye."

He took out a machete and cut them out of their seat-belts. He grabbed Lilly by her hair and dragged her out with no regard for her leg injury. He then dragged Darren out by his suit jacket.

Zubov forced them to their feet and announced, "Running from Zubov is like running from death."

After a few parting words, and the assurance of no hard feelings, Zubov explained that this was a business arrangement and he was just doing his job. When he said all he had to say, Darren and Lilly McLaughlin flew off the high cliffs of Netanya.

Chapter 96

The cavalry arrived. Israeli Special Forces stormed the Sarvydas estate, clad in black, and assisted by high-tech night-vision goggles. It was a two-pronged attack, arriving from both land and sea.

The Sarvydas security force had no chance. The Special Forces unit was on orders to shoot-to-kill, and they did. The guards fell like raindrops to the floor, before they could even shoot off the rounds from their Uzis.

They found Nick and Natalie Gold tied to chairs in one of the bedrooms. They appeared more relieved than elated to be rescued, saying very little.

When the place was completely secure, Israeli Prime Minister Ati Kessler showed up to view the scene that had kept his country on edge for the past day. But now he was going to be the hero. The forceful leader who stormed the beaches to rescue the hostages.

It was the stuff that legends are made of, and Ati Kessler was a living legend. The key word being living—he knew how to survive. But he was also a politician and his approval ratings were about to go through the roof. It didn't hurt that his biggest political baggage was lying dead on the floor in a purple suit.

He requested to meet privately with Nick—the victim. He walked him outside, knowing that Viktor had every inch of the house bugged. "You look good for a man who endured a plane crash."

Nick smiled. "It was a risky proposition, but I never run from a danger. I've learned this past few months that living on the edge can be quite exhilarating."

Kessler smiled back at him, his capped, white teeth glowing in the dark. "I had no other choice. I had enough clout with the US government to get you out of New York, but with Viktor's continuing negative drag on my approval rating, I didn't have the political influence to authorize a safe landing at Ben Gurion, and a taxi to Netanya. I would have been overruled and none of you would've gotten off that plane without a few new holes in you. Believe it or not, the plane crash was the safest route."

Their stroll stalled at the cliffs. They looked down at the water below and took cautionary steps back away from the edge. Still looking down the treacherous elevator shaft to the deadly sea, Nick informed, "The hijackers are all dead. Died in the crash. The McLaughlins and Dava Lazinski."

"We captured Zubov on the grounds, trying to make a run for it."

"Zubov is loyal to me—I want him released."

Kessler shook his head. "I'm sorry, Nick, but I'm going to need some raw meat to throw to the animals. He will be a symbol of my strength. As if to say nobody comes into Israel and dictates terms as long as Ati Kessler is in charge. It's important to show that kind of strength in this part of the world."

"And how would such an arrangement benefit me?"

"If my power is strong, then your interests will be strengthened, especially since you have taken over your father's business. What is good for me is good for you, Nick," he said with a friendly pat on the back.

They headed back toward the lights of the mansion.

"So what do you want to happen now?" Kessler asked.

"I want to go home to New York. It's been a hectic couple of days."

"I will just need one more thing from you to make that happen."

"And what is that?"

"I want access to Viktor's secret video surveillance. The ones of Ms. Gold and myself are of specific interest."

They moved into the mansion and Nick disappeared into Viktor's bedroom to oblige the request. Kessler looked across the room at Audrey. He walked to her and slowly ran his eyes over her every curve. He whispered, "I hope Nick and I will be doing a lot of *business* in the future."

She turned away with disgust, understanding that business meant the same thing if it was father or son.

Nick returned with a package of disks. They stepped back outside and he handed them to Kessler.

"These are all of them, Nick? I want to think we're getting off on the right foot."

Nick looked offended by the accusation. "Have I not been honest with you every step of the way? If not for me, you wouldn't even have known about the tapes or any other blackmail tactics Viktor was using against you. And be sure to check the disks to see if copies have been made—I know you have such technology."

"Just remember that your father was an honest man at one point. Maybe not to his family or in his businesses, but to his fellow vors, and that is what's most important. I now consider you a vor, Nick, and it's important that we remain honest with each other." He stared menacingly at Viktor's dead body. "Because a relationship built on lies always ends badly."

Chapter 97

8 Days Later

Jessi Stafford smiled into the camera like a woman who just signed a multi-year deal with GNZ to host her own prime-time show. And her first assignment was an exclusive interview with heroic hijack victim, Nick Zellen.

They sat facing each other in the lavish but comfy living room of his Long Island mansion. He looked back at her with his intense eyes, his dark hair slicked back. He was dressed business casual in a button-down shirt and khakis, no tie.

"I'd first like this opportunity to welcome you home, Nick," Jessi started.

"Your reporting might have helped keep me alive. If I wasn't able to tell my story from the plane, who knows what would've happened."

"Your modesty aside, the courage you displayed likely saved not only your life, but the lives of the others aboard the plane, including pop sensation Natalie Gold."

Nick continued shyly, "I would love to tell you a heroic tale in which I was the brave protagonist, but the boring truth is that the plane hadn't been completely fueled when it was hijacked. So there was no other choice but to attempt a crash landing on the water. After that, survival instincts kicked in, just as they would for anyone put in such a precarious position."

"Tell me about the crash—many aviation experts claimed that it was a one in a million shot that anyone could survive it."

Nick turned emotional, his voice cracking, "It was horrible. I had never felt an impact like that—it was like someone had taken a baseball bat to my body. And I can still hear the noise pounding in my head over a week later. When we hit the water, the tail ripped completely off and Natalie was sucked out. I thought she was dead."

"While you and Natalie thankfully made it, we have confirmed that the three main hijackers—Darren and Lilly McLaughlin, along with Dava Lazinski—are all dead. And that the fourth hijacker, the assassin Zubov, is being held in an Israeli prison."

"It is a great relief to know they will no longer be able to hurt innocent people."

"But your ordeal didn't end with the crash."

"That's right. Darren McLaughlin, who was piloting the plane, had instructed Viktor Sarvydas' men as to where the plane would likely go down, based on fuel estimates. So while we withstood the crash, we were taken to face Sarvydas. Thankfully, Prime Minister Kessler had the courage to send troops in to save us."

"The man he saved you from, Viktor Sarvydas—what do you think his motivation was to harm you?"

"While many knew Viktor as a music producer, he also had a dark side that was hidden behind the legitimacy of his work. In fact, he was responsible for the murder of my parents."

"You witnessed the murder of Karl Zellen, which was carried out by his son, Alexei Sarvydas. It was also the reason why you were in the Witness Protection Program in Arizona under the name Brett Buckley."

"That is correct."

"In the program, you were protected by a US federal marshal who has been identified as Chelsea Fitzpatrick. Initial reports were that Ms. Fitzpatrick might be involved in the kidnapping plot, but we have since learned that her shooting of Alexei Sarvydas actually saved your life."

"I owe her a debt of gratitude. Her bravery is the reason I'm here to talk to you."

"All attempts by GNZ to contact Ms. Fitzpatrick have been unsuccessful—all we know is she has resigned from her position. We would like to have her tell her heroic story, do you think you could help us locate her?"

Nick shook his head. "I've had no contact with her since the incident at Sarvy's. And I learned from my time in witness protection that those working in the program often use aliases to remain undercover, so Fitzpatrick might not even be her real name. And I wouldn't want her, or anybody connected to the program, to be put in any danger created by a media storm."

"This past week, the agencies involved have come under intense criticism for their handling of your protection, but it doesn't sound like you harbor any ill will."

"Despite what happened, including the leaks, I believe everyone involved did their best to protect me. We are talking about one rogue agent in Dava Lazinski, who was responsible for my cover being blown, and is not a reflection on the many hard working people in the FBI, US Federal Marshals, and the US Attorney's Office, especially US Attorney Eicher who was in charge of the case."

Jessi smiled, hoping to lighten the proceedings a little. "This might be a little off the subject, Nick, but one of the things that fascinated me about your journey is that you had to return to high school. That would have been the scariest part for me."

He laughed. "I tried to make the best of it. My first time in high school, the biggest obstacles were my social awkwardness and battles with acne. This time it was my teacher and her husband luring me into their web to deliver me to a Russian mob boss. So I guess you could say it was different types of challenges."

Jessi's smile faded, her look turning serious. "Since you brought up the now deceased Lilly McLaughlin, your affair with a married woman seems very out of character for you."

Nick turned emotional once again. "It was stupid, I know. Not that it's an excuse, but it was a very vulnerable time for me—my mother and girlfriend had been murdered—and in some strange way, Lilly took on both their roles—a mother-figure and lover. I guess I was an easy target for her, and I'm sure Viktor Sarvydas knew that."

"One final thing—what I find to be the most ironic twist to this whole case, is that due to a legally binding contract between Karl Zellen and Viktor Sarvydas, you are now in charge of the businesses vacated by the man who tried to kill you, including Sarvy Music."

Nick nodded. "Karl and Viktor went back to when they were young men held captive in the Soviet Union. When they came to America, they vowed to always keep the Russian roots in their businesses through family. While their union ended in tragedy, the agreement between the two men lives on, as does their legacy in the business world. And with Viktor having no heirs to the throne, so to speak, it was left to me and my sister Sasha."

"Critics say with your lack of experience, you are unqualified to run a multi-national corporation."

"Well, I am qualified enough to know one thing—that integrity has nothing to do with experience. It's what I plan to return to the business. That's what Karl Zellen wanted to bring back to the company before Viktor..."

His words trailed off.

Jessi reached across to him and patted his hand. "This must have been such a terrible experience for you."

A smile appeared on his face. "It wasn't all bad, I guess."

Jessi looked surprised. "Talk about the glass being half full—other than your ultimate survival, what could you possibly take as a positive from this experience?"

Nick's smile turned coy. "I met a great girl."

As if on cue, Natalie Gold walked into the room. They kissed and sat cozily on the couch. It was like the ratings gods were smiling down on Jessi.

After Jessi finished her questions about their relationship, Nick took a knee before Natalie and opened a ring box. Jessi had never seen a diamond that big!

"When Audrey died," Nick began, eyes welling with tears. "I never thought that I could fall in love again. But the minute I met you on that airplane, I knew I wanted to spend the rest of my life with you. Natalie Gold … will you marry me?"

Chapter 98

8 Months Later—December

The man strolled down Boston's Newbury Street as a light snow fell. The famed street was decked out for Christmas with elaborate decorations, and festive carolers sang on street corners. But the man wasn't in the holiday spirit. The past year had taken a toll on him.

He took note of the 19th-century brownstones that lined the street. The neighborhood—now called the Back Bay area, built after the harbor was scaled back in 1860—reminded him of his own life, surrounded by the past, but still marching forward.

As he continued toward his destination, he entered the shopping district. It was full of trendy fashion shops—Chanel, Donna Karan, Armani, and Prada. But there was nothing fashionable about his own look. He wore a black skullcap pulled low on his head, along with a ratty sweater and jeans. Heavy black army boots warmed his feet.

He dropped some spare change into the cup of a street Santa, and when he looked up he noticed the young woman in the crowd. She wore a weathered Red Sox cap and had a backpack slung over her shoulder. She looked like a student, perhaps at the nearby Berklee College of Music.

His plan was to go to the opening of the new Sarvy Music store up the street. He wasn't interested in purchasing any new CDs; his intent was to thank an old friend for saving his life, or at least trying to. But the woman in the Red Sox hat changed his plans. The last eight months had proven to him the old axiom—*man plans and God laughs.* If anything, he'd learned that you have to be fluid in life and be able to change on the fly. This was a big change from his past thinking.

He followed the woman past the Exetor Street Theater, which looked more like a Tudor mansion than a movie theater. Then into an area made up of deconstructionist buildings. They were designed at crazy angles, looking as if they were colliding together. After walking a few more blocks, he concluded that the woman was going to the same place he was.

The Sarvy Music store was a forty thousand square foot, high-tech entertainment retailer. It was opened last night with a midnight ribbon-cutting ceremony attended by CEO, Nick Zellen. But he wouldn't be there for the first full day of business, as he was attending the US Figure Skating Championships being held in Boston. The man was counting on that. And besides, the big crowds spilling out the door weren't there to see a businessman; they had come to see Sarvy Music recording artist, and Zellen's wife, Natalie Gold, who was signing copies of her latest CD.

The man waited in line for almost an hour, about ten spots behind the woman in the Red Sox hat. When he was able to examine her face, he confirmed that his mind wasn't playing tricks on him—it was her. She looked antsy, which wasn't unusual, but what surprised him was that she appeared nervous. That wasn't her style.

When she finally got her meeting with Natalie Gold, they both tried to act nonchalant. But they couldn't fool him—this was a planned meeting. And when Natalie shook the woman's hand after she signed her CD, he noticed that Natalie had stealthily handed her an object, which the woman quickly hid in her pocket. If he weren't observing their interaction so closely, he never would've noticed. The extensive security cameras might not have even picked up the sleight of hand.

He was desperate to follow the woman, but had to remain patient for another ten minutes to get his audience with Natalie. When he did, he handed her his CD like any other fan.

"Whom should I sign this to?" she asked, looking at him, but not seeing him.

"Zuckley, Brick Zuckley," he said.

The unique name caught her interest and she took a closer glance. When she did, it was if she'd seen a ghost.

He was prepared for this. "It's good to see you again, Audrey. Just act normal."

"I thought you were…"

"Yeah, and let's keep it that way. What are you up to?"

She faked a smile. "I'm just here to meet my fans, Mr. Zuckley."

"I saw her here. You gave her something. Where's she going?"

Natalie held her smile as she opened the case of the CD titled *Naughtily Gold*, with the obligatory sexy photo of her on the cover. "That would be Zuckley with an *e-y* or just a *y?*" she asked.

"If she fails—which is the most likely outcome—it won't be long before he figures out that his wife was the one behind it. But if she succeeds, you will both face a much worse fate—you will become just like him."

"Thank you, Mr. Zuckley. I hope you enjoy the CD," she replied indifferently and looked to the next in line.

When he got outside, he opened up the case and read what she wrote. It gave him their suite number at the ritzy hotel just up the street, and the room code to get in. He ran up Newbury Street until he came to the Taj Boston, which used to be the famed Ritz Carlton on the corner of Newbury and Arlington. It was all the way at the other end of Newbury, near the Boston Public Garden.

He had no patience for the elevator, so he ran up the stairs, his boots echoing with each heavy step. He arrived at the top floor, and came in contact with three of Nick's guards. But all of them were knocked out and gagged in the stairwell. The woman's covert attack had worked.

He punched in the room code to gain entrance. The elegant room looked more like a luxury townhouse than a hotel suite.

He checked the marble bathroom and then ventured into a guest room that included rich fabric wall coverings and a pricey-looking armoire. He moved to the window that provided a view of the park. He took note of the ice skaters gliding atop the frozen frog pond. It sparked his urgency to find her before Zellen returned from the skating competition.

That is when he felt the cold steel of the gun on the back of his neck. He put his hands up in surrender.

"Hey Nick, welcome to the South Chandler High Reunion. I just voted you most likely to get a bullet in your head," she stated and pushed the gun harder.

Darren spun around and removed his skullcap. She had the same look as Natalie. Like she'd seen a ghost.

"Oh my god, Darren—I thought you were dead," Becks exclaimed.

"Darren is dead, and so will you be if you don't get out of here."

"Sorry, I have a job to finish."

"Then you are going to have to kill me, too."

Her face turned angry. "I can't believe after everything he did to you, that you would risk your life to save his sorry ass. He stole your wife and then he stole your life."

"I'm not saving him, I'm trying to save *you*. If you go through with this, your life is over either way."

She looked at her gun and then up at Darren, contemplating. She surprisingly lowered the gun and ran to him. She wrapped her arms around him. "I thought you were dead, you big idiot."

It felt good, but there was no time for sentiment. Darren pushed her toward the door. "Let's get out of here."

The minute they stepped into the hallway, the elevator at the end of the hall dinged. Out stepped Nick Zellen, his sister Sasha, with a pair of ice skates slung over her shoulder, and a team of sinister-looking bodyguards in long leather coats. The only good thing was that by coming up the elevator, they'd yet to discover his security detail tied-up in the stairwell.

Darren urged Becks to move to the stairs before they came into view. But she refused, walking directly toward the new leader of the Russian Mafiya. Darren had no choice but to follow. As they crossed paths, Darren avoided eye contact. But Becks had always believed life was a contact sport.

She "accidentally" bumped into Zellen and staggered him. He caught himself, before falling to the floor. He appeared taken aback, while his guards looked trigger-happy.

"Sahry, didn't see ya thahr," she uttered in her deepest Boston accent.

Nick looked at her and his eyes softened. "Don't worry about it—just watch where you're going next time." His bodyguards scrambled to help their leader back to his feet.

She then pulled down her baseball cap, and followed Darren to the elevator.

Chapter 99

Nick's first sign that something was out of place was that no guard was on duty in front of his door. So he sent his bodyguards in. If someone were waiting for him, they would never get a chance to deal with him.

But it was strange. Nobody was inside, and nothing was missing. They found the guards tied up and unconscious in the stairwell. They never saw who hit them from behind. Nick was thankful for this "fire drill," which taught him that these men couldn't be trusted with his life.

He mentally Rolodexed his many enemies, and felt relieved that Zubov was still incarcerated. The question nagged at him—*who was trying to send him a message?*

After a long afternoon of promoting her new CD, Natalie arrived to the suite. She looked surprised to see him, which he found peculiar. But it was consistent with the strange vibe he'd received from her lately, especially the part where she had started to give in to his every whim without a struggle. He made a mental note to watch her very closely in the future.

He grilled her as to whether she'd noticed any suspicious behavior at the store that might be connected to the attack on his guards. She claimed nothing or nobody appeared out of the ordinary, which was the expected answer. But not being the trusting type, he would call over to get copies of the surveillance tapes to take back with him to New York tomorrow.

He wouldn't let the incident ruin his evening. Nick still planned on taking Natalie and Sasha out to celebrate the opening of the new Sarvy Music store, Natalie's new album, and Sasha's runner-up finish in the US Figure

Skating Championships. They had a lot to celebrate, which made it more puzzling as to why he felt no joy. In fact, he felt empty.

The one thing he took satisfaction from was the knowledge that his mother would be proud of how he and Sasha had thrived in her absence, even if she wouldn't have been a fan of the tactics they were forced to use. And even though she tried to shield him from who he was, everyone eventually becomes who they are. He thought of her constant motherly advice, "Just be yourself, Nick." That was what he was doing, even if it wasn't the life he'd chosen.

Nick rented an entire restaurant on Newbury Street for just the three of them and a couple of bodyguards, whom he called the *oprichniki*—based on the name Ivan the Terrible referred to his merciless palace guards, who were the precursor of the KGB. Throughout history, danger was always around the corner for Russian leaders, and protection was a priority.

Nick raised a glass of Stolichnaya Gold vodka. He toasted today's triumphs, again noticing Natalie's distant demeanor. Nick and Sasha held their own private toast for their mother. Nick could only hope that he had gotten her the justice that allowed her to rest in peace. He then swigged the vodka, savoring the bittersweet taste, which was symbolic of his life.

When they returned to their hotel suite, Nick's lead bodyguard informed him that the men who failed to guard his room had been dealt with. It was a good reminder to the others that it was a privilege to work for Nick Zellen, and if their job was not done correctly, people could die. Before retiring for the night, he received a call from Pavel Kovalenko, who ran Nick's businesses in the western United States, to discuss an urgent business dealing in Los Angeles.

It seemed like his days never ended, but that was all well and good, because all downtime did was give him time to think of the life he'd left behind, and how much he missed both his mother and Audrey.

He had come to grips with the fact that his life from birth until law school was nothing but a fantasy. All it did was hide what lurked within him, and ran through his veins. When the layers were peeled away after his mother's death, he looked in the mirror and saw who he really was. And that person was no different than Karl and Viktor, whether he liked the reflection or not.

Natalie was drunk again—the memory of Audrey slipped further away with each passing day. Either she was turning into an alcoholic or she was acting to avoid being with him. Neither was acceptable, and he would put a stop to it. But he didn't have the energy tonight for one of their fights.

As Natalie fell into a drunken stupor, he prepared for bed. When he took off his suit jacket, he reached into his pocket to remove his wallet and cell phone. But what he found froze him.

It was a note. It read: *Becks + Posh = TLF*. The F in the *True Love Forever* acronym was underlined. He understood the symbolism—she would be chasing him forever. There was also another line written on the other side of the note. *Sorry to hear you killed your father. Both of them. My condolences.*

How did she know that? Everybody who knew that secret was dead, and Zubov was locked away in solitary confinement. He would get those answers when he found her. And to find her, he would have to figure out how she got the note in his pocket.

Could she have been at the skating competition? He doubted she was at the restaurant, it was only his group and the wait staff, and he'd have recognized her. No person escaped his scrutiny these days. Maybe she paid one of them to do her dirty work.

But then it hit him—*the woman*. The one who bumped into him with the heavy Boston accent. She was the one who had sandbagged his guards. She put the note into his pocket when she walked by, just to prove that she could get to him. But who was the man she was with?

Nick's initial instinct was to scour the streets of Boston until he found her. But she was a former marshal. So she was smart enough to be halfway around the world by now.

"What are you up to, Becks?" he muttered.

Chapter 100

After leaving the Taj Boston hotel, Darren and Becks traveled to the other end of Newbury Street and picked up a subway. They took it to the hilly village of Chestnut Hill, near the campus of Boston College. Becks led him to one of the seemingly endless number of Murphy's Pubs in the Boston area. She claimed it had the best burgers in New England.

She took off her baseball cap, revealing a short bob of brunette hair. She looked at least ten years older than when she sported a mishmash of blonde and pink, and light years in the sophistication department. Darren removed his skullcap and she couldn't resist rubbing her hands over his completely shaved dome. If she had gained ten years, he had taken ten off, except for the gray that was creeping into his goatee.

They were seated at a booth table and just stared at each other, still too shocked to say anything. Finally Becks broke the silence. "So is this one of those *It's a Wonderful Life* glimpses into an alternate existence? Christmas *is* only two weeks away. What's going on here, Darren—I thought you were dead?"

"I'm not Darren."

"Then who are you?"

He pushed his Massachusetts driver's license across the table for her to read.

She started laughing. "Brick Zuckley—you must not be Darren because he didn't have a very good sense of humor. In fact, I'm not sure he had one at all. But you do know that Brick Zuckley isn't a real person's name, right? It's like a spy novel name."

"That might be fitting."

"So are you going to tell me what happened to Darren?"

He shrugged. "The hijacker? From what I heard on the news, he died in a plane crash."

What he didn't tell her was that when they came to the end, looking into Zubov's soulless eyes, they found out that he really did have a soul, or at least a principle he lived by. He claimed to never have killed an innocent person—it didn't go with his brand—and he considered Darren and Lilly to be innocent victims in the battle for control of the Russian Mafiya.

He told them the tale of how he came up with that philosophy. When he was a young Russian immigrant in Brighton Beach, he worked for Psyk Miklacz, a man he detested. But he put up with his crap because his comrade, and fellow vor, Viktor Sarvydas, had married Miklacz's daughter. But when Trina found out that Viktor had gotten his mistress pregnant, she ordered that Zubov kill Paula Branche, or Trina would have her father kill Viktor. He'd killed hundreds before coming to the United States, he had never killed anyone he believed to be innocent, and Paula and her child were innocent. So he informed Viktor of his wife's intentions, and together they planned the ambush on Trina and her father.

But just because he wouldn't kill Darren and Lilly, didn't mean he planned on helping them. He gave them one chance to leap off the cliffs into the sea below, hoping for God's mercy. If they went against his wishes, he would no longer consider them innocent. It was a business deal. They would get the opportunity to live, albeit slight, and Zubov would get to claim to Nick that he completed his job, while not going against his principles.

Before they took the ultimate leap of faith, Zubov mentioned that Natalie Gold always left a second set of scuba gear at the bottom of the cliffs. He was suspicious that she'd been preparing for a quick getaway, so he decided to keep an eye on her. He never shared this information with Viktor or Nick. Zubov knew to always keep an ace in his hand.

Even though they'd never done it at this height, or in darkness, this wasn't Darren and Lilly's virgin voyage in cliff diving. It was a pastime that Lilly and her brothers did growing up in Mexico, and perhaps where she discovered her love of the ledge. When Darren took a vacation with Lilly to Acapulco while they were dating, Lilly convinced Darren to take a turn at cliff diving. He was scared out of his mind, but there was no way he was going to let Lilly see any weakness in him. It was one of the photos he used during his interview with Jessi Stafford. Who knew it would save their lives one day.

They leaped into the darkness, praying that they wouldn't go splat on the rocky shoreline. And for better or worse, they hit nothing but freezing water. After locating the scuba gear, Darren swam with Lilly riding piggyback, due to her leg injury. His scuba and water-rescue training from his Air Force days came in real handy. Somehow they made it a mile down the coast. They laid low for a few days, hiding in the cliffs, before making their way to Tel Aviv. Their escape was helped by the belief that they were dead, by both the authorities and Nick.

After receiving new identities in Tel Aviv, they made their way to the coastal city of Haifa, where they began their new lives. The McLaughlins were now dead.

Darren and Becks ordered burgers and spoke over two drunken college girls who were butchering Elton John and Kiki Dee's "Don't Go Breaking My Heart" on the karaoke stage.

"It's nice to meet you, Brick Zuckley. But my parents taught me not to eat Murphy's Pub burgers with strangers. Tell me about yourself and then you won't be a stranger anymore."

"I moved to the area recently, and live in an apartment out in Bedford. I fly tours for a helicopter company."

"A pilot...I'm impressed. I love a man in uniform. Where did you learn to fly a helicopter?"

"I got experience flying Cobra helicopters when I was in the Air Force."

"A military man...the more uniforms the merrier. You have a very interesting background, Brick. I'd like to learn more about you. Tell me about these tours you give."

"We fly out of the Hanscom/Bedford Airport. Usually day-trip sightseeing tours, about two to three hours. Cape Cod and the North Shore, the Newport Mansions, Martha's Vineyard and Nantucket, and even down to Foxwoods Casino in Connecticut."

"Maybe I'll take a tour sometime. You seem like you'd make a good pilot. Like one who might be able to ditch a commercial airliner into the sea and live to tell about it."

"And who exactly would I be taking on this tour? I checked with the US Federal Marshals, and there seems to be no record of any Chelsea Fitzpatrick who ever worked there."

"It's nice to know you care, Brick," she said with a smile. "I don't know who this Chelsea chick is, but my name is CJ LaPoint."

He chuckled. "If my name is spy novelish, then yours sounds like a middle reliever for the Sox."

"It's actually my real name...well, kinda sorta. I got CJ from Chelsea Jane. And Fitzpatrick is my mother's name—the one she has used since she got divorced. My birth name was LaPoint, but I've gone by Fitzpatrick for as long as I can remember."

"Why did you do that?"

"Why should I use my father's name when my mother did all the work, while he was out globetrotting? It also made it easier when I started at the Marshals. Federal law enforcement is a small fraternity, so I didn't want it held for or against me that my father was..."

Darren cut her off with a grin. "Agent LaPoint is your father?"

Becks looked irritated. “Technically, yes. From putting any time into raising me, no. But after Alexei Sarvydas got in the way of my bullet, the powers-that-be worried about my safety, so I quasi-changed my name back to my birth name. I guess Chelsea Fitzpatrick is as dead as Darren McLaughlin.”

“LaPoint is your dad,” Darren said again with an amused look.

“He was an absentee landlord my whole life and now he’s Mr. Overprotective. He sends a couple of feds by my apartment each night to check on me. Total overreaction—I did the Ruskies a favor by shooting Alexei. From what I’ve heard, the guy was universally hated, and the only reason they’d want to find me is to buy me a vodka shot for doing the deed. I’m not in any danger…well, until today, anyway.”

“What did you do in that hotel room?”

“I would tell you, Brick, but then I’d have to kill you.”

“You almost did—on a couple of occasions. How did you figure out that Nick was the one behind Karl’s murder?”

“There had to be a reason why Viktor had Trina killed—otherwise it made no sense, and Viktor only did calculated. Then it hit me—what if he had gotten Paula pregnant? Once Trina found out about the pregnancy, and threatened retaliation, the only logical move was for Viktor to launch a preemptive strike. I then did the long division until I got to Nick. Karl wasn’t his father, Viktor was.”

Darren nodded, impressed by her thought process. “A house built on lies. Sort of like the story of Darren and Becks. Once Lilly disappeared, it wasn’t an accident that you popped into my life. You tracked me, thinking I’d lead you to her. Was everything a lie?”

“You’re the one who came to the Buckley house—sorry about the punch, by the way—and you were the one who showed up at the school. Nobody held a gun to your head and forced you to follow me around like a puppy dog. And for the record, it wasn’t a lie when I pushed you out of the way of Alexei’s gun.”

"Would you have really shot me?"

"Based on the way you acted after your wife ripped your guts out, you probably would have fallen in love with me if I did."

"So you weren't really offering me drunken revenge sex that night at my house?"

"Totally sober, and not a chance." She smiled. "Maybe I have a future in acting."

"If you're not babysitting criminals anymore, and you haven't started the acting career yet, what are you doing with yourself these days, CJ?"

"Doing what I always wanted to do. I think I became a fed to prove a point to my father. I'm teaching at BC—assistant professor of criminal justice—and also working on my doctorate. I'm an alum—got my undergrad and masters there." She smirked, a look he knew too well. "You should come in and be a guest lecturer—I'm sure the students would love to meet a real life hijacker."

"So if you left the crime fighting to others, what was today about?"

"Unfinished business. I told you that when someone screws me over, I won't stop until justice is served." Her face turned deathly serious. "And I thought he killed you."

Darren didn't want to go there. He changed the subject as their burgers arrived. "So you did go to BC in the fall. You actually told me something that was true."

"Honesty is the best policy. Look at Darren and Becks, they just didn't work out because it wasn't based on the truth. But I see some hope for Brick and CJ."

Chapter 101

"Since we're on this whole honesty kick, how old are you?" Darren asked.

"You should never ask a woman her age. You are doing some bad will hunting, my friend."

Darren gave her a disappointed look.

She sighed. "If you don't ask me things, then I won't have to lie to you. Twenty-eight, I'll be twenty-nine in February. I guess the whole 'perpetually looking sixteen' thing finally paid off."

"Wow—you could have qualified for the cougar hunt. Too bad they didn't know."

"Those boys couldn't handle this eleven pointer," she replied with a laugh.

"Eleven, wow! I married a ten pointer. I didn't think it was possible to top that."

"Maybe you just didn't look hard enough." She glanced at the finger where his wedding band once resided. "But looks like your single now, Brick. So I guess there's hope for you."

"My wife died."

"I'm sorry to hear that. How did it happen?"

"A hijacking gone wrong."

"You think you know someone and then they turn out to be a hijacker. But I bet you were loyal to the end, Brick. You seem like the type of guy who would stick it out even if your wife cheated on you with the future head of the Russian Mafiya."

It was still too surreal to believe. He and Lilly parted ways in Israel and eventually found their way back to the United States, separately. She found safety in the border town of Columbus, New Mexico, a farming town along Highway-9, with one road running through the endless desert. She was now in her own version of the Witness Protection Program, doing her penance under the name of Maria Banuelos, and living with the fear of her true identity being discovered. Although, it probably also feeds her danger addiction. She teaches English to the numerous Mexican immigrants who flee past the border to Columbus. At least that's what he gathered from her last, and final, correspondence. He couldn't be sure that she was still there.

There was no need for a divorce, since they were both listed as dead. Their house and assets went to their only remaining family—Lilly's mother. Darren read online that crime enthusiasts made pilgrimages to see where the hijackers once resided.

Upon returning to the States, Darren did what most people do when a spouse dies. He mourned, he questioned why, but eventually made peace with it and moved on the best he could, hoping to find love again.

"How about you, Professor LaPoint?"

"How 'bout me, what?"

"Married? Boyfriend?"

"I was dating a guy this past summer," she said and then stopped, and an ironic look filled her face. "He was actually one of my grad students."

"I've heard about those teacher/student relationships. They don't always end well. You said 'was'?"

"He dumped me—said I was too intense for him."

Darren couldn't help a playful smile. "I don't know where he got that from. You seem like the laid back type to me."

She looked at her watch and frowned.

"Hot date?" he asked.

"No, I've got class."

"Class? It's Saturday night."

"It's an individual study session for my criminal justice nerds. They're freaking out because finals are next week. I tell them that real life experience is more important than book learning, so they should go rob a bank. But they never listen to me."

Darren took the last chomp of his Murphy Burger, which was tasty, but no Cholla Burger. He swigged the remainder of his soda and said, "Well, it was nice to see you again, CJ LaPoint, even if it was the first time we ever met."

"You too, Brick Zuckley. Perhaps we'll run into each other sometime around the Old Towne. Or maybe I'll take one of your helicopter tours."

She put her Sox hat back on and headed toward the door.

Then like a scene out of an old-time movie, she energetically turned and ran back to him. "C'mon, it's killing me. You gotta tell me what happened on that plane. And at Sarvydas' house!"

"If I told you, I'd have to kill you."

"If you don't tell me, I'm going to drag you on stage for some karaoke, Run DMC, and you'll wish you were dead."

"Is that a threat?'

"It's a promise," she said with a get-her-way grin, and headed for the karaoke stage.

Darren grabbed her arm and stopped her. "Oh no you don't."

"Says who?"

"Says the clock. You're late for class and I'm going to make sure you get there on time."

"Who do you think you are?"

He smiled a hopeful smile. "I'm the truant officer."

Acknowledgments

In many ways publishing a book is a lot like The Truant Officer (although, less drama) – a race against time with many moving parts, and the only way to survive is to have trust in those around you. And I was very lucky to be surrounded by a great team.

Thanks again to Charlotte Brown, The Pedant of Oz, for her magnificent editorial work. It's a much better book because of her efforts, and I'm a much better writer for working with her.

Thanks to Carl Graves for another great cover. I was getting compliments on the Truant Officer cover before it even came out. That's why he's the best at what he does.

Making Truant Officer into an ebook – formatting, uploading, etc – is the work of technology guru Curt Ciccone. Another great job by "Dirt"

And a special thanks to American Airlines captain Peter Jeffrey, whose expertise helped shape the flying/pilot scenes and make them as real as fiction will allow. I really appreciate his time and knowledge!

Like all my stories, Christina Wickson turned my handwritten words into a typed page. That normally makes her the first to read and comment on the story. The second person to read it had always been my grandfather, AJ Mays. Unfortunately, Grandpa Jay has passed away since the last book and was unable to read The Truant Officer. But I promised him that one day I'd work his hometown of Devol, Oklahoma into a book, and because of that I think his spirit lives on in The Truant Officer.

And of course, every book I'll ever write is dedicated to my parents – who only find fault in me when I don't pursue my dreams.

Excerpt from The Trials of Max Q

Chapter One

Perfection is like the mechanical rabbit used to lure greyhounds at the dog races—tantalizing, but unobtainable. It seduces you into believing you can catch it, only to ruthlessly dart away at the last moment. As I peer into the perfect blue sky of a late July day in Saratoga, New York, it's a reminder of how I know this all too well.

The crowd is bubbling with anticipation for the next mad-dash of thoroughbreds at Saratoga Racecourse. I strain my neck to look for my friends, Mac and Ashley Cirillo. They left to place wagers on the upcoming race, what seems like twenty minutes ago, even if my watch tells me it has only been five. But having known Mac since college, I know the only sure bet is that he stopped off to purchase a beer and a plate of nachos.

No sign of Mac and Ashley, just another postcard-esque view of the Victorian grandstand. It's another packed house at America's oldest racetrack.

I sit at a picnic table in the general admission paddock area. I'm not far from where my family, the Lawsons, normally sit with the flamboyantly rich in the luxurious box seats at the finish line. The same seats the Lawsons of yesteryear once sat in, arm-in-arm with the Vanderbilts and Rockefellers. But from a social-class point of view, my seat is a galaxy away. I can't avoid the obvious symbolic separation from my old life.

The Lawson legal dynasty began when Thomas Lawson arrived in Boston Harbor from the mother country in the first half of the eighteenth century, eventually settling in what is now Greenwich, Connecticut. He set up a small law office on nearby Manhattan Island, and after years of chasing the horse and buggy version of ambulances, he grew to be one of the most powerful lawyers in the New World. He was so taken with the law (more precisely, its lucrative rewards) that he decided that all future Lawsons would follow his lead, coining the phrase "Lawsons are lawyers." To ensure his mission statement would be carried out, he linked each descendant's inheritance to their joining the family business.

Over the years, the mechanical rabbit the Lawsons chased became narrowly defined. The acquisition of unimaginable wealth was part of it, of course, but my family views true perfection as being *perceived* as perfect by those around them. Or what I like to refer to as the meaningless quest for the approval of others.

The thoroughbreds are led into the starting gate. One feisty colt is having second thoughts and puts up a fight, but eventually gives in—the rebel always seems to lose in the end. As bugles signal the race is about to commence, I spot the oversized white hat of Ashley Cirillo. She strolls through the thick crowd with her usual grin and the grace of an old-time movie star, the haughty Saratoga background fitting her like a Vera Wang dress.

Walking alongside Ashley is her husband, Mac. He is looking frat-boy scruffy, as if he didn't get the memo that states you aren't supposed to look and act the same at thirty-two as when you were twenty-two. They are an odder couple than Felix and Oscar ever were, their only noticeable commonality is the "in-love" smile they wear for each other.

"I love the smell of trust funds in the afternoon," Mac jokes upon reaching me, dramatically sniffing the air for effect.

I smile and grab one of his cheese-glazed nachos.

"So who'd we bet on?" I ask Ashley. I always follow her lead on such matters. Her success often exceeds that of the so-called experts, even though her technique of picking the horse with the "prettiest tail" has yet to become an accepted technique of professional handicappers.

"Mac bet on a three-to-one shot called Old Wino, not exactly going out on a limb," she begins.

"I couldn't resist, Jack, it reminded me of your grandmother," Mac states. He looks proud that he extracted a grin from me. Lately it's been a challenge.

"The combination of my family and your lifelong losing streak doesn't exactly scream winner," I reply, and then get to the all-important bet. "Which one has the pretty tail, Ash?"

"Actually, I'm going away from the plan this time, Jack."

Before I can question this dramatic change of course, Mac explains, "It's destiny, Jack—as big of a lock as you in the courtroom. The horse's name is Clotheshorse!"

For years Mac has playfully referred to Ashley as "the Clotheshorse" in response to her expensive addiction to shopping.

"It's fifty-to-one, Jack, but I don't know how it can lose," Ashley adds with enthusiasm.

We walk to an outside grill that's situated right next to the track, and is VIP only. I use my Lawson influence to get us in, so we can stand by the rail. It is one thing to watch the race, it's another to feel the horses thunder past you.

A ringing of bells halts our conversation. The gates burst open and the rumbling of hooves crackles through the thick summer air. Those in the grandstand rise out of their seats. "And they're off!" shouts the track announcer.

It feels like the earth is shaking as the horses bend around the first turn. "Old Wino shoots to the lead!" belts out the announcer.

Ashley excitedly urges Clotheshorse on, "C'mon baby, mama needs a new pair of shoes!"

"Mama has a whole closet of shoes she has never worn," Mac reminds her. He is trying to remain confident, but I can tell he's already sensing another bad ending.

I maintain my cool demeanor that has always served me well in the courtroom, but sometimes gives the perception of aloofness outside of it.

At the halfway point, Clotheshorse, the fifty-to-one shot, has done the unthinkable by overtaking Old Wino. Mac nervously chain-eats his nachos as we watch the horses head down the home stretch, while Ashley cheers on with a knowing grin.

It's Clotheshorse by a nose ... Old Wino makes his move on the rail ... Old Wino moves to the lead ... Here comes Clotheshorse ... It's too close to call...

That's when a seven-to-two shot named Bossy Cow makes a move on the outside. She is a dark brown filly with a white stripe down her nose. She passes with ease and cruises to a three-length victory.

Old Wino takes second, giving Mac slight bragging rights over Ashley, who watches Clotheshorse drop to fifth and out of the money. She curses herself for abandoning her system.

"Typical woman," Mac impugns the victorious filly. "Just when you're feeling good about things, she sneaks up behind you and ruins all the fun."

The comment leads to a group laugh—a nice moment between friends. One that's been lacking during the recent stage of my life, which officially is being called a "sabbatical," while the whisperers behind my back tend to prefer the term "mental breakdown."

I currently live with Mac and Ashley at their house on Otsego Lake in Cooperstown, a small village ninety miles northeast of Saratoga, and known for being the home of the Baseball Hall of Fame. That is where Mac works as the Assistant Director of Marketing, a step on the path to his dream job, which is to be the curator of the museum.

Ashley followed Mac to Cooperstown after graduation, and the city girl became so bored in rural upstate New York that she began doing errands for everyone she met to keep busy. This attempt at curing boredom developed into a profitable business she aptly named Ashley's Errands, making her the true breadwinner of the family. Mac often jokes that the errand business is just an excuse for Ashley to go on shopping sprees, even if they are for others.

We all met at Brown University, thirteen years ago. Mac chose Brown because the Ivy League education allowed him to pursue his dreams and escape the blue-collar town of Poughkeepsie. Ashley chose it because Providence was near her Boston home and she considered it a "hip college town." I went to Brown because my aristocratic mother patterned her life after Jackie Kennedy, and if Brown was good enough for her son John Jr., then it certainly was good enough for Jack Lawson.

Having grown up at the corner of rich and delusional, I rarely interacted with real people. This changed when I met my college roommate, a sophomore named Mac Cirillo. He was nothing like anyone I had ever met before. He was funny, comfortable in his own skin, and wasn't overly concerned what others thought of him. He is known for being a little "out there" with his offbeat theories that he calls Macademia—combining his name with academia, because in his words, he is educating us. I more associate the term with macadamia nuts, which I think might be a better description of Mac. His belief that man never landed on the moon is the one he is most passionate about.

The big favor I did for Mac was introducing him to Ashley Armstrong, a gorgeous leggy blonde with grace, style, and pedigree. In other words, way too good for him. Ashley will be the first to admit she is girly, but if you call her high maintenance you'll have a fight on your hands. She can fish and talk trash with the boys as effortlessly as she can pick out a pair of designer shoes. Her father owns a private airline company called Armstrong Airlines, and Ashley is an accomplished pilot herself, giving lessons on the weekend. But most importantly, she has always been my biggest source of support—a support I've needed the last couple of years.

I consider them to be my real family. So when I took a leave of absence from my family's firm, Lawson Baird & Gentry, I ultimately migrated here. It's where Mac returned the favor by reintroducing me to a great love of mine—the law. It's the one great legacy of my family's incessant shove in that direction. But I don't love the "Lawson Law" of money, schmoozing wealthy clients, and making partner. The law I fell for was the one that represents justice, and speaks for those who can't speak for themselves. Which is what led me to stay in Cooperstown, and take the job as Chief Assistant District Attorney for Otsego County.

Lightning Source UK Ltd.
Milton Keynes UK
UKOW042249040313

207142UK00001B/61/P